SEVENTH BORN

SEVENTH BORN

THE WITCHLING ACADEMY SERIES
monica sanz

Entangled Publishing, LLC
2614 South Timberline Road
Suite 105, PMB 159
Fort Collins, CO 80525
rights@entangledpublishing.com

Entangled Teen is an imprint of Entangled Publishing, LLC.

Visit our website at www.entangledpublishing.com.

Edited by Karen Grove
Cover design by Fiona Jayde and Wesley Souza
Cover images by
CoffeeAndMilk/iStock
svetikd/iStock
vladimir_karpenyuk/iStock
iiievgeniy/iStock
Xsandra/iStock
lenanet/iStock
ThomasVogel/iStock
peangdao/iStock
rotofrank/iStock
Mypurgatoryyears/iStock
FOTOKITA/iStock
Mimadeo/iStock
Mikesilent/Getty
redheadstock/www.obsidiandawn.com
Interior design by Toni Kerr

ISBN 978-1-64063-192-2
Ebook ISBN 978-1-64063-193-9

Manufactured in the United States of America

First Edition September 2018

10 9 8 7 6 5 4 3 2 1

To anyone who's ever been a seventhborn.

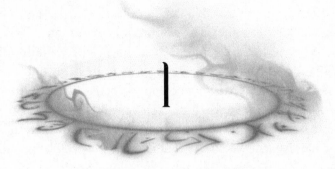

the unmitigated truth

Relegated to a small, dark alcove in a corner of the Aetherium's Witchling Academy library, Seraphina Dovetail shifted on her small wooden stool, plucking a fingernail against the frayed edge of the black book on her lap—the only book she was allowed to read for leisure: *The Unmitigated Truths of Seventhborns*.

She rolled her eyes and kicked the pointed tip of her battered black boot on the stone floor. She needn't read an entire book on the subject, not when she lived its content every day. She was the seventh-born daughter to a witch, her birth the cause of her mother losing her powers and in turn, her life. If she ever cared to forget, the thin black line on her wrist would remind her. And—she glanced about the library at students sitting in plush chairs and wearing warm cloaks—so would the world.

Unable to stomach reading more about the faults of her *irreparable condition*, Sera looked across the room to the stool opposite hers. Hazel Flemings, the only other seventhborn in the Academy, sat with her back spear straight, her shoulders relaxed and brown eyes downcast. No signs of hostility issued from her frame and demeanor. Had Sera not been fully aware of Hazel's presence, she might have missed her altogether. The girl was no better than a shadow.

Sera shook her head. Hazel had clearly taken *The Unmitigated Truths of Seventhborns* to heart. Namely the chapter on the proper decorum expected of their *cursed birthright*, from keeping oneself invisible to maintaining a pleasant mien lest anyone consider them ungrateful of the mercy bestowed upon them. In other words, keep a low profile and be thankful they were allowed to live.

Perhaps feeling the weight of Sera's stare, Hazel lifted her lashes and met her gaze. Sera smiled, though inside, her heart twisted at the fourteen-year-old girl's innocence. It would never last. Sooner or later, she would learn that regardless of how invisible she tried to be, the world still saw her, and that world was full of monsters ready to devour her at first chance.

A harsh gust of cold air lashed Sera, blew the horrid book from her lap, and shoved her sideways against a neighboring bookshelf. She hissed as sharp pain rushed down the side of her face when it collided with the bookcase.

Stiff silence settled over the library, all eyes focused on Sera and the ladies' matron, Mrs. James, towering over her.

"Socializing between seventhborns is strictly forbidden," the woman hissed, one hand on her hip and her face pinched in disgust. She pointed her wand at the book on the floor. "And so is mistreating school property."

Sera's pulse quickened. Magic roared through her veins, a fierce heat coursing out from her belly and burning the underside of her skin. "I was not socializing." She lifted her face to Mrs. James. "And I didn't mistreat the book."

Red flushed the matron's cheeks, her face matching her hair. She moved closer, her eyes narrowed to tiny slits, her hand tight around her wand. "What did you say?"

Sera dug her fingers into her knees to keep them from clenching, to keep from channeling the heat in her core into a gale to blow the beastly woman through the stained-glass window behind her. The headmistress wouldn't allow her another transgression, not after the fire she sparked last month in a fit of rage.

"Nothing, Mrs. James," she muttered through clenched teeth. She swallowed thickly, suppressing the magic that squeezed hot, sour bile into her throat. "I'm sorry about the book."

Mrs. James scoffed, her thin lips pulled to a snarl. "Don't apologize to me but to all the seventhborns who wished they got the opportunity to study at a prestigious school such as this instead of rotting away in whatever hovel they've been cursed to, and rightly so. Any goodness that comes to your sort is great kindness, indeed."

Sera snorted. Better kindness could be found at the zoo, under the claws of a ravenous tiger.

Mrs. James gasped at the sneer, but Mary Tenant swept beside her and interrupted. "Perhaps Miss Dovetail can show her appreciation by helping me carry a few books to my table?" She flashed Mrs. James a practiced smile, a meek spread of the lips and batting of the lashes that seemed to grant her whatever she wanted—well, most things. "They are rather heavy."

Mrs. James remained still, seedy brown eyes fixed on Sera and her knuckles white on her wand. When Sera made no attempt at retaliation, the woman sheathed her wand in the metal holder hanging from the side of her dress. "Pick up your book and assist Miss Tenant. Unlike you, the students in this school hope to contribute to the magical community. At least have the dignity to appreciate your mother's sacrifice…or stupidity." She spun and clapped her hands twice, prompting students to refocus on their studies.

Sera's glare remained fixed on Mrs. James's back. The woman's last words spurred her magic, a beast clawing at her insides for release. The candles flared on the chandelier above, making the shadows throb in tune with her heartbeat. Nearby students reached for their books, others carefully moving closer to the door. If last month's events were any indication, they had less than a minute before she snatched out her wand and set something—or someone—on fire.

"Steady, Sera," Mary whispered, standing close. "You don't want to do this." She tilted her head toward the back of the library. "Think of your family."

Family. A wave of stark cold washed through Sera. Though she could not remember them, she focused on the phantom faces she'd imagined as those of her siblings and father. She hauled in a steadying breath. They were out there, somewhere, and blowing Mrs. James through a window wasn't going to help her find them. She exhaled, picked up the cursed book, and followed Mary.

A kaleidoscope of color shaded them momentarily as they passed the stained-glass windows portraying the seven guardians, the goddesses believed to be the founders of magic. The women's mournful faces were turned down to one of the seven elements they cupped in their hands. Each window was a different color, representative of the element: red for fire, yellow for air, blue for water, green for earth, gray for metal, brown for wood, and a clear pane for aether— the study of light and darkness, of emotions and matters of the soul.

Mary guided them behind a bookcase and tugged Sera

closer. Sera snatched her hand away, but glancing around, she breathed freer. They were alone, and no one saw the forbidden affection.

"How are you, dearest?" Mary whispered.

"Wonderful and ever so grateful for the Academy's *kindness*." She mocked a bow to the nearest window, the image of the Aetherium founder, Patriarch Angus Aldrich, imprinted on the glass. He sat in a throne chair, surrounded by the seven elemental signs.

"Stop it." Mary giggled, her skin reddening. She plucked a book from the shelf and handed it to Sera. "How was class this morning?"

Sera took the book in her arms to start their fraudulent pile. "Boring as ever. The sooner we're done with these Aether-level courses, the better. I don't know how much longer I can deal with the *influence of magic on the soul*."

"Yes, well, you don't know which elements will be represented during assessments, so you have to pay attention to them all…and perhaps charm a professor in the process to sign your referral papers?"

Sera frowned but hummed in agreement. To be admitted to the Aetherium School of Continuing Magic, she had to first take their entrance exam…and that required a referral from a professor.

"You're doing well in Mysteries of the Mind. Maybe ask Mrs. Aguirre? A referral from an Aether-levels professor is impressive."

"Maybe last quarter she would have agreed…before the spell-book incident." Sera shook her head. After attempting to transfer a negative thought into a stone unsuccessfully, she had thrust her spell book aside in frustration and unknowingly too close to the flame beneath her cauldron. The book caught on fire, and, though a simple mistake, no one else saw it as such. Seventhborns weren't allowed mistakes.

Mary wrinkled her nose. "Ah yes, I forgot about that."

"But enough about me. How are you?"

"Spent. Mrs. Fairfax was in the infirmary last night," she said, setting another book into Sera's arms. "She fell down the stairs and got herself a nasty gash. She didn't want to wait for Nurse, who was tending to an emergency in the kitchens, and so I tended to her myself."

Sera waited until they were shielded behind another bookshelf to reply. "That's fantastic, Mary. Your own patient, even if it is Mrs. Fairfax. That woman is a tyrant." Though Sera conceded it was only logical the housekeeper disliked her when it was the housekeeping staff who were burdened with cleaning up her messes, like last month's fire. Or the explosion in the potions room. Not to mention the rubble from the statue she'd blasted two months prior. It was a wonder she hadn't been expelled, she mused.

Mary shrugged and dropped another book into Sera's arms. "Yes, well, Nurse will never know. She doesn't like us healing without her supervision, but it was good practice for assessments. I'll surely deal with worse as an Aetherium healer." She blew out a sigh, her black bangs waving upward. "Now I'm positively exhausted. It took nearly all my reserves to heal her wound."

Sera adjusted the growing pile of books. "Why don't you ask Mrs. James to be excused to your room?"

"Are you mad?" Mary stopped abruptly by the Astral Studies section. "It's a full moon, silly. All big decisions should be made today, and today is the day I'll be asked to the Solstice Dance. But first I must be noticed, though it will be impossible with all of that." She motioned out to the room.

The tables throughout the library were filled—an

inordinate number of girls squeezed into the seats. Other girls pretended to search for books in the bookcase nearest the boys' half of the library, while the boys did the same on their side. Split into two towers, the boys' and girls' wards were joined only by the library.

Sera rolled her eyes. Another reason why she despised the library, during the day at least. The last thing she needed was contact with a silly boy.

"Then perhaps being seen with me will not improve your chances," she muttered. "Go, I'm fine. I've endured worse than Mrs. James's wrath. I'm sure someone will ask you."

"And that's the problem. My mother does not expect me to go to the dance with *someone*. She expects me to go with *the* one. Only a Delacort will do."

Sera peered around the corner to the boy of topic. He lounged in a leather armchair in the sitting area nearest the great fireplace, where most senior magicians tended to gather. With a hand over his mouth and blue eyes squinted with laughter, he watched his best friend swing his wand while recounting an animated tale.

"Such beauty." Mary sighed, green eyes fixed on Timothy Delacort. She rested her head against a neighboring shelf. "Even you must admit to that."

Sera opened her mouth to deny it, but the clouds shifted and faint rays filtered through the arched window, bathing Timothy in warm light.

"Damned sun," she murmured. It would be a heinous lie to say Timothy Delacort wasn't handsome with his aristocratic features, mop of black curls, and big blue eyes. Not to mention his impeccable manners. Why he chose Hadden Whittaker as a friend evaded her; the arrogant boy was a nuisance, his ego as big as his mountainous frame.

But she turned away and stacked another book onto her

pile. Timothy's choices were no concern of hers. "Yes, he's handsome, but I have better things to worry about."

Mary sighed and lowered her head, pretending to leaf through a book. "Yes, yes, like becoming an inspector, I know, but there is more to life," she went on. "I would hate for you to wake up one day only to realize life has passed you by and left you an old spinster." She gasped and shut the book. "Come to think of it, you should come to the dance."

Sera blinked and blinked again as the animated brunette returned the book to the shelf and picked up another. "Are you mad? Perhaps you should be the one in the infirmary along with your patients."

"If this school is as progressive with the treatment of seventhborns as it claims to be, then why shouldn't you come to the dance?" Mary stacked the book on the five Sera held already. Sera's arms began to burn under the strain, but it was rare that she and Mary got to talk during the day. She could weather the discomfort a little while longer.

"Because as much as the Aetherium has *embraced* Pragmatism," Sera replied from behind the tower in her arms, "it's as prejudiced as when the Purists ruled. Pragmatism, Purism. Different religion, same nonsense. For seventhborns at least."

"That argument won't win you a reprieve," Mary muttered. "My mother wrote to say she is sending my gowns. I have a yellow one that's simply to die for. You will look like a ray of sunshine."

"Yes, well, I prefer black."

Mary sulked. "Black is death, Sera."

She grinned. "Precisely. I would rather be dead than go to that dance—"

A flash of light darted past her. Sera screamed and ducked as it blasted into the bookcase behind her. A rain of tomes tumbled down onto her and Mary, the corners of the books jamming into her head and back before joining the ones that had fallen from her hands to the floor. Specks of light flickered before her eyes.

Silence claimed the room a moment before it exploded into roars of laughter. Sera pressed her hands on the floor and centered herself, mastering the sting along her spine and throbbing pricks at the back of her head. A metallic taste tinged her mouth, and laughter rang in her ears as tears blurred the room around her.

Mrs. James rushed to them. She swept past Sera and helped Mary to her feet. "Miss Tenant, are you all right? Are you hurt?"

"I—I'm fine," Mary said, a hand pressed against her temple. "What was that?"

"It was a mistake." Timothy Delacort was suddenly beside them. He turned to Sera, a line marking his brow. "We were having a bit of fun, and Mr. Whittaker must have had a slip of the hand."

"We will speak of this later," Mrs. James said to Timothy. She drew Mary away to one of the secondary matrons. "Take Miss Tenant to the infirmary," she ordered the assistant. "We must tend to this cut and make sure it doesn't scar."

Timothy held out a hand to Sera, prompting a wave of murmurs. "Are you hurt?"

Rising alone, she looked beyond him, her gaze fixed on Whittaker celebrating behind the chaperone's back. "That was no mistake."

Mrs. James scoffed. "This is not the time, Miss Dovetail. No one is persecuting seventhborns anymore. If Mr. Delacort says it was a mistake, then it was a mistake." She clutched Sera's chin and, jerking it from side to side, inspected the cut on her cheek.

Lips pressed to a tight line, Mrs. James shoved Sera's face away and dusted her hands as if having touched something foul. "No need to bother Nurse with an insignificant cut. Go and get yourself cleaned up, and then help straighten this mess. Mr. Delacort, back to your section please." She spun on her heels and walked away, a chorus of snickers all around her.

"I'll talk to him," Timothy whispered. But lost to the swell of heat in her blood, to the laughter, Sera walked around him. A cyclone of warmth gathered in her belly, wildfire twisting with each beat of her heart. The beast that clawed her insides for release grew stronger, raw anger spurring her magic. Reason warned her to calm down. Hadn't she already caused herself enough problems under similar rage? She shouldn't do this. She couldn't. She wouldn't—

"Forgive me, Dovetail," Whittaker called out to her. His grin widened. "It was a…*mistake*."

Anger waved upward till redness shaded the fringes of her sight. Focused on the thrash of her heartbeat and on the vile boy, she envisioned plumes of fire, and her hands grew hot.

Preoccupied with celebrations, the stout, freckle-faced boy failed to notice the curls of smoke that whirled from the tail of his cloak.

Timothy gasped. "Whittaker, your cloak!"

When the burn in her hand grew to a scalding ache, Sera clenched her fingers shut.

A fire snapped onto the tail of Whittaker's cloak first, then upward along the black fabric. A collective gasp resounded, cut only by Whittaker's screams. A soothing warmth rolled through Sera, the release of magic intoxicating and comforting.

Thrusting off his cloak, he threw it to the ground, and

with a flick of his wand, extinguished it. He spun to Sera and advanced, his wand aimed at her. "You little—"

His eyes widened. He stopped and lowered his wand slowly, paling in equal measure. The room grew still; so did Sera's heart as Professor Barrington appeared from behind a bookshelf and moved in between them. Tall and lean, he took up little space in the vast room. His dark humor, however, seemed to obscure all light and air. At no older than five and twenty, he was younger than all the other professors, but this made him no less severe. He had a handsome, angular face, a strong jaw, narrow nose, and thin lips. Full black lashes made his gray eyes seem lighter, more intense. Uncomfortably so as he slid them back and forth between the two students, then lowered them to the smoking cloak.

Still, Sera held her head high as Professor Barrington scrutinized the scene.

"Mr. Whittaker, is there a reason your cloak is on the ground, half burned?" he asked, his voice a deep baritone. But while each word was smooth, cultured, and refined, Sera felt the tension in the room swell. Though Barrington exuded sophistication, there was something ominous and dormant beneath his surface. She shivered, having no desire to know what.

Whittaker speared a pudgy finger at Sera. "Sh-she tried to set me on fire!"

Barrington raised a hand and silenced the boy. "Do not bark at me, Mr. Whittaker." He lowered his hand. "Miss Dovetail?"

Sera glared at him and said nothing. What would be the point? The fire in his eyes told her he'd already gathered his answer.

Barrington's jaw clenched. "Well, Miss Dovetail?"

"That's not true, Professor." Timothy swept up beside her, his chin a touch higher, as though to reach Barrington in stature and intensity. "I was next to her the entire time, and she never drew her wand."

A strange look overcame Barrington's eyes, offense that Timothy would dare speak to him mixed with something else Sera couldn't quite place or care about at the moment. She could only gape at Timothy Delacort defending her. No one ever defended seventhborns, especially someone of his standing, and against his best friend no less.

"I know she did it," Whittaker hissed, nostrils flared. "If she didn't use her wand, then...then...she did it wandless."

The crowd gasped, and murmurs erupted once more.

Barrington's icy scrutiny slid from Timothy to Whittaker. "That's a serious accusation. Use of magic without a wand is grounds for severe repercussion for a student...as is blaming an innocent witch." He held out a hand. "Your wand, please?"

Whittaker's eyes widened, but under Barrington's steely gaze, he relinquished it. His wand was fashioned out of ash wood, the same school-issued wand as Sera's, but it was splintered and its casing tarnished. Sera pursed her lips. Just as ugly as its owner.

Barrington twirled the worn rod between long fingers. Sera's gaze fixed on his Invocation ring, an honor bestowed on graduates of the Aetherium School of Continuing Magic and a sign that he was highly trained and able to manipulate magic without a wand. The mark of a true magician. More, a requirement to becoming an inspector.

"You understand that performing a wandless spell requires expert focus and control, Mr. Whittaker?" Barrington asked.

"Yes, Professor, but how else—"

"And you also realize that Miss Dovetail has limited

training, nowhere near the likes of that needed to perform wandless magic…were she foolish enough to try."

Though he was focused on Whittaker, Sera stiffened under Barrington's peripheral glare. Surely he hadn't seen her illicit use of wandless magic. She turned her eyes down, hoping this was the case.

Whittaker nodded. "I understand, sir—"

"And you would still risk your wand over this accusation?" Barrington asked above him.

Whittaker gulped, a thin sheet of sweat glistening at his wide forehead. He looked to his wand in Barrington's hand, and then to Sera, and swallowed again. "I…I…"

"Don't be stupid," Timothy whispered. "Maybe you mistakenly brushed your wand against your cloak."

"I would never make a mistake with my wand," Whittaker barked.

Barrington hummed, one black brow arched. "Then what should we call this?" He motioned coolly to the mess of books scattered just behind them. "Intentional? Did you go against the oath you spoke over your wand to never use it for ill? Tell me it is so, Mr. Whittaker." He lifted the wand, long fingers gripping the ends tightly. The wand slowly illuminated blue, and Whittaker's eyes widened the brighter it grew. School-issued wands were designed for the power levels of a student. If Barrington flooded the rod with his more mature, stronger magic, the wand would burn and wither to ash.

"No!" The round-faced boy pressed his lips into a tight line, his hands fisted. "It was…a mistake."

"As was the matter with your cloak." The wand's glow dimmed, and with the whirl of a wrist, Barrington presented it to Whittaker, metal handle first. "Do be sure to sheathe your wand when not in use. You wouldn't want to fail assessments over something so simple." He turned to the horde. "Back to your studies."

Murmurs of protest resounded, but everyone obeyed and returned to their tables.

Sera did neither, focused on Whittaker walking away, Timothy beside him.

"Is there a problem, Miss Dovetail?" Barrington stepped into her line of sight like a black brushstroke, his shadow swathing her.

She clenched her hands, the need for revenge hot in her fingertips. "He did it on purpose. He could've killed me."

"Yes, well, strike him and you'll lose everything. Is that what you want?"

"No."

"No, what?"

Her jaw tightened. "No, it's not what I want."

He arched a brow.

"*Professor.*"

"Then off with you." He spun, his black robes billowing behind him. "And Miss Dovetail," he said over his shoulder, "I will not save you again."

Her face grew hotter with each of his retreating steps. Save her *again*? Her pulse quickened, panic replacing her anger. Did he mean save her from Whittaker, or had he seen her use wandless magic? No, it couldn't have been possible. She would not be standing there if so; he could have burned her wand and expelled her, but he hadn't. He must have meant save her from Whittaker, but as she watched him vanish out of the library, all she could wonder was why bother saving her at all?

2

strange evening call

"No one's persecuting seventhborns anymore," Sera mumbled bitterly as she strode down the wide, arched corridor of the female dormitory where throngs of girls snickered, pointed, and whispered. Portraits of previous pupils lined the walls in gilt frames, and even they seemed to stare down at her with bright, jovial eyes and small grins.

Her hands tightened, cramped. How did Mary expect her to walk down the hall with these pompous hogs and not lose her temper? Anger-laced magic pricked her insides, little nudges to bend and break. To burn and destroy. She clutched *The Unmitigated Truths of Seventhborns* to her chest and stifled the urge. She couldn't. Professor Barrington was right; one more strike and she would lose everything. All that waited if she got expelled was work as an Aetherium official's secretary—if she were lucky. Seventhborns were often not.

She *could* always go against Aetherium law and become a medium. It was no secret a seventhborn's magic was inclined to clairvoyance, empathy, auras, and the other types of Aether magic. But singular to seventhborn girls was the darker aspect of Aether magic—death, including the ability to see the dead.

There were rumors of seventhborns who chose to use this magic for personal gain through mediumship. They hosted secret séances, used their magic to evoke the dead through spirit boards, and told fortunes through crystal balls. Unfortunately, Sera's connection to the Underworld was as dead as the people she would attempt to contact. Not that she minded. There were some dead she had no desire to see.

Sera pulled open her door, then slammed it shut behind her. She stomped up the stairs and into her tiny dim room in the dormitory's tower. None of the other scholarship students were forced to live in such cramped and squalid quarters. It was small and damp, and her decor an amalgamation of broken and dated furniture, but it was hers. And on days like this, she treasured the solitude found within its four walls, however crumbling they were.

With a hefty sigh, she fell onto her chair, the legs wobbling under her weight. Her hard-set face gazed back at her from the metal pitcher in the center of the wooden worktable. She set down her book, dragged the jug close, and shook her head. Her fair skin was blotchy, and brown strands of her hair had slipped out from the bun on top of her head that was now askew thanks to Whittaker's *mistake*.

"Never mind if I would have gotten hurt." She brushed away the hairs that fell onto her face and wiped the smear of blood on her cheek. Hot tears pooled in her eyes, and her reflection blurred. "They wouldn't have cared. No one does, and you must remember this."

Hating the break in her voice, she set down the jug just as the bells tolled the hour.

Five.

If she was going to pass her Aetherium entrance assessment, she would need to increase her magic reserves. The exam was a tedious week-long affair, and fatigue simply wouldn't do. She scrubbed away her tears, rose, and turned to lock the door. With Mary in the infirmary—no doubt milking the small cut for all it was worth—no one would come to see her. But better to be safe than sorry. The last thing she needed was to blast the poor girl by mistake if she came to visit, as she often snuck in to do.

Sera paused. A note had been slipped under her door. She frowned. Had it been there when she entered? She approached it slowly; no one ever left her notes.

Kneeling, she picked it up and held it to the light. It was addressed to her, though the handwriting was horrendous. She turned it over. A red wax seal kept the note closed, a scripted *B* embossed upon it. Sera hummed. She didn't know anyone whose surname began with a *B*, no one who would write to her anyway.

She slid her finger under the seal and opened it.

My office at eight. Not one minute late.
Barrington

Sera eyed the words, then set the note down slowly on her lap. *Barrington?*

Before the thought had settled, the edges of the note erupted into flames. Sera yelped and thrust it off her lap. Licks of white fire devoured the page as it floated down. Soon all that remained was a small mound of ash and a charred sliver of paper, a *B* on its ash-stained facing.

She ran her eyes along the loops of the letter. Her nerves tangled the same. Why would Professor Barrington summon her? She'd never had him for any classes and hadn't ever had any contact with the man before that afternoon—well, other than moving out of his way as all students did when he stalked across the campus wearing his usual black cloak and frown.

Unless he *had* seen her use wandless magic...

Sera leaned back against the door and covered her face with her hands, feeling sick. Maybe he'd been pressed for time that afternoon in the library, headed for class or a meeting, and hadn't the time to consider her actions. But now he had, and he'd changed his mind. He wouldn't save her at all. What for? She was nothing to him but a seventhborn.

Three hours later, Sera peeked out from under her hood and surveyed the fourth-floor corridor. The cold gusts of a November rainstorm had swallowed the torch flames, rendering the Academy hall a tunnel of shadows cut by intermittent shafts of moonlight. Curled into her cloak, she emerged from the staircase, reached the end of the hall, and rounded the bend. One door marked the end of the short hallway, a *B* carved into its dark oak.

Her fingers clenched. She had to knock, but the war between her mind and gut left her as frozen as the shadows lining the hall. Nothing good waited on the other side of that door. Of this she had no proof, but what good could come of being summoned by Professor Barrington?

She hauled in a breath and knocked on the Alchemy professor's door.

"Come in," he spoke from the other side.

Sera rubbed her fingers together and opened the door.

Firelight painted the room in dancing shades of amber and gold, yet Professor Barrington stood in the shadows of the curtained window like a man afraid of light. His face was downcast, focused on the book in his hands. He tapped a finger on his thin lips, his brow furrowed.

Sera cleared her throat. "You wished to see me, Professor?"

The rap of his fingers stopped, and he raised his head to her. "Yes, come in. Close the door behind you."

Sera lowered her hood and entered the cramped room, closing the door. Shelves crowded the walls, stuffed with books upon books. Various tables were strewn about the room, their tops laden with multicolored jars, mortars, vials, and retorts. Whatever he had brewed last left the earthy scent of cinnamon lingering in the space.

Weaving her way through his mess, she sat before the desk dominated by more books and papers. Some sheets were crumpled into balls, others torn. Were it not for the iron-tipped legs on the table, she would have thought it all to be nothing more than a mound of books and parchment.

Barrington tossed the tome on his desk with a loud thud and sat. Slipping a brown file from somewhere within his mess, he flipped it open.

"I have heard much about you, Miss Dovetail." He put on wired spectacles and stared at her in silence, as though waiting for a reply.

Sera opened her mouth. She closed it. There was no need to say she hoped it all to be good. The thick file before him proved otherwise.

"An orphan of notable raw power found after setting a building on fire." He shook his head. "Careless."

A flush crept into her cheeks, but she folded her hands on her lap and kept her silence. No matter how many times she explained the incident, she would still be found at fault.

He flipped to the next page. "Highly emotional, insubordinate, and confrontational—heavens. Nearly burned down the library in an argument...*twice*." He turned a page and the next.

Blowing out a sigh, he shut the file and pushed it away as if having touched something toxic. "Surprisingly, none of this is your worst fault." He motioned to the seventhborn tattoo at her wrist, a thin black line that wrapped around the flesh like a shackle. "Yet, in spite of this, it says here that you've chosen to pursue one of the most challenging positions in the Aetherium. You aspire to become an inspector. Why? You could pursue an Aether-related career. It would be much easier considering your...condition."

Sera bristled. "I have no desire for telepathy or divination, sir. Majoring in Aether studies will keep me from all Metal, Fire, and Wood levels. Strength, defense, and law courses are all required to become an inspector."

He scoffed. "I'm a professor, Miss Dovetail. I know how Aetherium course-levels work. But that still doesn't explain why you want to become an inspector."

Sera hauled in a steadying breath. The man was a beast, but she wouldn't lose her temper.

"I'm interested in becoming an inspector and applying my studies to finding out more about my family—"

A low laugh rumbled in his throat, the amber firelight reflected in his wolf eyes. "What's there to know? Your mother died giving birth to you, as is the story with every other seventhborn that isn't aborted."

She tightened her hands in her lap, prickling heat crawling through her veins like knives beneath her skin. "Yes, but my father—"

"Gave you away in his heartbroken misery, surely." He sighed away his laughter, slipped off his glasses, and set them on the desk. "You should thank him for being so kind. Many of you are found dead."

Hot tears stung her eyes, but she forbade them to fall. Not here, before this despicable man. Sera summoned her strength and held her chin high. "Perhaps, but there are still—"

"Your siblings? Do you dream that at least one of them will forgive you for leaving them motherless, probably begging in the streets because their father was too drunk to hold down a position since his wife's demise?" He sat back and pressed a finger to his thin lips, regarding her keenly. "I wonder if perhaps they should've added masochistic tendencies to your file as well."

She bolted to her feet, and the hanging candelabras flared. "I beg your pardon, *Professor*, but if you asked me here to ridicule me or think I'm here for your amusement, then you're a sadder man than I thought. Feel free to add *that* to my file." She turned. Surely she'd hear from the headmistress at that—but, blast it all, the chances of her graduating were practically nonexistent, anyway. If the fire in the library hadn't sealed her fate, surely breaking the statue of Patriarch Aldrich in the dining hall had.

"That's it, then? That's all it took to send you running?" He chuckled behind her. "To think I credited you with having more spine. I'm disappointed, really."

Sera spun, heart crashing against her ribs. "Is this a game to you? You think what's written there makes you an expert on my life? You know nothing about me."

"And yet I know it all," he said mildly, contrary to the darkness in his eyes. "I know that if you don't control your anger, there is no way you will ever graduate or get the referral you need for the Aetherium entrance exam." Barrington stood and, hands held behind his back, paced around his desk. "But run if you must. Just like getting angry, it's your escape." He stopped at the window and, with a finger, brushed aside the black velvet curtain as though to ascertain the sun was gone.

"And why do you care?" she asked, teeth clenched.

"Because you need a referral." He slid off his teaching robe and hung it on the coat-tree by the window. Sitting on the edge of his desk, he clasped his hands in his lap and met her eyes. "A referral I'm willing to give you, in exchange for something, of course…"

Sera paused at the word "referral." "Excuse me?"

"Surprising, yes, I know, but I believe this is an arrangement we will both enjoy greatly. You get the referral you need, and I get your services whenever I need them. A mutual benefit."

Taking in his words, his stance, and his slow exhale as he regarded her, she flinched. Memories crept from the darkest pits in her mind, and the countless scars along her body tingled to life. She knew well how men treated seventhborns—mere things for their own wicked pleasures, to be used as if…as if they were something less than human.

"How dare you?" she seethed, trembling. "Regardless of what you think of seventhborns, I am a respectable woman. Never contact me again, or I swear upon my wand, I will set you on fire." She made to leave.

"Well, this is surprising." He spoke over the *whoosh* of her skirts and the taps of her boots on the hardwood floor.

"Despicable brute," she muttered.

"I didn't imagine you would reject my offer to refer you to the Aetherium…"

Sera pulled the door open. "Wayward boor—"

"…in exchange for your help on a case."

She stopped.

"But," he went on, "every day does come with its own surprises—"

She snapped the door shut and silenced him. "What do you mean *help on a case*?" She turned, yet still alert, she remained by the door.

"Well, in my spare time, I am a consultant of sorts and"—he motioned to his desk—"my workload is great. Sadly, there is only one of me."

Sera frowned. "A tragedy."

He clicked his teeth. "Indeed. It's this terrible and tragic lack of *me* that has left me in need of an assistant. I invited you here to ask if you would be said assistant." He straightened and ventured around his desk. "As payment, I would give you the referral needed for your exam. Seemed like a good idea when I thought of it, but, well"—he sighed heavily, adjusting his cuffs—"no respectable lady would ever associate with a *despicable, wayward boor* like myself. I should've known better, and I apologize. Good night, Miss Dovetail."

Heat waved from her feet to the crown of her head. Oh, she could have thrown something at him, but she braced her spine and strode back to the chair. "Perhaps I'm not so respectable. What type of assistance will you need on this case?"

He held up a hand. "First, an order of business."

He slipped his wand from within its holder at his waist and held it out to her. "This is an oath, and every word spoken in this meeting is for us alone and bound to secrecy between us. We have entered into this agreement freely and must both be in agreement to break it. Agreed?"

Sera brushed aside her cloak and drew her wand the same. She paused, her hold tight on the cool metal handle. Oaths were no small matter. If she uttered even a word of it, she could lose her ability to speak for years.

Yet she ran her gaze along his wand fashioned out of rosewood, then fixed on his ring. She would never hold a wand like his, and she would most certainly never wear an Invocation ring, if she didn't first pass the Aetherium entrance exam to become an apprentice and then a proper witch.

More, an inspector.

But could she really trust this man?

She swallowed. It was a risk…

…and her only chance.

She touched her wand to his. "Agreed."

His wand glowed blue as though he held a bolt of lightning. At once, his magic streamed into her wand and illuminated each thread of wood in blue. A warm sensation then tickled up her body, little pinpricks traveling from her belly to her fingertips. Her magic seeped out, crept up her wand, and overtook his, amber like the firelight. Their respective wands absorbed the foreign magic, their oath made.

Sera lowered her wand and exhaled. "Now then, Professor, what does this position entail exactly?"

Barrington sheathed his wand. "Murder."

She blinked. "*Murder?*"

"Yes, yes, lots of it, in fact. Apparently it's quite a profitable business," he said with the ease of one speaking of the weather. "Our job is to investigate those no one seems to care for."

"And why does an Alchemy professor care for murders?" she asked slowly. "Especially those no one else cares for?"

"The same reason you will care for them, Miss Dovetail. The same reason you're here: *need*." He snatched up a piece of paper. "Tomorrow, you'll report to me at the same time, only you must come a different way. I can imagine the gossip if anyone sees you entering my office again and closing the door." He held the page out to her. "You will use this spell. If you cannot execute it properly, I will find another assistant. If you knock on this door, I will find another assistant. If you ask anyone for help—"

"You will find another assistant. I know."

"I was going to say it would break our oath, but also that."

Sera rolled her eyes and took the paper. A protection circle dominated the page, and within it, a transfer spell. She eyed the chain of circular ciphers, each one containing parts of the travel coordinates. "But we aren't allowed to use transfer spells without permission—"

"Permission granted." He walked to the door and opened it. "Now, I have things to do. Dismissed."

She tucked the spell into the pocket of her cloak and walked out into the hall. "Good night, Professor."

He inclined his head once and closed the door between them.

Left alone in the newly settled night, Sera leaned back against the stone wall beside the door. What on earth had just happened? Her mind swam with questions, with words of agreements and murders and spells. With the infuriating Professor Barrington.

But however strange and inappropriate, one truth coaxed a smile from her lips: she had been wrong. Good had waited on the other side of that door.

3

impressions

A thick concoction bubbled and popped in the small cauldron before her with the pulse of an agitated heart. Sera sighed and pushed her grimoire away. If only she could dip her head into the Rhodonite potion instead of listening to Mrs. Aguirre drone on. Of all Aether-level courses, Mysteries of the Mind was her favorite, but after last night, her concentration splintered between class and Barrington's spell burning a hole in her inner mantle pocket.

Even worse, thinking over the rather odd visit with Barrington had chased away all sleep, and come morning she still wasn't sure what exactly had happened. When he could have expelled her and burned her wand for using wandless magic, he'd instead asked her to be his assistant — in dealing with murder, of all things. *Need*, he had said. But... Sera settled back. What need could be so great that he would seek her out? And above all, *why her*?

Mrs. Aguirre set down her large wooden spoon on her workbench and picked up a vial of Rhodonite crystals. The round, silver-haired woman then turned to the class. "If everyone would please pour the contents of your vials into your spell dishes. What I am about to show you is an alternate method to the potion we've brewed."

Sera twisted the cork off the narrow tube and sprinkled the pink dust into the black dish on her worktable. A hairline crack ran the length of the dish, but without any funds, she had been unable to secure a new one.

"If at any time your patient cannot drink the Rhodonite elixir and gives you permission to access their memories, you can always sprinkle the crystals on their forehead as you've done on the dish," she said, her tone an excited, secretive whisper. "If they are completely unconscious, chances are it will not work. But if they show the slightest bit of consciousness—even if just a murmur—you can appeal to them, as their spirits can still hear you. They can then allow you entry into their minds where you can uncover whatever it is they're unable to tell you due to injury or illness."

Sera made a mental note to research the method later on, when she could think beyond Barrington's spell. Perhaps she could use Rhodonite crystals to summon some of her own memories? It was worth a try. Aetherium doctors could have attempted it, but who would waste precious resources on a seventhborn?

Images flitted through her mind of that terrible night she was rescued two years ago. Of those Aetherium doctors in their stark white robes who poked and prodded her with their wands to heal her cuts, not caring that they inflicted pain themselves.

Still, the pain they caused had been nothing compared to...*him*, and the cruelty he'd inflicted on her for a year. Though she had not one memory of her life or her family when he'd found her, he'd taken her under his wing and given her a place beside him. He became her everything, the only person she trusted. But then she learned he was no person. He was a monster. A knot jammed firmly in her throat. She didn't need Rhodonite crystals to remember his viciousness. She bore the proof of it on her skin. But Sera shook her head. She wouldn't think of him. He was dead, and she was free. As free as a seventhborn could ever be.

Mrs. Aguirre circled the much larger cauldron dominating the front of the room, her black skirts dragging behind her. With the vial of pink crystals in hand, she motioned the proper application along her forehead. "You sprinkle the crystals on their brow just as you've done in your dishes. If some spills off the side, that's fine. All that matters is proximity to the mind. Then, with your wand, slowly ease out your magic. This will ignite the crystals, and if you've acquired their permission, their memories will linger in the smoke. But I stress, this requires a great deal of skill and will work only with permission. Also keep in mind that any information recovered in these sessions is confidential. Betrayal of this trust could cost you your wand." She lowered her hands. "Now, set your wands above the dust and feed your magic out slowly, covering the crystals…"

Sera drew out her wand and held it over the dish, her magic already racing within her. Magic manipulation was part of Water-level courses during the first year of schooling—a year she missed entirely, along with Earth levels, which made this class all the more taxing, considering half was dedicated to brewing potions. Still, she took a calming breath and imagined her magic as a spinning reel, a tip from Mary to help Sera control her vast reserve of magic. She envisioned herself winding it back…back…back…until it stopped.

She hissed. Denying its release forced her magic to gather in her fingertips. Her hands burned and trembled under the strain, and sweat sprouted at the back of her neck.

"Remember, slowly," Mrs. Aguirre echoed, pacing through the rows and nodding in satisfaction. "Not all birds soar on their first try."

Sera winced. Mrs. Aguirre had meant it to be kind, but of all the words she chose to say... Sera shut her eyes tightly against the memories threatening to surface. This was not the time.

Sera, Sera in a cage...

No, she wouldn't think of him.

She focused on her mound of Rhodonite crystals and thought of her magic as a small stream, trickling from her fingertips. A cloud of red smoke seeped from the tip of her wand.

Sera, Sera wants to fly...

Her magic rattled for release, but clenching her teeth, she held it back.

But her pretty wings are broken...

Refusing her powers burned her fingers. The heat then swept up her arms and into her head like claws biting into her skull. But she had to hold it a little...bit...longer...

Mrs. Aguirre drew closer.

A little longer...

Look at her fall from the sky...

Sera cried out, the pressure in her temples feeling as if it might crack her head in two. Magic burst to her fingers, hot and burning. Fire flared from the tip of her wand like a torch and consumed the dish and crystals. The force thrust the wand from her hand.

Mrs. Aguirre rushed beside her and whirled a hand over the dish. "Extinguish!"

The flames died with a hiss. Curls of thick, gray smoke swiveled from the Rhodonite crystals, now black instead of pink. The class grew quiet, but Sera's pulse beat wildly in her ears.

Mrs. Aguirre stared at her, her ochre complexion deepening, her brown eyes wide behind her glasses.

"I..." Sera started, but struggled through the smoke and memories clenching her throat.

She snatched up her wand and rushed out of class, hurrying back to her room in the tower. Kicking the door to her room closed behind her, she slid to the floor, her maroon skirt spread around her like a pool of blood. Folding her legs to her chest, she bumped her forehead against her knees. If only it could dislodge the stupid, stupid memories. He was dead. He couldn't hurt her anymore...

And yet, here she was once again.

Fumbling with her cloak, she pulled Barrington's spell from the safety of her mantle's inner pocket and set it before her. These ciphers—this spell was all that mattered. Her memories wouldn't ruin this.

When it was time to see Barrington, Sera dragged herself to her feet, paced the room, and eyed the page. There was a circle with symbols along the border of the shape, a few she could decipher as a basic protection spell. On the outside rim of the circle were the coordinate ciphers of Barrington's location. The character in the middle of the circle, however, she had never seen before. When they studied elementary transfer spells during Air-level courses—moving simple objects like onions and radishes—there wasn't ever anything written inside the protection circle.

She hefted a sigh. The transfer spell was not going to draw itself. Eventually she would not need to draw or speak the spell, once she memorized it and could focus enough to spark the spell with her mind. In the meantime, she grabbed a stick of red chalk, flipped aside the corner of the rug by the window, and knelt. Then she drew a circle around her. The next few minutes were spent copying Professor Barrington's words onto the floor, checking and rechecking his atrocious letters against her finished diagram. The last thing she needed was to end up in the wrong place.

The spell perfect, she set down the chalk and wiped her hands on her skirt. Standing in the center of the circle, she drew her wand.

Her breaths grew shallow, her insides jittery. It had been ages since she'd transferred, the last time being when she was brought to the school, but she remembered the nauseating suction and drop sensation she'd felt in her stomach. Comingled with the fact that she was about to see Professor Barrington again, bile rushed into her throat.

Don't be stupid, Sera, she chastised herself, swallowing down the bitterness. She wasn't going to meet any danger at his hand…was she?

She steeled her spine and closed her eyes. Perhaps he was dangerous, perhaps not. But cowardice would get her nowhere, most definitely not into the Aetherium School of Continuing Magic. She tightened her hold on her wand and closed her eyes. Should Barrington have any ill will, she'd fight like hell to live, just as she'd done before.

"Ignite," she whispered.

Ready for the plummet she remembered, she drew in a breath. A moment passed, when…nothing.

She exhaled and snapped her eyes open. That wasn't right.

Brushing back to her work desk, she reviewed the spell, then her rendering on the floor. Everything matched.

When Madame Rousseau had done it, she had lit candles, though that had all been to help them focus. Barrington's spell didn't call for candles. Whatever the case, Sera set out to gather what candles she could. Of all the Air-level courses, transfer spells were not her forte, but tonight that spell was going to get her to Barrington even if she had to dig her way out with a spoon!

She positioned candles around the circle and, with a quick snap, lit a fire at their wicks.

Back at the center of the diagram, she closed her eyes and flicked her wand. "Ignite."

Nothing.

Sera grunted and stomped her foot. The candles had been lit, the protection circle drawn, and the coordinates were right. "Why isn't it working?"

She paced away from the circle. Had Barrington made a mistake? Had she?

Thrusting the page aside, she gripped her hair and dissolved the loose bun into a mass of curls. Her fingers brushed against a small cut on her scalp from Whittaker's *mistake*, and she paused.

Or could it be that Barrington was making fun of her?

She dropped her hands from her hair, a tumble of curls cascading onto her shoulders. Had she been deceived once more?

Perhaps they should've added masochistic tendencies to your file as well.

"Of course," she whispered. It made perfect sense. No wonder he had chosen her. He didn't need an assistant. He thought her a simpleminded, desperate seventhborn there for his own amusement.

Fists clenched and her pulse loud in her ears, she looked to the page, then to the perfectly drawn transfer spell. Every symbol was the same, down to the small curvature of his squares. But of course it didn't work. He meant to make a fool out of her. He was probably in his office, laughing at her pathetic efforts. Oh, she should've known better than to believe him.

"That good for nothing…" She crumpled the spell and threw it to the floor. "Despicable cur!"

She aimed her wand and blasted the sheet. The bolt ricocheted from the paper and sent it floating about the room. Sera lowered her wand, her eyes narrowed. Why on earth would Barrington proof a sheet of paper against an attack? *Unless…*

"You were expecting me to get angry, weren't you, *Professor*? You think you know me so well? I'll teach you. Get back here, you dratted sheet!"

She targeted the spell once more. A bolt of light flashed from the tip of her wand. The paper swiveled from its path, and the bolt crashed against the Aetherium crest over her bed. "Damn!"

Sera blasted freely at the page, angered more with each failed attempt. She chased it until blinded by the smoke filling the room. Until falling onto her knees, weary, spell books and vials scattered about her.

The room blurred in her eyes. As with every time she lost her temper, she would now have to clean up the mess. Slumping down onto the protection circle, surrounded by symbols, extinguished candles, and her self-pity, she curled into herself as the drain of magic settled in her bones, and her body grew cold, her reserve depleted. She would clean up later. For now, she would rest. No one would come. Everyone was used to her fits of rage…

But not to the tears that fell from her eyes as fatigue dragged her to sleep.

Sera woke with a start, the pull on her magic tight at her core. She pressed her hands down as the world righted itself before her eyes. Hardwood floors stretched beneath her just like in her room, but this ceiling of painted elemental signs was not hers. She rolled over and sat up. Neither was this room.

There was a large desk and behind it a floor-to-ceiling bookcase. Along the adjacent wall were more bookcases, only these reached mid-wall, where three arched windows covered by thick maroon curtains dominated the rest of the space. Behind her was a fireplace, and displayed prominently atop it was a painting of two young boys, twins, dressed in dated fashions. Both had striking gray eyes…

Her jaw clenched, as did her fists. "Barrington."

A gasp resounded behind her. Sera stood and spun to face a short, older woman. Puffed white hair peeked out from beneath her white cap.

The woman dropped the folded linens she'd been carrying and drew her wand from her apron pocket. "Who are you? Where did you come from?"

Sera raised her hands in surrender. "I mean no harm."

The woman jumped back. "Drop your wand this instant!"

"But I—"

"I said drop your wand!"

Sera loosened her grip on the wand and let it tumble to the floor.

"Now kick it here." The woman inched into the room, her wand pointed at Sera. "You chose the wrong home to steal from."

"I'm not here to steal, I came to—"

"Kick your wand this way!"

"What on earth is this commotion? Oh." Barrington appeared at the doorway, an apple in hand. He wore a white shirt, silver brocade waistcoat, and black pants, and looked much younger when not cloaked in his black professorial robe.

He leaned against the doorframe, his feet crossed at his ankles. "Miss Dovetail, you made it."

"*Miss Dovetail?*" The older woman looked at her, blue eyes wide. "You mean…you mean you know her?"

"Yes, yes. Put down your wand, Rosie. All is well. I was expecting Miss Dovetail, only…" He slid out his watch from his vest pocket and flicked it open. "It took her longer than I expected."

Sera's cheeks burned, and she eyed her wand. Rosie might blast her, but if she were quick enough, maybe she could strike him first. It would be worth the pain.

Pushing off the doorframe, he passed the quavering woman and entered the room.

Rosie adjusted her cap and smoothed down her apron, her cheeks and nose flushed. "I'm terribly sorry, miss."

Sera bent and gathered her wand. Sheathing it, she walked to the door and helped Rosie with the tumbled linens, but not before she glared at Barrington. "No apologies needed," she assured her. "No one was hurt. I'm sorry I frightened you."

They rose, and she set the folded pile into the woman's arms. Rosie bowed her head and exited.

Sera turned to Barrington by his desk, and her anger crested once more. "You should have told her I was coming. She could've killed me, you know."

"Rosie wouldn't hurt a fly—well, she would, actually. She hates flies. But not you."

"Well, I could have hurt her. Did you ever consider that I could've scared her to death, or mistakenly immobilized her? She's an elderly woman. She may not have survived."

Barrington pondered on this a moment, twisting the apple stem in slow rotations. A slight grin tipped his lips. "No, she has dealt with a lot worse than you in her years here."

Sera frowned, not doubting that one bit.

"So then." He motioned to the chair of red plush velvet across from his desk. "How were your travels? It seems you had some problems."

"And whatever gives you that idea?" She harrumphed, sitting. "The scent of smoke or the ash on my face?"

"Neither, really, though they're clear indications that I was right in protecting the spell as well. I time-altered it, you see."

Her fists gathered. "You did what?"

"Time-altered—the symbol in the middle. It delayed the time the spell took to work—"

"I know what time-altered means."

"Ah, good," he said plainly, ignoring her anger. "I also proofed it. I imagined once you gathered your wits, you might have wanted to give it another go. Had you burned it, you would have lost your chance at a referral." Small crinkles gathered at the sides of his eyes. "You're welcome."

She fixed him with a scowl. How could someone be so infuriating and irritating and boorish all at the same time and not explode?

"What do you think my test was, Miss Dovetail?"

"To torture me, I'm sure," she grumbled.

He walked around the office, much neater than his one at school. "I like torture as much as the next man, but no." He bit into his apple and chewed with precision, as though analyzing every burst of flavor, the same way he assessed her. "The first lesson is patience, which you lack in abundance, as evidenced by the way you nearly walked out of my office without so much as hearing my proposition and the way you almost destroyed the spell. Not to mention, the way you nearly set a boy on fire." He looked at her pointedly.

A blush pricked Sera's cheeks. He had seen her use wandless magic, of this she was sure. But if he was willing to overlook it, so would she.

"Remember always, Miss Dovetail, *a quick temper hinders understanding and brings about regret.*"

Sera smothered the urge to roll her eyes. If she wanted to listen to Pragmatic scripture quotes and judgments on her character, she would have gone to church service—were seventhborns allowed to attend.

He set down his apple. "But I must say, I'm happy you're here, however late you are."

She thought to say something. Perhaps, *thank you.* There had been a compliment somewhere in his words.

He clapped his hands together. "Now to discuss the reason you're here…" He stopped, his gaze fixed at her shoulder. "There is blood on your collar."

Sera raised a hand to the back of her head and winced. The cut wasn't bleeding but was still rather sore. "It's old, from yesterday. Having books fall onto one's head may do that to a person."

"You didn't go to the infirmary?" He reached a hand toward her.

Heart pounding, she rushed to her feet and shifted away. "What are you doing?"

Barrington retracted his hand. "I thought I might heal you, but I take it you prefer to be in pain."

Sera watched him for a moment as her heartbeat slowed and her mind registered his words.

A blush pricked her cheeks. Goodness, she had to relax, memories be damned. If they were to work together, she couldn't flinch at his every move.

Steeling her spine, she nodded her acquiescence. "Thank you."

Barrington's brow dipped, but he neared her and lifted his hand to her head. Sera cursed inwardly, hoping to all in heaven he didn't question her behavior.

"Pardon me, I…I thought your nearness improper…" she lied before he was able to ask.

"I'm afraid this pales in comparison to everything that is improper between us, Miss Dovetail. Now, relax."

She let out a breath. If only it were so easy. It wasn't every day she was alone with a man, her reputation and virtue in danger…not that she had any reputation to ruin or virtue to keep. But banishing all thoughts of her past to the deep, dark hole where she housed them, Sera blew out another breath and deflated. She was safe here. She had to believe it. If he had wanted to hurt her, he could have done it already.

Barrington closed his eyes. His jaw, shadowed by light stubble, clenched, and his brows gathered. From this close, Sera considered the brooding professor. There was a slight curve to his lips that hinted at a pleasant smile should he ever decide to stop scowling, and he had a nice nose, sculpted, but not too severe. His hair was thick and full, though he did little to tame it. It was always unruly, as if he spent his days caught in a windstorm. Still, he was handsome, Sera conceded but pursed her lips. A man with his ego already knew that.

Warmth stung Sera's scalp like tiny needles. The sensation grew to a wave of heat that clouded her mind and rolled down her limbs, slowly, until she felt sure she could float in it.

Hard as she wished not to, she stared at him openly,

knowing he traveled the threads of her life, seeking out the blackened ones that marked her injury. She'd always found healing such a fascinating art, and were she not in search of her family, she may have even taken up the study.

Her neck quickly wearied. He was taller than her by about a head, and she was forced to look up at him. Left staring at his chest that undulated with each breath, she surveyed the room instead. The painting above the fireplace called her attention, yet her eyes kept moving. Nothing to see there but the possibility of more Barringtons. Heaven knew, one of him was enough.

He lowered his hands and opened his eyes, a strange mix of grays with golden flecks. "There."

Sera touched the back of her head. No pain. "Thank you."

He nodded a silent *you're welcome*, turned on his heels, and walked back to his desk. "Now, for the reason you're here." He reached into a desk drawer and set out a file on the table. "I can't recall if I asked, but I do hope you have a strong stomach."

He opened the file, and her breath died in her lungs. Two bodies lay beside an exhumed grave. One was a skeleton, the other a charred, mangled corpse. Smoke curled out from the burned body, a frozen cloud of white in the picture.

He spread the impressions out on the table one by one. The scenes were the same, though the locations and victims varied.

"So many," she whispered, nearing the table. "Who did this?"

"That's what we're here to discover. So far, I've found no connection between the corpses and the burned witches, nor between the burned witches themselves. With the witches burned beyond recognition, I need a new pair of eyes to look through these photographs and point out anything I may have missed. Tell me what you see."

Sera spread out the pictures, trying to separate her emotions from the task at hand. "In every picture, a body has been exhumed," she said, analyzing the gnarled and dusty skeletons beside the graves. She focused then on the burned bodies beside them. "I think the burned corpses died most recently; there's still smoke emanating from their bodies. Their clothes are burned, but their dresses are still somewhat recognizable—"

"Yes, yes, I know this. Using your eyes is for ordinary humans, Miss Dovetail. You're far from ordinary. Embrace it." He was standing now. "*Look* at the picture."

She lifted one before her eyes.

She set it down and picked up another. There was nothing there she hadn't described. A dead body. Smoke. A coffin unearthed.

"Focus on the photograph," he repeated, pacing behind his desk.

Jaw tight, she picked up another and stared. Putting it down, she tried the next. This was impossible.

"Do not force the answer," Barrington said. "Let it come."

She dropped the impression back onto the desk. "I am waiting. I'm staring until my eyes dry…and nothing."

He brushed a hand aside. "We're done for the night. If you don't want to learn, I can't force you." He stacked the images into a pile. "Take them with you, and under no circumstances are you to show them to anyone. A spell will not help you, not in this case, at least. Sit with them. Study them. Come back with your analysis, and we will continue. If not, I'll take the impressions and you're relieved of your duties."

Heat gathered in her cheeks. "If you will replace me so

easily, why not do it already? Why did you bother choosing me, anyway?"

"I have needed an assistant for quite some time, but, for one reason or another, no one has wanted to take up my offer of employment."

One reason or another. Sera stifled a snort. His boorishness and conceit were reason enough.

"And aside from my need, I haven't replaced you because everyone is wrong about me, Miss Dovetail. I had hoped, perhaps, they were wrong about you as well. So far, I fear I may need to accept they were right."

She gasped. "You—"

"I know nothing about you, yes, I know. You have told me before." He held the stack out to her. "Prove me wrong, then. You have a week to find something for me in these impressions. In the meantime, you will report to me every evening to commence your training."

"Training?"

He scoffed and lowered the impressions. "You didn't think I fancied for myself an untrained assistant, did you? If we are to work together, you will be on your best behavior during your classes, and at night you will report to me. No outbursts. No wandless magic. No setting things—*or people*—on fire. Come to think of it, we will begin with wand training."

Sera pursed her lips. "I know how to use my wand."

His brows rose in mock amusement. "Do you now? Then you must have us all fooled considering you typically leave an explosion or fire in your wake."

"You—"

"Wayward boor? Yes, I've heard it before as well. But I've a better one for you. You're brilliant. Your power is vast and your reserves impressive. But you're careless and impulsive, and soon you will learn that all the raw power and talent in the world mean nothing in magic if you don't know how to use them. That will require hard work"—he looked at her levelly—"and patience. Losing control may give you a semblance of power, but you will realize that when you need your magic most, it will not work. It will scatter and be utterly useless. Only with focus and control can you achieve what you need it to do."

Sera stared at him, once again taken by his fierceness. Her suspicions flared. There was indeed something dormant beneath his stoic surface, and she had a sense that whatever it was had once lost control, too. "Do you speak from experience, Professor?" she ventured.

He turned his eyes down, but not before Sera noticed the undercurrents of sadness within them. "Yes, I do." He straightened, his mask in place, and handed her the impressions. "As I said, you have a week to find what I need in those impressions."

She snatched the pictures from his hand. "So this is another test, then."

He walked to her and pointed his wand at the floor. "It is. Only, if you fail these tests, other witches may die."

"What—"

"Dismissed."

Sera yelped, the ground beneath her vanishing. A blink of black and she crashed down onto her rug. Her hands loosened on the impressions, and they scattered around her. Stumbling back, she collapsed onto her window seat to steady herself as she gulped to dislodge her stomach, which had since found a home in her throat.

"You will get used to it, Sera," she coaxed herself as she knelt down. That, however, depended on whether or not she figured out what on earth was in these impressions that

Barrington had missed. He believed she could find it. But what could it be?

She gathered the photographs and shook her head at the unfortunate scenes.

"Who did this to you?" she whispered, and wished for once that the dead could speak.

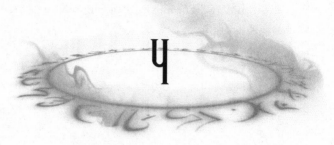

an ocean within him

Dark clouds lingered on the horizon, speckled by black ravens gliding along the countryside. Gray, muted light filtered in through the small window at the back corner of the classroom. Winter had clamped its bite down early; a cold breeze wheezed through what cracks it could find in the glass panes.

Sera burrowed into herself and hugged her arms about her torso to keep from fidgeting. After an entire evening of staring at photographs, images of dead witches had invaded the darkness of her closed eyes and made it impossible to sleep. She stifled a yawn and looked around the classroom. Worst was knowing that in a few hours she would start training as Barrington's assistant, which only made class that much more unbearable. With him, she would learn real magic and inspector work, not the useless drivel and theories she was forced to endure in some of her classes — she glanced at her History of Clairvoyance professor and frowned — especially this one.

"Next page," Mrs. Norton called out, her whispery voice a nuisance. Half of the time Sera couldn't hear her all the way in the back corner, and whenever she raised her hand, she was ignored, which had led to last month's altercation.

The Aetherium gave you a place, Miss Dovetail. Not a voice. Be grateful for what you have, Mrs. Norton had said, to which Sera could not quite remember what she replied, only that her face grew hot, the redness washed over her sight, and the next moment she was in the headmistress's office, explaining the obscenities she'd hurled at Mrs. Norton and the book she'd then thrown at the now-repaired window. Thankfully, Headmistress Reed had been much too busy to issue a real diatribe and punishment, and had Sera write an apology to Mrs. Norton on the blackboard, three hundred times over. It had taken her all night.

Sera turned the page, and her stomach tightened. As if her day couldn't get any lousier. Caricatures of old Purist officers were drawn along the page. With their beaked plague masks and all-black attire, they looked like ravens. And, like ravens, the old Purist officers were harbingers of doom, especially to every seventhborn who crossed their path.

Mrs. Norton sighed. "Which brings us to the Persecution."

A heavy silence settled over the room, one Sera was sure would not exist were she not present. A cold sweat pricked the back of her neck, her wool dress suddenly too constricting.

Pacing the room, Mrs. Norton read the tragic history of the plague that afflicted seventhborns, their skin riddled with pus-filled boils and their flesh turning black, as disease devoured their bodies. The Aetherium feared it was punishment on the magic community for allowing seventhborns to live. They eradicated its provinces of seventhborns, infected or not, lest the plague spread to everyone else.

The words mingled with the images of dead bodies in Sera's head. She squirmed in her seat, picturing hordes of seventhborns corralled and killed because of fear, because of a damned mark on their wrist and a birth order they had no control over. Their lifeless bodies tossed side by side, united in death as no one dared stand with them in life.

She swallowed thickly. Though the Aetherium government now embraced a Pragmatic religion, favoring reason over myth, Sera glanced about the room. They weren't fooling anyone. Whether Purist or Pragmatic, the role of the seventhborn would never change.

Mrs. Norton set down her book, her coal-black eyes resting on each student as though she meant to burn a hole through them. "How does this make you feel?"

Mary raised her hand, but Mrs. Norton glossed over her, pointing to Susan Whittaker in the front. Sera stifled a groan; the girl was as insufferable as her brother.

The tall brunette turned her eyes down and pressed a hand to her heart. "It pains me to think what those poor officers were forced to endure, how hard it must have been for them and taxing on their magic to rid our provinces of disease. They must have been so frightened to contract it themselves, but they did it for the sake of our people, and all magic is indebted to them and their valor."

Sera's throat dried. Curses swelled and surged in her chest. Barrington had warned her to stay out of trouble, and speaking would only negate that, but damn it all, how could anyone possibly stay quiet in the face of that?

Mrs. Norton nodded. "Yes, yes, many lives were lost, but the Aetherium was forced to take action."

Sera gazed down at the photographs of dead seventhborns spread about the page and clamped her mouth shut. She wouldn't say a word…

"Their kindness is what allows us to live free of the plague."

"Kindness?" The word grated her throat on the way out. Sera curled her fingers to fists, her pulse loud and fast in her ears. "They were *forced* to kill innocent seventhborns over a disease Pragmatics have since ruled questionable, and you call it kindness?"

Mrs. Norton slammed down her book on the stand. "Miss Dovetail—"

"Young girls—mere babes—were gathered in fields as if they were cattle taken to the slaughter, and you think Aetherium officers did it out of the *goodness of their hearts*?"

Heat flushed her body, concentrated on her back, on the marks of *kindness* someone felt compelled to leave upon her skin.

Students toured their eyes between Mrs. Norton and Sera, except for Mary. She kept her gaze focused on Sera, slowly shaking her head no. Sera wished she could have listened.

"Miss Dovetail, you will quiet down this instant!"

Sera bolted to her feet. "I will do no such thing! If you appreciate their kindness so much, how then would you like that kindness bestowed upon you?"

Mrs. Norton gasped, eyes wide. She unsheathed her wand, the tip illuminated in amber. "Is that a threat?"

She marched around her desk, her skirts swishing as she moved, as if warning Sera. *Shh, shh, shh...*

In the spaces between her pulse, reason wedged through, Barrington's voice whispering in her mind, *You will lose everything.*

Mary's words, *Think of your family.*

Sera's gaze trailed to her open book, to the Purist officers standing proudly before fields of dead seventhborns. As an inspector she could help the seventhborns who truly had no voice. Could help other witches avoid a similar fate.

She gulped down her rage, acid sloshing in the core of her stomach, and hauled in a breath. Heavens, how would she ever survive till assessments? "It was not a threat."

Mrs. Norton opened her mouth to speak, yet seeming to realize Sera's concession, she stumbled on the words that came, and the hue of her wand dimmed to its normal brown. "Y-yes, then. Very well." She eased back, her brow knit and confusion shading her stare.

An uncertain tension made the room crowd around Sera, and she sat down, winded. Hot tears filled her eyes, and she dug her nails into the heels of her palms, taming the heat that gripped her so tightly it felt as though her bones were breaking.

Nine o'clock found Sera on her knees, a stick of chalk in her hand. Lightning illuminated the room in flashes, while thunder chased it and rattled the windowpanes like warring giants. She drew out the various symbols of Barrington's transfer spell, sure to avoid the time-altering rune this time. He wouldn't trick her with that one again.

Setting aside the chalk, she picked up the impressions, aimed her wand to the floor, and closed her eyes. "Ignite."

The floor vanished beneath her. A second later, her boots tapped on the wooden floors, and she cringed at the sourness in her mouth. Goodness, would she ever get used to transferring?

She opened her eyes and gasped, startled by Professor Barrington leaning against the doorframe, his legs crossed at his ankles and arms folded over his chest. Dressed in all black, he looked like death come to claim her.

He slid gray eyes along her in one cool appraisal. "No progress with the impressions, I take it."

Sera glanced down at the macabre photographs in her hands and sighed. "I tried for hours last night but didn't see anything."

He was quiet for a moment, and Sera dug her nails into the grooves of her wand. Damn. Was he debating whether to send her back?

"Very well." He pushed off the doorway, walked into the hall, and out of sight.

Sera blinked, a hollow ache spreading in her chest. That was it? But she'd only just arrived. What of her training—

"Any day now, Miss Dovetail," Barrington called from the hall.

Relief rushed over her. She blew out a breath and followed him. He stood at the end of a long, dim corridor next to a large bay window. The storm that poured rain over the Academy appeared to have followed her to this place— whatever province Barrington called home. Come to think of it, she could be anywhere in the world. Lightning flashed, and thunder quickly followed. The white hue illuminated acres upon acres of moors before it was thrust into darkness once more. Nothing could be seen in the intermittent flash, not even the lights of other houses in the distance. And if that were at all a possibility, blinding sheets of rain began to fall and stole away the chance.

A deep-red runner stretched down the corridor and covered the dark pine floors all the way to the staircase at the center of the hall and beyond it. Recurrent exposed beams of the same wood framed the hall. Symbols ran the length of the beams, engraved ciphers that would look like simple vine-like decorations to a non-magical eye. Sera knew them to be protection spells. She observed them warily, then watched Professor Barrington walking before her. How much protection could one professor need?

Barrington stopped before the last door on the opposite end of the hall and pushed it open. The room inside was long and narrow and sparsely decorated save for a few tables along the blue damask walls. On the tables were spell books and various wands, some broken, others splintered. There were also empty platform stands clustered in a corner among old mannequins.

"This is my training room. We will work on focus and magic intensity." He strode to the corner and dragged a mannequin to the middle of the room. Then, taking the impressions from Sera, he set them on the table one by one. "You must look at the photos and let them speak to you."

She groaned. "I told you, I spent an entire night staring and saw the same things you do: charred corpses, mangled skeletons. What more do you want me to see?"

"Death, Miss Dovetail. I need you to see death. I could have asked any other witch, but I have asked you because of a seventhborn's ability to see death."

Sera stiffened and shifted back, her pulse quick. "I don't have the sight." She turned her gaze down. "And I don't want it."

Barrington was quiet. Sera didn't raise her eyes. No doubt he'd see the truth there, the stark fear that her enemy in life would now find her in death.

"The dead cannot hurt you," he said gently, clearly missing nothing. "The spirits you see are only those you summon. And should a spirit arrive uninvited, then you send them away and forbid their return. You are in control of them, just as you must be in control of your magic. You are thinking of magic as something needed to defend you. You need no protection here, Miss Dovetail. I can assure you, you're safe."

Sera lifted her lashes. His gaze bored into hers, an open stare where she sensed no deceit. Reason told her he could have hurt her already, yet memories rattled in her mind of others she had trusted, and her stomach twisted. But for her sake, for that of finding her family, she nodded. "I understand, Professor."

Barrington scrutinized her for a moment longer, then said, "Because your magic has always been your shield, it is tightly bound to your emotions, which in turn leads to…well, mishaps. You must learn to use it in other ways. In order to learn what is in these impressions, magic must be your eyes. This requires you to be calm and receptive. Using magic will not always be a manic, destructive endeavor, but rather…"

He held out his wand. It illuminated blue, then a stream of magic curled from the tip slowly until a thin cloud hovered above them, a universe with sparks of magic dashing within it like shooting stars.

"Controlled…"

Wherever he moved his wand, the mist followed and spread until it encircled them.

"Gentle…"

Twines of his magic curled out from within the cloud, whispering past Sera—soft, cool caresses against her cheek, phantom fingers brushing through hers. She lifted a hand, awed at how delicate magic could be. It had always been separate from her, as if a sword she had to carry at all times. Yet, as Barrington moved his wand, overhand and under, his wand illuminating just before a flare of magic joined the collective around them, a slow smile spread on Sera's lips. He was one with his powers, and it was beautiful to witness.

In these moments, his brow eased and the lines of his mouth relaxed, and nothing else seemed to exist but him and his magic, together. She lowered her hand, wanting to feel the same with her powers.

"You must be unafraid." He met her gaze through the strands of smoky magic weaving between them. "Are you ready?"

Sera nodded, more ready than she had ever been.

Barrington whirled a hand above him, and the mist dissipated with a whisper. Sera frowned at the void of his magic.

"You will do what I just did, but instead wrap your magic around that mannequin there. First we will work on controlling intensity, then flow. Now, aim your wand, close your eyes, and find your magic." He spoke smoothly, pacing around her. "It is a part of you that will feel…different. Some say it feels like a whirlwind in their soul. Others say it is like a boulder they must chip away at."

She didn't need to think hard on her answer. "Fire," she replied. "When I get angry or scared, I feel it sloshing within me."

"I thought so. Imagine yourself touching that fire. If you don't want it to burn you, then reduce its intensity."

Sera focused on her breathing, falling deeper into herself…deeper…until finding the wild flame that hummed and churned in her belly. She visualized her hand reaching out to touch it. It flared, and she gasped, spearing a blast of fire at the mannequin. Her eyes snapped open just as Barrington held up a hand and with a twirl of his wrist extinguished the flames.

Damn. She clenched her jaw, her grasp tightening around her wand.

"Calm, Miss Dovetail. I did not expect you to get it on

the first try. You have been on the defensive for a long time."

"And I bet you think I shouldn't be angry," she seethed, but cut herself off with a sigh. "Sorry, I…"

"On the contrary. I want you to use that anger to control your magic, not spur it," he said, his tone sharp and brow furrowed, though Sera didn't sense any anger. For a second, she could imagine what he was like in the classroom, stern and focused as he swept up and down the aisles with a fierceness and determination that made his students want to succeed, to be better.

He motioned to the mannequin and stepped back. "Again."

Sera aimed her wand and closed her eyes. She would succeed.

She reached for the fire within her—

It crested, and another blast of magic shot out from her wand.

Damn it.

"Again," Barrington ordered.

Flames, wilder and hotter, dashed from her wand and consumed the mannequin.

No, no, no.

"Miss Dovetail—"

A flare *whooshed* out from her wand, a hotter surge of heat. Barrington waved a hand, and the fire extinguished, but Sera raised her wand once more. Her insides vibrated, shame and anger colliding within. She wouldn't fail. She couldn't.

A blow of heat spread from her belly, rushing to her fingertips. She aimed her wand.

"Miss Dovetail, stop."

She would control her magic if it was the last thing she did.

Magic exploded from her wand, a flood of bright red fire. The flames engulfed the mannequin, spread like wings, and billowed, igniting the surrounding tables.

"Miss Dovetail!" With a wider sweep of his arm, Barrington snuffed the encroaching flames. Thick smoke gathered around them, whirls of white that drifted about like ghosts.

He yanked her wand from her fingers, and Sera startled. Goodness, she had forgotten he was there. Shame flushed her cheeks, and hot tears clung to her eyes.

"Were that our last shred of evidence, you would have destroyed it." Barrington raked a hand through his hair and sighed. "You cannot force it to happen. You must channel that anger if you wish to ever become an inspector. You will see things that will make your stomach turn, your skin crawl, and will shatter you to pieces. But you must master your emotions to do your job or you will never succeed."

He shook his head to himself and handed her back her wand. "We are done here for now."

Sera gripped her wand, her knuckles white. A vast, hollow ache spread through her chest, and her next breath hitched. He was worried she might eventually destroy a last piece of evidence, and she had proven him right. "Good night, Professor." She aimed her wand at the floor, wishing her heart would vanish instead. "Ignite."

A moment later, nothing.

"Miss Dovetail," Barrington spoke behind her, much softer. "Only I can transfer you out of my home. A protective measure. And…" His footfalls approached, and he stopped close behind her. "You're forgetting something."

Sera turned. He held the stack of impressions out to her.

"You…you still want me to take them? What if I…?"

"Burn them?" A small smile tipped the left side of his lips. "Give me some credit, Miss Dovetail. I did not become a professor at my age for lack of smarts. They've been fire-proofed."

Of course they had. She reached out and grabbed hold of them, but Barrington didn't release them. "Remember, your anger is neither your enemy nor your master. Work with it, and keep practicing." He relinquished the impressions. "I will see you on Monday."

She frowned. She had forgotten it was Friday. In spite of her failures, for the first time, she couldn't wait to try again. "Good night, sir. And I'm sorry for…" She motioned to the smoke that had since thinned and the black scorch marks on the tables.

Barrington slid his hands into his pockets and surveyed the damage. "If I feared fire, I never would have asked you to be my assistant."

Which made her wonder, "What do you liken your magic to, Professor? Fire, a boulder, or a whirlwind?"

He meditated on this a moment, where Sera wondered if she'd overstepped her boundaries.

"An ocean," he replied finally.

She nodded; an ocean, indeed. Ominous and mysterious, Barrington had been a calm sea at the school with Whittaker, yet an undercurrent had emerged when he looked at Timothy. Tranquil when he used his magic, yet intense in teaching her. But remembering the protection spells along his home, his *need* to solve these murders, she couldn't help but wonder what secrets lay in his depths.

5

the prettiest eyes in the world

Two days.

Sera leaned her head back against the rough bark of a tree, smothered her face with her hands, and groaned.

Two bloody days and nothing.

The smoky images of dead and gnarled bodies danced in the dark behind her closed lids, the same way they haunted her dreams each night. Her eyes now open, she sighed and shut her Divination book with a loud *thump*, stuffing the edges of the impressions inside.

Professor Barrington had said no spell would help her uncover what was in the photos, and, damn it all, he was right. There was nothing in any of her books about impressions or what she should look for. Worse, there was no spell that would uncover hidden objects or meanings in the photographs. Besides, how could she know what to research if she didn't know what to look for? He hadn't even given her a hint.

"Useless book," she muttered, and tossed it onto the

dew-damp grass.

"Are you sure? I sometimes like to use them as paper-weights," a voice spoke from behind.

Breath caught, Sera jumped to her feet and spun to find Timothy Delacort just beyond the brush, his dark coat and black curly hair camouflaging him in the shadows. He gave a small, hesitant wave and smiled…a very nice smile that made his eyes a little brighter, bluer, prettier. Still, Sera stifled the thoughts, took a step back, and then another. Pretty eyes or not, the last thing she needed was trouble with Timothy Delacort, of all people.

He moved out of the bushes and into the soft morning light that flashed through nearly barren branches. "It was a joke. I meant that you could perhaps find another use for the book."

"I know what you meant," she clipped and shifted back more.

His brows dipped, and he halted his approach. "I've frightened you. Forgive me, that wasn't my intent. I was reading down by the lake," he said, holding up a book, "and was heading back before everyone woke when I saw you here."

"Then why did you stop?"

He opened his mouth to speak but stumbled on fragmented words.

"Forget it. It doesn't matter." She picked up her book. "I have to get to class."

"On a Sunday?"

She paused. "I meant to say I have—I should…" A burn crept up her cheeks, and it was she who now muttered unintelligible nothings. "Never mind. I have to go. Good day, Mr. Delacort."

"Call me Timothy, please. And don't go. I didn't mean

to disturb you. I, too, like to get out a little earlier. Can't really think with everyone around, and the forest is always so quiet at this time. But I much prefer reading by the lake, by the waterfall there." He pointed to the south with his book, his gaze sweeping in the same direction. "It's a bit cold, and the spray always dampens the pages, but it's quiet." A sense of peace overcame his features, and she could see he found calm and freedom there, the same she sought when she snuck out into the forest that dawn.

Silence trailed his words, one where even the song of the birds died away, as though the forest watched this secret meeting.

"Miss Dovetail," he said then, his knuckles white on the book, "I confess my reasons for stopping were not entirely of curiosity. Yes, I wondered how you were—are, but I also wanted to...to stop and talk to—with you, talk with you about, well, about things that I've been thinking of for some time. I was going to ask Mary but didn't know how to phrase it without sounding like a fool."

Sera took in his strange nervousness, the way he paled and grasped his book as if the words about to be spoken would gut him alive. "You want to talk about Mary and the dance. Well, she will say yes if you ask her. Very happy, indeed. Good morning."

She spun and walked in the opposite direction.

"Oh, I'm flattered," he spoke from behind, "but that wasn't what I meant. I did not mean to speak of Mary."

"Then we have nothing to discuss," she said over her shoulder.

"Will you at least allow me to escort you? It would be terribly ungentlemanly of me to let you walk back on your own." His footsteps neared her from behind.

Heartbeat in her ears, she unsheathed her wand and spun

to him. Her eyes darted all around, to the spaces between the trees and the shadows beyond them. Critters skittered and rustled the thickets and dead leaves surrounding them, their bright golds and ambers overcome by the brown of death. "Where are your friends?"

Timothy's brow dipped. "Friends? I don't understand—"

She aimed her wand at him, halting his words and approach. "I may be a seventhborn, Mr. Delacort, but I am no fool. I know who you are, and you would not risk your reputation on the basis of talking to, no less walking with me. So I'll ask you again…" Her grip tightened on her wand. "Where are your friends? Do you plan on an ambush? Fancy tying me to a tree for target practice? Sorry to disappoint you, but it's already been done."

He held his hands at surrender. "I'm not here with anyone. I swear upon my wand."

She scoffed. "Don't insult me. You can just get another."

"You're right, but this one is irreplaceable. I inherited it from my grandfather this summer. It's not helping me too much in Aether-levels, but…" He shrugged a shoulder. "I would not risk it damaged for fear of my life." He lowered one hand slowly. "I'm going to toss it over to you as a show of goodwill."

Sera braced, her breath suspended as he reached for his wand. *If he dare try anything…*

He drew his wand and tossed it a good distance before him. Eyes fixed on his, Sera tucked her book under her arm and retrieved it.

The wand was beautifully fashioned out of branches twisted into a braid-like form. Much magic had flowed through it for many years, told by the highlights upon it. He would be a fool to bring damage to such a fine piece.

"Do you believe me now?" He shrugged. "You have my

wand. If I had any friends here—which I don't—I wouldn't risk my wand any harm."

She eased away, the hairs on the back of her neck still on end. "Regardless, I will hold it. You walk ahead, and when we reach the edge of the forest, I'll return it to you."

"Please, Miss Dovetail. This is wholly unnecessary. I would never hurt you."

She bristled at these familiar words once spoken by a monster in her past who sought to make her magic his own. The myriad scars along her body tingled to life as if her horrible memories sought to bleed out through them. Though she doubted Timothy—and even Whittaker—had the cruelty, much less the knowledge to drain her of magic, she wouldn't give them the chance to prove themselves.

"Walk." She flicked the wand and motioned for him to move. He deflated with a resigned sigh and turned, leading the way into the forest. Sera lowered her wand, lest anyone see them and think she meant to hurt him somehow, and followed some yards behind.

In the distance, early morning light swathed the two towers jutting up from the Academy that stretched across the countryside. Between the spires, a string of gargoyles dotted a stone archway. Though the sight once terrified her, Sera fixed her eyes on the monstrous stone creatures and found some comfort. They were not monsters but sentinels, the runes etched on their bellies protecting the grounds.

"I take it I'm not allowed to talk, either?" he spoke into the open before him.

She shrugged. "As long as you walk, you can say what you want. It's your forest."

"It's not *my* forest."

"Ah, so it's a coincidence that it's named after your family, as is the rectory and the girls' dormitory?"

Book in one hand and his other hand at his side, he strolled before her, a cool ease in his demeanor. She frowned. It was as if he enjoyed their walk.

"My family has close ties with the school. That I won't deny. I'll be a sixth-generation graduate."

"Impressive," she muttered.

He smiled over his shoulder. "You may be pretty, but you're not a very good liar."

She rolled her eyes. "Flattery will not get you your wand back."

"I merely speak the truth in hopes of overcoming this… *impediment* we find ourselves in. An obstacle I have found us in for quite some time. When I said I wished to ask Mary something, it wasn't about the dance but about this barrier between us."

"I wasn't aware we had an *impediment*," she said, focused on the Academy entrance coming into view through the trees.

"You acknowledged it yourself. You said you knew nothing about me and therefore could not trust me. But we could change that. Quite easily, too. I tell you about my life, you tell me about yours, and then we can't claim not to know each other, thus banishing this impediment. And perhaps then, we wouldn't be so lonely."

Sera chuckled bitterly at this. "What do *you* know of loneliness? You aren't alone, ever. And you not knowing me and my being alone is not an impediment, it's a conscious choice I make every day, the same way I make it now." She tossed the wand beside him, keeping hers close at her side. "As promised, we've reached the edge of the forest. Take your wand and go before anyone sees us here."

He bent, and in retrieving his wand, he smiled, though this time the gleam didn't reach his eyes. "You can be surrounded by hundreds of people and still be very much alone." He sheathed his wand and shrugged. "Still, I'd hoped that perhaps for one night, for one dance, we could set aside our differences and not be so alone...together."

Cold rushed down her spine and fixed her to the damp ground.

"But a man should know when to count his losses, and I've accepted mine." He inclined his head. "Thank you for the walk and for my wand, and forgive me for disturbing you. It will not happen again. Good morning, Miss Dovetail." With no more words, he turned, walked away, and never looked back.

Sera watched him grow smaller with distance, though his words echoed in her mind as though he stood beside her, whispering them into her ear: *Perhaps for one night, we could set aside our differences and not be so alone...together.*

Together.

Did Timothy Delacort mean to say he wanted to go to the dance with *her*? She shook her head and watched him disappear into the school. It had to be a ruse. Timothy Delacort would never go to the dance with her. He would have probably laughed if she'd agreed, and then he would have told all of his friends. Mary would be sure to find out a short time later. She could clearly see the heartbreak in Mary's eyes, hear her sobs mixed with the echo of laughter that would follow her down the halls.

No, it made no sense to pay mind to his words, however genuine he seemed to be. Honest or not, she could never go to the dance with him. Nothing changed who she was. Not magic, not common loneliness, and not a boy with the prettiest eyes in the world.

6

puppets

That evening, Sera spread the photographs on her worktable and swore. She should have just sent Timothy away, or ran away herself. If so, she wouldn't have heard his stupid, stupid words that now played at the edge of her consciousness. She wouldn't have doubted her actions. Focusing on the death spread before her, she banished him to the abyss where her heart lived. She wouldn't ever trust him. Nothing was going to get in the way of her dreams or her friendship with Mary, especially not a boy.

Pin by pin, she released her rigid bun and shook out her hair. *Patience*, she reminded herself while massaging her temples in even, circular strokes. Last night, she had stared at the pictures for hours and nothing happened. Tonight, it had to work.

Firelight danced along the walls, washed out by recurrent flashes of lightning. Sitting on the edge of her bed, she pressed bare feet on the floor and held her wand tight at her lap. She would stay there and stare as long as it took. Come Monday,

Barrington would expect answers, and answers she would give him.

An hour later, the clock marked eleven. One hour closer to Monday. Sera rolled her shoulders, ignoring the peals. Lightning lit up the sky, and an answering thunder rumbled. The whitish light spilled over the pictures she focused on intently. As always, the steady hush of rain and moan of the winds calmed her, carrying away all thoughts save for Barrington's words that she replayed as a mantra in her mind.

She breathed in...

Do not force the answer.

Out...

Let it come.

In.

Do not force the answer.

Sera paused. A slow trickle of numbness rolled down her spine.

Let it come...

Upon her next breath, the seep grew to a wave of fatigue that spread to her limbs and joints. The room took to a sudden and slow spin around her, much like when she used a great deal of magic and her reserves of power dwindled. But she wasn't using any magic. Yet she grasped at her sheets as blackness framed the edges of her sight and proved the opposite.

A loud crash resounded in her ears, that of metal hitting stone. She winced and shut her eyes at the sound that pierced her eardrums. When the echoing sound faded, she opened her eyes and gasped. The room around her was changed. Her bed was no longer a bed but rather a wooden chair. And her room was no longer her room but a dim, rounded chamber of stone.

She stood slowly, her hands clasped tight on her

nightdress. In this room, gas lamps hung from hooks, and under their gilded light, the seams of the stone glittered, telling of magic. She spun in place and hesitated. There was a short hallway behind her and beyond it another chamber, only there were doors in this other room, many gated doors.

A cold chill of awareness rooted her to the ground.

"A binding-chamber spell," she whispered, inching closer to the corridor whose stone walls glistened under a thin sheet of condensation. She pressed her fingers to her lips and recalled all she'd learned of binding-chamber spells during her Air-level courses. Abilities or memories could be locked away within a magician's mind. Whenever the magician needed the confined ability or memory, their magic would remember where it had been bound, and with much concentration, the magician could break it. A survival mechanism, Mrs. Pewter had called it.

Once broken, the magician mentioned falling into a vision or a trancelike state where they encountered a hallway or a tunnel of gated doors—the number of doors dependent on how many memories or abilities had been locked away. An unlocked gate represented an unbound memory or ability that the magician would retrieve upon walking through the door.

Sera sucked in a breath. No wonder her powers dwindled rapidly before. To break the spell took a large amount of concentration and vast reserves of magic. Something in the photos must have made her magic believe she needed whatever memory or ability had since been unlocked. She gulped. What on earth could it be?

Taking one of the gaslights in hand, she held it before her and started down the hall. The beveled stone floor was damp beneath her bare feet, and the stark cold bit at her toes. She eyed the encircling shadows but found herself very much alone. Droplets of water echoed in the deep silence, and beyond it, nothing but the flicker of torches.

Through the arched doorway, another chamber spread before her, long and narrow and lined with gated doorways on either side as far as the eye could see. Lit torches flanked every door…except for one set a slight distance away. A strange sensation coiled at Sera's core, an invisible reel pulling her closer to the door.

Lamp clutched tightly in her hands, she walked down the center of the hall. A cool mist roiled along the stone ground, and she shivered, her tattered nightdress no match for the damp chill. Door after door was shielded with wrought-iron gates closed with black padlocks. With each locked door she passed, her heart sank a little more. She didn't have just one memory or ability bound, but countless. She shook her head. Why, at only eighteen, did she have so many secrets sealed within her? Surely behind one of these doors was the memory of her father and siblings. One of the gates shielded the first fifteen years of her life before she woke up on the ship with no recollection of ever boarding.

She detoured and neared one of the lit doorways. The torch fires flickered, agitated by a fierce, phantom wind. Sera let out a breath and hesitantly reached for the gate. She hissed and retracted her hand, the metal scalding.

A feral pain pulsed in her palm with each heartbeat. She turned it upward and swore. The skin there was burned, a blister already formed, surrounded by pink, inflamed skin. With the injured hand at her chest, she stumbled back from the gate. It would be impossible to open it, not until she somehow broke the spell that kept the door shut. After one last side-eye at the offending door, she focused on the only unlit doorway.

She stood before the entryway and swallowed. Shadows

swathed the small, tunneled entrance. She lifted her lamp and chased away the darkness. A broken padlock was on the ground in pieces. More worrisome, the gate and door were ajar.

A shiver shook her frame, her pulse loud in her ears. This must be the spell she had broken. One sliver of memory or an ability set free. All she had to do now was walk through the door. The burn on her palm pulsed as a painful reminder, but Sera inched forward. Sidestepping the broken padlock, she stopped before the gate and held her hand over the metal. No heat radiated from it. Still, she quickly tapped the gate with a finger. Perhaps the burn muddled and numbed her senses, but no sting met her finger.

The gate groaned as she pulled it open, the hinges stiff.

She hauled in a breath and tapped the knob quickly. This too was cool. But while the metal did not burn her, Sera withdrew her hand and hesitated. She could taste her fear, an acrid thing that soured her stomach. Could hear it screaming *danger* in the back of her mind. What if that door had been locked for a reason, done by someone who knew its contents would hurt her? Barrington's words assailed her next, a deep-seated worry that she herself had wondered many times. What if her family didn't want her? What if she remembered them casting her out, cursing her existence?

That was a possibility, but she opened her palm and glanced at the singed skin. Something in Barrington's photos brought about this experience, unwittingly caused her to break the binding spell, and led her to this door. Images of the witches flashed through her mind. She had but a burned hand. Those victims died, their whole bodies incinerated. Was it not the duty of an inspector to face trouble head-on—whatever the danger—as long as it uncovered the truth?

She lowered her hand to her side and steeled her spine.

Yes, in spite of what waited on the other side of that door, the knowledge would not benefit just her but those whose lives had been cut short.

She stepped forward, clutched the doorknob, and pushed the door open. Darkness. Sera gulped.

"I will be an inspector," she whispered to herself in prayer. "I will be an—"

She swept inside.

"Inspector."

The vision vanished, and she was in her room once more. Sera bolted to her feet and spun in a circle. Yes, this was her room entirely. She stalked to the window and yanked the frayed curtain aside. The world outside also remained unchanged under angry sheets of rain that slammed against her window and thunder that made it shudder. She turned, and her gaze locked on the clock on the mantel. Not even a minute had passed, though it felt like she had been in the binding chamber for hours.

Leaning back against the windowsill, Sera closed her eyes and braced, gripping her wand like a lifeline. This was it. Whatever memory or ability she had unlocked in the binding-spell chamber was at her disposal now.

Years of wonder swelled her throat, but she whispered, "Father?"

She searched the darkness of her closed eyes and found nothing. Bitter pain twisted her insides.

"Sisters?" she whispered, her voice weak. "Brothers? Family?"

A moment passed.

Nothing.

The heaviness in her chest vanished, leaving a painful void. "Serves you right for getting your hopes up," she whispered to herself. A hot tear spilled through her lashes and trickled down her cheek. "What did you think to find?"

Voices echoed far away—faint sighs that reached her as unintelligible murmurs. Throat dry, she pressed back against the wall, fear welding her eyes shut. The temperature in the room plummeted, and awareness pricked the back of her neck.

The second sight.

All seventhborns were not only burdened with a cursed birthright but with the dreaded second sight once they came into their full powers. While some were rumored to have premonitions of death, others even able to see glimpses of the dead, Sera had manifested neither. Now it all made sense why. This ability had been bound and locked away with her many, many other secrets. And now it was unbound.

A wheezing breeze whispered past and rustled her hair against her cheek. A tart, sickly sweet scent filled her nose and squeezed bile into her mouth. Sera hugged herself, arms pressed tight against her body. She knew exactly what it was that burned before her and willed herself to be brave. She had to open her eyes. Whatever it was, it couldn't hurt her. Ghosts could cause no physical harm.

She clutched her wand tight. *One…two…three.*

Her eyes snapped open. A broken breath left her. Another one didn't come. There was no one in her room, material or immaterial. Instead, a white fog, similar to that which hovered over the corpses' mouths, curled out from the impressions on the table in the middle of the room. The pungent smoke spilled over the edge of the table in continuous waves that now blanketed the floor.

The twirls of white slithered toward her, ghostly fingers preceded by a thin sheet of rime. The ice crackled and splintered like breaking bones as it approached her. Whereas once she would have run or blasted the impressions into a pile of ash, she slid against the wall and held herself still as the smoke wound about her feet. The mist, cool and damp against her skin, shackled her leg now covered in gooseflesh. It rippled then, much like a taut string being pulled from within the impression. Understanding the ghostly summons, Sera abandoned the wall and followed the mist to its origin. Heaven help her if it was the wrong choice, but there was only one way to find out.

With each step closer, the room grew colder and the scent of scorched flesh intensified, as the whispers became clearer. Face contorted from the horrible smell, she cupped a hand over her mouth and nose and turned her ear. The myriad of voices were different, yet all were feminine and urgent and scared. Some shouted *no, please don't make me*. Others cried, *don't do this*. Most disturbing, beneath their cries, a collective of voices whispered the same thing: *puppet*.

She stopped a few inches away from the table and peered over the pictures. The smoke spilled out from each impression and into the room like fog rolling in through an open window. Her eyes narrowed. Through the thinning smoke, she noticed the scenes in the pictures were still the same, but unlike before, the impressions were now riddled with ciphers. She lowered her face to the pictures slowly, her breathing suspended in fear that one breath would blow the circular symbols away. The markings were everywhere, scattered over the dead bodies and on the ground.

Rubbing her fingers together, she reached out to shift aside a photo that partly shielded another.

A hand burst out from somewhere in the smoke and clamped down on her wrist. "Puppet!"

Sera screamed and yanked her hand free. The force sent her backward and, tangled in her nightdress, she tripped and slammed to the floor. Sharp pain pulsed at the back of her head that she hit on the leg of her bed. In spite of the ache, she scurried to retrieve her wand and clambered to her feet.

The fog was gone. So were the voices, the scent, and the cold. Around her, the floor was dry in spite of the frost that had covered it moments ago. Her wand trembling in her hand, she approached the impressions once more. The scenes within them remained immobile, from the bodies to the smoke, and the symbols were gone. She shoved one picture aside with her wand and shifted back.

Nothing.

She spun and eyed the spaces around her, from the shadows in the corners to those underneath the bed. Satisfied that the nightmare was over, she crashed down onto the chair by her reading desk, deflated. She searched for answers in her mind—things she had read, stories told to her by others—and nothing could explain the living nightmare she'd just experienced. She had not seen any ghosts; at least the hand that gripped her had not been cold nor pale, no.

Remembering it, she reached blindly for a paper and quill pen, sure to keep the image fixed in her mind. The hand had been thick and masculine. She shivered. No, that had been no ghost. None of the voices that chanted had been masculine.

She paused. And what of those voices? She jotted down *Puppet* and a question mark. What could they have possibly meant? She proceeded to write the ciphers from memory. It was a spell. Of that she was sure, but what kind of spell?

Breathless at the questions that seemed only to multiply, Sera wrote them all down quickly, her handwriting perhaps as bad as Barrington's. Was this what he expected her to see? How could he have known she would see it—the smoke, the hand, the symbols? Perhaps it was another test…but if so, why could she see the symbols now but hadn't been able to see them before? Why had her second sight been bound?

Pen tapping against the sheet, she shook her head. Questioning herself would not bring about anything but more questions. If she wanted answers, she would have to see Barrington, regardless of proprieties and the time.

She dressed quickly, gathered up the impressions, and hurried to the corner of the room. Chalk in hand, she lifted the rug and quickly drew out the transfer spell minus the time-altering symbol. With the impressions held tight at her chest, she hauled in a breath and aimed her wand.

"Ignite."

anchors

The heels of her boots thudded on a wooden floor. Sera stumbled forward and gripped the mahogany fireplace mantel to keep from falling. She lifted her eyes, and a frown found her mouth instantly at the picture of the twin boys just above the ledge. A thin rectangular gold plaque marked the bottom of the frame, one she had missed her previous time there.

Nikolai and Filip Barrington.

Abandoning the painting, she spun to the empty room. A part of her wished Rosie would happen to come in, or better yet, Barrington himself. Though missing from the room, his aura remained in the space, a brooding yet intelligent air that seemed to linger from his things, from the books stacked on his desk to his professorial robes hung on the coat-tree at the corner of the room. Clutching hard at the impressions, Sera strode to the door. His books and robes were not the ones solving murders. She needed to find the man.

She traveled down the hall, past numerous closed

doors. He could be in any of those rooms, if he was even on this floor. If he was even home! She bit her lip. Had she overstepped her boundaries in coming unannounced on a weekend? What if he sent her away, not even bothering to transfer her back to the school? She didn't need impeccable manners to know it improper to seek him out in his home.

But he had said a witch could die in the time it took her to find what was in the pictures. Her hand tight on the photographs, she hurried to the training room. Upon not finding him there, she rounded back to the staircase and descended.

"Damn," she muttered, reaching the ground floor. The grand stairs led down to a large parlor dominated by a round table in the middle with a vase of white flowers on top. Through an archway before her was the entrance hall. There was a closed door to her left, and to the right, an empty dining room. Two hallways stretched beyond either side of the grand staircase.

She spun in a circle and crossed her arms over her chest, mulish. "What now?"

A yelp resounded. "Miss Dovetail!"

Sera spun to Rosie, who clutched a silver tray tightly, her pallor as white as her hair. "Oh, forgive me, Rosie. It seems I'm always frightening you with unannounced arrivals, but I swear I wouldn't be here if it weren't important. Is the professor in?"

Rosie's brows rose. She gazed down to the bottle of sherry and two tumblers beside it, and a hint of panic flashed over her eyes. "I...the Master...well, yes, but..."

The doors to the adjacent room swung open, and both women jumped. Barrington made to step out, but upon seeing Sera, he stopped short, his eyes fixed on hers unblinking. "Miss Dovetail?"

"Professor, I…" she began, but trailed off, noting his cravat was undone, shirt partly untucked, and hair tousled— more than usual. Her eyes narrowed. And was that lip rouge on his neck and collar?

Someone giggled from inside. "Dovetail? What sort of a name is Dovetail? I thought your maid's name was Rosie." A brunette head came into view from behind the sofa, but Barrington closed the door quickly before Sera could see the woman's face.

He cast a glance at the grandfather clock beside the entrance hall doorway. "It's past midnight, Miss Dovetail."

Sera's face burned at the gentle scolding, yet a scolding nonetheless. "Yes, I know, Professor. I wouldn't have come, but I…" The events of the night washed over her. Unable to sort through and make sense of all that had happened, she held out the stack of impressions and her notes. "Here."

Barrington took in the slight shake of her hands. "You saw," he said, his irritation washed over by his interest.

The door opened behind him before she could answer. She drew back the impressions as a woman strutted across the threshold. Dressed in a purple gown that did little to hide her breasts, the woman draped herself against the doorway like a lover, her brown hair disheveled. Red and black eye paint made her wide brown eyes wider, and her swollen lips were smeared in red rouge. Sera's cheeks warmed, her suspicions confirmed.

The woman glanced at Rosie's tray. "Is this the sherry you promised me, Barry?"

Sera raised a brow. *Barry?*

"Barrington," he said pointedly, then snatched the bottle from Rosie's tray and shoved it into the woman's arms and breasts. "Thank you for your help, Gummy. I'll look into… matters and report back."

Her red-stained lips bowed to a pout. "You mean the party's over?"

Barrington sighed. "Rosie, can you escort Miss Mills out, please?"

Gummy gasped. "Miss Mills? Why, you haven't called me that in ages, since before we—"

"Please, Gummy." He went to straighten his cravat, but seeing as it was undone, he merely smoothed it down and adjusted his waistcoat. "I've work to do."

She scoffed. "Work, I'm sure." Lips pursed, she eyed Sera from under painted brows. Sera eyed her the same, cleared her throat, and looked away.

Gummy chuckled. "What's the matter, young 'un? Never seen breasts before?"

Beside her, Rosie flushed and stuttered unintelligible words, then set the tray down on the round hall table with a loud *tap*. "Heavens be, Miss Mills. This way, please."

The woman gritted her teeth. Chin high and dress dragging behind her, she followed Rosie through a doorway, the bottle of sherry in her arms like a babe.

Barrington cleared his throat and drew back Sera's attention. He stepped aside and motioned for her to enter. "I take it the answer to my question is yes for you to come by so unexpectedly. I didn't expect to see you until tomorrow."

Sera blew out a breath and strode into the parlor. "Yes, well, you're not the only one not expecting to see certain… things."

He shut the door and said just as sharply, "Miss Dovetail, may I remind you, I am your superior, and what I wish to do on my own time in my home—"

She held up the photographs. "I meant these," she lied. She set the impressions on the round drawing room table and her page of notes beside them. "There were ciphers everywhere, but I can't interpret them."

"I wouldn't expect you to," Barrington murmured, perusing her notes. "Advanced cipher translations are years into Wood-level studies."

He picked up one of the impressions. Sera spun away, not yet wanting to look at them again. She paused, caught by her reflection in the quatrefoil mirror over the crowded mantel. If her arrival hadn't frightened Rosie, she was sure her appearance would have. The events of the night were imprinted on her; her usually fair skin was even paler and her brown eyes wide. The messy braid she'd managed with shaky hands had slipped, and now her hair tumbled wild over her shoulders. The firelight cast shadows on her face, and in the amber light, she looked haunted, scared, fallen. Had she still been in her white nightdress, she would have mistaken herself for a ghost.

"You can see it, then." Barrington rubbed his lips, a strange sort of smile marking his mouth behind his fingers. "Fantastic."

"It took me some time, but yes. Why did you need me to see them if any other seventhborn could have—"

"Did you tell anyone? Does anyone know you've developed the sight?" he asked from over the photos. "Anyone at the Academy? A friend, a teacher, anyone at all?"

"So that the Aetherium could swoop in and suggest I join their seers? Once a seer, always a seer, and never an inspector." Part of why she'd been happy not to develop the sight was not being recruited by the Aetherium as a seer the way other Academy seventhborns had been, forced to examine crime scenes for spells by criminals but never allowed to investigate the actual crime. To have her dream stolen away? Never. "No, Professor. No one knows. It happened just before I came here. I—"

Before she could dive into her list of questions, Barrington swept up the pictures and her notes and exited the room like a man being chased. She took off behind him, up the stairs, and into a workroom beside his study. He tossed the impressions onto a long table and strode to a bookshelf, one of many in the room. The rest of the shelves were dominated by vials and instruments. A telescope was before the window in the back of the room where there were two doors on either side of the chamber, one black and one wooden.

Barrington hovered before the bookshelf, fingers drumming at his lips. "Ah, here we are." He drew out a black tome squeezed onto the shelf and tossed it down on the table. Sera neared the workbench, sat at one of the stools, and watched him flip through the yellowed pages. Upon reading the title, she flinched.

"Necromancy?" She thought over the photos, the burned bodies next to exhumed graves, and the residing corpses. It made sense, but goodness, of all forbidden magic…

"Yes. I imagined that to be the case but couldn't be sure—not without the full investigative notes anyway. Sadly, a friend was able to get a hold of only the impressions and a handful of reports for me, but they had nothing of importance."

Sera's eyes widened. "You mean these are stolen?"

He shrugged off her alarm while comparing her notes to the book. "I rather prefer borrowed from the Aetherium, and when I no longer need them, I will have my friend return them."

Sera pinched the bridge of her nose. It was bad enough to be found dealing with anything necromancy related, but to be in possession of items stolen from the Aetherium? She sank into herself, feeling sick.

Barrington set down his pen and sat back. Small lines formed at his brow. "Well, aside from confirming the victims to be female, Aetherium inspectors also believed it to be a series of necromantic rituals gone wrong. Once a necromantic ritual has started, it must be finished. You can't partly open a connection to the Underworld. They assumed these women started the ritual without proper training, then realized they were out of their depths but couldn't turn back." He shut the book heavily. "But the cyphers here are a blend of magic, white and black, and older runes coupled with newer ones. This spell was crafted by a knowledgeable magician. It will take me some time to decipher the runes and test the various combinations to uncover the spell and its purpose. Did you see anything else that could help us?"

Memory of the hand that gripped her flushed ice through her veins, and she rubbed her wrist. After a moment, she lifted her eyes from the ciphers in the book and realized she hadn't answered him. But she didn't need to. Barrington set down his glasses, clearly gaining his answer from her silence.

He leaned forward, hands clasped on the table. "We are bound under the same oath, Miss Dovetail. While our arrangement is a secret, there can be no secrets between us. What did you see?"

She stood and paced the room. "It wasn't what I saw, but what I heard. Voices echoed in the smoke, girls—or women—*feminine* voices. They were sobbing and scared, and all repeated the same word: *puppet*." She stopped at the head of the table, goose bumps sprouted along her arms. "I believe I heard the girls in the impressions, which is why I think the Aetherium is wrong. They all screamed *no, please, don't make us*…as if they were being forced. And then there was a hand…"

Gazing at her wrist, she shivered at the memory of the

phantom grip. "When I touched the photograph, the hand reached out and grabbed me. It was only for a second, and I know it's impossible for ghosts to physically touch those of the living realm, which is why I know it wasn't a ghost... rather a memory, only it wasn't mine." She turned to him, but he stared down at the table, troubled. "I know you must think I'm mad, and I admit I would think the same, but I felt it. The hand was warm and masculine."

Barrington's gaze grew distant. "Interesting."

"What does it all mean?"

He rose. "It means that in hoping to solve one mystery, I've stumbled upon another: *you*," he clarified. "What you accomplished—a summoning—is something done years into Aetherium studies, yet you managed to do it on your first try, with various spirits at once." A small smile curved his lips. "A mystery, indeed."

"But I didn't try. It just happened." She shook her head. "Did it say anything about a summoning in the investigative notes you stole—"

"*Borrowed*."

Sera rolled her eyes. "Borrowed."

"The Aetherium inspector who was assigned to the case did have one of the seers summon the spirits, but they refused to cooperate. Spirits can be fickle and elusive, and yet they came to you."

"I'm beginning to think I imagined it all."

Barrington leaned back against the table, arms folded at his chest. "You didn't imagine it, Miss Dovetail. I'll admit, I'm as confounded by your abilities as you are, but you're in luck that I'm quite fond of mysteries and that I'm a rather magnificent magician. Worry not, I'll guide you through it."

"You want me to try summoning the victims? I don't know if I can do it again, much less what I did to make it happen."

"A seventhborn's second sight allows her to see dead things. Sometimes that's an executed written or spoken spell, or spirits, or visions of experiences in the past. It all depends on your training. Based on your level of schooling, I assumed you'd be able to see the spells used at most, but instead you summoned our victims."

He spread out the impressions. "If you will allow me, I would like to help you channel your powers, to see if we can summon them again and get any more information that will help us. If I'm right—which I am—these impressions will serve as your channeler. But," he said before she could speak, "what you did tonight was dangerous, and I never would've had you search the pictures alone had I known you would summon. You should never fully immerse yourself in a summoning without an anchor. Some spirits are wicked and will lure you deep into a vision so profound you may never find your way back. You will be lost in your mind forever. Do you understand?" His face was serious, eyes dark and mouth set hard in wait for her answer.

Sera swallowed through a thickened throat and nodded. What on earth had she gotten herself into?

He sighed, satisfied. "Hopefully we'll be able to learn more about our mystery hand or about the victims." He rushed back to the bookcase and gathered another book. Sera's eyes widened. It was an Aetherium book—more, a year-four Aetherium book, one year before Aetherium graduation. Her heart nearly ripped from her chest as he set the book before her.

"This is the spell we'll be using. Please gather the materials while I write down some notes." Barrington sat at a small side table along the wall and began to scribble furiously in a notebook.

Sera could move only enough to lift her hand to the thin

pages. She smiled, her fear replaced with wonder and hope. One day she would own a book like this. If she kept learning and getting stronger, there was no way the Aetherium wouldn't accept her, wouldn't let her become an inspector.

Barrington cleared his throat. "Sometime tonight, Miss Dovetail?"

"Oh!" She stood and spent the next moments locating all the supplies needed for the spell and also memorized their locations for future reference. She set the sky-blue and purple candles on the table at the appropriate places, then set off to find the required crystal.

She searched through the curio of vials and paused. "The spell calls for dissolved Rhodonite crystals."

"In the pantry, there," he said absently, waving a hand to the back of the room. She walked to the back of the chamber and reached for the black door's knob.

"No!"

Sera sucked in a breath and stumbled back as Barrington straightened sharply. "Not that door. That one." Frame tense, he pointed to the wooden door. "The black door is locked, and even if it weren't, it is off-limits. Is that understood?"

Normally she would have seethed at his tone, but Sera moved to the other door, her stare fixed on Barrington, who turned back to his work. "Yes, Professor." Touring her gaze between him and the door, she abandoned the mystery and entered the pantry.

The supply room was immaculate, no doubt of Rosie's doing, if Barrington's office at the Academy spoke of his cleanliness. She located the Rhodonite crystals quickly as the vials were in alphabetical order, next to herb bunches, also classified.

"I've found all the materials," she announced.

He set the impressions in the middle of the workbench.

"Rhodonite crystals are ideal for—"

"Memory," Sera interjected.

"Very good. Once the victims are summoned, a bond is created between you and them. The Rhodonite will work through you to enhance our victims' memories. That way you will not have to delve too deeply and remain in the vision for long." He motioned to the vial. "Would you like to do the honors?"

She nodded, a small smile twitching at her lip. Finally, she was learning actual inspector work, the same she would be doing in the Aetherium. A spark fluttered in her belly. This was more than she could have ever hoped for. She sprinkled the Rhodonite over the pictures.

"Perfect." He drew his wand. "First things first; you must remove the casing at the handle of your wand."

He held his wand before him and, with a twist of the wrist, popped off the metal case and set it on the worktable. "Normally our magic flows from the blunter end to the tip for more focused magic. However, this will burn out the dust quickly and sever your connection even faster. That is why you hold on to the pinnacle and send out your energy through the wider end."

"So you want me to use my wand backward?"

He frowned. "Precisely, though I rather like how I explained it."

Sera rolled her eyes, but he flipped his wand and continued. "By using it this way, the release of power is gradual and gives you more control of the burn and the vision. Even when you've mastered wandless magic, it is recommended you use your wand. The outflow of magic must be precise."

As he explained, Sera wished Mrs. Aguirre would have explained using Rhodonite crystals the way Barrington had. Perhaps then her attempts wouldn't have been so disastrous.

He set down his wand. "Now, take off your casing, and I will guide you through the spell."

Nodding, she spun to the table, her pulse in her ears. This was it. No tests in books, only the real-life display of magic, which she could not botch.

Barrington came close behind her. Sera startled and shifted away. The professor was quiet a moment, and her heartbeat quickened.

She swallowed tightly. *Damn, damn, damn.* He may have overlooked her behavior the first time, but how would she explain this? Perhaps she should have explained somehow—something, anything—but no doubt he would see the panic in her eyes. Instead, she gripped her wand tighter. *I cannot fear him. I cannot fear him…*

She resumed her place by the table.

"I do not wish to overstep my boundaries, Miss Dovetail," he spoke from behind her, a gentle sort of awareness in his tone. "But I suspect something in your past makes our proximity…distressing."

Sera winced. "It isn't what you think, I can assure you."

"You need not explain it to me; it is none of my business. But while I know that trust is earned in time, for the sake of us working together, I will have to ask it of you before earning it fully. Be a little mad and trust me, Miss Dovetail," he said, his voice low between them. "I swear on my magic, you are safe here, and I mean you no harm."

They were mere words, but Sera thanked the heavens she stood by a table, for they hit her like a blow to the gut. She pressed fingertips on the table to steady herself. He'd asked for trust. Not about her life before the Academy. Not of her behavior. But…*trust*.

She met his stare over her shoulder. Light eyes bored into hers, and he nodded.

Exhaling, she turned and extended her arm in answer.

Barrington straightened her elbow and turned down her wrist. He wrapped his fingers around her wrist then. His touch was firm, though also kind, as if his hands were determined to prove that he had been honest in his words.

"When you ignite the spell, do it measuredly, in rhythm with your breathing. Your magic should blanket the crystal fragments and impressions slowly. If the glow of the crystals is too bright, then you know you're using too much magic. Now, whirl your wrist slowly like so." He led her wrist in a continuous loop, demonstrating the proper rotation. "It helps you keep a rhythm and more control. I'm lighting the flame now."

Releasing her, he snapped and lit the candles.

Sera focused on the whirling of magic at her core instead of the void left by Barrington's hand no longer on hers. A warm sensation hovered like humidity over her skin as she allowed her magic to flow in controlled waves as opposed to her usual manic rush. She directed this down toward her wand, slow and easy like her breathing.

Her palm burned; the energy pooled in her hand for release. "My hand is burning."

"That's normal. Your magic is used to a wider entry point into your wand. Focus and lead it in through the tip."

She did as told, and within moments, every strand of wood in her wand illuminated red, filled with her magic.

"Fantastic," Barrington said. "Now, guide it toward the crystals, slowly."

Sera directed her magic—a mist of amber—down toward the crystals. A thin sheet of magic floated over them that suddenly took on the Rhodonite's pinkish glow.

"Wonderful. Now focus on the impressions. Think of nothing else."

Exhaling, she stared down at the gruesome photos through the pinkish haze. Gnarled skeletons. Charred corpses. Heaps of dirt. Pain. Screams. Death. Her pulse quickened, prodded by memories of her night, of the screams and the hand.

Her magic crested. The dissolved crystals flashed brightly and extinguished with a hiss.

Damn. She lowered her wand, her cheeks warm and stomach a sour pit.

"Too fast," Barrington said, waving away the smoke with a hand. "Much too fast." His tone was harsher, but she knew it wasn't personal. Still, she thrust down her wand and pinched the bridge of her nose.

Barrington swept to the back of the room and into the pantry. He reemerged with another vial of Rhodonite. At the table, he waved his wand in an arc motion. A weak gust snuffed out the candle flames and whisked the now black Rhodonite crystals to the floor. Sera moved back, crestfallen. She'd failed, and now Rosie would have to clean up her mess.

He held out the vial. "Patience," he said, drawing back her gaze. "We do not excel at everything on our first go. Well, I do, but I've always been rather brilliant."

She fixed him with a scowl, but the small smile at the side of his mouth eased her, and she took the vial from his hands.

He snapped again and lit the wicks as she sprinkled the dissolved Rhodonite crystals over the impressions. Sera drew in a deep breath, then exhaled slowly. She could do this. She had to.

Gnarled skeletons. Charred corpses. Heaps of dirt...

The crystals ignited, glowed like embers. The mist of her magic took on their hue, steady and warm.

Gnarled skeletons. Charred corpses. Heaps of dirt...

Within moments, the smoke above them washed out

the world from around her, save for Barrington's steady breathing.

"I can't see anything," she said, her voice a soft echo in the mist. "Nothing is happening. Just fog."

"Do not force it," he said, his voice a whisper. "Let it come."

Feeling weightless, a soul void of a body, she waded in the fog. Whispers eased in just as smoothly. *Puppet, puppet, puppet...*

Their whispers grew to screams that collided against one another, multiplied, and crowded Sera's head. "I hear them, so many of them. They're whispering *puppet*, but one is also screaming while others cry *help me* and *please, no. Oh God.*" Pressure mounted in her temples. She pressed a hand to her chest, the agony too much to bear.

"It's all right. You feel it much more now because of the Rhodonite, but their pain is done," he said in her ear. His voice sounded far, lost within the cries. "Listen to them. They need you, Miss Dovetail."

Sera swallowed and, following the voices, she felt herself float in the fog, deeper into the vision. The farther she dropped, the more distant the screams, but the individual whispers grew clear. The temperatures also plummeted, and she shivered uncontrollably.

"What are you saying?" Sera asked into the smoke. "I can't understand you."

Agatha Beechworth, whispered one.

Briar Wakefield, said another.

Catherine Yates.

Elsie Godwin.

Harriet Adams.

Winnie Forge, said one, and then added, *Portia Rees.*

"What do you see?" Barrington asked softly, his breath a

warm fog on her cheek, the warmth welcomed in the frigid smog surrounding her.

"Just fog, but they're telling me their names, over and over." She repeated the names to him and heard the swift stroke of his pen as he wrote them down.

The hand burst through the smoke and took hold of her wrist. "Puppet!"

Sera screamed and jerked back, but Barrington's hands came onto her shoulders and held her steady. "I'm here. Relax and remember, I am your anchor. I will not let you go. Focus on their killer. Help me avenge these girls."

With the sound of their screams all around her, she held fast to Barrington's words and looked to the hand clutched around her wrist. "The hand from before has gripped me."

"I need you to focus on it. Are there any identifying marks, an Invocation ring perhaps?"

"No, sir. No ring, but…there's something on his cloak sleeve. A crest of sorts." She focused her mind's eye. "It's an emblem of ravens. I hadn't seen it before."

Barrington bristled behind her, his hands slipping from her shoulders. "Ravens? Are you sure?"

Sera nodded.

The hand evaporated from around her wrist. The screams grew further apart, the voices withering to distant echoes. The smoke dissolved around her, slowly revealing the impressions on the table once more. She gathered a few breaths as the white mist of her magic curled back into her wand, and the crystals extinguished their glow.

A small smile spread on her mouth, though she still trembled. She had done it. She spun to Professor Barrington but did not find the same satisfaction on his face. He leaned forward onto the worktable, his hands flush on the surface, his head turned down.

Her smile faded. "Professor, is everything all right?"

He lifted his head slightly, his brows pulled in. "I need you to be completely honest with me, Miss Dovetail. In trying to figure out the impressions, did you suspect necromancy and in turn research the art at all? Did you look into its history?"

"No, never. I searched in my divination books, but never once considered necromancy. Why? Did I do something wrong?"

Barrington shook his head and straightened, his mind far away. "I've grown tired and must rest." He picked up her wand casing and handed it back to her. "We've covered a great deal today. Take tomorrow off and replenish your reserves. We will continue on Tuesday."

He led the way out of the room, dismissing her. She slipped her casing back on, followed him into his study, and stood at her previous entry point, sure he didn't see her as he stared up at the painting of him and his brother.

He let out a long, helpless breath that extinguished all of her previous mirth. If she had done so well, why was he so sad?

"Should I take the impressions with me?" she asked, hoping to add some sound to the terrible silence. "Perhaps see if I can uncover anything else?"

"No need. You've given me more than I could've hoped for. Good night, Miss Dovetail." He unsheathed his wand and pointed it at the floor beneath her.

"Good night, Professor." Sera lowered her head and braced, her stomach already in tangles.

"And Miss Dovetail…"

She lifted her head.

"Well done today." A small smile touched the side of his lips, though wells of sadness echoed in his eyes. "I know I've made the right choice."

Before his words settled between them, the floor vanished beneath her. The next moment, Sera sagged back against her bedroom window, her stomach still knotted within. But through the nausea, she smiled. She had helped with a case—real help that led them in a new direction. This may have been the best night of her life—save for the hand and the voices.

Yet later that night, just before she fell asleep, it was Professor Barrington who haunted her thoughts. His abrupt change in mood. His solemnness as he stared at the portrait with a look of pain, loss, and regret. No, he hadn't been tired, she realized. He'd wanted her gone. A sinking feeling settled in her stomach. Something about the raven crest had changed things, and whatever it was, it made the case personal for Barrington. But what could murdered and burned witches have to do with him, she wondered as she rolled to her side and watched the shadows. And why hide it after asking for her trust?

hope or nightmares

Books. She needed books, and lots of them.

Sera woke up that morning like a woman possessed. If she was to be an inspector — a great inspector — she had to follow the clues. Barrington had left more than his share of them. The hand had upset him. More, the crest of ravens. Upset him to the point that his stoic mask had all but shattered, and he'd been too pained to hide it. She needed to know what the crest meant, and for that she would need books. Necromancy books.

But by that evening, there had been no time for books. After Mary snuck into her room as she did on Tuesdays and Thursdays, before and after her infirmary duty, there had only been time for Mary, and Mary's gossip about Timothy. Not that Sera could blame her. The rumors were everywhere.

"He was so quiet in the library and skipped supper and evening prayer," Mary said from the vanity where she inspected the path of freckles on her cheeks in the old mirror, in spite of the black spots that blemished the glass. "It was all the girls spoke about at the Solstice Dance committee meeting, you know?"

Sera smothered a pillow on her face. It blocked out all light. If only it would do the same for the guilt and frustration in her heart.

"No one knows who the girl is who broke his heart, but I'm determined to find out. Some say he's fancied her for some time now. I wonder if that's why he's having such a hard time with his Aether-level courses? He's never gotten low marks before, but this year he's been struggling."

Sera stifled a groan. He could have any girl he wanted. It couldn't be he was heartbroken because of *her*.

"It's just a rumor, Mary. Maybe he's tired or stressed about assessments." Remembering the peace he exuded in the forest, she sighed. "It must not be easy being a Delacort. He has no choice but to succeed."

"*Stressed?* As if he'll have any problem getting into the Aetherium. His father is the chair of the seventhborn program. Besides, it's not a rumor. Susan Whittaker heard it from her brother."

Sera clenched her jaw. Damned Whittaker. She could have set him on fire again. "Yes, well, this is Whittaker we're talking about. The boy is a beast. He's probably jealous of Timothy, and what better way to embarrass him than to spread rumors that Timothy Delacort can't get everything he wants."

Mary quieted, no doubt mulling this over. "Yes, yes… you're right. How could a girl possibly turn down Timothy Delacort? It is rather ridiculous now that I think of it. Timothy must be sick, then, as I can't imagine him choosing another girl," Mary went on through Sera's self-imposed darkness.

"We're both of the same status; our fathers are well-known, respected, and successful in their ventures. True, my father doesn't work for the Aetherium, but his medical practice is one of the grandest in our province. And not to be vain, but I have the loveliest skin—not that your skin isn't lovely, Sera, you really are quite lovely, but I do think those creams Mama sent me have given me a rather nice glow. I'll be sure to bring you some. Come to think of it, you're in desperate need of it, no offense. You've been rather pale lately, and those bags under your eyes. How are you feeling?"

Sera slipped the pillow from her face and heaved a sigh. What was she to say to that? She couldn't possibly tell her friend about her work with Barrington, or about the hellish fear twisting her insides at the thought of seeing Timothy at some point during the day. The horror of Mary finding out about their encounter in the forest made her jump whenever Mary called her name. Oh, she'd be so angry and hurt.

Maybe it was best if she told her outright. Wasn't it worse to let her friend weave dreams in her mind of a romance that wasn't ever going to happen? She frowned. What kind of friend was she to not be truthful and forthcoming? Mary had never been anything but kind to her, honest, trustworthy.

Which was precisely why she wouldn't tell.

Sera set her jaw and sat up. "I'm fine, Mary. Perfectly fine."

"Are you sure?" she asked, now chasing fingers through her hair. "You seem distant. To be honest, I've felt as though I've been speaking to myself this entire evening." She paused, eyes turned up in thought. "Maybe you have whatever Timothy has, which means it must be spreading. How else would the two of you have it? It's not like you're ever *that* close in proximity."

Sera forced a chuckle through the rising panic. "Believe me, I'm fine. And I've heard your diatribe—all two hours of it." She rose and walked to her open spell book. Maybe she could figure out a spell that would make Timothy fancy Mary instead?

"How about we talk in the morning?" Sera asked, thumbing through the pages. "If he hasn't asked you by then, we'll consult the stars."

Mary shook her head and stood. "You're horrid at Astrology. But your inattention has plagued you for more than just today. You've been distracted all week. What are you keeping from me?" She clutched her chest, as if the room suddenly lacked air. "It's a boy, isn't it?"

Sera paused mid flip but forced her hands to lower the page. "Mary, please."

"It is!" Mary spun her by the shoulders, wide eyes fixed on her with the look of a hungry fox eyeing a hare. "Who is it? When did it happen? Why didn't you tell me?"

"Do you know how ridiculous you sound?"

"But you're not denying it!" Mary pouted, and her hands fell from Sera's shoulders. "I thought we were the best of friends."

Sera shut the book with a pat. "Heaven help me, Mary. I met no one. I'm tired is all. I still have a lot left to study for the Aetherium exam, and not to mention my reserves must be up to par. What good of an inspector will I be if one flare of magic leaves me without power for hours?"

"You're not *that* bad," she replied, seeming appeased by Sera's answer. "But your reserves will never increase if you keep losing your temper. Now, come." Mary drew her wand and held it out. "Let us see how your reserves are doing."

Sera eyed her friend's wand. Reserves were a private matter. Anyone knowing of a magician's levels could purposely tire out an opponent and, when left without magic, disable them—or worse. There was also the chance a magician could tap into another magician's reserves for information or to possess them.

But she sighed and unsheathed her wand. She could trust Mary. Mary was a healer, and matters such as reserve levels and anything she may discover during healings and reserve checks was confidential. Betrayal of trust was against Aetherium law and would have her banished to one of the Null regions—provinces where magic was wholly forbidden.

Sera touched the tip of her friend's wand. A blue twine slid from Mary's wand and wrapped itself around Sera's. Warmth trickled up her fingers, arms, and down to her stomach.

A frown settled over Mary's brows, her gaze distant as it traveled the web of Sera's powers. "Yes, you've gotten stronger, Sera. And your magic seems...different."

Sera forced a smile. "I've been working on controlling my anger in preparation for assessments, so maybe now it's not as wild?"

"Perhaps." Her eyes narrowed, but in meeting Sera's stare she smiled, and the blue twine evaporated with a hiss. "You've nothing to worry about. Your reserves are vast, and for a seventhborn, quite impressive really. You'll have no problem on the exam—that is, if you manage to tame your anger." She sheathed her wand. "I'll leave you to your studies, then. I have the Solstice committee in the morning, and I want to try something new with my hair, so I need to wake up early. I hope Timothy will like it."

Sera set down her wand and opened the door for her friend. "He'd be a fool not to."

Rosy cheeked, Mary squeezed her hand in passing and descended the narrow tower stairs. "Hopefully Mama will think the same thing instead of her usual *you're not trying hard enough*." She sighed weightily. "Good night."

Once Mary's footsteps faded and the downstairs door closed, Sera waited a moment. When certain her friend would not return, she locked the door and dashed across the room to her wardrobe. She shifted aside her dresses and cloak and reached for a trunk in the back—a present from Mary so Sera would have somewhere to store her things.

She pressed her wand to the lock, and the clasps snapped open. Setting aside the cloth herb bags that rested on top, she swallowed thickly as she beheld her only belonging from her time before the Academy—a cloak given to her by one of the Aetherium inspectors she'd met the night she was found two years ago. It had been cold and damp that terrible night, and she had been shaking and freezing, scared of what the officers would do to a seventhborn with no memory of her past beyond a year prior, who was now guilty of killing another. But while all the other inspectors had regarded her as a measly, filthy seventhborn—however scrawny and dirty she may have been—this one guard had given her his cloak, his compassion, and allowed her to sleep on his shoulder once the drain of magic set in.

Casting aside the cloak and memories, Sera reached the object she desired. She lifted the stolen servant's uniform from the trunk, one of her earliest and best transgressions.

Having been admitted into the Academy midsummer, Sera had been made to help the servant staff prepare the school for the fall semester. The staff had been so ready to get rid of her, they forgot to collect the uniform. Sera held up the brown woolen dress and grinned. Their loss.

She slipped on the dress and tied the large white apron behind her back and neck, then arranged her hair into a low bun parted in the middle, the way it was worn by all the female house staff. Satisfied with her appearance, she snuck down the stairs, sure to avoid the squeaky third step.

Underneath the stairs, she moved aside the brooms and buckets in the housemaids' closet and pressed her wand to the stone wall as she'd seen them do throughout the secret doorways along the floors, lest any students encounter a maid in service.

"Safe passage."

The outline of a door glittered blue, and the stone faded to slight transparency. Sera hauled in a breath and peeked through. All should be asleep at this time. Still, it was best to be safe. The staircase was empty, and peering over the banister, she breathed freer at seeing no one there.

She descended the stairs to the library level undetected. Rounding a corner, she stopped and neared her wand to the wall.

"By the stars," she whispered. Each doorway had its own password, though she knew only a few. There was a slight *click*, and the wall opened outward. She neared her face to the crack and peeked inside. Moonlight slanted through the windows but still offered her shafts of shadows to hide in. The darkness made mountains out of the bookcases that vanished into the encroaching blackness above. Outside the winds howled and wheezed, and the trees groaned, their shivering branches and gnarled fingers *tap-tapping* on the glass. All else was quiet. Night Flaggers usually cleared this floor early, as no one ever wanted to break into the library. She pushed the Astronomy bookcase a bit more and ducked inside.

Crouched by the many books of planets and stars, she exhaled. Normally she knew what she wanted, which made for a quick exit, but this time she gazed all around. Where should she start? Her eye caught on *Recipes for Celebrating the Planets*, and one thing was for sure: she was most certainly in the wrong section.

Determined, she sank into the shadows and darted

behind the first bookcase. She dashed behind the next one, and the next, until in the avian section. She examined countless books on ravens, until a footnote gave her pause.

Also adopted by the Brotherhood as a talisman.

Sera hummed. The Brotherhood. She hadn't heard of them before. Locating a reference book, she stooped and flipped to the *B* tab but found nothing about the Brotherhood. She tapped a finger on the page. Perhaps in necromancy...

She flipped to the *N* tab. Any information, however little, was a start.

Necromancy: The practice of communication with the dead by calling on their spirit or raising them bodily for divination or to discover hidden knowledge. Outlawed by the Aetherium, post persecution. See Persecutions.

Sera thumbed to the *P* tab.

Persecutions: At a time of heightened influence, Purists convinced many that seventhborns were a curse on the magical world and must be cleansed. Purists thought them to be bad omens, evidenced by the seventhborn plague. Whereas seventhborn males were spared for their ability to heal, females were swiftly executed. See Purism.

Sera shook her head. To imagine so many seventhborns dying over an ability they had no control over was a painful thought. She trailed the thread and flipped to Purism a few pages away.

Purism: Outlawed after the persecutions. Roots in Magical Creation Mythology. See Persecutions.

She scowled at the text and flicked feverishly to Magical Creationism. Her glare deepened.

Magical Creationism: Belief of the Purists. See Purism.

She cursed in a heated whisper, shut the book, and put it back on the stand. Hurrying to the mythology section, her search resulted in the same dead end of basic information.

She blew out a breath as she opened the final book. "Let me guess...of course," she muttered, her finger paused under the single sentence beside Purism:

Outlawed after the Persecutions.

"You're not going to find that here."

Sera spun and gasped. Eyes wide, she stared at Timothy standing before her, blue eyes focused on where her finger marked. She took in his blue robe with a moon crest at his breast and mumbled a curse. Of course he was a Night Flagger, and of course he'd be the one to catch her.

She closed the book, shoved it back onto the shelf, and rose. "Must you insist on sneaking up on me whenever you get the chance?"

"No, but you looked in desperate need of something, and I thought I'd help."

Sera lifted her chin. "I don't need your help. Go on, report me. If not, then I'd like to get back to my room."

"Without finding what you were looking for? Seems to me you were rather upset at not finding anything about Purists in your search."

Her jaw tightened. "How long have you been watching me?"

"Long enough to know that you really want to learn about Purists. Why?"

"Why do you care?"

He chuckled. "You wouldn't believe me if I told you, but like I said, you won't find anything about Purists here."

"Yes, well, I've already gathered that all on my own, so thank you very much for your *help*. Now, if you'll excuse me." She made to move past him.

"Not in *this* library…"

She stopped short. "This is the only library."

He was quiet a moment, and though dark, Sera noted his intense internal debate.

Timothy met her eyes. "How important is this to you?"

"Why do you care if it's important to me? And if it is, why would you help me?"

"Like I said, you wouldn't believe me if I told you. We haven't much time before the next Flagger is due. How important is this to you?"

Sera fisted her hands, uncertain. If she was to help Barrington, she needed to know about this—the Purists, necromancy, ravens—about all of it. Besides, what inspector didn't walk willingly into a bit of trouble now and then?

"Very important," she answered. "I want to know about Purists and what they believed in." And what it had to do with ravens that made Barrington so glum.

He nodded once and jutted his head to the side. "This way then, and quickly."

They flitted to the back of the library, to the Ethical Magic section. Timothy pressed his wand to the bookcase. "Right above all else."

The bookcase creaked open. Sera suppressed a smile. Another password to add to her arsenal. At least this one had been much easier to come by. Much easier than prying when assisting the servant staff each time she got into some kind of trouble.

They hurried inside the small alcove, and he closed the bookcase behind them with a quiet *click*. Darkness swallowed them. Lanterns illuminated a hall just outside of the shallow alcove. They waited in silence a moment. When they heard no sound but that of their own breathing and the distant soughs of the wind, Timothy ushered them against the wall and inched forward.

He peeked around the corner. "It's clear. Come on." He held out a hand to her, but she never took hold. Exhaling, Timothy darted into the hall and kept tight to the stone walls as he navigated them through this hall, another, and the next. Sera did her best to remember everything—anything that would tell her how to get back, but it was impossible. With every turned hallway, directions became a tangled mess in her mind.

"We're here," he announced finally and pressed the tip of his wand against the wall. Various lines illuminated in the stone, very much like the branches of a tree. All of the lines came together and formed a symbol. A shiver coursed down Sera's spine.

"Ravens," she whispered.

Timothy nodded, unaware of her raising a hand to her sheathed wand. "It was the sign of the Brotherhood, a cult of Purist extremists. You said you wanted to know why Purists did what they did. Well, what better way than to study their own teachings? It's a load of rubbish, if you ask me, but I need to know all of these things if I'm to take over my father's chair in the Aetherium council." A sadness very similar to what she'd seen the day in the forest touched his eyes. "He says that to beat your enemy, you must know everything about them, though we beat the Purists a long time ago."

"A very pragmatic thought."

"The founders of Pragmatism are my ancestors. After the Persecutions, they dedicated their lives to changing the way seventhborns were treated, eventually initiating the seventhborn program."

The jingling of keys resounded somewhere down the hall. Sera looked to Timothy wide-eyed. There was only one person known to carry such an abundant set of keys. "Mrs. Fairfax."

Timothy held out a hand to her once more. "Are you coming?"

She stared at his outstretched fingers.

"I can help you find what you're looking for," he said, the lamplights making a halo over his head.

The jangle of keys drew closer.

"Either come with me or we get caught. Mrs. Fairfax has been head housekeeper since before my father attended the Academy. I'm sure she knows all the servant staff, no matter how convincing your costume may be."

The steps neared.

Sera's breaths quickened.

Heart pounding, she thrust her hand into Timothy's, and he walked them through the wall as if it didn't exist.

Her mouth gaped. The stout Mrs. Fairfax walked right past them as though…as though she couldn't see them or sense the magic at all.

The housekeeper rounded the corner and paused. She toured a glossy, unfocused gaze along the hall, and Sera's brow furrowed. Something about the woman was…off. Her skin was pallid, and she twitched her neck, then each arm as though adjusting her skin onto her bones. She shook her head then and marched away.

"She can't see us," Timothy confirmed. "Or hear us. The magic used to conceal this place is strong."

Sera stared back at the mirage-like wall. Strong magic indeed. Yet she inched close to the wall, trailing Mrs. Fairfax until she could see the woman no more and the sound of her keys vanished.

"Did you see that? She looked pale and…" Sera struggled with the word. Strange was too light a definition.

"She had a bad fall recently. Maybe she isn't feeling her best. I'm sure if she's sick, she'll go to Nurse. Come on."

Realizing he still held her hand, Sera yanked it away and stepped back. Above, lanterns hung from a web of twisted vines that ran the course of the secret hall. There were various wooden doors along this short corridor, closed out by two massive, gated doors.

"What is this place?" she asked.

"We are still at the Academy, at least a wing of it from many years ago. When Purism was banned, the Brotherhood remained faithful and created this place to hold what remained of their teachings. Once they were discovered by my father, he decided to protect this place instead of burn it. He believes that in order to rule effectively one must not only understand the good but the motivations of the enemy." Timothy led the way to one of the smaller doors along the hall. "Come on, the library is just here."

"And there?" Sera pointed to the double doors at the end of the corridor.

"The dungeons. Many witches met their end behind those doors at the hands of the Brotherhood."

Sera stared at the massive doors. Her arms tingled, her skin remembering the ghostly hand clamped on her wrists, the cries and screams.

"But you don't want to go in there. The pain that was experienced…" He trailed off, pale and visibly shaken.

"You can feel it, can't you?" she said with some relief

and surprise. "You're...you're an empath?"

He nodded over his shoulder. "If you could keep that between us, I would be much obliged. Besides, I'm not a very good one. I haven't honed my power much and can sense only extreme emotions accurately."

"Is that why you're struggling in your Aether-level courses?"

He averted his gaze. "Partly, yes. My father was mortified when he learned of my inclination. I'm sure he never imagined his son's magic would follow an Aether path, but he's determined to rectify it. He ordered me to fail on purpose so no one will suspect my magic is prone to Aether—no offense. I know seventhborns are apt to the element, but Father thinks it will hurt my chances to ever become chancellor if I'm associated to it. Many will think me weak and unable to rule with emotions clouding my judgment. He says if I suppress it for long enough, the ability will fade until I no longer feel it." He opened the door and stepped aside to let her enter.

"Is that what you want?" she asked, relieved to get away from the dungeon and glad to know there was no way Timothy could harm her. The pain and guilt of it would hurt him as well.

"Does it matter? It seems I never get the things I truly desire."

Sera swallowed under his warm stare and averted her gaze, touring it along the library instead. A wall of bookshelves mastered one side of the wall. On the other hung tapestries of the seven guardians of magic. At the far end of the room was a fireplace, two armchairs just before it. Two narrow windows flanked the fireplace, and through the glass was darkness. A strange darkness that felt alive and made her magic hum.

Timothy cleared his throat and walked to the center of the room. "And here we are. Whatever you wish to know about Purists, you will find it here."

She paced, taken by the immense number of books that, though old, were in pristine condition. She trailed her hand along the tomes, thought of how many hands had once touched them. How many of those hands had later turned murderous, stained with the blood of seventhborns? A sick feeling lurched in her stomach, all joy gone at finding the secret library.

On the second level, Sera stopped before a tapestry on the wall and shook her head. Stitched into the fabric was *The Fall of the Seventh Sister*, written by Patriarch Aldrich. Of all the chapters in *The Unmitigated Truths of Seventhborns*, Sera had always been drawn to this story. The seventh sister, guardian of Aether magic, learned of a stronger power kept in the Underworld: the power over time. Desiring it for herself, she traveled to the Underworld where she was corrupted beyond measure.

To protect magic and unable to kill the seventh sister, the other six sisters locked her behind a gate in the Underworld, never to be opened again. Her evil, however, spread to all seventh-born girls, and soon mothers began to die upon birthing a seventh-born daughter. Believing them to be bad omens, Purists decided to keep track of all seventhborns with a tattoo.

Sera glanced at the bust sculpture of Patriarch Aldrich beside the tapestry. "Bastard."

"Indeed," Timothy said. "There's no better name for a necromancer."

Sera arched a brow. "Necromancer?"

"According to all my father learned from the Brotherhood who were captured, Patriarch Aldrich raised body after body in hopes of learning the strongest of magic."

"Power over time," Sera injected.

He nodded. "Life, death, strength, knowledge—magic itself are all slaves to time. Control time and you control everything. You can go back and fix your mistakes or keep the ones you love alive. You can alter the past to shape your future. The possibilities are endless. Patriarch Aldrich recognized this and drained countless witches until gaining enough magic to summon the seventh sister to learn how to obtain this magic for himself. She bargained with him; if he freed her, she would share her power over time. She told him how to open the gate, but his daughter stole his writings, *The Scrolls of the Dead*, and with a powerful spell she locked him inside a labyrinth in his mind. He couldn't remember anything at all, and those who wished to help him met only madness themselves. Some of his disciples took it upon themselves to recover the Scrolls and established the Brotherhood. Ultimately it became a cult of black magic and murder, mainly against seventhborns whom they used for their own evil ends, from draining to magical experimentation, all under the guise of religion. Because they targeted seventhborns, Purists merely turned a blind eye."

Sera shook her head. She'd suffered through that doctrine at the hands of her own pious monster. Though he never mentioned the Brotherhood, she had no doubt he would have joined them given the chance. She remembered his fervor, how he'd drain her of magic, claiming it was for her own good, even though it only made him stronger.

Her hands clenched. The desire to blast Patriarch Aldrich's statue to dust jabbed her skin with heat.

Timothy handed her a book and pulled her from her brooding. He drew two others from the bottom shelf and stacked them beside her. "But you can read better about it in these books."

"Could I not just take them to my room?" she asked. "I promise to return them."

"Sadly, no. They would age and wither away."

Her eyes widened. "This is a time capsule? That *is* strong magic." Only the strongest mages were known to dabble in the magic of time, way beyond the tinkering of time-altering spells. No wonder her magic pulsed when she stared out the window. It was not night but a void.

He smiled. "Beautiful and smart."

She opened her mouth to ask a question, but at Timothy's nearness, it faded. She turned her face down to the books she held.

"Miss Dovetail, I—"

"I should get started on these," she cut him off.

"Oh yes, yes, of course. I'll be downstairs. Let me know if you need anything."

She refused to look at him until his back was to her and he walked down the stairs. Knowing him to be an empath was supposed to have relieved her, and yet she was more lost than ever. His reaction near the dungeons told her he hadn't stifled his powers the way his father wished for him to, which meant he wouldn't purposely hurt her by lying and making a mockery of her in front of everyone. Although that was comforting, it also meant that in asking her to the dance, he'd been genuine…and genuinely heartbroken when she said no.

She blew out a breath and forced her eyes to the first book on her lap. Matters of the heart would have to wait. There were others who were waiting for her to uncover why their hearts didn't beat anymore.

For what felt like hours, Sera read about the horrible Purists' beliefs, mainly propaganda blaming seventhborns for partaking in death magic, including necromancy. They believed that in contacting the Underworld, seventhborns dragged disease and evil into the realm of the living, which in turn led to the plague. Yet Sera couldn't find Barrington's connection to it all.

Stressed, tired, and frustrated, she met Timothy at the fireplace.

He set down the book he was reading. "I take it you didn't find what you sought."

She frowned. "How perceptive."

He grinned. "I am an empath."

She mirrored his smile, but as she glanced about the room, it quickly withered. "This is unbelievable, that this place—these philosophies were accepted. It all seems so fictional when studying it in class, but to see their teachings with my own eyes…" She exhaled, the breath rattling on the way out.

"It was a dark time for our people, but thankfully other Purists, like my ancestors, didn't agree with the persecutions. They had the sense to think beyond myth, that maybe it was a chink somewhere in our magical makeup. That perhaps there was something in a seventhborn's birth other than a myth that led to their mothers' powers and lives being drained. Sadly, progress is slow. It has taken us decades to get this far, and we've yet to eradicate prejudice."

He glanced at the clock. "I'm afraid the servants will be waking up soon. But if you need to come back, just say the word. I usually make it to the library at midnight, if you ever need to find me."

Sera rose. "Thank you."

Timothy followed suit. "The pleasure is all mine."

He walked to the door and began to open it, but she put a hand on his shoulder and stopped him. A portrait hung on the wall. A group of men sat in a row, staring straight ahead with plague masks on their laps. Sera drew closer, her eyes fixed on the man sitting in the middle. He looked like Professor Barrington, perhaps a little older, though the icy glare and arrogance were the same.

She glanced down at the plaque below it, and her suspicions were confirmed. "Barrington," she whispered.

"Yes. Like me, Professor Barrington comes from a long line of Purists. It's said his father became rather obsessed with uncovering the *Scrolls of the Dead* and eventually went mad, adopting the Brotherhood's extremist ways. This was never proven, though. If there was any evidence, it burned down in the fire that killed him and the professor's brother."

Sera's breath caught. "Professor Barrington's brother is dead?"

Timothy pulled the door open. "Some say he tried to save their father. Others say he dabbled in the same black magic."

Breathless, she followed him out. "Where was Professor Barrington?"

"He was always the black sheep of the family. Even got expelled from the Academy. He vanished for some years, and when he returned, he was the moody professor you see today. Professor Barrington never believed his father capable of black magic, but those who knew him spoke otherwise."

"Do you believe it?"

"I have to," he said, closing the door behind him. "If not, I'd be calling my father a liar. He discovered what the professor's father was doing."

Memory of Barrington's reaction that morning in the library crossed her mind, the glare now making perfect sense. Like many who judged him for the crimes of his father, Barrington disliked Timothy for the same reason.

"I'm sharing these things with you in the strictest of confidence, of course."

"I'll tell no one."

Sera eyed the dungeon doors, and a chill trailed down her spine. Sorrow followed for Professor Barrington. It was no wonder his sadness the night before had consumed him. Seeing the raven—knowing the Brotherhood was involved— must have stirred up all the horrible memories.

Lost to thoughts of Barrington, his father, his brother, and the Brotherhood, Sera followed Timothy out into the hall and back through the labyrinth until they reached the Astronomy section in the library.

"Thank you for tonight," she said, pressing her wand to the bookcase, eager to find her way back upstairs to sort out all she'd learned.

"It should be me to thank you, as I greatly enjoy your company. And that's not flattery. It's the truth, same as my words to you the other morning."

She sighed. "Timothy, I...this—you and me... I appreciate what you did for me tonight, and your words the other morning, but..."

A crestfallen look overcame his eyes. "But you will never feel for me what I feel for you?"

"You can't feel anything for me. How could you? You don't know me."

"I know enough. I know enough to know that we are not so different. We are both in positions of birth we did not wish for and are burdened by things we wish we could erase. But I simply want to know how you feel." He neared her a little, eyes very blue. "Are we a possibility, whether in secret or for everyone to know?"

Sera groaned. "It doesn't matter what I feel—"

"It matters to me," he said. "You asked why I helped you, and this is why. It matters to me what you feel, what you think, what you say. You matter to me. But if we're never to be, then tell me to go, and I won't bother you again."

The answer was simple: no, they could never be. There was no way she could bind herself to him. He was perfect, yes—kind, smart, handsome—but something was missing. Whenever Mary spoke of him, she mentioned how her heart fluttered and palms dampened, and how she spent every waking moment thinking of him. Sera frowned. Her heart didn't seem the least bit agitated, her hands were perfectly dry, and quite frankly she hadn't thought of him at all— save for worry that Mary might have learned of their secret morning meeting. Though she hadn't much experience in love, surely, *surely* it had to feel more than the void she felt with Timothy.

Indeed, the answer was simple, and yet Sera stepped back against the wall. Timothy's words conjured the various possibilities of her future in her mind as though they were a vision.

She could tell him to love another—to love Mary, for heaven's sake, but whereas Mary could always find another blue blood, what of Sera? Would anyone ever care for her, wish for her the way she wished for so many things? Would anyone look beyond the black ring at her wrist and the history it told as Timothy was willing to? He was kind, and an empath of all things. And if matters with Barrington didn't work out, would Timothy not be the ideal person to help her find out about her family? He would be on the

Aetherium council, and though she was a seventhborn, she would never have to worry another day in her life... She would be safe. *He* was safe.

"Tell me what to do," he said. "Is there hope?"

Pulse pounding and fingers digging into the wall behind her, she felt all of his promises just a breath, a kiss, a word away.

Is there hope?

Distant bells rang. Sera sucked in a breath, the spell broken between them.

"I must go."

She spun and slipped through the ajar bookcase. Timothy may have called for her, but she heard none of it as she hurried up the stairs, his words in her mind like the ghosts of nights past. *Is there hope?*

9

the man in the smoke

Timothy's question haunted Sera all night and throughout the next morning. By History of Clairvoyance, she was sure it would consume her entire day, until Mrs. Norton shut the book she lectured from and said to the class, "Not all of us possess the gift of clairvoyance. Most of us are given only a touch." She paced before a long table at the front of the room. A white blanket was draped on top, and whatever she'd hidden under it formed lumps beneath the fabric.

"Those of you whose magic tends to be Aether-inclined—and seventhborns, of course," she said as a bitter afterthought, "will find concepts of divination come easiest to you, but that, too, requires much practice. Visions can at times be abstract and influenced by many factors, which is why the Aetherium tends to shy away from it as a serious subject of study." She gripped a corner of the white sheet and smiled at the class. "That does not mean one cannot have a bit of fun now and then."

She whisked the sheet up from the table. The girls in

the class clapped and whispered in delight at the array of divination tools revealed. There was a stack of tarot cards, a crystal ball, tea leaves and teacups, a spirit board, a pendulum, and a scrying mirror. "There are many tools used for predicting the future, as you can see, and I would like for us to have a little demonstration." She tapped a spindly finger on her chin and glanced about the room. "Do we have a volunteer?"

Every girl speared her hand into the air, but rolling her eyes, Sera settled back in her chair. Though curious about whether or not she would ever find her family, she decided against volunteering in class. Mrs. Norton was right; visions were sometimes abstract. She needed facts to find her family, not images to get her hopes up, then dash them when it proved to be something else. It was a waste of magic, and for Mrs. Norton to indulge these girls was most irresponsible and—

"Ah, yes, Miss Dovetail," Mrs. Norton said, waving a hand forward.

Sera ground her teeth. Of course, the woman pretended not to see her all year, except for now, to put her on display for the gifts for which she was often shunned and criticized.

"Perhaps you can shed some light on the topic and show us which of these tools your people use to glimpse into the future?"

Your people.

Seeming to notice her discomfort, Mary raised her hand. "Mrs. Norton, seventhborns are known for their second sight, not for divination so much."

"Yes, yes, but her kind are quite skilled in the Aether-related fields. Now, Miss Dovetail, come demonstrate for us."

Sera's heart pounded. *Her kind?*

Mrs. Norton clapped her hands, addressing the class.

"How lucky we are to have a seventhborn in class with us. Not many have the pleasure of a live demonstration such as this, of that you can be sure."

Sera chuckled bitterly; she may just as well have been on display at the zoo. Mary turned in her chair, her gaze apologetic. The other girls merely stared expectantly.

"Well, then. Come forward, Miss Dovetail. We haven't all day," Mrs. Norton said.

Sera rubbed her fingers, every fiber within begging her to refuse, to remain seated. She was not their sideshow at the circus. Still, meeting Mrs. Norton's resolute stare, Sera knew the woman wouldn't let this go, and she couldn't afford an argument, not now when a referral and finding her family was in her future.

Hauling in a breath, Sera stood, wiped her damp palms on her skirts, and spun to the class. Their stares pierced her skin with cold, and though fully dressed, she shivered. For the first time since she stood before Aetherium doctors two years ago, she felt naked and exposed. Anger twisted her insides but, focused on the table in the front of the room, she raised her chin high and set one foot before the other, her boots tapping sharply on the hardwood floors. She did this for her family.

She reached the end of the aisle and followed Mrs. Norton behind the table. Though she'd never come into contact with any divination tools, a strange energy hummed from the instruments, as though calling to her magic. Sera swallowed. As long as she kept calm and controlled her magic, she would be okay.

"Move your hand over them and choose which you'd like to use." Mrs. Norton then said to the class, "Unlike our wands that grow with us and we trade in as our powers mature, a magician will find that items such as these and other scrying tools choose them. Which one of these speaks to you, Miss Dovetail?"

Sera walked down the line. When she passed the crystal ball, her stomach tightened and, against her best attempts, she stopped, rooted to the ground. *Damn it.* She'd hoped to have no connection, but her flaring magic said otherwise.

"Yes, yes," Mrs. Norton moved forward. "An orbuculum. Very tricky. Used for both fortune-telling and scrying, it requires a keen sense of control, as we must feed our magic into it slowly, something I am afraid you lack. But we will try anyway."

Sera's cheeks warmed, but meeting Mary's gaze and soft smile, Sera's anger simmered, and she was thankful not to be alone.

"Put your hands upon it and clear your mind. You must fill it with your magic, creating a bond. Come along, girls," she said, motioning the class forward.

The class congregated around the table, their excitement palpable. Sera's hands trembled. As if the new lack of personal space wasn't nerve-racking enough, now she had to use a crystal ball to tell her fortune. What would it show? Would she somehow see the faces of her family? No, she wouldn't get her hopes up, however much her heart stuttered at the possibility.

She set her hands flush on the cool orb. The glass vibrated beneath her fingers, and although she tried to remove her hands, the crystal seemed to suck them against the surface. At once, she sensed an emptiness in her consciousness and knew it was the crystal ball now linked to her. The void tugged at her inside, like a taut string pulling at her powers. Beyond the void, Sera sensed a veil, and if it was lifted, she would find spirits waiting to speak. It nudged at her soul, begging her to reach out to them, but rejecting it, she let her magic flow into the crystal until it droned in her ears, low and constant.

Mist filled the orb slowly, twisting and curling within. By and by, the smoke thickened. Unsure of whether she was supposed to guide her magic or not, Sera simply let her powers wade in the void, focused on the openness and freedom she sensed within the crystal.

The smoke pulsed and thinned in parts, and a slender face formed within the glass.

"What do you see, Miss Dovetail?"

"Nothing yet," Sera lied, as a fine mouth, nose, and lovely gray eyes revealed Barrington's face. Sera stifled her shock as his image floated in the smoke.

The mist throbbed, and Barrington's image twisted and reformed into a figure with shoulder-length brown hair. Sera gulped, her hands trembling.

"Clearly you see something, Miss Dovetail. What is it?" Mrs. Norton snipped.

"Probably the hovel she'll end up living in," Susan whispered. The other girls laughed. But Sera couldn't care about the girl and her damned prejudice. Not when she was supposed to be predicting her future, and yet it was her past that drenched the smoke.

"I see…smoke and…"

Sera, Sera, in a cage…

Her breath caught in her throat, as though it were hands—his hands wrapped tightly around her neck. There was no way he could be in her future—he was dead, done by her own hand. Yet his smoky figure turned to her, those beautiful brown eyes boring into hers, those lips capable of the sweetest kisses pulling up into that cold grin.

Sera trembled. Had she summoned him by mistake, the same way she had with the murder victims? This didn't feel like her previous summonings, but she'd experienced only two. Surely there were variations. And Barrington warned her against summoning without an anchor. How would she find her way out of it without an anchor? Her breaths quickened.

"Oh, do stop being so dramatic and tell us what you see," Mrs. Norton chided.

The smoke vibrated. *Sera, Sera wants to fly.*

"No!" Sera pushed away the crystal ball and shuffled back from the table.

"Put your hands on the ball, Miss Dovetail. We are not finished," Mrs. Norton said.

Sera shook her head. "I didn't see anything."

Mrs. Norton unsheathed her wand, her thin lips pressed tightly. "I will not have your insubordination today. You will put your hands back on that orb, or so help you."

Sera glared at the woman. Whatever pain Mrs. Norton thought herself capable of inflicting, Sera was certain she'd met worse. And if not, she would weather it not to see that face in the smoke again. "No."

The woman clutched Sera's hand, her teeth bared. Sera struggled, but Mrs. Norton jerked her forward to the table, forcing her hand onto the crystal ball. Sera's magic rattled and crested, and the moment her hand touched the orb, it flew off the table.

Mrs. Norton gasped and lunged to reach it, but it slipped through her fingers. A sparkling crash resounded as the ball shattered on the floor now covered in shards of glass glinting like diamonds.

"You stupid, useless girl!" Mrs. Norton grasped Sera's arm, digging her nails into her seventhborn mark, and shoved her aside. Sera tripped on her own feet and crashed onto the floor. She hissed at the pain radiating up her arms and the shards of glass puncturing her palms. Small beads of blood sprouted from the cuts, quickly gathering into pools in her hands. Yet, she'd much rather see blood. She would rather see death before beholding that face again.

Sitting across from Headmistress Reed later that morning, Sera was certain seeing death was a possibility, if Headmistress Reed had her way. The woman already hated her, and as per Mary, every other seventhborn, including her own sister. As the eldest of seven children, Headmistress Reed had been forced to care for her siblings after her father met his demise at the end of his own wand. Though Sera's academic career hung in the balance—as well as her employment with Barrington—her thoughts strayed toward more fearsome contemplations. Did her siblings hate her the way the headmistress abhorred her own sister? Had Barrington been right? Did her father find solace at the bottom of a liquor bottle, leaving her siblings to fend for themselves? She gulped. Was he even still alive, or did he willingly vacate life like the headmistress's father?

Sera pushed the thoughts from her mind. Though her palms ached from the cuts and crackled under the now-dried blood, she pressed her hands together, her mood sinking. How could she let a mere spirit get her into this mess? He was dead, and even if he manifested without being summoned, all she had to do was order him to leave. She needn't fear a ghost, especially of the monster who had taken so much from her. She couldn't allow him to take her dream away as well.

As Mrs. Norton explained the day's events with much

hysterics and theatrics, Headmistress Reed stirred her tea with measured twirls around the cup. She was a rather pretty woman, with long limbs that she moved gracefully, like a dancer. Sadly, she constantly wore a pinched expression, as though she spent her day tasting bitter things.

And just as bitter were her punishments. She'd already had Sera go days without a meal, forcing her to sit in the dining room as everyone else indulged. And after Sera blew up the bust of Patriarch Aldrich, she'd had her stand at the crux of both the girls' and boys' towers for an entire day, holding a portrait of Patriarch Aldrich above her head, without rest, for everyone to see. Headmistress Reed was never one to favor corporal penalties. No, humiliation was her preferred method. Still, Sera sat up straight. She would accept whatever the headmistress wished, so long as it wasn't expulsion. Heaven forbid, expulsion.

Once Mrs. Norton was done, the headmistress tapped her spoon on the side of her cup, a delicate *ting* that was much too loud for Sera's tattered nerves. "Destroying school property *again*, Miss Dovetail?"

"It was a—"

"I didn't ask you to speak," she said calmly, though Sera sensed an undercurrent of violence. She brought the cup to her lips, took a small sip, and set it back on the saucer that she then moved aside. She smoothed a hand along her desk delicately, then clasped her small hands on top, so tight her knuckles blanched. "Apparently you think because I can't expel you, that you are free to behave as though above your birth order."

Sera blinked. The headmistress couldn't expel her?

"You are a stain on this Academy, Miss Dovetail," she went on, "as is your kind on the magical community. If it were up to me, I would send you to the nearest pit to live out the rest of your disgraceful existence. But seeing as you are under the Aetherium's jurisdiction, I am allowed to discipline you only within my means."

In spite of her imminent punishment, Sera's mind caught on the headmistress's words. She often wondered why she hadn't been expelled, and now it made sense. She was under the Aetherium's authority, and if her guess was right, that meant specifically under Mr. Delacort's direction. But surely even Mr. Delacort had his limits. Could it be Timothy had something to do with it?

"I should forbid you to go to the Solstice Dance," the headmistress spoke through Sera's thoughts, "but I doubt anyone will go with you, much less dance with you, anyway." She stared at Sera for a minute, her black eyes glittering as her mind clearly worked through suitable penalties. "No, no. We need something more to quell this peculiar fire within you."

The headmistress's chair creaked as she stood up and walked to the large window behind her desk, her boots tapping on the floor like nails into a coffin. The trees shook under a strong gust, and what leaves remained on gnarled branches brushed across the courtyard in a curtain of brown. The headmistress smiled, a little too slow and wide for Sera's liking. "I think a bit of time outside will be ideal to cool you off."

Her gaze swept to Mrs. Norton. "She is to stand outside and not come back in until she has read the entire *Unmitigated Truths*, cover to cover." She looked at Sera. "And don't think I won't see if you try to leave. I'll have a wonderful view of you right here from my window."

Sera's jaw clenched, her magic bubbling within. Curses rose into her mouth, but she fought against them. She did this for her family, whether they hated her or not. "Yes, Headmistress." Sera stood and turned to a waiting Mrs. Norton.

"Ah, I almost forgot. Your cloak comes off."

Sera paused, her hands trembling now. She took off her cloak and draped it over her arm. She would bear the cold, just as she suffered her year with Noah and her past two years at the Academy.

She took a step—

"And your shoes."

Anger grew to a venomous thing, spreading through her, fraying her self-control. *Would you like my stockings, too*, she wanted to ask, but instead she knelt down and undid the ties to her boots. The headmistress was testing her, to embarrass her and break her. Sera slipped off her boots and picked them up. If Headmistress Reed expected tears or begging, she could die waiting.

Sera turned to leave once more.

"Twice," the headmistress said. "You will read the book twice, and you are not allowed to come back in, not for supper or for rest."

Anger shaded the fringes of Sera's vision in red, her magic roiling in her veins, but before she could retaliate, Mrs. Norton seized Sera's shoulder and tugged her away. "Come, ungrateful girl."

Downstairs, she led Sera to the back garden doors and pulled them open, pushed the book into Sera's chest, shoved her outside, and closed the door. Sera stumbled back, the cold blades of grass like jagged icicles underfoot. She hissed but trudged forward into the courtyard. When at a good distance from the school, she spun around and glanced up to Headmistress Reed's window. The woman glared down at Sera, her teacup in her hands. The desire to burst the dish in her fingers flitted through Sera's mind, but she set down her cloak and shoes beside her.

A bitter wind blustered and found its way beneath her

skirts and collar. Sera stiffened and curled into herself, the cold like teeth gnawing at her skin, desperate for her bones. Hands trembling, she flipped open the book.

"*The Unmitigated Truths of Seventhborns*," she began, her breath a thick white cloud hovering at her mouth.

By the third page, her teeth chattered so hard, she was sure she'd grind them to dust by the end of her punishment.

By the fifteenth page, Sera was doubtful she would live that long. Her body jerked as though wishing to conjure heat with every spasm, but it was useless, and soon she glanced down to make sure her limbs were still attached to her body. How would she ever survive?

Anger twisted within her, but shivering with cold, she was unable to grasp it. She closed her eyes and tried to focus, to touch the fire within as Barrington had taught her. Maybe she could conjure up a bit of magic to warm her insides, but the fire had waned, now a teardrop-sized flame dancing at the end of a wick.

Sera blinked her eyes open to find students pressed against the windows, all too happy to watch her suffer, but she had expected that. She looked away, and her gaze fixed on the first-floor window. A shiver coursed down her spine. Mrs. Fairfax lingered before the glass, her eyes focused solely on Sera. The woman tilted her head and raised a hand to the glass as though wishing to touch her. Sera gulped. Mary said Mrs. Fairfax had a terrible fall, and Timothy mentioned she might have been sick, but neither of those explained the longing and sadness in the housekeeper's gaze as she slid her hand down along the window.

Sera glanced behind her. Maybe she looked at someone else? Finding herself wholly alone, she spun back to Mrs. Fairfax, but she was gone.

10

again

It was a wonder she'd made it up to her room later that night, Sera mused. Her feet were like icicles, and every step jolted pain up her body. Not to mention, the memory of Mrs. Fairfax standing at the window nudged her stomach with wrongness. Something wasn't right with the woman, of that Sera was sure.

She opened her door and upon encountering the folded white note at her feet, both the cold and worry over Mrs. Fairfax vanished. Dropping her cloak, boots, and dreaded book, Sera collapsed before the letter, struggling to unfold it with trembling hands.

9:00 in the evening.

Like the previous notes, a flame sparked on the edge and quickly consumed the page. Sera held it cupped in her hands, glad for the warmth and that the crystal ball had been right about one thing. Barrington was still in her future.

Two hours later and curled beneath her blanket, Sera flipped through the Water-level spell book she'd borrowed from Mary some weeks before. Though her position with Barrington and his subsequent referral would help her take the assessment, whether or not she passed the entrance exam was entirely up to her, a feat made more difficult after missing the first two years of school. With the entrance exam being a cumulative test, surely Water and Earth levels would be covered. But Sera sighed. Of all the Water-level topics, healing had proven to be the most frustrating to grasp, especially tonight with partially numb fingers and an empty stomach. She glanced at her cut palms. She couldn't even manage to heal herself. Breaking things was much easier than fixing them.

"This is impossible," she muttered, glancing at the clock. She gritted her teeth. In a little under an hour, she was to meet Barrington, and Mary still hadn't arrived. She was never late.

Timothy's question filtered through Sera's mind.

Is there hope?

Worry drummed her pulse. Did Mary find out about her and Timothy's meeting in the library, about his secret affections and desires?

There was a light rap on the door. Pushing aside her blankets, Sera struggled to her feet and moved to the entryway, her movements stiff, as cold lingered in her bones and toes.

She pulled the door open.

"Dearest!" Mary swept into the room and threw her arms around Sera, her scent of honeysuckle filling Sera's nostrils. "I was so worried; I could barely concentrate in the infirmary. Nurse was even concerned, but I lied and told her I was hungry so that I could get you this." She pulled away and stuffed her hands into her cloak pocket, pulling out a handkerchief. Within was a chunk of bread and cheese. "I thought you might be hungry."

Sera's heart twisted, guilt threatening to swallow her whole. Oh, her sweet, sweet Mary. Why was Timothy such a fool? Why couldn't he just love Mary instead? She took the offered food, fighting against the tears in her eyes. "Thank you, Mary."

"Of course, dearest. Now come, let me see your hands. I can't stay for long. Nurse expects me back," Mary said and closed the door behind her. They moved to the bed, and as Sera ate, Mary healed the small cuts on her hands until there was no sign they ever existed.

"Does anything else hurt?" she asked.

My heart, Sera wanted to say, but shook her head and ate her last piece of cheese. Hungry as she might have been, guilt rendered the food tasteless.

"Good." She squeezed Sera's hand. "I have to go, but I need to tell you something, and you have to promise you won't say or do anything."

"I promise I won't tell my imaginary friend. You know how much it loves to gossip."

Mary pouted. "Sera."

"Yes, yes, I promise. Now what is it?"

"Hadden Whittaker is planning something—something bad as payback for the library incident, but Susan won't tell me what. I've asked her a million different ways, but she says it will be a surprise. I don't think he'd try anything too severe; his family is poor, you know? No offense, of course. His father has a small medical practice—nothing as grand as my father's, but enough to pay for Hadden's and Susan's tuition here. But that is all the money they have. He would be a fool to sabotage his academic career on silly payback, not to mention his sister's future."

Mary arched a brow. "Let's face it, her chances at marriage are abysmal and her grades are lacking. Their best chance at success is Hadden working for the Aetherium and supporting his family. It's why he befriended Timothy, I'm sure of it. Susan said Timothy will put in a good word with his father." She sighed, pressing a hand against her heart. "Such a kind heart my Timothy has. Anyway, don't worry. I'll find out more soon."

"I'm not worried." Sera stuffed the last piece of bread into her mouth and dusted her hands. "I can take care of myself."

"Exactly! You can't afford to get into any more trouble, and that is why I made you promise. I'll try to get more information, but I want you to stay out of it."

"That's not fair. You made me promise *before* you told me what he means to do."

Mary cupped Sera's cheek, stroking it gently. "That's why. How will I survive this last year here without you? We're a pair, remember? Now, I have to go. Maybe I will see you tonight if Nurse lets me go early enough...and if Mrs. Taylor is on her sixth dose of"—she cleared her throat—"tonic."

The girls shared a laugh; the overnight ladies' matron kept a flask of brandy in her desk, just outside the girls tower. Most girls knew not to sneak out before ten—the woman might have been drunk and old, but she had peculiar intuition and often caught students the moment they set a foot on the floor with the intent to sneak out. All except for Sera, forgotten up in her tower room.

"I may be sleeping; all this studying has me exhausted,"

she lied. Any time before midnight and she might still be at Barrington's.

"Good night, dearest." Squeezing Sera's hand, Mary rushed from the room and closed the door behind her.

When certain Mary would not return, Sera locked her door, rushed to the corner of the room, and prepared her transfer spell, her spirits much higher after Mary's visit. Seconds later, she slammed onto Barrington's floor, gripping the mantel as she toppled sideways. Practice was clearly not making this any easier.

"If you use too much magic to power the transfer spell, it will affect your landing," Barrington muttered. Sera spun to find him sitting at his desk, his glasses low on his nose and his eyes turned down to a notebook. Though his usual frown marked his lips, whatever sadness possessed him their previous night together was gone, of which Sera was glad, though she didn't understand why. His moods were none of her business, especially his sorrow.

"I'll be sure to try it next time." She approached his desk and sat down. There were two stacks of notebooks, one taller than the other. He shook his head and drew a line across the page. Closing the book, he set it on the shorter stack, then plucked another from the taller pile. "Are those for the case?"

"Unfortunately, no." Snatching a sheet out from beneath his mess of books and papers, he scribbled something quickly and handed it to Sera. There were symbols on the page and formulas she didn't understand.

"Those are the symbols for base metals. Anything that looks different from what I've drawn for you is incorrect."

Sera arched a brow over the notebooks. "I'm helping you grade schoolwork?"

"Indeed." Barrington plucked another notebook from

his now smaller pile and flipped it open. "Are you not my assistant?"

Sera grabbed the pen and the first notebook. "Yes, but I thought…"

"Not everything is murder and mystery, Miss Dovetail."

Sera glanced down at the answers he'd scribbled for her and sighed. Not everything was a mystery, but his handwriting sure was. She opened the first notebook and immediately frowned. Hadden Whittaker. Sera struck a line through the page without a second glance. Whether it was right or wrong didn't matter. It was Hadden Whittaker, and that was wrong enough.

Barrington scoffed and thrust down his pen. "Cases I can solve, this, however, I cannot. You would think after two weeks on the same formula, they would have grasped it by now, especially with me as their professor." He sat back and squeezed the bridge of his nose.

Sera peered over the notebook she graded and shook her head. How someone so young could have such an enormous ego was beyond her, but noticing his hands trembled slightly and a light sweat dampened his forehead, though the room was rather cool, Sera set down her book. Perhaps she was wrong, and he wasn't yet over his sadness.

Barrington lowered his hands. Sera returned to grading and abandoned her musing, lest he find her staring.

"This time of year is always difficult with everyone's attention gone to that blasted dance. It's all they seem to talk about, though it's not for another month. It's a nuisance," Sera said, comparing the cipher on the page to Barrington's.

"I take it you don't like dancing?"

She set the book aside. "I'd rather sit through a week of Mrs. Norton's lectures on the Persecution."

He smiled over his papers, a boyish grin that made him

look more his age than his usual constant scowl did. It was a nice smile, and Sera was glad to see it.

"Speaking of Mrs. Norton…" He settled back. "I thought we agreed you'd stay out of trouble."

Sera sighed. "We did, but Mrs. Norton insisted I use a crystal ball to see my future, and I started summoning by mistake, and so I stopped. She then sent me to Headmistress who thought I had a *peculiar fire* that needed to be quelled."

His brow gathered, and he set aside his work. "A summoning with a crystal ball? That's not possible. Crystal balls are used for scrying and divination. What made you think you started summoning? Did you see our spirits again?"

"Who I saw is someone I never wish to see again. And I know it was a summoning because he's dead, so how could he possibly be in my future?"

"Yes, yes, indeed." Barrington stood. He removed his coat, draped it on the back of his chair, and turned to Sera. "I think we will practice basic forms of detainment."

Sera blinked at the sudden change in topic but was glad to finally move away from summonings, crystal balls, and the nightmares of her past. "Don't we need to finish grading these papers?"

He walked to the door. "They will be as hopeless tomorrow as they are today. There is promise in you, however. Come along."

Sera smiled and followed him to the training room.

Once again there was a mannequin in the center of the room, this one with a cipher on its chest. Barrington lifted his wand.

"There may come a time when we will encounter situations where we must detain a suspect or delay them so that we can get away. In those instances, you will do this."

Three dashes of white snapped from the end of his

wand and wrapped around the dummy. The whips shone white, pulsing like a heartbeat. "These binds will respond to you, so the tighter you envision them" — his hand tightened around his wand and the binds responded, digging into the mannequin — "the snugger on your captive. That is why focus is so important. One slip of magic and you can kill your only suspect."

Sera pursed her lips. "Would that be such a terrible thing?"

"Yes, especially if that suspect has information needed to solve a case. Now, let's begin. In the real world, you will have no time to gather focus so you must master your magic. The world can come crashing down around you and you must remain calm, ready to take the appropriate action with the necessary force."

Again, his voice grew sharp as it tended to do when he started teaching. And like before, Sera was rapt by his intensity as he paced before her, his eyes steeled and every word passionate. She sensed teaching was more than work for him — a mission. No doubt being the youngest professor in an Academy wasn't easy. Most other professors already had one foot in the grave. They probably thought him a child, and like her, Barrington had to prove himself worthy of his role. And surely being surrounded by peers and students who thought his father a murderer added to the burden on his shoulders. Yes, Sera realized, teaching her was as important to him as learning was for her.

"The method of tapping into your magic is the same as with channeling and every other type of spell you wish to execute, but this time, you must shape and command it, and prepare for the kickback your magic will produce. If you grasp your wand too tightly, it will also affect aim. It's a balance. You cannot be too stiff or too loose." He reached for her arm but paused. "May I guide your arm into the appropriate form?"

He met her eyes at this, as though to gauge her answer and any fear, but Sera found not one ounce of herself afraid. "Yes, Professor."

Barrington swept behind her, his chest touching her back with each breath. Though he was brooding and strict at times, Sera relaxed, feeling a sense of safety stemming from his person. They were in this together.

He lifted her arm and bent it at the elbow, his touch delicate as though she might break if he tried any harder. "When you send magic through the wand at a fast speed, your arm will jerk back, and this will affect your aim." His hand rested gently on her shoulder, the other beneath her elbow. "Now send out a flare of magic, and as it leaves you, shape it. Imagine it as binds wrapping around a felon."

Sera grasped her wand tighter. Heat rushed up her body to her fingertips, but remembering her manic flares and how she'd nearly burned down his training room, she stifled its force. A small cloud of magic fizzled at the tip of her wand.

"Interesting. When I ask you to feed your magic out slowly, you nearly incinerate the room. Now I ask for a flare, and you give me a small stream." Barrington hummed. "You truly are a mystery."

She turned her head over her shoulder, her lips pursed, but Barrington smiled.

"Again, Miss Dovetail. With a little more intensity this time. You must feel it here." He slid his hand from her shoulder and splayed it on her belly. Sera's insides tightened, and a blast of magic dashed from her wand, knocking her back into him. Fire engulfed the mannequin.

"Precisely," he said, his breath warm on her ear. "Again."

• • •

Again became the fuel powering her days in spite of her fatigue every morning. She worked readily and stayed out of trouble during the day, all for the chance to hear Barrington speak the word come night.

Though, days later, she had yet to master forming her magic into detainment binds, Sera relished the opportunity to try and looked forward to her lessons. More so with each of Susan's smirks and Whittaker's stares in the library. Whatever they had planned, she would be ready.

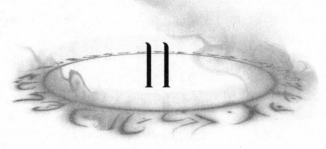

fairmount

Whereas once she relished the weekends, forty-eight glorious hours where she could pretend the world outside of her room didn't exist, now the prospect of two days without training or investigating was downright depressing. Sera glanced at the clock and gritted her teeth. It was only five minutes later from the last time she'd looked, though it felt like hours.

She thrust her Water-levels book on the bed, strode to the window, and sat. Below, students ambled along the gardens in spite of the cold, chaperones sprinkled throughout the field to monitor all contact. Sera rolled her eyes. If there was one thing she dreaded more than the Solstice Dance, it was the weeks leading up to the blasted celebration. The halls were aflame with the chatter of dresses, hairstyles, and escorts, and classes were no better.

Sera turned away from her window, happy to leave their vanity and nonsense outside. She had more important things to think about, namely why Barrington couldn't meet her on the weekends. What was he doing anyway? Maybe he was with Gummy, but wasn't their case more important? He'd told her that in the time it took her to find something in those impressions, a witch could be dying. She was glad no other witches had died, but what of this source of his? Had they found something—anything from the names she'd gathered from the spirits? She gripped her hair as the questions multiplied in her mind. How on earth would she survive two whole days? Maybe a walk would do her good.

She dropped her hands and stood, when she noticed a note at the door. Sera rushed across the room and picked up the letter. She bit her lower lip to stifle the smile that tugged at her mouth and tore open the seal.

8:00 in the evening.

Though only four words, her pulse quickened, faster than any boy or dance invitation could ever make it race.

Sera spun away from Barrington's mantel just as the grandfather clock marked eight. She grinned. Right on time. The room was empty, and she strode to the chairs before his desk and sat. There were, as always, stacks of papers on every surface. Sera shook her head. Poor Rosie. The man was a tempest. She trailed her eyes along the many papers. Was his mind the same, a chaos of ideas clashing with mysteries, murders, and memories of his father and brother?

After Timothy's revelation, she was certain it was. She inched forward. Alchemical equations marked various sheets, some scribbled and tossed aside. A newspaper was folded in half, his wire spectacles beside it. News of Aetherium Chancellor York's declining health dominated the headlines, but the rest of the story was shielded by a book. Sera tilted her head to read the spine: *Clairvoyance*. A sheet was stuffed within the book's pages, his atrocious handwriting visible on the edge. She neared a finger to open the book. He'd called her a mystery—was he attempting to learn more about her abilities in hopes of solving her? She jerked her hand back. No, no. It was none of her business. Standing, she walked to the door. Heaven forbid she attempted to snoop as he walked in.

She reached for the doorknob but paused. He'd invited her back to his home, but did he mean for her to wait here in his study? She dropped her hand. *Damn*. She couldn't once again travel his home uninvited. And then there were other things one simply couldn't unsee. Remembering Gummy's breasts and disheveled state—and not to mention the rouge on his collar—Sera scoffed and rolled her eyes. No need to see *that* again.

She strode to the chair and sat back down. She would remain where she was, even if she had to bind herself to the chair.

A while later, the door slammed open. Sera's head jerked up, startled. She rubbed her eyes and turned to Barrington at the door—black top hat, black cloak, and hard-set expression.

He set down his walking stick with a *tap*. "You're late."

Sera glanced at the clock.

9:30 p.m.

She had fallen asleep. Still, her eyes widened. "Late? I have been here since eight, as you instructed."

"If that was the case," he said, crossing the room to his desk, "why didn't you come downstairs?"

"Because I thought it improper to roam about the house uninvited."

He pulled open a drawer and retrieved a velvet maroon bag. The contents clinked and jangled as he secured it in his inner coat pocket. "When has that stopped you before?"

She fisted her skirt. Normally it took long minutes to test her patience, but it seemed Barrington had it down to an art.

"I imagined there was a chance you were otherwise engaged," she said through clenched teeth. "And what does it matter? Clearly you were out anyway."

"No, Miss Dovetail, I was not *out*. I was in, downstairs, waiting for you." He slammed the drawer shut, his foul mood more than palpable.

Sera glowered. He was an ocean, indeed. One day he was a raging sea, the next calm waters. She shook her head. How Rosie kept up with his moods was beyond her. She made to argue more, when Rosie entered the room, rosy cheeked and out of breath. Silver hairs slipped from beneath her cap and framed her round face. She smiled at Sera, a weary smile.

"Miss Dovetail, so lovely to see you," she said through labored breaths, her voice whispery. "How are you, dear?"

"Did you find what I asked for?" Barrington interrupted.

Rosie sighed. "Yes, sir. I've set it all out in the guest chamber."

"Perfect. We leave immediately. Help Miss Dovetail change, please, and escort her to the workroom when she's ready."

"Ready?" Sera surveyed Barrington and Rosie. "Ready for what?"

"We're going to Preston, in the Fairmount province." He grabbed a small notebook and pencil from his desk and slipped it within his cloak.

"Fairmount? But that's a no-magic province."

"Indeed, and that is where our investigation leads us. And had you been here earlier, we could have had more time to meet the transporter who will get us in."

Get us in...

Ever since no-magic provinces were established for those who grew weary of the feuds between Purists and Pragmatics, strict rules were decreed for travel in and out of these jurisdictions. It took days to get the proper paperwork to travel to no-magic provinces. How could Barrington have secured them without a special appointment and surrendering of their wands unless...

She swallowed. "We're being smuggled in?"

"It is not smuggling; we are merely visiting...after hours."

Visiting, of course. "And who exactly are we *visiting*?"

"Portia Rees," he said plainly, adjusting his cuffs and picking up his walking stick.

"Portia Rees is dead. The spirits spoke her name."

"Not exactly. After you heard the names, I passed them along to my source, who promised to contact the families once the case has been solved. In searching for their families, he discovered a Portia Rees requested a transfer to Fairmount three weeks ago, just *after* the last body had been found. She'd also filed a report that she had been kidnapped, but officers failed to corroborate her story. I do not think this is a coincidence. If the dead witches mentioned her name, she must be of importance, and tonight we will find out why. Rosie will help you prepare," he said from the door and walked out. "Hurry, then. We haven't much time."

Sera pressed a hand to her stomach, her nerves tangled. Though she was unsure of the penalty should they get caught, one punishment was certain—her expulsion from the Academy. They'd tolerated more than she'd ever expected—from fires to explosions—but surely even the Academy had its limits. Yet, Barrington would lose his position, too. No way would he allow them to get caught, not without a good fight. Sera sighed. If she didn't trust him before, for the sake of her dream, she'd have to trust him now.

Rosie motioned down the hall. "If you would follow me, Miss Dovetail."

Sera didn't argue and hurried behind the woman. The house became a tangled blur of hallways, stairs, and doors as she struggled to keep up with Rosie, who moved faster than her years should have allowed. The halls were all similar, spells intricately carved upon the exposed beams and gilt-framed artwork on every wall. There were no more portraits. Save for the one in Barrington's study, she had noticed no other pictures of Filip. Not even one of his father.

"Hopefully the things I've found will do. He asked for everything so suddenly." Rosie flustered over her shoulder, pulling Sera from her thoughts. "I didn't know where to begin looking. I have some things, but I haven't been as thin as you for some time, so I doubt they would fit you." They stopped before a room, and she pushed open the door.

The guest room was quaint, blue damask wallpaper lining the walls and a maroon rug on the floor. Two windows flanked an ivory-colored vanity on the wall opposite her, and upon it, a veiled black hat and a pair of black gloves. On the bed to the left of the door were two gowns spread on the ornate patchwork blanket.

"Thankfully I found some garments amongst the old Mistress's things."

"Mistress?" Sera echoed, somewhat breathless after their dash across the house. "The professor was married?"

"Master Barrington, married? Oh, goodness no." She cupped her mouth and laughed merrily. "I meant his mother, Mrs. Barrington. A lovely, lovely woman, may she rest in peace. I found these gowns that I'm certain will fit. The veil and hat are mine. The Master insisted you wear all black, but mourning dresses were disposed of after the funeral. Heaven knew we didn't need any more bad luck. These will have to do. Now, which would you prefer?"

Sera stared down at the two gowns spread on the bed and dithered. One was a burgundy dress with beautiful buttons running the length in two rows. The neckline revealed much more than she'd ever dare, but it was a lovely dress. She sighed and instead pointed to the navy-blue dress with full sleeves and a high neck.

"Wonderful choice. Now let's get you changed." Rosie picked up the gown, but with heart pounding, Sera reached out and stopped her.

"I can get dressed on my own, thank you. No need to trouble yourself."

"It's no trouble at all, dear. You won't be able to tighten it from behind without some help. No magic for personal gain, as they say."

Sera froze. There was no way she could lower her dress. Rosie would undoubtedly see her tattered chemise; she hadn't the funds to secure a new one. And surely she'd see the marks along her body.

But Barrington was waiting downstairs. And this was her dream.

She turned, unable to look at the woman, and accepted Rosie's help out of her school gown. The dress slid off her shoulders. A chill pricked her skin, her upper back exposed through the scoop in her shift. Rosie's hands stilled on Sera's forearms, the healed cuts now visible. If it weren't for Rosie's shuddering breath, she would have thought the woman gone.

Rosie recovered quickly and helped her into the new dress and over to the vanity. She had yet to say a word and never once met Sera's eyes in the reflection as she took the pins from Sera's hair.

The silence between them too much to bear, she touched the woman's hand and stopped her. "It happened some time ago... I'm fine. The Aetherium doctors tried to heal me, but..."

"But you're a seventhborn, and they didn't try very hard." Rosie squeezed her shoulders and finally lifted her gaze. Her stare was strong and held no judgment. "I'm sorry for the way your kind are treated. Not all of us are so heartless."

Sera forced a smile at Rosie's reflection and shrugged. "I suppose it's not all bad. The Aetherium wanted to show they didn't support the abuse of seventhborns, and I was accepted into the Academy soon after."

"And now you're here, and I'm glad of it." She squeezed Sera's shoulders, and the matter was put to rest. The mood lightened, and though the rest of her night promised gruesome things, it wasn't every day her hair was done for her and her clothes adjusted to perfection, and so Sera allowed herself to be fussed over this once. The way other girls were fussed over by their mothers, she thought with some hurt. Mothers who, while tending to their daughters' hair, spoke of magic and their place within that world.

Her heart grew heavy. Even if she found her family, her mother would be forever lost to her. Swallowing the knot in her throat, she slipped on the gloves and forced herself to ignore the black ring at her wrist. A reminder of the reason why she had no mother at all.

Rosie adjusted the hat and veil over her head. "Wonderful. Now let's get you down to the Master before he comes up here to fetch you himself."

A strange concoction of nerves and excitement brimmed in Sera's stomach, mixed with sorrow for the victims. Being an inspector was all she'd ever wanted, and yet witches had lost their lives for her to get closer to achieving it. Caught in this inner debate, she put on the cloak and followed Rosie down to the workroom just as Barrington strode out from the black door.

He gave her a cool once-over and expressed approval with a single nod, then closed the black door behind him. "That will be all, Rosie. Thank you."

Once Rosie was gone, Barrington faced Sera, his warm presence hovering before her like a shadow. "I will transfer us together, but in order to do so, I must hold your hand and you can't let go," he said gently, as though to prepare her for the contact.

Sera swallowed through a thickened throat, excitement and fear fluttering within her like a flock of birds in her stomach. Barrington said his methods were unorthodox, but she'd never imagined that *visiting* no-magic cities and *borrowing* crime scene photos factored into the equation. Still, she nodded and slipped her hand into his. Fear would not help her find her family.

Barrington drew closer, his scent of sandalwood and musk enveloping her. He folded his fingers around hers, and though he wore gloves, the pressure and warmth of his touch tamed the torrent in her stomach, and she relaxed.

He aimed his wand at the ground, and his body grew tense, bracing. Unlike transferring to his house where the floor merely felt to vanish beneath her, here the ground rumbled as Barrington fueled their transfer. His magic surrounded her, a potent charge of cool energy swathing her skin. She glanced up and met his eyes, shadowed by the brim of his top hat. He gave her a small smile and squeezed her hand, as though to ease her worries. To tell her with no words that she was safe here, with him.

The world around her faded like smears of watercolor until blackness enveloped them. She blinked, and they now stood within another room. She'd barely felt the transfer in her stomach, a testament to Barrington's control of his magic.

They stood upon a platform of black marble, within a large gold-metallic circle embossed on the floor—a transfer wheel. A series of ciphers were carved along the gold band. Sera recalled learning of them during her Air-level course on transferring. A magician merely needed to rotate the rings to their destination's coordinates and ignite the spell. The first she'd ever encountered had been two years ago, when transferring into the Aetherium with a guard at either side of her.

Muffled music resounded from outside the cream double doors bordered in ornate gold. Sera spun to the foreign room. There were four more transfer wheels next to hers and five circular red banquettes, one positioned before each wheel. An older man with white hair and a deadpan expression stood at the end of the platform. He moved toward them as they stepped off the transfer wheel and onto the blue Persian carpet spread over polished cherrywood floors.

"Good evening, Professor. Miss," he said with a curt bow. "Your cloak, madam?"

"We won't be staying long, Barnaby. Could you tell Miss Mills we've arrived."

Sera grimaced. Though she'd met the woman only once, it was more than she'd cared for.

"Of course, sir." Barnaby bowed and quickly exited through the only door.

"Gummy is our smuggler?" Sera whispered for Barrington's ears only. She'd heard smugglers were fugitives who never stayed in one place for long and earned money by transferring clients between provinces. Gummy didn't seem like a fugitive from what she last remembered.

He motioned to the settee, but she shook her head.

The nerves knotting in her stomach would never let her sit. "No, she is our facilitator. She owns a number of these establishments in various provinces with a vast clientele."

Just then, a transfer wheel activated beside theirs, and a man appeared in the middle. He walked down the stairs and met another butler who promptly took his hat and overcoat, then led him to the double doors.

When he opened them, the stifled music, chatter, and laughter grew louder, as did intermittent giggles and shouts. A woman in a low-cut emerald-green gown appeared at the door, her skirt hitched high and her stockings visible.

The door closed, and Sera spun to Barrington. "You've got to be joking. Her network of information is a brothel?"

"Indeed. You wouldn't believe the number of secrets a man will spill with just the right amount of liquor and… persuasion."

Sera wrinkled her nose and turned away. Figures. If *visiting* and *borrowing* were a part of Barrington's vocabulary, why wouldn't this *establishment* and its *facilitator* be as well?

The door opened again. Gummy stood on the other side. She looked regal in a red silk gown and nothing like the woman Sera remembered from the other night. With her hair swept up and cascading curls framing her round face, she was youthful and rather lovely.

She strutted to Barrington, smoothed a hand down his chest all the way to his vest pocket, where she drew out his pocket watch. She clicked open the watch, then glanced up at him through thick lashes. "This doesn't look like eight fifteen to me, does it, Barry?"

"Barrington," he clipped and drew back the watch, his frame bristled and jaw tight. "Miss Dovetail had to get ready."

Gummy cast her a side-eyed glance. "Right, Miss Dovetail. A pleasure," she said, though her small smile told

Sera it was anything but. Sera stared back at her but didn't bother with formalities.

"Now that you're here, you have only one hour." Gummy snapped her fingers, and a short man walked into the room, ushered by Barnaby. His coat and pants were stained with soot and patched together with odd scraps. He held a drink in his hand, his eyes glassy and fingernails black.

"This is Crenshaw. He will be your transporter. The Aetherium scries for magic incessantly, and patrol is constant throughout the province. When you arrive, you must move away from the transport location quickly, after which you have an hour. If you don't get what you need, it doesn't matter to me; you get back to your return transfer point or you get left behind. Understood?"

"Understood." Barrington reached into his inner coat pocket and handed her a velvet bag. She gave it a shake. It jingled, but not like coins, rather like glass vials clinking against one another. "A week's supply."

Her red lips spread as she pulled open the drawstrings and examined the contents of the bag. "Safe travels, Barry."

Crenshaw downed his drink and handed the empty tumbler to Barnaby whose frown deepened. Sera glanced at Barrington. Could they trust this man? Alcohol was known to have negative effects on magic, and Crenshaw was most certainly not drinking water.

If Barrington noticed, he didn't say a word. He walked back onto the platform.

Crenshaw surveyed Sera's outfit, squinting his eyes as though to see through her veil. "Who died?" he asked, the tangy scent of liquor wafting from his lips.

Sera glanced around and scowled. "My morality, I'm sure."

She met Barrington on the transfer wheel, and Crenshaw

stood before them. Gummy lingered at the foot of the stairs, her eyes focused on the professor.

Crenshaw extended a hand in wait for Sera's. Sera remained unmoving.

"I'm certain holding one of us is enough," Barrington said, his eyes never one to miss anything, including her apprehension.

Crenshaw shrugged. "Suit yourself."

Barrington gripped the man's shoulder firmly, then took hold of Sera's hand and drew her to his side. He leaned in close to her ear. "Remember what I said, do not let me go."

Sera met his eyes, bolstered by the strength and safety she found in his stare. "I don't intend to."

Gummy pursed her lips and chuckled. "I'll see you when you return, Barry."

Sera's skin prickled with heat, sure Gummy said it to Barrington but meant it for her.

Crenshaw placed his other hand above Barrington's, and a minty scent overtook Sera's nose as his magic enclosed them.

The floor gave out, a longer flash of black, and then they landed neatly on their feet. Sera sighed. She had to get better at controlling her magic, which would make for smoother transferring and not the crash landings she was used to when transferring into Barrington's home. That is if they ever got out of this alive.

A putrid scent met her nose, and Sera stifled a gag, her eyes watering. They were in a small room, tattered and stained rags hanging before them to create a division. Based on the scent alone, she had no desire to know what was on the other side.

"The address is three streets over," Crenshaw said. "I trust Gummy gave you your return location."

Barrington nodded, and with a tip of his hat, Crenshaw was gone.

After assuring the coast was clear, Barrington led them quickly into the night. He drew out a small notebook with a hand-drawn map. "It's this way," he said with a nod.

Although the narrow road was relatively quiet, uneasiness crept up Sera's back. Buildings of crumbling brick flanked the winding avenue. Dark alleyways fed off it like black veins. The sky above was an impregnable ocean of black fog and soot, an encroaching heaviness that felt alive. Noxious fumes seemed to flare up from the slick streets. Sera's stomach tightened, and she pressed a hand to her mouth as if to physically keep herself from vomiting.

Nothing about this place seemed safe, save for Barrington. She couldn't use magic, she knew this, yet her insides churned and warmth flared within her, ready for release.

They kept a steady pace to create distance from their arrival point, until Barrington stopped before a rundown building, a clothesline tethered to the opposite building with stockings, aprons, and trousers flailing in a passing pungent breeze.

He neared the door and knocked. Sera kept watch, her hand tight at her side. She rubbed her skirt, finding comfort in the feel of her concealed wand beneath the fabric.

A moment later, a latch was released and the door opened. A girl no older than sixteen stood before them, wiping oily hands on her stained white apron. She toured dark eyes between Sera and Barrington, her brow gathered in a scowl.

"Miss Portia Rees?" Barrington asked in the absence of her greeting.

Her eyes widened slightly, and she glanced behind her. Sera attempted to follow her stare, but the girl closed the door to where only she was visible through the seam. "That's me. What do you want?"

"The Aetherium has secured my services in regards to your ordeal last month."

She leaned against the doorframe, her full lips pursed. "Is that so? They didn't care much then. Why should they care now?" She held out her arm, and Sera's brow rose. A seventhborn tattoo marked her wrist. "When have they ever cared for a seventhborn?"

"They care now, I can assure you," Barrington replied. "Could we please talk inside?"

She scrutinized him, touring coal-black eyes along his frame. She crossed her arms over her chest. "I have nothing to say. Those bastards caught me, and I got away, and I never want to think of it a day again."

"Please, it will take only a few minutes of your time, and I will make it worth your while." He reached into his inner coat pocket and drew out a gold coin.

She snatched it from his hand, turning it over in soiled fingers. "Isn't like an Aetherium guard to bribe a seventhborn. Most would throw me in jail for being *hostile*," she said, inspecting the coinage. "You have five minutes. A coin for every answer." She moved aside and allowed them to pass.

The room inside smelled of mold, though compared to the stench of refuse outside, for Sera it was a welcome relief. The space was much smaller than her tower room at the Academy. She hadn't imagined anyone could ever live in a lesser space. To the right was a bed, two tattered gray wool blankets on top. A single gas lamp lit the room, but even so the space was cloaked in shadows. To the left was a chimney stove with a small table and two chairs before it. Sera glanced fleetingly at the table and then at Barrington—there were two plates. As usual, Barrington's stoic expression remained fixed and gave away nothing.

Portia slumped into one of the chairs, stacked the plates together, and motioned to the opposite chair. "So, what do you want to know?"

Sera sat, Barrington towering beside her. Drawing out a few more coins, he handed them to Sera. The gold weighed heavy in her hand. She'd never been in possession of so much and pondered the things she could do with that money. A new cloak, new shoes... But, she conceded, a referral was worth more than all the gold in the world.

"Can you tell us what happened, in detail?" Barrington dug into his inner coat pocket and pulled out his small notepad and gold mechanical pencil. Portia's eyes roamed to the pencil, and she pursed her lips. Barrington nodded to Sera, and she set a coin on the table.

Portia yanked it away greedily and stuffed it into her pocket. "I was kidnapped, that's what. They hurt me, kept me in a big house, and drank my magic. The other girls, too."

Sera's heart tightened, but she forced herself steady. This was her job, memories be damned.

"Big house where? And what other girls? Did you know them? Can you recall their names?"

Sera put another coin down. Portia swiped it before Sera had a chance to slide it across the table. "Polly, I think. Or was it Martha?" She turned brown eyes up and tapped her chin with a dirtied finger. "I don't remember. But their names didn't matter, only that they were seventhborns. The lot of them were."

Sera's face burned beneath her veil. After the years of horror experienced by seventhborns, now they were being targeted again by these monsters.

"All of you were seventhborns?" Barrington reiterated.

She nodded. "Some for draining, others for killing, but

they were all seventhborns."

Sera's brow gathered. *They*, not we.

Barrington jotted this down. "And by killing, you mean…?"

She glanced at Sera, but Sera's hand tightened on the coins, a nudging feeling in her belly. Something wasn't right. Still, she set a coin on the table, then slid it over slowly.

"They took some of the other girls, who never came back," she said, pocketing the coin. "They must've killed them."

Barrington hummed. "And you say they drank your magic. Can you tell me exactly how this happened?"

Sera let out a shuddering breath, turning her face away.

Sera, Sera in a cage…

She didn't need to hear how a warlock drank of his victims—drank from her. Of the way he'd invade her mind, searching out her reserves.

Sera, Sera wants to fly…

And if she dared try to block him out, how his beautiful eyes glinted with pleasure as he forced his way into her mind, pushing so hard against her reserves that it felt as though her skull cracked in two. As she screamed, focused on the pain, he tapped into her reserves and absorbed her screams and her magic. He'd drink so much that her lifeline weakened, and cuts and bruises bloomed along her gray and gaunt skin.

But her pretty wings are broken…

Finished, he would then sing that damned song.

See her fall from the sky.

Maybe if she'd stopped fighting, he would have been kinder. Sera's hand tightened around the coins. She would've rather died.

Barrington took a coin from Sera and set it on the table himself, pulling her from the nightmarish daydream.

Portia eyed the coin, then Barrington. She shifted in her

chair and cleared her throat. "Well, they, um…they held me down and put their wands on my belly and told me to use my magic so he could absorb it." She nodded to herself, her face downcast. "Yes, yes, it was terrible."

Sera's brow furrowed. That wasn't how it was done, but before she could speak, Barrington took another coin from her and set it on the table. "What else?"

Portia reached for the coin, but Barrington seized her wrist. The girl gasped and struggled to pull away, but he tightened his grip.

"How about the truth, Miss Rees—if that is even your name? There is only one way to drain a witch of her magic, and what you described is not it. Now, you are in possession of more coin than you'll see in a lifetime. Tell me the truth, and you will be allowed to keep it. Lie to me, and you will be charged with stealing from an Aetherium officer." His voice was cool, lethal, his eyes just as cold.

Her frantic gaze swept across the room toward the bed before shifting back to Barrington. "I don't know what you're talking about. I told you the truth."

Sera stood, moving slowly toward the bed.

"What is your name?" Barrington asked.

Portia gulped, staring at Sera approaching the bed. "Fine, I lied. My name is Rowena Rees. Portia is my twin sister, but she isn't here. Now please leave."

"Where is Portia?"

Sera reached for the wool blanket—

"Run, Portia!" Rowena screamed.

A gangly girl in a white nightgown darted from under the bed. Sera startled and jumped back, drawing her wand.

"Miss Dovetail, no!" Barrington said.

The girl froze, her chest heaving with juddering breaths. "I can't leave you, Rowena," she moaned, glancing at her sister.

Sera's grip tightened on her wand, her magic a vicious beast clawing at her insides for release. *Steady, Sera. Steady…*

Rowena pulled away from Barrington, but he jerked her back against his chest. "Go, Portia!" she yelled.

Portia dashed to the door, yanked it open, and ran outside.

Damn it! Sera raced after her.

"Miss Dovetail, wait! You stay here, I will go after her," Barrington ordered, struggling against Rowena.

Sera stopped at the door. She looked at Rowena scuffling, at Barrington keeping her fixed while gray eyes bored into Sera's, at Portia running into an adjacent alleyway.

He would fire her for this, she was sure of it. But he would have an easier time holding down Rowena. And Portia didn't need a man to chase after her, not when it was a man who had hurt her.

Sera ran out into the night. The last she heard was Barrington growl a curse before the door closed behind her.

12

monsters to find

Portia hadn't run very far.

Sobbing, she shuffled down the alleyway, groping the walls to remain upright. Sera gathered her skirts and chased her down the street, reaching her in a few fast strides.

She grabbed her hand. "Portia—"

The girl wrenched her arm away and scrambled back against a brick wall, eyes wide with fear. Her skin was gray and pallid, her lips cracked and dry. Dark circles hung like half-moons beneath her eyes, and her cheeks were sunken. Even her hair hung limp about her shoulders. She was a breath away from being a walking skeleton. Sera's heart twisted; it was like looking into the mirror two years ago. After months of having her magic drained, it had taken her double the time to gain weight and strength, and longer for the cuts to heal.

"I won't go back," she moaned and lifted a hand to the air. Bruises covered her arm, and on her wrists were linear burn marks as though she'd been bound. "I'll use what magic

I have left and make the Aetherium arrest me before you take me back to those men."

Sera held her hands up in surrender. "I'm not here to hurt you, Portia. All we want is to help capture the men who took you."

Portia tucked her bottom lip between her teeth, considering Sera's words, but shook her head and made to turn.

"Portia, wait!" Sera hissed and glanced about the avenue. At any minute a patrol guard could pass by. She had to earn the girl's trust so she could bring her back inside. And quickly. Pulling down her glove and lifting her sleeve, Sera revealed the trail of scars along her arm. Portia's brow gathered, tears trailing down her deep-set cheeks. She didn't try to run away.

Sera inched forward. "They did this to you, didn't they? I know what you went through. My attacker is dead now, and I want to catch yours. Help us make sure they don't drain another witch again."

The girl's body was wracked as she shielded her face with her hands and sobbed. Her knees buckled, but Sera caught her before she collapsed and helped her back down the alley and into the house.

Rowena was sitting now, Barrington towering over her, the very fires of hell in his eyes. Sera averted her gaze and moved Portia to the bed. The cold of night clung to her clammy skin. Sera draped one of the wool blankets over the girl.

"What did you do to her?" Rowena cried, struggling to stand. Barrington released her, and she ran to Portia's side, glaring at Sera. "What did you do?"

"She's here to help," Portia whispered, her voice hoarse. She curled into herself and gripped Rowena's hands, her own knuckles white and pronounced.

"I know this is hard for you, Portia, but can you tell us what happened? You can trust me…and him." Sera looked over her shoulder to Barrington. His jaw was clenched tight, but he sat down and picked up his pencil.

Sera stooped next to the bed, at eye level with Portia. "Please, tell us everything."

Portia took a few steadying breaths that rattled in her chest, her eyes filled with tears. "I was on my way back home from the bakery where I worked—I cleaned there sometimes. The baker was nice, and I was able to bring home food. These men were waiting for me, said they were from the Aetherium Seventhborn Program. I had applied last month—Rowena said I had more power in a pinky than she had. It was worth a try. When I saw them, I thought I had gotten in. One of them asked to test my reserves, and I let him. That's when they nabbed me, said they were taking me to the Academy." Her face contorted as she suppressed a sob.

"How?" Barrington asked. "It's impossible for you both to be seventhborns."

Portia reached out her arm. Sera and Barrington exchanged glances. Her seventhborn mark was fading.

"She was trying to help me," Rowena said, smoothing down Portia's hair. "We figured if she got into the program, even if she didn't graduate, she could get a better job with what she learned, so we used dye and made her seventhborn mark. Had I known…"

"Pretending to be a seventhborn?" Barrington scoffed. "Are you mad?"

"No, sir. We're hungry and desperate," Rowena hissed, tears clinging to her lashes. "We're not all as lucky as you," she said, glaring at Sera. "We don't got no fancy job and dress. They still find us and kill us, and the Aetherium pretends it never happened. Purist or Pragmatic, you're

all the same. This was our chance. But then they took her…
Those bastards."

"Do you remember where they took you?" Barrington
asked.

Portia shook her head. A tear trailed from the corner
of her eye, down her temple, and vanished into her matted
hair. "When I woke up, I was in a room with two girls. The
curtains were drawn; we weren't allowed to look outside.
But there were spells everywhere on the walls, and the men
wore blue robes with a raven on the breast."

Barrington's grip tightened around his pencil.

"One of the girls they drained right away. They then took
me and Winnie—she was a nice girl from Clewiston."

Sera shivered. Though she'd heard Winnie's name during
the summoning, to know she was real—that she had existed
and now spoke to her from death—made the hairs on the
back of her neck stand on end.

"They dragged us to a cemetery where they'd exhumed
a grave and made me touch the dead body." She trembled,
hugging herself tighter. "It was terrible. They said I would
help them raise the corpse."

Barrington set his pencil down slowly. "Did they say
exactly what you would do?"

"No," she whispered, "but it didn't work. They needed
seventhborns, and I'm not. That's when Winnie told me to
run. She knew I wasn't a real seventhborn. I'd told her. She
had a bit more training and blasted them with magic, and I
was able to get away. Thankfully there was a constable close
by. They would've caught me otherwise."

Barrington inched to the edge of his seat, his anticipation
brightening his eyes. "Miss Rees, would you be able to
cast out your memory of these men? I will pay for all
transportation to whichever Aetherium magic province

you'd like and can guide you through the spell. It wouldn't take much magic—"

"No, no, no. No magic, no magic." Quaking, she burrowed into her sister's side. "No magic."

Rowena scoffed. "You're mad if you think we're setting foot in a magic province again. Our condition may be no different in Fairmount, but at least those bastards will have a harder time nabbing her here. If they come for her, she can use magic, and the constables will be here at once and protect her. No, she's told you all she can. You need to leave. I said five minutes, and you've had thirty."

Barrington drew out his pocket watch. Opening it, he gritted his teeth. "Indeed we have, and yes, we need to leave." He stuffed his watch back into his pocket, his eyes steeled with disappointment. "Can you tell us anything about these men? Anything that can help us identify them?"

Curled up in her sister's side, Portia stared, seemingly at nothing. Sera's heart tightened, and she gripped the girl's hand.

"My sister is finished. Please go," Rowena said, stroking Portia's back as if to warm her. But Sera knew there was no warming her, not until her reserves recovered from the abuse. Even then, the chill lingered.

"Perhaps you can draw them, then, or jot down whatever you remember, whatever at all? Drop it off at Trousseau, down in the Lower District. You've heard of it, yes?" Barrington spoke quickly.

Rowena nodded. Barrington reached into his pocket and set a stack of coins on the small table. "You will receive triple that amount upon delivery."

Putting on his top hat, he strode through the door. Sera squeezed Portia's hand and hurried after Barrington but stopped and glanced back at Portia shivering in Rowena's arms. Her hand tightened on the doorknob, a fierce ache in her heart. Never before had she wanted to be an inspector so badly. She yearned to locate her family, but now there were monsters to find.

There would always be monsters to find.

Sera imagined he would have dismissed her the moment they set foot outside the Rees's hovel, yet an hour and two transfer spells later, they entered Barrington's study and he had yet to say a word.

He slid off his cloak and hung it on the coat-tree, then relieved his pockets of his notebook and wand. Walking to the side bar, he grabbed a glass and set it down with a light tap, then poured himself a drink. He picked up the goblet and stared at the amber liquid but didn't drink. Didn't speak.

Sera slipped off her veiled hat and dropped it on his desk. He hadn't even recognized that they had new information—good information, thanks to her! She shook her head. "You can't possibly still be angry with me."

Barrington's grip tensed on the glass, his knuckles white. "Don't tell me who I can and cannot be angry with, Miss Dovetail. In case you've forgotten, I'm the superior here, and when I ask you not to give chase, you do not give chase."

His words were glacial, sharp icicles stabbing Sera's skin. She scoffed and tore off her cloak and thrust it on the chair beside her. "You're unbelievable. Why can't you just admit that I did a good job? That if I would have listened to you, our only witness may have fled, and we never would have learned what we did today?"

Barrington said nothing, transfixed by his glass of brandy

and whatever thoughts crowded his head.

Heat seared Sera's insides. "I did what was right."

"You did what you wanted," he said, his voice eerily calm. "Without thinking of consequence."

Sera bit her nails into her palms. There was no pleasing him! "I did what was right, and it bothers you because you take pleasure in trying to make me feel small and worthless, just like everyone else."

Barrington spun to her at this, his wolf eyes narrowed. "*Pleasure?* No, Miss Dovetail, it isn't pleasure I feel in scolding you, but inordinate frustration. More than you can imagine. Nothing about you is small and worthless—on the contrary, you are a brilliant witch and can be a spectacular inspector, yet you continue to jeopardize your future. You ran after Portia and never once considered that an Aetherium patrol could have been right outside. What would you have said then?"

Sera's cheeks flushed at the reproach, but she set her jaw. She hadn't thought of that. Still she said, "I would have stalled so you could get away, then taken the blame for transferring in illegally."

"It is not about the blame," he said, his voice a harsh whisper. "It is about this—about us. What is the point of us working together if you will sabotage it at every turn? What I tell you to do isn't to order you around for *pleasure*. It is to keep you—to keep us—alive and able to move on with our investigation. And in the end, it isn't about us at all. It is about Portia and Winnie and Agatha and Elsie and every other witch whose lives have been cut short. They are the ones who need us to find these men."

"They aren't men. They're beasts, and if we'd let Portia run away, we would have lost our chance at finding out they are targeting seventhborns."

"I would rather lose a chance than lose you, Miss Dovetail. When I ask you to do something, above all, it is to keep you safe, and I need you to understand that. Yet you insist on drawing attention to yourself without realizing it will bring only…"

He met her stare and, seeming to remember himself, he raked a hand through his hair, squeezed at the nape, and said no more. Focused on the ground, he shook his head and paced in an aimless circle. Sera watched him, reminded of an ocean in the midst of a storm, dark and tormented. But why?

She gulped through a thickened throat, his apprehension suddenly contagious. "Will bring only what?"

Barrington stopped. "Will bring you only more trouble," he said without looking her in the eyes.

Sera's brow furrowed, a sense of dread settled in her belly. This wasn't what he meant to say. "Professor?"

"I'm tired, and you have class in the morning." He drew his wand and aimed it at her feet. "I will be in touch. Good night, Miss Dovetail."

"But Professor—"

Blackness surrounded her, then she stumbled back onto her window seat.

"Damn it," she whispered, sitting. Kicking off her boots, she drew her knees to her chest and stared out to the darkness as Barrington's words and abrupt change chased one another through her mind.

Will bring you only more trouble…

She shook her head. No, this wasn't what he'd meant to tell her. Her soul stirred with this awareness. His words didn't match his solemnness…or had it been fear? But what could he have possibly meant to say that he'd been too scared to share?

13

forgive me

The sheets clung to her sweaty skin.

Sera, Sera in a cage…

A torrent of memories swarmed Sera's mind, hazy recollections of pain whisking by like wisps of smoke and whispers.

Sera, Sera wants to fly…

She turned her head away and willed her eyes to open, but sleep burrowed its claws into her consciousness, wrapped its tentacles around her joints, and pressed its claim. Sera's body tensed, but after her night with Barrington her mind was too weary to fight, and she fell deeper into sleep's darkness.

But her pretty wings are broken…

The blackness became a vortex of smoke that pulsed like a heart. With each beat, it gained shape and form until a familiar room materialized. Noah's room.

Look at her fall from the sky…

Black floors stretched beneath her like an ocean of

dried blood, and black walls spread around her. A candle chandelier of skeletons hung overhead, the only light in the dim room. Black velvet curtains denied all signs of day and weather, but time and season didn't matter. Noah would never let her experience them, he would never let her go.

Sera lifted onto her elbows. Her black dress crinkled as she sat up. She glanced to the bedside table. Relief spread through her chest. His wand wasn't there, and he was never without it, the horrible piece of black wood painted with the blood of his victims.

She kicked off the black silk sheets and made to stand, but her hand was taken in a firm, frigid hold.

Sera...

Her muscles tensed, and a cold wave rushed down her spine. She let out a shuddering breath and looked to the side.

Noah knelt beside the bed, his head bowed over her hand. His lean body shuddered as he sobbed silently, his warm tears spilling over her fingers. He turned his face up; beautiful, angular brown eyes stared back at hers, a dual promise of pain and tenderness in his gaze.

"I'm so sorry, Sera," he whispered. "I'm so sorry."

Sera shook her head, her breath breaking. This was wrong. This was all wrong. Noah never apologized. Noah didn't feel remorse.

"Forgive me, please." He lowered his head and sobbed again, his shoulder-length brown hair shielding his face.

"What is this?" She wrenched her hand away but hissed as he dug his nails into her skin and kept her fixed.

"I'm sorry, forgive me."

"No, you're not him," Sera whispered, breathless. She tugged her hand away, harder. "You're not him."

Consciousness descended on her mind like a bird of prey.

"This is all a dream," she whispered. "You're not real.

You're not him…"

With each denial she issued, he faded away, and then his room, until Sera once again waded in smoke and shadows.

The splintering crackle of lightning exploded, and she bolted upright, her heart hammering in her chest. She lifted a hand…but it was seized by another.

A scream lodged in her throat. She glanced down to who held her hand, and couldn't make a sound. Mrs. Fairfax knelt beside the bed, the housekeeper's shoulders trembling and her keys jingling at her side as she wept.

A chill of awareness trailed down Sera's spine, wound around her stomach, and squeezed. Was…was Mrs. Fairfax dead and this her ghost?

The housekeeper sniffled, and warm tears spilled onto Sera's hand.

Sera shook her head. No, it couldn't be. The dead didn't cry warm tears. The dead couldn't touch the living. But then what on earth was wrong with her? Mary said she'd had a fall, and her appearance had been strange when Sera hid with Timothy in the secret library. Was she sick?

Heart pounding, Sera slipped a foot out from under her blanket and set it on the opposite side of the bed. She inched to get out, but the mattress groaned, and Mrs. Fairfax's head snapped up. Glossy eyes bored into Sera.

"Sera," she moaned and gripped Sera's wrist. "Forgive me."

"Mrs. Fairfax, let me go!" She wrenched her arm away, but the woman clutched her tighter, tearing her sleeve. Freed, Sera scrambled backward off the bed.

Mrs. Fairfax clawed thick fingers into the tousled sheets and tried to stand, her plump face flushed and chin quivering. "Forgive me, please. Forgive me."

She lunged and reached for Sera again. "Forgive me!"

"No!" Sera lifted a hand. Panic gripped her stomach, and a blow of magic burst from her hand in the form of binds. They whipped around Mrs. Fairfax so fast, the force pushed her into the air and across the room. She slammed against the door and crashed onto the floor, unconscious.

Sera shifted back, her frame heaving. She grasped her wand from her bedside table and aimed it at the motionless woman. "Mrs. Fairfax?" She panted, her hands trembling.

Wild winds wheezed outside, and thunder rattled the windows, but Mrs. Fairfax didn't make a sound.

Breathless, Sera inched forward toward the woman. The white binds of her magic were snug, their hue pulsing to the tune of Sera's frantic heartbeats. Moving a little closer, she saw that Mrs. Fairfax was breathing, and the tightness in her chest eased slightly. But for how long? And what would she do if she woke up? This was bad. It was very, very bad. How would she ever explain this? Though Mrs. Fairfax had come into her room, surely she'd be blamed for it somehow. Unless someone could help her...

Sera called back her magic, and the binds around Mrs. Fairfax vanished with a hiss. She aimed her wand at the floor and, a moment later, stumbled into Barrington's dark study. The embers in the fireplace barely emitted a glow, and the room was cloaked in shadows.

She started for the door. He may have been angry at her, but surely he wouldn't turn her away. Barrington was moody but, so far, never cruel.

Reaching for the doorknob, she paused at a light snore. She spun to find Barrington asleep at his desk, his head down on his forearms. His frame undulated with even, rhythmic breaths of sleep.

Sera hurried to his side. He slept over an open case file, impressions of charred bodies and exhumed graves spread out beneath him. Beside him was an empty decanter and a half-filled tumbler.

"Professor, wake up," she said in a stage whisper.

He didn't rouse.

She gritted her teeth and gripped his shoulder, shaking him. If he didn't wake up soon, they might have another dead body on their hands. "Wake up, sir!"

Barrington jerked upright, his hair spiked on one side and his eyes narrow with sleep. He still wore his clothes from earlier in the night, his black robe the only addition. He took one look at Sera, and all bleariness vanished.

He rushed to his feet and seized her shoulders. "What is it? Did you see something?" Lightning flashed, highlighting the alarm on his face before thrusting them back into darkness. "Speak quickly, girl."

"Mrs. Fairfax. I—I woke up, and she was there, in my room. She's still breathing, but I fear she may be hurt."

"Mrs. Fairfax, the housekeeper?" He shook his head. "Miss Dovetail, tell me exactly what happened."

"I was asleep, and when I woke up, she was in my room, crying and asking for forgiveness." Sera shivered, clasping her hand against her chest, haunted by the sensation of Mrs. Fairfax's warm tears. "She lunged for me, and I used binds to detain her, but they came out so fast, she slammed against the wall, and now she's unconscious."

Barrington's eyes darkened, and Sera braced. He would help her; she was sure of it. But would he also scold her for using what he'd taught her to harm a fellow staff member?

"Are you hurt?"

She reared back to defend herself, yet stumbled upon the question that came with his words. In her silence, Barrington pulled her away and scrutinized her. His eyes locked on the torn sleeve.

"Did she do this?" He took her arm, his touch firm yet gentle, and pushed aside the frayed fabric to inspect her skin. He paused, his fingers stilled over her scars. His jaw clenched.

Sera yanked her arm away and tugged down her sleeves. "I'm fine. She didn't hurt me."

Clearing his throat, Barrington nodded and whisked off his robe, then draped it over her shoulders. Warmth and the scent of musk and sandalwood enveloped her. Sera sighed. A sense of safety rolled through her, chasing away the chill of fear.

Barrington reached for his wand. "Where is she now? Did you fetch Nurse?"

"She was still by the door when I left." She remembered the woman crumpled on the floor, and her chin quivered. She hadn't meant to hurt her—not fatally anyway. "I thought to get Nurse, but they'd find a way to blame me, I'm sure of it, so I came here. I didn't know where else to go."

"You did well in binding her, and in coming to me. You can always come here."

Sera lifted her head. Though the room was dim and his face set hard, she could see the honesty in his stare. She lowered her head and clasped the robe around her tighter, a strange twinge in her belly. "Thank you, Professor."

He touched her shoulder and aimed his wand to the ground. She blinked, and the darkness of her small room surrounded them.

Barrington shifted back, taking in the burn marks on the wall and her amalgamation of dated furnishings in one glance. He moved to Mrs. Fairfax's side and, kneeling beside her, he brushed her white hair from her ashen face and set a hand at her temples.

His dark brows joined in concentration. "She has no serious injuries," he murmured, much to Sera's relief, "but she's weak. I must get her to Nurse immediately. I'll say I found her on the back stairs. And you must speak to no one about this, not to the Tenant girl...nor to Mr. Delacort."

Sera's heart pounded, her mouth wound with unintelligible words. "How did you...?"

"There are eyes everywhere, Miss Dovetail." He slid a hand beneath Mrs. Fairfax's shoulder and eased her into his arms. "Thankfully, silence is a commodity. Now, lock your door and use magic if necessary. If any trouble comes to you, transfer to the house."

Sera nodded and moved back. He vanished into darkness with Mrs. Fairfax, and though Sera was still wrapped in his cloak, the room grew colder around her.

News of Mrs. Fairfax dominated all talk that morning, though with every whisper Sera heard, the story changed. Some claimed she was found in the library, while others said they saw her from their windows, unconscious in the back gardens. The tales followed her into Mrs. Aguirre's class, where Susan Whittaker leaned in to Mary.

"I don't care what anyone says, she was properly drunk. I heard she was found in the pantry some days ago without a memory of how she got there. Isn't that what drunks usually say?" She pursed her lips and nodded once, wholly satisfied with her answer. "I bet if they search her room, they'll find all sorts of liquor there. I say she should be fired."

Mary glanced at Sera and offered her a fleeting smile before turning back to Susan. She looked tired, her skin missing its usual glow and her eyes their gleam. Sera glanced at Susan. The girl was a pest, and after a morning of hammering the same subject, Mary must have been annoyed.

"Come to think of it," Susan went on, "she might have seen a ghost. I heard those stairs weren't always servant stairs. Purists used them to go down into the lower levels and sacrifice seventhborns in a secret room. Maybe she saw the ghosts of dead seventhborns? Surely they can haunt us, with their link to death and all."

At this, Susan glared back at Sera.

Sera sighed, but she didn't have the energy to care about the girl today.

"You sure do hear a lot, Susan," Mary snipped, gaining the girl's attention once more. Susan stared at Mary, her mouth agape.

Sera grinned, her heart warm.

"She was probably tired," she added. "She works hard and barely rests, especially now with the Solstice Dance approaching. Nurse warned her about exhausting her reserves. I suppose it's finally caught up to her."

Susan tipped her chin and spun to her cauldron. "I still say she was drunk, and the dance better not be ruined because of her."

Mary sighed but didn't reply. *Just as well*, thought Sera. No one knew the truth of what was wrong with Mrs. Fairfax, not even her.

his name was noah

Later that day, Sera sat in her corner in the library contemplating things. Mrs. Fairfax could have been sleepwalking, but that still didn't explain the crying, the apologies, and why she was calling Sera's name. Sera sighed. Mary had asked to be excused to the infirmary to help Nurse; hopefully she learned something of Mrs. Fairfax's condition, anything to explain her strange behavior the previous night.

A peculiar heaviness settled on Sera, as though she were being watched. She glanced up from her book. Whittaker stared at her from across the room, his seedy eyes narrowed and lips pulled into a smile. A shadow swathed Sera and drew her attention. She spun to Susan Whittaker holding an impression, a smile similar to her brother's on her lips. "I believe this is yours."

Sera's stomach sank to her feet, and the floor seemed to spin and sway beneath her. The impression was of Sera's back, taken when she had been rescued by the Aetherium. Myriad scars marred her skin, some of the newer ones still inflamed.

Standing, she tore the image from Susan's hands. "Where did you get this?" she snarled, her magic flaring. She gripped the girl's arm and yanked her forward. "Where did you get this?"

"I found it," Susan replied, impervious to Sera's grip and blatant anger. "But it's only one of eleven impressions. I wonder where the others are?" She looked over Sera's shoulder.

Sera followed her stare to the students along the tables. They stared down at something—pages that they exchanged with one another.

No...

Sera shoved Susan aside. With each impression that was passed along, she cringed. It was as if they'd taken her body, cut it into pieces, and parceled it out, and now their merciless hands touched the deepest parts in her soul.

No, no, no.

Anger, humiliation, and sorrow battled to possess Sera, and her magic scattered under their fight. She growled and rushed to the tables, snatching away the impressions that had been distributed. "Give that to me!"

"Miss Dovetail!" The girls' matron, Mrs. James, rushed to Sera, gripped her shoulders, and yanked her around, quickly seizing the pages. "What is the meaning of this...?"

She glanced down at the impression, and her breath caught. Her brows gathered, and she looked at Sera, a mix of shock and anger, but for once, it wasn't directed at her. She whirled to the students surveying the various impressions, to the assistant matrons standing idly by. "Collect them, now!"

She swept to the nearest table and grasped the notes of Sera's file that had also been distributed.

Across the room, Timothy wrenched Whittaker's cloak and pulled him close. Whittaker shrugged and shook his head, clearly denying any involvement. But Sera knew this was done by his hand. Mary had warned her that he sought revenge, but while Sera had been ready in case he tried to hurt her physically, he'd instead come after her soul. Timothy shoved him aside and glanced at Sera, genuine pain in his eyes. *What can I do*, his stare screamed, *is there a way for me to fix this?*

Tears distorted him in her eyes, the answer a painful no. Nothing could make this better. She was broken, and now everyone knew. After being shattered so many times, she was unsure how she fit together, much less what anyone could do to help.

She focused on Whittaker, her body trembling. Each quiver spread heat through her body, crumbling her self-control. Reason begged her to think of her family and her position with Barrington. But lost to her memories and dissonant rage, she snatched out her wand. Magic, hot and cruel, waved up to her fingertips, ready for release. She would bind him, squeeze until he begged for mercy, but she would refuse him until his screams drowned out her own heartbeat in her ears.

Yet, digging her nails into her wand, Sera ground her teeth together and suppressed her sinister desires. Noah had taken her magic. She wouldn't allow Whittaker to take away her chance at finding her family.

Barrington rushed into the library, a shadow in all black. His wolf eyes fixed on Sera, then briefly lowered to her wand. Seeming to understand what she could have done but hadn't, he stalked to Whittaker. The boy's eyes widened, fear devouring his complexion. He held his hands at surrender, but Barrington fisted the boy's cloak and dragged him out of the library.

"Professor Barrington." Mrs. James rushed to him and

handed him the stolen impressions and notes she'd recovered. He took them from her blindly and shared quick words Sera couldn't hear. Glancing briefly over his shoulder at Sera, his jaw clenched, and then he stalked out of the library, Whittaker sniveling beside him.

Sera gripped the nearest chair. The ache of refusing her magic burned her insides, while the sudden change in events stole her breath.

"Come away, now," Mrs. James said, in an uncharacteristic soft tone, and with a gentleness unlike her, she touched Sera's elbow, guiding her out of the library and upstairs to the tower door. She pulled it open and nodded Sera inside.

Sera hesitated a moment. Mrs. James was going to let her go? Even though the events at the library weren't Sera's fault, she was certain she'd be blamed one way or another. A seventhborn was always at fault, even when they were innocent. Perhaps Mrs. James was the one unwell, taken by whatever plagued Mrs. Fairfax. But too tired to consider it further, Sera moved into the tower stairs and ascended.

"Miss Dovetail."

She stopped and turned. Of course Mrs. James wouldn't let her go so easily.

"Will you be all right?" She looked Sera in the eyes, shame and pity brimming in her stare.

Sera's heart twisted. No, she wouldn't ever be all right. Not until she found her family and her memories, until being a seventhborn didn't mean a life of persecution and torment.

"No, but I'll have to be," she replied. It's all she could do. Whatever the pain, she had to fight and survive.

Mrs. James pressed her lips together and nodded. "Indeed, and just so you know, Professor Barrington said a maid saw Mr. Whittaker in the records room last night, rummaging through files. She was afraid to say anything but came to her senses and reported it. Now, get some rest. I will have Miss Tenant bring up your supper and will speak to your teachers about your assignments for today."

She walked away. And though she didn't apologize for her previous behavior and prejudice, Sera appreciated her thoughtfulness, however briefly it might last. With her spirits as low as they were, a little kindness went a long way.

Once Mary had come and gone, Sera transferred to Barrington's home. Upon further reflection, she suspected the maid who'd exposed Whittaker's involvement hadn't come to her senses alone. Remembering Barrington's words and his knowledge about Sera's meetings with Mary and Timothy, she was sure he had his sources in the school. And if silence was a commodity, then information was, too. And however much it was worth, Barrington had paid it for her.

The scent of smoke and sulfur pushed the thought to the back of Sera's mind. Clapping a hand over her nose, she followed the offensive scent out into the hall, where she then trailed the white smoke billowing out from the workroom.

Barrington stood by the worktable, his sleeves rolled up to his elbows. He held his wand above a black dish resting on a spirit lamp in the center of the table. His magic was draped over the dish like a dome of blue mist. White smoke twisted up to the ceiling, joining the thick clouds already there and those escaping out the door or through the open windows in the back of the room.

Sera watched him move around the workroom, his stride confident and movements graceful as he observed his experiments and jotted down notes, unaware of her presence.

She started to enter, but trepidation rooted her to the floor.

No doubt he'd seen the impressions, and surely he'd already suspected something terrible had happened to her, though he'd never prodded in spite of her reactions. Yet, he always asked for permission before he touched her, and when she conceded, his hands were always gentle as if her acquiescence was a gift and he was grateful for her trust. But what would he think of her now that he knew what had been done to her, that the scar he'd seen on her arm was only one of many?

Sera's hands tightened, and she eased back. This was bad. She shouldn't care what he thought of her and whether she disgusted him or not. They had a working arrangement, and it didn't extend beyond that. But while she wished his imminent reaction didn't scare her, her thundering pulse beat with sharp spasms of truth. She didn't care about what the rest of the students thought of her; they meant nothing. But Barrington had somehow carved a place into her life with kindness, and as arrogant and boorish as he could be, his opinion mattered more than she ever would have thought. Beyond what she would have liked.

She sighed. *Heaven help me.*

Perhaps feeling the weight of her stare, he lifted his gaze and straightened sharply. "Miss Dovetail—"

Flames burst from the dish like a torch.

"Damn it!" Barrington tore a rag from the table and plucked up the plate now emitting plumes of black smoke. He rushed to the window and set it on the sill. He snapped the window shut, the smoke outside like storm clouds pressed against the glass.

He turned and raked a hand through his hair, and she sensed her apprehension was contagious. "Miss Dovetail, you startled me."

"Sorry." She entered the room, glad the smoke had dissipated, though the sulfuric scent lingered. "And sorry about your experiment."

He turned down the flame in the spirit lamp and dropped the rag on the table. "It probably wouldn't have worked anyway. I haven't decoded the entire spell but got impatient and thought to test out what I have so far."

Sera's brows rose. "You, impatient?"

A small grin tipped his lips. "Shocking, I know."

Silence stretched between them. Unsure whether he wanted to speak of what happened or not, Sera walked around the table crowded with retorts and crucibles, flasks and funnels, and preservation jars, half of which were empty. The others contained dead rodents, reptiles, and other specimens. She neared her face to the jar of a dead rat and wrinkled her nose. "What on earth are you doing?"

Barrington leaned back onto the edge of the side counter and sighed heavily. "Well, based on the ciphers you gathered from the impressions, I've been attempting to piece together the spell, to see what our necromancer attempted to do." He reached beside him and picked up his notebook. She moved to his side, and he started to explain. "Typically they're in a chain, each circular cipher containing different information. You see how the ciphers here are reversed? That indicates black magic. The hook here determines temperature, here signals time of day. In your spell books, the spells are already translated. But when we are investigating a case, we must decrypt them ourselves, and that"—he sighed weightily—"is where the work is. I must deconstruct these random snippets of spells until I find the correct combination."

He pointed at a peak in the circle. "This indicates the type of wand used, which can tell us what element the magician is inclined to. If there is no symbol here, then it was wandless, which makes things a bit trickier. This curve here measures intensity of magic, and the swirl here is length of time the spell was cast. And—"

He cut himself off and shook his head. "Forgive me, I'm sure the last you want after a day of lessons is another lecture."

"You are much more entertaining, believe me, unless you are about to tangent into a discourse on the persecutions."

He arched a brow. "I will spare us both the punishment."

She smiled and leaned in closer to study the ciphers, preferring his scent of sandalwood over that of sulfur lingering about them. "What have you discovered so far?"

Outlining a cipher with his finger, he said, "Here it says it rained the night this spell was used. Of course, we are in the middle of our wet season, and so I'm not sure whether rain is essential or was just coincidental. But since it is not raining now"—he motioned to the cylindrical canister over one of the spirit lamps—"I was attempting to recreate the atmospheric balance by other means. The rest of the ciphers deal with objectives."

He tapped a portion of the circle that looked like two loops with a line through them. "I see here they bound our victims with magic, which reinforces what Portia said about her touching the body."

"And she also had burn marks on her wrist, many tiny lines."

"In necromancy, you must bind yourself to the body you attempt to raise. But there are two ciphers that indicate binding, and they happen minutes away from each other. Why bind the victims once, then again?"

Sera considered the ciphers in question. "Maybe they broke through it, and so they were forced to bind her again?"

He smiled. "Good theory, except the cipher is not broken.

The spell — as seen by a complete circle — is still intact. Were the binds severed at any point, it would show."

Sera frowned. "I wish they would teach us this instead of Rhodonite potions."

"Soon enough. Ciphers take years to learn, but you've a brilliant professor to teach you."

Sera rolled her eyes. "So is this what we'll be working on today?"

"No, actually." He closed the notebook and set it down. "I didn't expect to see you today after what happened with the Whittakers and Mrs. Fairfax."

"What will happen to the Whittakers?"

"Well, after Mr. Whittaker blamed his sister for concocting the entire affair, he accused Mrs. Fairfax, said she was the one who let them into the records room."

Remembering the woman's odd behavior, Sera hugged herself. "Do you think he tells the truth?"

"Mr. Whittaker is a coward and an opportunist and would blame his own mother to save himself. But it was all Headmistress Reed needed to hear to practically exonerate the boy and his sister. She felt forbidding them from going to the Solstice Dance was punishment enough."

Sera shook her head, her cheeks growing hot. "Of course she would think it punishment enough, all they did was torment a seventhborn." She scoffed. "Prejudice has turned her blind."

Barrington hummed in agreement. "But worry not, I've spoken to Mr. Whittaker. They won't hurt you again," he said with a conviction that told Sera that although Headmistress Reed refused to punish the Whittakers, Barrington had delivered his own warnings. She stifled a smile, her heart warm. How she wished she could have seen the damn boy tremble as Barrington towered over him, issuing secret threats, all in her honor.

"As for Mrs. Fairfax, she claims to have no memory of how she got to your room. Nurse said she's suffering from exhaustion and was most likely sleepwalking. She's being kept under observation for a few days and hopefully, she will remember more soon. But just in case she harbors any ill motives or something else is afoot—whether of the magical variety or an undiagnosed mental condition—I've secured my own surveillance."

Thinking back on the woman's behavior the previous night, Sera shivered. Mrs. Fairfax had looked at her with a strange mix of sorrow and guilt, not malice. While Barrington was right to think Mrs. Fairfax's condition warranted some added concern, Sera did not find magic or prejudice to be the culprit, no. Mrs. Fairfax hadn't meant to hurt her, she realized now. Her incessant apologies and tears confirmed this. But what on earth had been wrong with her? Sera clasped her hands together, still feeling the woman's warm tears on her skin. Perhaps some illness had gone undiagnosed?

"In the meantime," he said, through her thoughts, "if you don't feel up to training…"

She arched a brow. "Give me some credit, Professor. I've encountered worse."

His frame tensing, he lowered his head. "Yes, of course. Forgive me for implying…"

"No, that isn't what I meant. I…my scars…the impressions you saw today—"

"I didn't look. I had my suspicions, but I never looked, and I never read that portion of your file." He met her gaze at this. "What happened to you is a private matter that I will hear only from you, should you ever desire to tell me."

Tears welled in her eyes, and she spun away from him, as if it were possible to put distance between him and her memories. Yet knowing he stood there behind her, silent and willing to listen or abandon the subject should she choose, she pressed a hand to her chest, her heart twisting. Every fiber in her wanted to tell him, wanted more than guarded conversations and apologies. Wanted no more walls built of nightmares and secrets.

"Miss Dovetail—"

"All I knew when I woke up alone in the cargo hold of a ship was my name, age, and that I was starving. Nothing existed before that moment, not even the knowledge of my tattoo."

She motioned to the dead rat within the preservation jar. "A rat darted past, and in my hunger, I reached for it. Next thing I knew, I had slaughtered it without ever touching it. I was so scared. Not only did I not know who I was, but *what* I was. And then he found me." She let out a shuddering breath and turned to him. "His name was Noah."

Barrington said nothing, his gaze firm and steady on hers.

"He said I was special, but that the world would try to hurt me. He told me about my tattoo and the way all seventhborns were treated, and he promised to protect me while teaching me to increase my powers. In spite of my state, he offered me his arm. I was young and stupid and scared, and with a simple gesture, he gained my trust.

"I shouldn't have trusted him so easily, but"—she shrugged, a sad smile on her lips—"he was beautiful and kind and brilliant, and in weeks, I'd learned so much, and my reserves grew. All I wanted was for him to be pleased with me, but then he changed."

Her smile fell. Hot pinpricks bloomed along her body, the memory of his savageness alive on her skin. She approached the impressions slowly, each step dragging her deeper into memory. "He began to drain my powers, claiming that my magic was a sin and what he did was to save my soul. I felt like death afterward, unable to eat or walk. Deep down I knew what he did wasn't right, and one day, in a moment of clarity, I refused…"

Her chin quivered, hot tears spilling from her eyes. "Whereas once his touch was gentle, it became vicious and cruel." She pointed to the impressions of the dead girls. "He turned *me* into nothing more than a body. It was then I realized he built me up for the sole purpose of later breaking me and draining me."

"A warlock," Barrington said.

She nodded. "He made himself out to be a pious saint, but he was evil incarnate, and my greatest mistake. So you see, I do not fear a touch because my virtue was stolen. I gave that to him freely." She swallowed, the sight of the impressions blurred behind her tears. "My magic and humanity, however…"

Fingertips brushed her arm. Gasping, Sera flinched back.

Barrington startled and retracted his hand. "That was careless. I'm sorry," he said with some difficulty, his hand taut on the handkerchief he had intended to offer her. "And for the things I've said in the past."

She shrugged, just barely, and gazed back to the impression. "You knew only what the Aetherium put in my file, but now you know the truth. Noah found me and drained me until I finally came to my senses, and in a manic flare of magic, I killed him and burned his house down around him. That's when the Aetherium took me in and shortly after brought me to the Academy." She motioned to the worktable. "But while he may be dead, I can't have what happened to me and these girls happen to another witch, seventhborn or not. That is why I don't mind your lectures on ciphers and summonings and anything else you want to talk about. I know I can be impatient at times, but it is only because I want to learn. I want you to teach me."

Barrington stared at her in silence, and Sera found it impossible to breathe as she waited for his reaction. Had she shared too much? Did he somehow think her used and tarnished? Still, she steeled her spine and stood there, firm, her heart both heavy with worry and light from secrets revealed. She would not fear Noah's ghost, should he come again. She would not be afraid of Barrington's rejection, should he issue it. With or without him, she would become an inspector and find her family. With or without him, she would protect seventhborns from monsters like Noah.

He nodded once, his jaw clenching and hands in taut fists. "Thank you, for trusting me."

He moved to the worktable and, picking up his wand, tapped the spirit lamp, and a flame *whooshed* to life. "We will begin with the basic construction of a cipher…"

For the next days, once her classroom studies were complete, she and Barrington studied symbols, compared impressions against the results of their experiments, ruled out possibilities of what "puppets" could mean, and shared the pleasures of simple conversation. Sera learned how mere lines on a cipher could change an entire spell and what different shapes upon a cipher meant. They spoke at length and experimented for longer, absorbed in magic and death to where nothing else existed…until days later Sera arrived to Barrington standing at his desk, her veiled hat in his hands.

She reached out and took the hat, her pulse quickened. "Are we to interrogate another witness?"

"Sadly there is no one left for us to interview this time." He stopped at the door, his frown deepened. "Two more bodies have been found."

15

absolutely and all at once

A gust of winter air wrapped the veil about Sera like invisible fingers meant to keep her from going. She embraced the cold and walked out of Barrington's home to where a black carriage waited. A brown-haired boy stood before it, not much older than she. He was tall and lanky, awkward like he didn't know what to do with his long limbs.

"Miss Dovetail, this is Lucas Davenport. Our coachman," Barrington said. "Don't let his age fool you. He will get us out of trouble, both of the magic and the non-magic sort."

The boy tipped his hat. "A pleasure, miss."

Sera paused. It was not his age that would have fooled her but rather his frame. Slip thin, he looked incapable of surviving a strong gust of wind. Inclining her head to say hello, she entered the carriage. She of all people knew not to judge one by appearance and circumstance. If Barrington trusted him, she would as well.

Barrington followed behind and sat opposite her.

"Why don't we transfer there?" she asked as he opened

the black curtains at either side of the carriage.

He tapped on the roof with his walking stick. The wheels groaned, and the carriage jerked into motion. "Large spells and use of magic leave remnants of power. We try our best not to leave any traces near crime scenes, nothing that can lead the Aetherium to us."

He crossed one leg over the other and settled in for the ride. Reaching into his coat breast pocket, he drew out the small notebook.

Sera bit the inside of her lip. Should she have brought something to write on?

He reached inside his pocket again and took out a writing instrument. She frowned. She hadn't brought anything to write with. What if she saw symbols? Worse, what if she didn't see anything at all? Perhaps the door that had unlocked in the binding chamber had since relocked itself and she lost the sight. Professor Barrington was risking his career because she had the sight once, and yet she hadn't seen anything else since then. She hadn't even felt what Timothy did when near the dungeons. She pressed fingers to her lips. This could turn out to be a disaster.

Barrington lifted his eyes and lowered his pencil. "You look rather ill, Miss Dovetail." He pressed his lips tight, a look of disgust washing over his features. "You're not going to be sick, are you? I'll admit, I've seen my share of gruesome things, but vomit is my undoing."

"I'm well, a bit worried is all, but nothing vomit inducing."

"Glad to hear it." He turned back to his notes and brushed a lock of his disheveled hair into place with his pencil. "A dead body is nothing to fear. You may see and hear spirits, but they can't harm you."

"I fear that I won't be able to see anything again." Her list of questions became a tidal wave that rushed to the forefront of her mind. "Has anyone ever lost the sight?"

He hummed in question while perusing his notes.

"The second sight. I stared at the picture for days, but nothing happened until I unlocked it somehow."

He arched a brow from over his book. "Unlocked?"

Sera nodded and divulged all that had happened that night, from the drain of magic, to the gates, to the burn mark that had since healed over. With each of her words, Barrington slowly lowered his book until it rested on his lap.

Moments after she had finished, he had yet to speak. The horse's hooves beat on the earth, and disturbed ravens squawked, but Barrington remained silent, his gaze fixed on her.

"I take it from your silence that this is also a mystery?"

"A seventhborn's second sight, like the ability to perform certain spells, manifests as your powers and reserves increase," he said finally. "I was certain you had reached the threshold. When I first asked you to look at the photos and you were unable to see anything, I thought it was your temper and impatience that blinded you, but now you tell me your powers were in fact *bound*." He tapped his chin in thought. "You mentioned there were many doors?"

"Gated doors, yes. Black ones. More doors than I have years."

His eyes narrowed. "Peculiar. Sadly, binding magic of that caliber is an ability beyond my expertise."

Sera sighed and molded back into the plush velvet seats, dejected. "Yet another mystery to add to my list."

"I said it was beyond my realm of knowledge, Miss Dovetail, but I'm a scholar. Quite a fantastic one at that. If there's something I don't know, it will not remain a mystery for long. Don't lose hope. We'll uncover what it all means."

The carriage stopped rocking. Barrington slipped the pencil and notebook into his inner pocket. "But, my little anomaly, it appears your mystery will have to wait, as we have arrived."

The scent of fish and cold met her nose, as did the sound of roaring oceans her ears. Lucas opened the door, and she lowered her veil. Murky puddles reflected the moon on the pier, the flags atop the ship sails waving like phantoms. It had been a long time since she'd been to a harbor. A shiver tore down her body, bringing with it very present memories and pain. She took hold of Barrington's offered hand and stepped out of the carriage.

A darker expression claimed his eyes, his look no longer that of a scholar but of a man alert and ready for danger. "Whatever you do, keep your veil down, your gloves on, and mind your magic. You must listen to what I say, and do only what I ask. There is no room for argument. Is that understood?"

She swallowed deeply. "Yes, Professor."

"Well, well, if it isn't the great Barrington," a deep voice spoke from behind.

A man leaned back against a waist-high stone wall, a ramp behind him leading down to the pier. Curls, blond and unruly, peeked from beneath his hat. He flashed a smile and walked over, his rakish, confident air preceding him.

Barrington met him halfway. "Rowe. Thank you for meeting us here."

"Whatever Gummy wants." He turned emerald-green eyes to Sera, and his smile widened. "Now, Barrington, you know better than to bring a lady to these affairs."

Barrington cleared his throat. "This is my assistant, Miss Dovetail."

"A pleasure, Miss Dovetail. Tell me, what on earth possessed you to work with Nik of all people?" Rowe leaned closer to Sera and said in a stage whisper, "I heard he can be quite moody."

Sera grinned, to which Barrington arched a brow. "I thought we were here to discuss something about a body. First time one has been found away from a cemetery. What made you think to contact me?"

"Yes, yes," Rowe said. "You shall see."

He led them down the damp stone ramp and onto the pier. Docked ships dipped in the water that sloshed against the port pillars. Briny breeze wheezed past, then thrust them into an echoing quiet, cut only by their respective footsteps.

"Any word from the Aetherium?" Barrington inquired.

"They're just as baffled as the last time we met and can't fathom why these witches are so adamant about raising these bodies when their results have been dismal."

"Then they've gathered nothing from the impressions? No identifying facts about a culprit, perhaps?"

Rowe shook his head, to which Barrington gazed down at Sera and nodded once, a small grin at his lips. Warmth bloomed in her cheeks, and she mirrored his smile. They were ahead of the Aetherium in their investigations, and it was all because of her summoning abilities.

"All they know is that the witches aren't alone, since the scenes are cleansed afterward," Rowe added.

Cleansed. Sera gulped. Only one beast was known to devour lingering magic. A Barghest. She knew about these hellhounds, demon dogs said to be tortured into submission by warlocks who used them for their own dark deeds. Rumor was magicians rarely lived after an encounter with them, and those who did were haunted by nightmares of them forever.

They rounded a corner to a gated tunnel. Two questionable characters stood beside the gate. The men were haggard, their beards wild and unkempt, and their coats, riddled with holes and muck, hung from their gaunt frames.

Rowe stopped a distance away and jutted his head

toward the men. "These are the two who discovered the bodies and reported it to Gummy."

Barrington handed him the small velvet bag to which Rowe tipped his hat. "One second." He walked to the men.

Sera eyed the men's dingy and wan appearance. It seemed unlike someone of Barrington's standing to associate with vagabonds. "How do you know these men?"

"The two there are employed by Gummy. Rowe was a friend when I was in the Academy. After some…incidents, he was the only one who remained true. Some years later, he encountered problems of his own and, well, it would be terribly wrong of me to leave him in distress, no?"

"Then he's this friend you have within the Aetherium, the one who secured you the impressions?"

"He's not a magician—well, not a magician anymore. Now he's a thief-taker and a drunk, amongst other things, but a damned good source. I wouldn't work with him otherwise."

She nodded, pity settling in her heart for Rowe who seemed to be a sibling of hers in ill fate. To have been born and raised in magic only to come of age and lose those powers was nearly as difficult as being a seventhborn.

She spoke no more of it and turned to where Rowe shared some words with the vagabonds. He handed them the bag. They pulled it open and surveyed the contents. Satisfied, they handed Rowe their lanterns and walked away.

Rowe waved them over. The gate screeched as he pushed it aside. He turned the knob at the base of the lantern, and shadows came alive along the stone walls. "Just through here."

Lantern raised before him, he ushered them into the tunnel cut by streams of light. In one of the patches of light, Sera noticed Barrington had, at some point, drawn his wand. She quickly drew hers as well and held it tight at her side. Her other gloved hand she pressed against her mouth. The stench of mold, urine, ash, and brine burned her nostrils and squeezed at her stomach. Not to mention these soft mounds and fetid puddles she was stepping in.

Several minutes later, Rowe held out his lantern, and Sera's hand dropped from her mouth. Whereas in the previous crimes, the burned victims lay beside the graves of the exhumed corpses, the scorched figure before her now rested beside another dead body in perfect state, that of a young woman with her throat severed. She lay slumped against a wall smeared with her blood, vacant eyes glazed over in death.

"I told my men to let me know if anyone came round asking about burning witches or necromancy like you instructed. They say this girl here, Isobel Weathers, went to the Aetherium, claiming she had information on the exhumed graves and dead witches but refused to speak to anyone but the chancellor. She visited offices in nearly every province, demanding the same. Most thought she was mad and turned her away, but she claimed her life was in danger."

Barrington gritted his teeth. "Damn it."

"Sorry, Nik. I tried to get to her as soon as I heard, but it was too late."

Barrington approached Rowe and the corpses, but Sera stared at the streaks of blood and the charred corpse, unable to will her body to move.

"So she was killed, and then our necromancer tried to raise her instantly," Barrington said.

"Not just killed." Rowe moved his lantern and shifted open the girl's cloak. "She was tortured as well."

Sera recoiled beneath her veil. Cuts split the girl's skin in various places, the other parts of her skin marked by bruises and burns. The scent was disturbing, but no more than the thought of the poor girl screaming as the criminal sliced her skin coupled with the seventhborn's cries as she burned to death.

Barrington illuminated his wand and surveyed the body. His scrutiny stilled over the signet of a dove on her cloak sleeve. His brow gathered. Straightening, he pulled out his notebook and flipped through the pages, examining each sheet with a finger. "Yes." Another sheet. "Yes, yes, of course. The files mentioned a bird on the headstones, another had a bird necklace, but it wasn't just a bird. It's a dove."

Rowe arched a brow. "And that matters because?"

"It's the signet of the Sisters of Mercy—a group of nuns devout to the seven guardians of magic. They helped shelter many seventhborns during the Persecutions. In short, they were sworn enemy to the Brotherhood, but they're an enigma. You do not find them unless they want to be found—or so it's claimed, as I doubt this Sister wanted to be found, much less killed. It seems all the bodies our necromancer has raised have been Sisters."

"Do you think it was a vendetta?" Rowe asked.

"No, this is more than a grudge. Torture and necromancy are both extreme ways of getting information by force, one while alive, the other while dead. Our victim here was tortured and killed, and then"—he pointed to the burned seventhborn—"our necromancer forced this seventhborn to raise her. Whatever the Sister refused to talk about in life, he forced it from her in death. Just as he's done with the other exhumed corpses. There is some valuable knowledge our necromancer seeks, and the Sisters of Mercy have it."

He looked at Sera, a small smile on his lips, but her mind could process only the girls.

Barrington straightened, awareness in his stare. "A minute, Rowe, if you please."

Rowe nodded and walked down the tunnel to an iron

ladder a distance away leading up to a manhole cover.

"I know, I know, I will see things that will shatter and break me," she said before he could speak, "but how are we supposed to control our emotions when someone felt it okay to do this?"

Barrington reached into his coat breast pocket and retrieved a vial of Rhodonite dust. "We remember that their pain is done, and our job is to find their killer. These victims have trusted you. I trust you." He met her eyes through her veil. "You can do this."

She nodded and took the vial. She could do it. She had to.

"What do I channel my magic on? Before, I used the impressions."

"It was more than the impressions, Miss Dovetail, but what was in them. Their pain, their blood, their deaths—that was your link to them then. That is your link to them now."

Sera uncorked the vial and sprinkled the crystals over the bodies. She slipped off her wand casing and handed it to Barrington. "I am here. I am your anchor," he said, folding his hand over her casing. "Focus and let them come."

She stooped beside the girls and held her wand between them. Her magic churned in her belly, but she hauled in a calming breath and forced her heartbeat to steady. She looked at Isobel. At the burned seventhborn. They were different, yet the same. Witches. Murdered.

Pain, blood, death…

She gazed down at the girl, at her vacant expression.

Pain, blood, death…

At the seventhborn contorted and charred.

Pain, blood, death…

She eased her grip on her magic. It pulsed out from her stomach, up to fill her chest and her limbs. She directed it down toward her wand, and her fingers burned. She hissed

at the magic gathering in her fingertips but swallowed down
her discomfort. The bodies before her had endured more
pain. The fibers of her wand ignited, every strand white and
filled with her magic. Smoke whirled out from the tip slowly.

Pain…

Her magic covered the bodies, and the Rhodonite crystals
illuminated, shading the tunnel in pink.

Blood…

The fog encircled and shielded the world around her.

Death…

Her own memories threatened to invade her mind, and
her pulse quickened. The crystals brightened, but she pushed
her memories aside. They had no place here. Neither did
Noah. The crystals dimmed to a steady, pink glow.

"Wonderful," Barrington whispered, but his voice
sounded far away, lost to the smoke that washed out the
world from around her.

Pain, blood, death…

Her body felt like it would dissolve around her, leaving
her but a soul in the sea of warm mist. Ciphers floated in
the fog, but unlike before, the ciphers were linked together
as they floated past. Sera trailed them, committing every
loop and line to memory.

A whisper breezed past. *Puppet, puppet, puppet.*

She spun and gasped. A shadowy figure lingered in the
shadows. Fear gripped her bones. It wasn't Noah, and if it
was, she would order him to leave.

Puppet, puppet, puppet…

"It's okay," she whispered. She would not force it. "Come
to me. I am listening."

The mist pulsed and billowed, revealing a young girl not
much older than Sera. She was lovely, with a heart-shaped
face and golden-brown skin. She wore a simple brown dress,

her hands clasped before her. A seventhborn tattoo marked her wrist.

Ophelia Crowe, she whispered, though her mouth didn't move. She lingered by the mist, as if afraid to step out.

Sera reached a hand to her. "Come, Ophelia Crowe, you can trust me. I'm listening."

Ophelia's eyes lifted, and she slid her hand into Sera's, cold and firm. *Show you...*

Cold washed through Sera's veins at once, and she sucked in a breath, feeling her soul pulled within Ophelia. She glanced down. She no longer wore her black dress and veil but Ophelia's brown dress and golden skin.

"What is this?" Sera stiffened and struggled to get out of the vision. The wall of fog encircling them trembled and pulsed, agitated like Sera's heartbeat. "What did you do?"

Show you, Ophelia spoke into Sera's thoughts. Though she could barely breathe through her panic, Sera nodded. She could do this. Barrington would bring her back if she fell too far into the vision. He was her anchor, and he asked for her trust. He wouldn't fail her.

Warm fingers wrapped around her wrist, a firm, savage hold. She gasped and looked down. The same hand from her previous summoning held her. She gazed up to a tall, cloaked figure wearing a plague mask. She struggled to pull her hand away, but black binds whipped around her wrist, tethering her to the necromancer. Nausea clenched her stomach, his magic worming into her consciousness. She felt him everywhere—in her soul, in her blood, in her thoughts. Her will to fight waned, and her magic grew cold and acrid—foreign. Not her magic anymore, but his.

No longer in control of her body, Sera reached to the other side of her and gripped something firm, warm, and slick. She turned her head, and a scream wedged in her throat. Isobel stood beside her. Streams of blood poured from her severed throat and melded with the blood seeping from her other wounds. Sera wished to release her, to no longer feel Isobel's open skin and blood beneath her fingers, but her intentions fell into a void.

Tell me the secret you keep, the hooded man whispered into Sera's mind, his voice ragged and raspy.

"Tell me the secret you keep," Sera echoed aloud, compelled to repeat it.

Isobel shook her head. Blood spewed out with each wrench of her neck.

Tell me your secret...

"Tell me your secret."

Isobel turned her face away, her mouth clamped shut. Sera winced, sharp pressure pushing down on her temples. She wished to release Isobel, but her body didn't understand the command, and if it did, it had no power to execute it.

The hooded man growled. *Your secret, now! I order you.*

"Your secret now, I order you!" Sera cried out, her pain that of a thousand knives being stabbed into her stomach.

I raised you, you cannot deny me. What is the secret you keep?

"I raised you," Sera struggled to say, her lungs collapsing within. She coughed out sprinkles of blood. "You cannot deny me. What is the secret you keep?"

Isobel clutched Sera's arm, her chin trembling. A tear spilled onto her cheeks, and in her stare was an apology, echoes of regret, and stark fear. "My broken oath, your broken life."

Tentacles of fire crawled from where Isobel held Sera. Whips of fire wound about her arm, dug into her pores, and wrapped around her bones. A scream grew in Sera's chest as the flames broke her bones and melted her joints. Fire, blue and white, engulfed her. Consumed, she screamed until empty of air and her throat raw.

Her guttural cry became the shrieks of many in her ears, a chorus of agony and laments. The mist shivered and rippled as the shadows writhed within it. Peaks formed in the fog as hundreds of dead spirits reached for her, and Sera knew deep within that they wanted her to understand their anguish. But she couldn't bear that much pain, or she would die, too.

"Release the spirit, Miss Dovetail," Barrington screamed from somewhere in the mist. But Sera couldn't see him—only the shadows and the licks of flames as her body burned. "You must order it to leave!"

Sera clenched her teeth, another feral scream gathered in her chest. *You...are...released!*

The flames vanished with a hiss, and the vision burst into wisps of smoke and fading cries. Air rushed into Sera's lungs, sharp and burning, and she rounded upward with a deep gasp.

Barrington wound an arm about her waist to keep her upright, and with his other hand he frantically lifted her veil. "You're safe. Listen to my voice, I am here, and you're safe."

She closed her eyes briefly, anchoring herself to him—to his strong hands holding her as her body shivered with the aftershocks of pain. To him towering above her, shielding her from terrors he'd never see and pain he didn't understand. To his soft tenor of voice as he whispered, "Feel me, Miss Dovetail. I am here."

He pressed a cool hand to her cheek. The trickles of his magic curled along her skin and bones and chased away the memory of them breaking and burning. Proprieties aside, she clawed her fingers into his arm and rested her head forward onto his chest as his magic reached her limbs that slowly gained feeling. His heart thundered beneath her ear, a welcome reprieve from her screams and those of the dead haunting her mind.

"I saw them," she said, her voice hoarse. She clutched his lapels, frustration and anger roiling in her belly. He didn't deny her and clasped his hand above hers, squeezing it gently. "I know why they showed me the hand."

She pulled away and glanced back at the bodies, hot tears in her eyes. "That bastard, he turns seventhborns into puppets. He not only lets their bodies burn, but he takes away their will."

She explained her vision quickly, and Barrington paled with each word. "That is why there are two binding ciphers in the spell. One is for when the necromancer grabs the seventhborn. The other is for when he forces the seventhborn to grip the Sister of Mercy. They form a chain, and using the seventhborn, the necromancer forces the Sister to break her oath."

"Not just an oath, but a blood oath," Barrington muttered. "If you break a blood oath, you forfeit your life. Usually an oath breaker bleeds to death, but seeing as the Sister was already dead, whoever forced her to break her oath suffers her penalty, which in this case was burning in the fires of the Underworld, I presume. That's why he uses these seventhborns—to form a bridge between himself and the bodies. And once he learns the Sister's secret, he leaves the seventhborn to suffer the consequences." He met Sera's eyes. "Tremendous work, Miss Dovetail."

She swallowed through a thickened throat. "Thank you, Professor. Would you like me to take note of the ciphers now that they're fresh in my mind?"

His brows gathered. "You've done enough. I don't want to push you."

She gave him a weary smile and held out a hand. She

would do anything to find this necromancer and make him pay. "I can manage."

"I know." He slid out his pen and notebook and handed them to her. She jotted down the chained ciphers.

Barrington leaned in close beside her. "The ciphers were linked and not scattered?"

Sera nodded, careful to depict them correctly with shaking hands. "Why does it matter?"

Barrington snatched the notebook from her hands and stuffed it in his pocket. "When a Barghest cleanses a scene, the symbols are disrupted."

He met her eyes at this, the answer glaring in the panic there.

Her stomach dropped to her feet. "It hasn't been cleansed."

"Precisely. We need to go—"

The sound of ice cracking silenced him.

They spun to the wall where frost vines spread out from a pinpoint. The ice fractured the damp stone as it traveled along the surface like a spider web. The hole at the center enlarged, and the pungent scent of rotten meat and sulfur engulfed them.

Sera stumbled back into a puddle, her fingers stiff on her wand. Barrington swept in front of her and held out his hand. Magic whirled from his palm and gathered before him. With each second, the magic spread and formed a translucent wall.

Rowe ran up alongside Sera. "Bloody hell," he muttered.

"Take her to Lucas," Barrington ordered, "and regardless of what you hear, neither of you is to turn back!"

"You mean to stay here?" Sera asked, her voice a frantic whisper.

"They will chase us and will not stop," Rowe said, already retreating. "Compared to the scraps left behind in these victims, our magic is a feast, even my measly bit."

"But—"

"I need to stay and reinforce the protection barrier," Barrington said. "We don't know how many of these beasts mean to come through, and this protection spell may not be enough to hold them."

Fear wrapped itself tight about her limbs, suffocating her veins. "What if it isn't and you're here?"

Barrington held her stare. "I can hold them back, but I can't fight them and protect you at the same time." A light sheen glistened at his forehead, the strain of controlling his magic wall already taking its toll. He drew the notebook from his inner pocket and pressed it into Sera's hands. Folding her fingers around it, he gave her hand a gentle squeeze, then released her. "You must go."

Sera heard him, but she couldn't look away from the red eyes that glowed in the growing hole.

A loud crack resonated. Black fog exploded outward from the pinpoint that was now a doorway. The smoke doubled and stretched until a shadowy figure materialized in its depths, a massive reptilian-like dog with a bear head. Black tar dripped from its fangs and sizzled when it met the earth. Sera gasped, but it was soundless, overpowered by the beast's growl.

"Miss Dovetail, we must go now!" Rowe touched her elbow. Torn from fear, Sera nodded frantically and trailed him down the long tunnel. Forgoing the route they used to get there, Rowe ran straight. "There is a manhole cover just down this way. You'll have to climb, but it'll leave us closer to Lucas."

A feral howl resounded. She glanced over her shoulder just as the hound lunged for Barrington. It crashed against an invisible barrier that glowed white when it slammed against it. The symbols of Barrington's protection spell glittered in the fog.

A rope of dread tangled down her spine, around her legs, and forced her to stop. Focused on the hound before him, Barrington was blinded to the wall that was turning to frost behind him.

"Miss Dovetail," Rowe hissed, "the professor ordered us to go!"

"We can't just leave him here!"

Another doorway exploded open in the wall. A beast lunged out, the frozen ground cracking beneath its feet. It crouched behind Barrington, oblivious of Sera and Rowe a distance behind it.

Barrington spun, his eyes wide. He lifted a hand, but the beast growled a warning, and Barrington stopped. Sera's heart pounded. There was no way he could create another barrier before the beast attacked. And use of his magic against this creature would weaken his hold on the other.

"We can still leave," Rowe whispered. "It hasn't sensed us yet."

The beast's spiked tail whipped the air around it as it hunched low, prepared to attack. Barrington swept his gaze beyond it and met Sera's eyes. Her hand flinched to her wand, but he shook his head no and mouthed for her to go.

She mirrored his gesture and drew her wand. A flare of white snapped from the tip. It slithered down the tunnel like a snake and exploded at the beast's feet.

The hound whipped around. A long split tongue glided from its mouth. It licked downward, frantic, and devoured the sparks of magic. From behind, Barrington instigated it, thrusting magic and insults at the beast, but the hound's red eyes narrowed, its gaze fixed on Sera.

What on earth was she to do now?

The hound lunged toward her. Sparks darted from its

claws that hit the stone with each step closer.

"Go, miss!" Rowe snatched the wand from her hand. "I will hold it back. Run to Lucas!"

Sera looked at the panic in Barrington's stare, at the beast slamming itself wildly against his magic, at the one that drew closer to her by the second, at the ladder some yards away.

Rowe aimed Sera's wand at the approaching hound. A small orb gathered at the tip of her wand, but fizzled with a *poof*. "Damn!"

The beast roared, lunged.

Sera shoved Rowe out of the way. With its speed, the hellhound tripped past them and tumbled down the tunnel, its momentum not allowing for a clean stop. It thrashed against the walls, splashed and splayed in murky water.

Forgoing the ladder, Sera darted into the tunnel to the left, Rowe quick on her heels. They rounded the bend that split the tunnel in two. Sera shoved Rowe to the right. "We have to split up. It can't follow us both." She knew who the beast would favor. She yanked her wand from Rowe, gave him a shove in the opposite direction, and rushed away before he realized this as well.

The howls echoed through the tunnels as the beast chased her left, right, right, left, until she was lost in the stone web. A low growl snuffed out her breath, a cold sweat dampened her shift. She stopped and speared a blast of magic down into the water, breadcrumbs for the villainous beast. As long as it chased her, Rowe was safe and Barrington able to focus his magic into defeating his own beast.

She turned her ear. Puddles splashed and the *tick-tick* of the beast's sharp nails on the stone answered, growing closer. She sent another flare of magic down the tunnel to the left, then dashed down the right one.

Her legs kept moving, running, carrying her away from the beast. She darted a glance over her shoulder. The orb of magic bounced and collided against the walls, the ceiling, giving off a faint light that haloed it in the darkness.

The beast dove into the intersection and caught Sera's eye in the distance. The orb sizzled, but before fading, the Barghest leaped toward it, snaked out its devil tongue, and slithered it up, taking the bait. It was too hungry not to.

She shot another bit of magic and turned. Gathering her skirts, she ran. There was no chance to look back. Not this time. Sweat beads rolled down her back, her breaths quick, harsh, raw.

She spun to the right and ran—

The light of her wand reflected against the sleek wall before her.

A dead end.

Sera turned, made to run in the opposite direction, but the Barghest pounced into the intersection and slammed down into the murky water. It growled, its sound bouncing off the walls. Sera set one foot behind her and then the other, until flush against the wall. Trapped. Caught.

The Barghest lowered onto its front paws, its hind end arched upward. Her heart pounded. There was no way out.

Sera aimed her wand.

The beast roared, then lunged.

She held up her free hand and shielded herself. Eyes shut tight and face averted, she braced for death.

A rush of heat seared her palms, as intense as the redness that shaded the darkness of her closed eyes.

Sera opened her eyes. Her breath cut short. Luminescent light, silver and white, sparked out from the tip of her wand like wings of frosted fire. It chased the darkness from the tunnel and illuminated the beast before her. Its wet pink nose was an inch away from her wand but, bound in white ropes of her magic, it could move no farther.

"Good God…" Rowe stumbled into the tunnel, eyes wide. He slipped off his hat and raked a hand through bushy curls. "How are you doing that?"

She didn't answer, her focus on the hound whose claws scraped the earth as it attempted to free itself. A growl rumbled in its chest, the desire to tear her apart palpable. Her anger flared, and she clenched her hand around the wand. No one would hurt her again.

Her magic responded to her rage. The beast's growls died to screeches, the binds of magic sizzling as they bored into its scaled skin. Its stare met hers. In its eyes was all the fear in the world. Fear of her, fear that she could break him if she wished.

"Miss Dovetail!" Barrington called from afar, his voice an echo in the tunnels.

She ignored him, lost in the potent sensation of magic that coursed through her veins uninhibited, unchecked, wild and free. It pricked at her skin, a paradox of pleasure and pain. It promised to consume her and possess her, to cleanse and avenge her, to drag her higher and higher until all else ceased to exist.

"Miss Dovetail!" Barrington said again, much closer this time. Sera refused to look away from the writhing hound. She'd controlled her magic when refusing to exact revenge on Whittaker, and in the end, Whittaker and his sister had walked free. But not this beast.

Winds tore through the tunnel and whipped wildly around her. Frozen on this thin line between madness and what was right, she closed her eyes a moment. Barrington spoke of control, but would it be such a bad thing if she just let go and embraced the intoxicating rush? She could make them *all* suffer, make them pay—every last one of them, from the Whittakers, to the necromancer, to every person who hurt a seventhborn.

Memories made every scar on her body pool in pain, and her hold tightened around the beast. It howled and screeched and toppled over.

"Seraphina!"

Hearing her name, her gaze flicked to Barrington. He stood a measure away, clothes in shreds, a gash over her brow, but still very much alive.

"You don't want to kill this hound," he said. "Control it. Banish it to the darkness it came from."

Tears salted her lips, yet she turned back to the beast and clenched her hand tighter around her wand.

"We do not kill when we can," Barrington said. "We kill when we must. This beast is at your mercy. Its fate is in your hands."

She lowered her eyes to the hound. All animosity was gone, but the pitiful excuse of a beast remained. It was an animal. However magical and hellish, it was nothing but an animal. Yet her hand shivered. How could he ask her to let it go when she hadn't ever felt this free, this *powerful*? When in this moment, no one could hurt her? When if she embraced it, no one could hurt her again?

He neared her, steps slow and steady. "Banish it."

A sob caged in her throat. She shook her head no.

Closing in beside her, he said into her ear, "Show it the mercy that's not shown to you. Banish it."

She heard him close, his words tugging at her conscience. If she killed this beast, she'd be just as bad as everyone who'd ever persecuted a seventhborn. Like her, the beast could not help what it was. She pressed her lips together, and with the need for abandon clawing at her insides, she conceded. "I don't know how."

Barrington came around her and framed her extended arm with his. "Repeat after me," he said, his breath a fog at her ear. "I banish the body. I banish the soul. I send thee to the darkness that is thine home."

"I banish the body," she whispered. The whips of magic she held around the beast vanished, and its body curled away as smoke until once again immaterial, a spirit in a black fog.

"I banish the soul."

Dimmed red eyes in the cloud met hers, and where the thirst for magic had been before, now there was gratitude.

"I send thee to the darkness that is thine home."

A red-rimmed hole appeared on the ground. The cloud of fog twisted into a funnel and seeped into the hole. Within moments, the beast was gone. The hole shrunk until only a smoky burn marked the ground. The faint peal of harbor bells resounded through the tunnels, but aside from that and the trickle of water on the walls, all else was quiet.

Fatigue rolled through her limbs in a violent wave, her reserves depleted. With the weight of magic gone, exhaustion buckled Sera's knees, and she collapsed against the wall. Strong arms came around her in an instant.

"Don't touch me." She tore herself away from Barrington's hold and pressed her hand against the wall to keep from falling.

"Your reserves—"

"I'm fine," she said, a blatant lie to anyone who wasn't blind. The tunnel spun around her, and the ground waved beneath her feet, though they were both still. "My reserves are fine."

Barrington stiffened, and his eyes steeled, but respecting her decision, he didn't help her, though on their walk back to the carriage, he didn't remain far from her side. His shadow melded with hers for the entire journey, of which Sera was both glad and ashamed.

Once inside the carriage, she snatched off the veil and hauled in a deep breath, unbearably hot. Her shift stuck to her skin, sweat the glue. The air was heavy like dirt packed tight around a coffin.

The door swung open. Barrington entered the carriage and sat nearest the door. He slipped off his hat, soundless. His hair was damp, matted to the sides of his face with sweat, his hands stained with mud. His trousers were torn and shoes indiscernible through the thick layer of muck. The drain of magic rendered his skin milky white. But he wasn't spent. His magic hummed in the air. Or perhaps it was anger?

Deflating with a sigh, he rested his head against the plush leather, his knuckles white and fingers tight around his walking stick. Decisions weighed heavy on his brow, and he stared at the darkness above as if the answer were hidden there.

"Damn it all." He pushed the door open and leaned out. "There's a change in plans, Lucas. To Rosetta's."

"Yes, sir," Lucas called down.

Barrington slammed the door shut and sat back once more. He pounded twice with his walking stick, and the carriage groaned to life.

Sera braced. There was no need for pretext. She knew what was to come, and the look of him told her he knew as well. Everyone schooled or employed by the Aetherium was required to provide a sample of magic for official records. No doubt once the bodies were discovered, the Aetherium would investigate and find her signature within the magic used in the tunnel. Worse, Barrington's. And even if they were found faultless of the crimes, there was still the question of her relationship with the Alchemy professor.

She lowered her eyes to her dress, leaded by whatever putrid substances layered the tunnels. And blood. A dead girl's blood. A dead girl she would never avenge because she couldn't control her emotions and her powers.

"I..." she started, but the words died to the stiff silence. What explanation could she possibly give? What apology could she utter that would make any of this better? He'd asked her to go, yet again she hadn't listened. Now not only was her place at the Academy at stake but also his career, and when the scandal of their involvement broke, so would his investigative work. His quest at clearing his family's name.

Pain gripped her, spreading through her veins with each breath. He hated her. No doubt he regretted hiring her and ever meeting her. And as much as those days meant to her, he would grow to despise their time spent together, those evenings practicing magic and the comfortable silences they shared. He would leave her life as quickly as he'd come, and she would no longer wake up happy, knowing that whatever hate and prejudice she encountered during the day, that night she would see him and be around him, learning and growing in magic while drawing smiles from him and giving them in return. No longer would she be a balm to his moodiness and sadness and he a comfort to her memories and the ill she thought of all men. No, their partnership was dead now, and there was nothing she could do about it...

...but perhaps she could do one more thing for him.

"I'll tell them that...that I ran away," she managed finally, her voice low yet somehow still too loud in the small space. "I'll say that you saw me and tried to keep me from boarding one of the ships..."

Barrington's jaw clenched. "I will fix it."

"...but when I saw you, I ran into the tunnels and hounds

were there, and we were forced to protect ourselves."

"I will fix it."

"But the Aetherium—"

"I said I will fix it!"

Sera recoiled and heat pricked her cheeks from within, his tone and anger unfamiliar.

His sigh washed out the echo of his previous outburst. "Miss Dovetail," he started, much softer, but moments later, he had yet to say another word. Forcing her face to the curtained window and away from him, Sera succumbed to the same contagious silence.

The carriage rolled to a stop. Lively music resounded somewhere nearby, broken by laughter and chatter. Barrington straightened and retrieved his hat.

The door opened to reveal Gummy leaning against the doorframe of an establishment whose doors read ROSETTA'S. Her dress was cut dangerously low, and she lifted a hand to her waist, unashamed. Another woman dressed in a similarly revealing manner entered the building, leading a gentleman by the hand.

Barrington descended and turned at the carriage door, his eyes downcast. "Lucas will see you to the house."

They were simple words, yet Sera's fingers tensed on the folds of black tulle. Ache became an invisible hand. Its fingers laced into the hollows between her ribs and squeezed. She pressed a hand to the seat, grinding her teeth together to master the pain and the urge to clutch his arm and drag him back. To talk things over. To find a way to fix things, together.

She let out a shuddering breath, and a warm tear spilled onto her cheek. It wouldn't make a difference. This was it. She had proved all the naysayers right. She was untrainable, erratic, and Barrington was done with her. Now he would enjoy one last tumble before the world crashed down around them, his dreams finished and hers as well.

He started to close the door, and Sera winced, the imminent goodbye a jagged knife fraying her soul. Worse was knowing this was their final farewell, and he didn't even look at her. No doubt he no longer saw her, just her violence and lack of control when she hurt the Barghest. But she was more than that, he had to know. She wasn't cruel or evil or unfeeling like Noah. Barrington couldn't think this of her.

Sera stared at his back, struggling to breathe past the painful knot jammed in her chest. *Look at me.*

He had to turn and lift those eyes to her one last time. Perhaps if he saw her tears, he would know of her remorse and the shattered condition of her heart. One last glance and he would see her as he once did—the girl whose trust he'd asked for and sought with kindness. He would know the fear in her soul—fear of losing her dream, her freedom... losing him. But of all, he'd remember that in spite of the marks Noah left upon her skin and of what she did to the Barghest, she was human. He had to know that.

"I'm not a monster," she said just above a whisper. Barrington paused, turned. "What I did... I'm not a monster."

"I never said you were," he said over his shoulder, his face shadowed by his top hat. "Good night, Miss Dovetail."

He walked to Gummy, who held the door open. Her eyes lit up, and she draped herself against him and ran a finger along his lapel. He murmured something, and she tilted her head inside. Catching sight of Sera in the carriage, Gummy pursed her lips and entered the brothel.

Barrington lingered at the door, and after a moment, he had yet to move. His fingers folded to tight fists, hesitation clear in his frame. Sera inched to the edge of her seat, her pulse quick. *Look at me.*

He started to turn, but shaking his head to himself, he followed Gummy into the brothel.

No...

Still, Sera watched the entryway, clinging to her veil like a lifeline. The door was still open, and with it, a chance that Barrington would turn back to her, that they could still fix this. This wasn't their end. It couldn't be.

A second lurched past.

The front door closed and proved Sera wrong.

A broken breath left her, and the curtain slipped from between her fingers.

Though her insides vibrated as though she were about to crumble, Sera clenched her jaw and brushed away her tears, seizing what anger she could muster. If he wanted to leave, fine. She didn't need him. She swallowed tightly. She didn't need anyone. Curling her fingers into a tight fist, she punched the carriage wall, prompting Lucas to drive them away.

"Goodbye, Professor."

The carriage lurched forward and reality descended swiftly. Their partnership was finished, and he'd never even looked at her.

A gale of pain consumed her then, absolutely and all at once. Pressing a hand to her stomach, she clamped her lips shut to smother the cry born in her chest and rising into her mouth for release. It was useless, and as the carriage rolled forward and drew her away from Barrington, Sera doubled over and cried tears of shattered dreams and a broken heart.

16

burn or flee

Morning dawned with glum, gray skies, much like the mood Sera had woken to. She lay deathly still, thoughts of the previous night playing above her like smoke. Isobel and Ophelia. The Barghest. Barrington.

She shut her eyes tight, willing the spell chamber to appear once more. She would pull, shake, claw at the gates — cry and beg them to release the memories they held hostage. Regardless of how the hot metal scalded her hands. Of how it branded her palms. With her memories, she would no longer need to be an inspector. She would not need him anymore, and maybe, just maybe, the hellish ache in her chest would leave her be.

But there was nothing to be seen save the black of her closed lids.

Sobs came hard and fast on the heels of her thoughts. She rolled to her side, curled into herself, the emptiness and disappointment more painful than she could bear. It was over and, although Barrington said he would fix the scene,

Sera knew there was no fixing them. No magic or pain or regret in the world could reverse the hands of time, could take her back to the tunnel and force her mind to overrule her heart and heed Barrington's orders to leave him.

Tears fragmented her room into a crackled image as a subsequent cry emptied her of air. It was too late to change anything now. She had lost her dream. She had lost him. Gone were their evenings of practice and magic, of pleasant conversation where for hours she belonged, valued and unafraid. Gone was the man who'd gifted her those mere moments of beautiful normalcy in the midst of torture, murder, and death. Who had somehow integrated himself into her every day, burrowed beneath the walls she'd erected in her heart, built of the pain Noah left in his wake. Who'd swept into her life like a breeze but whose departure left her as the shattered ruins of a hurricane.

Strands of hair clung to her tear-dampened face. She brushed them away and, desperate, pressed her cold hands down on her face, her arms, her shoulders, if only to feel a touch of the safety and warmth she felt in Barrington's company and arms. If only to dispel a bit of the terrible, hollowing solitude.

Feeling nothing but cold skin, she let her hands slip away. What was the point? She had ruined things with Barrington. Once their magic was discovered at the scene, they would be blamed for the murders and be imprisoned, and she would never see him again.

She swallowed tightly and watched the embers die in the fireplace. There was no need to relight the firebox. Not even the fires of hell could warm the stark chill that covered her bones and stabbed at her heart.

Later that day, the sky was still a dismal painting, dark gray clouds on a light gray backdrop. The wind shifted, and with it, the temperatures plunged. Sera sat on a stone bench in the courtyard, curled into her cloak. Her body begged her to go inside, and she was ready to do so, but she gazed at her friend sketching out the details of her Wishing Tree and didn't dare. All that had kept Mary from tears over her mother's latest letter had been the tree she was to decorate for the Solstice Dance, and the wishes that were to be hitched upon it. Though she didn't have the energy to play the docile helper, there was no way she could have turned Mary down when she asked Sera to pretend to assist her in sorting out fabrics and materials, so she wouldn't be so alone in her heartache.

Pity dampened Sera's heart. If there was one woe that always seemed to rival her own, it was Mary's once a letter arrived from her mother. After this latest epistle of how Mary was a disappointment to the family, Sera wondered if the letter was not some sort of spell, for how else could Mrs. Tenant succeed so well at demolishing a person's entire spirit with the use of simple words?

"Maybe the headmistress will take notice and Mama will hear of my work." Mary thrust down a slip of lace that she considered for the base of the tree. "Heaven knows nothing else I do seems to please her."

"I'm sure she will. Mrs. Southerly wouldn't have assigned this project to you if she didn't think you were more capable than the rest." Sera slid from her stone bench and knelt beside her friend, pretending to sort through strips of lace. "Don't pay mind to your mother. She forgets what it is like to be our age."

Mary scoffed. "No, no. That's the problem. She remembers perfectly. You've seen her. They say beauty lessens with age, so can you imagine what she was like in her youth. All grace and beauty with suitors to spare. Not to mention I also have my sister's legacy to contend with. Here I am choosing lace for my tree when my sister, at this age, was choosing lace for her veil." She rolled watery eyes and rubbed away her tears before they fell. "I will be a spinster, Sera. Maybe it wouldn't be so depressing if I simply accepted it."

Sera gave her a small smile. "Then, as always, we'll stay together and be a pair. We will be *two* spinsters. We'll have a nice little cottage—"

Mary sniffled. "And lots of cats."

Sera wrinkled her nose. "I was hoping perhaps a bird, or a puppy. You know I'm not too fond of cats."

Mary deflated, her skin mottled. "Of course you're not. See, we're already having marital disagreements and we're not yet married—or unmarried, or whatever it is we'll be."

In spite of the solemnness between them, the girls laughed freely for a few moments. The mirth died, and Mary pressed a gloved hand to Sera's face. Sera startled, and she flicked her gaze all around, but thankfully they were alone and shielded by hedges.

"Promise me you'll become an inspector," Mary said, her voice jagged. She lowered her hand and her eyes. "Nothing will make my heart happier than to see an Invocation ring on your finger, for you to become a real witch."

Mary lifted reddened eyes, and Sera's brow knitted at the look there, one she couldn't quite decipher. Was it worry? Fear? Regret?

"Regardless of what happens," she said, "say you'll become an inspector for the both of us."

It was now Sera's eyes that watered as she clasped her friend's hand tighter. Oh, her sweet, sweet Mary. If she only knew how the previous night she had dashed all her chances at a referral and perhaps even at freedom.

Still, she sucked in a breath and nodded. "I'll do it. For us."

Mary smiled, and her eyes shone again with their old gleam. She patted Sera's hand. "Good. Now, enough of my woes. If there's something I shall do right, it's this blasted tree. I was thinking of having a small barrel full of leaf cutouts on which everyone can write their wishes and then bind them to the tree. What do you think?"

"I think it will look marvelous," Timothy said, coming from around the hedge. "It's a very clever idea, Miss Tenant. You should be proud. It'll make a beautiful addition to our dance." He stopped and tipped his hat to Mary and then Sera. Upon meeting Sera's eyes, he paused, an eternal second that wound about her stomach.

He turned to the tree and surveyed the strips of fabric Mary had pinned onto the trunk during her contemplations. "A fitting addition considering it's our last year here. Many of us have unfulfilled wishes that, if possible, we would trade many other wishes to attain."

The sensation of him watching her in his peripheral vision pressed on Sera's skin and set her cheeks aflame. She cleared her throat and turned her eyes down to the grass as Mary stepped forward.

"Y-yes, well, that was m-my intention," Mary said, smoothing down her dress. "We all hold secret wishes in our hearts. Now anyone who yearns for anything can set their wish upon a paper leaf and bind it to the tree with their magic. Hopefully they will find some freedom at not keeping this secret stifled inside."

"A grand idea." He stared at the skeletal branches as if he could already see the Wishing Tree in all its glory. "I'll be the first to set my wish upon it, then."

"Oh surely you mustn't," Mary said with a shy giggle.

"And why not?" Timothy turned his attentions to her, his eyes hard and frame bristled with offense.

Mary startled and paled. "Oh, well, a-a man such as yourself...I..." Cheeks red, she lowered her eyes.

"What Mary means," Sera said against her best plan to remain out of the conversation and his attention, "is that this tree is for those of us unable to voice our feelings out of propriety or fear. This tree will hold wishes for those of us who are bound by status or gender or fate of birthright. For those of us unable to speak what's in our hearts, who are not brave and courageous. People unlike you."

He was quiet a moment, his gaze softened, and when he spoke next, his voice was much softer, too. "But you're wrong, Miss Dovetail. Painfully so. Some of us have been brave and courageous, and yet we've failed. We're still burdened by our dreams, waiting for just one glance, or one word that will give us our second chance, and in turn, our heart's desires."

The passion of his words hung heavy around them and obscured Mary, the trees, the school, the world. All that remained were Timothy's eyes taking in every ounce of hers, searching for this one look, for his second chance.

In this quiet, Mary blinked, equal parts wonder and pain in her eyes. If she had any doubt his affections belonged to another before, Sera feared she knew it now, and her own heart ached. How could she have thought to hurt her friend by considering Timothy, even if it was out of necessity or mere curiosity?

She steeled her spine. "I think you should be first to pin your wish on the tree and, afterward, move on."

Timothy blinked, and Sera's heart stuttered at the look there. The same pain as that in Mary's gaze.

"Very well," he said, his voice a low whisper.

"Delacort." Whittaker came up and slapped him on the chest with a folded newspaper. "I've been looking everywhere for you."

Timothy snatched the paper from his hands. "What do you want?" he asked, clearly perturbed.

Whittaker answered, but Sera heard none of it, her eyes caught on the newspaper. Under the headline *Torture: Ghastly Murder* was an impression of a corpse—Isobel Weathers.

"Mr. Delacort," Sera called after him as he walked away. Timothy turned back, a bright gleam of hope in his eyes.

She cleared her throat. "I wanted to know if you were done with the newspaper. I'd like to read it if you're going to throw it away."

Disappointment washed over his features. He sighed and held out the newspaper for her taking. The paper gone from his hands, he walked away without another word.

"Did you know someone killed a witch, Dovetail?" Whittaker said, grinning. "They tortured her and then dumped her in an alley behind some brothel. A pity if that were to happen to you, wouldn't it?" His smug smile widened.

She stepped closer. "Is that a threat?" Sera looked over his shoulder. "I'm sure Professor Barrington might not appreciate that."

At the mention of Barrington's name, Whittaker's smile withered, and he shifted back, surveying the field. "It was a joke, Dovetail. You can take a joke, can't you?" He chuckled nervously and hurried after Timothy.

Sera shook her head. The boy was a fool. She lowered to the ground and unfolded the paper.

Mary sat down beside her and hefted a sigh. "It was true, then. Another did break his heart."

"What?" Sera asked absently, her heart in her ears as she read.

The body of Miss Isobel Weathers was discovered about 4:00 a.m. on Margot Street, in the back alley of Rosetta's…

Cold rushed down her spine. *Found behind Rosetta's?*

"Remember what Susan said, that he was interested in someone, but she turned him down?" Mary said.

Sera nodded.

A customer who wishes to remain unnamed made the discovery while exiting the establishment. No evidence was found on the scene.

She cupped her mouth. He had done it. Boorish and cold as he was, Barrington had fixed it. He had moved the body and covered up her blunder. A broken laugh escaped her.

"I know. It's unbelievable someone would break his heart," Mary said erroneously and leaned in to her. "Oh, Sera, why in the world are you reading about murder?"

"I'm not," she lied. Her eyes instantly caught on the photo next to the article, one of Aetherium Chancellor York and his wife at the doorway to an orphanage. Mrs. York wore a royal-blue dress that complemented her brown skin, standing regal beside the chancellor. "I was admiring the chancellor and his wife. It's good to see he's doing better enough to walk. Last I read, he was close to death, and his healers could do nothing about it."

"Yes, I heard." Mary inched closer to read the article. "But the chancellor's illness aside, can you imagine what it's like to be Mrs. York? This"—she plucked at the picture—"is

what waits for the girl Timothy chooses. This is what I want."
She scoffed. "Who would be so foolish to turn down Timothy
Delacort?"

Sera glanced back to Isobel Weathers's picture and
smiled, wishing she could say, "The same girl foolish enough
to doubt her professor."

That night, Sera marveled she had made it to Professor
Barrington's home and not an alley somewhere, given
how quickly she had written out the transfer spell from
memory. No doubt the writing was perhaps as bad as
Barrington's. But she rushed forward, not caring one bit.
She was here and, staring up at the painting of the twin boys,
she smiled. Grim as Barrington was, she could've hugged
him! Not that she would, no, but she could.

Newspaper in hand, she spun in place and relished how
wrong she had been the last time she'd stood there. Her smile
widened. Her previous visit wasn't to be the last time she
was in Barrington's home. And if he didn't dismiss her, she
would be sure to not risk it again. She would apologize and
thank him, and after, she would mind her powers, listen to
direction, and not test fate again.

Long minutes passed. Unable to wait for him any longer,
she strode to the door and yanked it open. She marched past
his empty workroom but paused at seeing Rosie sorting
through a crate of vials.

"Good evening, Rosie," Sera said.

Rosie lifted her head, and her lips spread in a smile.
"Miss Dovetail! It's always such a delight to see you."

"You as well. Is the professor in?"

"Yes, but he's downstairs with Mr. Rowe at the moment. I will tell him you're here—"

"No, no. I can wait." She moved closer to the table. The crate was filled with vials of various herbs and crystals. "May I help you with anything?"

Rosie sighed and picked up a handful of vials. "Just sorting these into the pantry. The order *finally* came in. You two have been going through supplies so quickly, but I'm glad of it. It means you're learning, and now with the pantry replenished, you can resume your lessons."

Sera reached for the vials. "Do you mind if I put them away, to better familiarize myself with the rest of the supplies?"

Rosie agreed and, emptying the crate, she set the rest of the materials on the table and left to discard it. Sera put down the newspaper and sorted out the vials, then began putting them away in the pantry. Once inside the storeroom, she closed the door slightly, to reach the rack of obsidian vials on the counter behind it, when—

"It will take me some time to produce that amount, but they'll have the delivery in a matter of weeks," Barrington was saying.

"As long as you keep up your end of the bargain, Rosetta's is at your disposal," Rowe replied, "though you'll have to be careful being seen there from now on. You know, with your history and all…"

Sera hissed a curse. Couldn't they have gone into his office? She grabbed the knob to open the door and walk out, but Barrington walked to the black door, while Rowe sat at the worktable and crossed his feet on the surface, a drink in hand. Curiosity piqued, Sera inched back into the dark pantry and prayed Rosie didn't return soon.

"It's a good thing Rosetta's is my least favorite of their

establishments," Barrington said. He pressed the tip of his wand to the handle and various *clicks* resounded, more than Sera could count. He walked inside, and she struggled to see into the dark room from her hiding spot. In the light filtering in, she noted another worktable in the middle, upon which were a mess of glass funnels, beakers, and retorts. If the numerous spells she had seen written all over the beams of his house weren't strange enough, now there was an abundance of locks and secret experiments.

Before she could see or think any more, he walked out of the room and closed the door. He set a black Gladstone bag on the table before Rowe. A quiet tinkling of glass upon glass resounded from inside. "This should do for a month. By then, the next batch will be ready, and we'll go back to our normal order. Once every two months, as is our agreement."

"Perfect." Rowe downed his drink and stood. Barrington shuffled papers aside, searching for something. "I'm sure you've dismissed Miss Dovetail after all this trouble?"

Sera bristled. Barrington froze over his papers. "Miss Dovetail remains employed by me should she still want the position."

Rowe's brows lifted. "You're serious?"

Finding the sheet he sought, Barrington straightened. "Why wouldn't I be?"

"She saved our lives, yes, but she nearly ruined you, Nik." Rowe grabbed the pen the professor handed him. "If the Aetherium ever found out you were in that tunnel…"

Barrington lowered the sheet and slid it across the table slowly. "They won't."

"Of course not, but she's a liability. I trust your judgment, but I must confess her appearance was rather surprising. You're always alone, have been for years. Suddenly there's an assistant — a *she*. How much do you know about her, about her abilities?" He signed the form before him in two quick strokes. "You wouldn't be the first man to be fooled by a pretty face."

"I'm wise in the company I keep," Barrington said, each word mounted with offense. "And her beauty is of little importance."

A flush of warmth crept into Sera's cheeks. Barrington thought her beautiful? She stared at the man through the small part in the seam. His light eyes were always steeled and sad. Lips bowed to a permanent frown, and his brow low. It seemed he lost the ability to sense beauty in the world and in any person long ago.

"She's a talented witch," he went on, "powerful and exceedingly necessary. I'll work with her to control her powers. But that's the least of our problems." He slid the Gladstone bag across the table and held out a hand. "You have something for me?"

Rowe reached into his pocket and drew out a sheet of paper. "With all that happened, I forgot to give it to you at the scene." He handed Barrington a folded page. "From Miss Portia Rees. She said she tried her best to draw the warlock who drained her."

The corners of Barrington's mouth bowed as he turned in place and unfolded the letter. He raked a hand through his hair and squeezed at the nape. "Damn it all."

"What is it, Nik? You know the bastard?"

Barrington gritted his teeth, glaring again at the picture in his hand. "Unfortunately, I do. His name is Noah Sinclair."

Sera's eyes widened, Barrington's words like claws digging into her soul. *Noah…Sinclair?*

She pressed a hand to the wall, her knees suddenly weak beneath her. Noah couldn't be alive. It couldn't be *her* Noah.

"He was rumored dead," Barrington went on, as though

hearing her doubts, "but there have been sightings of him over the past months. I had hoped they'd been mistaken, but apparently he is alive and well and, to make matters worse, in tandem with the Brotherhood."

Her legs gave way, and Sera silently crumpled to the floor. Noah was alive, and Barrington *knew*?

"Nasty business," Rowe muttered. "What did he do, or given your reaction, what *didn't* he do?"

Barrington sighed. "Murder, black magic, kidnapping, torture—he's done it all. What he *didn't* do was kill Miss Dovetail. Only two witches have ever survived him."

No, no, no. Sera cupped her mouth to stifle the scream building and spreading through her chest and into her throat. She rocked back and forth, memories devouring her magic to where she couldn't get a hold on it. It was scattered everywhere. Like her soul. Like her heart.

Rowe *whooshed* out a breath. "Damn, does she know?"

"Of course she doesn't know, and you're not to share this with anyone."

"Mum's the word. But are you sure you want to keep doing this, Nik? If the Aetherium knew that all the charred corpses were seventhborns and that he's involved, they might—"

"Might what? Protect a seventhborn?" Barrington chuckled bitterly. "Don't be ridiculous. They already think it's a cult committing the necromancy. I tell them this, and they will think it to be a cult of seventhborns. This will be the fire needed by every opponent of the seventhborn program. They hear of this, and they will shut down the program, after which they will demand all seventhborns be either killed or banished. We don't need another round of persecutions. We'll lose our only chance at luring these monsters in and finding out what they're after."

Luring these monsters in…

Sera pressed a hand against her mouth. Her fingers trembled against her lips. A mix of fury and hurt stabbed her within. Had he meant to use her? To lure in the necromancer? To lure in Noah?

Cold, she hugged herself, the earthy scent of herbs now set to suffocate her.

"You should at least tell Miss Dovetail. She deserves to know. After last night, I daresay she'd destroy him once and for all. Her power is…extraordinary."

"It is, but sadly she is all raw power and little control. Unless she can focus that magic, she will not survive him. She escaped him the first time due to a flare of power, but should she meet him again… No. We will find him and destroy him for what he did to her…to all the witches he's killed." He set down the paper. "I think we're done here. I'll see you out."

Rowe took the bag and, with a resigned sigh, followed Barrington from the room. Their footsteps and words soon faded, but Sera cared for none of it. She'd heard enough. She stumbled out of the closet, her joints numb. There was no doubt now, no mystery as to why he had chosen her. He had planned to use her.

Picking up the newspaper in shaky hands, she admitted it was worse than that. He had lied. And perhaps it wouldn't have hurt so much if he hadn't seen the scars, hadn't pretended to care when she told him of Noah's savagery.

She stifled a gag, the truth rolling through her in bitter waves.

If he hadn't asked to be her anchor.

No, no, no…

If he hadn't asked for her trust.

Feeling outside of her body, she struggled toward the

worktable. The page lay facedown on the open case file, the impressions of dead witches spread out beneath it. She neared her fingers to the sheet and hesitated, her body trembling as she beheld the proof of her folly. The evidence of his betrayal. It didn't matter whether she flipped it over or not, the truth beat loud in her ears and burned in her veins. He had used her in spite of this trust he'd asked of her. In spite of having told her she was safe.

She turned over the page.

A vast, broken breath left her lips.

Noah's face stared back at her, and she dropped the paper onto the table. The upward angle to his eyes, his strong jaw and fine features. An angel facade wrapped around the heart of a beast. A beast she thought was rotting in hell, and yet he lived—and Barrington knew.

She weaved her hands in her hair, dug her nails into her scalp. *He knew!*

The sight of Noah blurred and crackled in her eyes. It shouldn't have made a difference. Barrington had admitted to his betrayal in so many words to Rowe, but to see it with her own eyes…

Her breaths came in quick spurts, the room shrinking around her. She spun away from the horrid picture. Questions chased one another in her mind, trailed by deafening accusations. Where was Noah now? Was he coming for her? How long did she have till he arrived? Why hadn't Barrington told her? Why had she been so stupid as to believe he was different from all the others who saw seventhborns as something to be used, as something less than human? Why had she trusted him with the truth of her scars? Worse, with her dreams? Sound muted in her ears until all she could hear was the muffled thrash of her heart. The *whoosh* of her breaths. The voice of her conscience echoing *fool, fool, fool.*

Currents of fury-laced magic waved to her fingertips as she beheld the workroom. Heat flushed down her body, the prickling of magic seeking release. She could burn it. She could set it all aflame and burn it to hell. Reason warned her that Barrington had protection spells all over. Not to mention, it was undoubtedly Rosie who would have to clean up the mess after all was said and done. But she couldn't let him…let him hurt her and not hurt him in return. *Burn or flee?* she wondered.

She shook her head. In spite of Barrington, Rosie and Lucas had shown her nothing but kindness. Would she leave them without a home? Would she endanger their lives?

Burn or flee?

Footsteps neared and stopped at the door. While she may have wished it to be Rosie, the height and air of the person told her this wasn't so. Neither did the preceding sigh and scent of musk and sandalwood.

"I wondered when you would see the newspaper," Barrington spoke from behind her.

Her hand tightened on the paper. She sensed him enter the room, his steps measured. A moment passed. She had yet to turn, to speak, to decide what to do with the horrid ache.

Burn or flee?

"Miss Dovetail?"

"Send me back," she said before another thought.

He stopped behind her. "Pardon me?"

"I want to leave." She shut her eyes and braced her spine, her control and voice weak. "Only you or Rosie can allow for it, so send me back."

He sighed weightily and moved away. Sera imagined him leaning against the table as he so frequently did, considering her.

"Aren't there things we should discuss first?" he asked, at ease. "Namely, how you nearly cost us both our careers and our freedom?"

Her breaths grew tighter.

"What you did was noble but incredibly foolish. I've been through and have handled far worse than a Barghest. While I appreciate your effort, your powers are for the most part untrained, and I need to know that from this day forward, you will listen to instruction. I trust this will not happen again…" There was a long pause before he continued. "Is there a problem, Miss Dovetail? The newspaper in your hand tells me you've seen I kept my word."

She opened her eyes and spun. Barrington sat on the table, just as she'd expected. Dressed in all black, he was a vision of elegance and grace. Yet, beholding him, Sera thought of the devil—cold and manipulative. Selfish with eyes the color of the sky, fit to lure one to think they could fly, only so he could delight in watching them fall.

He lowered those eyes to the newspaper, whose edges curled in flames and floated down as ash beside her. "You're angry," he noted with some surprise. Black lashes lifted, and his gaze narrowed. "Do you think me wrong for moving the body? Think it unfair to the poor girl? I did what I thought was best."

"Best, of course," she returned. "It's always been about what you thought was best for *you*, regardless of anyone else." She looked at the picture beside him. "Most certainly not me."

His brow dipped slightly. He trailed her gaze. "Miss Dovetail—"

"I was in the pantry," she confessed before he spoke again. Before he lied again. "I was helping Rosie. I heard everything."

He made to speak, but she raised a hand. "Don't say a word. Everything you say is a lie."

Barrington's jaw pulsed, but he said nothing.

Sera shook her head, a bitter laugh in her throat. "Tell me, should I be more disgusted in you or in myself? After all that's happened to me—to my people at the hands of Purists—I should've known better than to fall for your trap. You're just like them." She pointed at Noah's picture. "Just like *him*."

At this he looked at her squarely. "I'm nothing like that monster."

"You're right," she seethed through gritted teeth. "You're worse, and don't you dare say you're not."

Light eyes hardened, a mix of gray, anger, and offense. If looks burned, Sera knew she'd burst to a cloud of ash, settling beside that of the newspaper. Still, she went on.

"He fooled me with promises of magic, and you...you tricked me with my dreams of becoming an inspector and finding my family. At least for the monster he was, he was brave enough to stab me while I faced him. But you're too much of a coward. You ask for my trust and then stab me in the back. You promised to help me become an inspector only because it was not a promise you would have had to keep. I would be dead before ever seeing it come to pass."

His shoulders lowered with a slow, measured sigh. "Not that it matters what I say, but know that I don't waste my time on failed experiments. If I didn't think you capable—if I didn't think *myself* capable of protecting you—I never would have chosen you as my assistant."

"Oh, that's grand! *Assistant?* You could have chosen any seventhborn to be your assistant, but you chose me because you knew he'd come after me. I'm not your assistant, Professor. I'm your bait."

"You have no idea what you're saying, and I won't do this with you right now."

He walked out of the room, finished. Snatching up Noah's picture and case file, she followed him to his office. "No, of course not. You don't spend time on failed experiments, do you, Professor?"

He shook his head, sat down at his desk, and moved a stack of folders before him. "It means I can't talk to you when you're like this." Calm, he opened a file and resumed his work.

"When I'm like what? Offended? Betrayed? Hurt?" Each word churned the anger in her belly. "Oh yes, you expect me to feel nothing at all because those feelings are reserved for humans, not monsters like me."

Barrington's hand tightened on his pen, but jotting down notes on the file, he remained quiet.

Sera pulled out an impression from within the file and threw it at him. "Was she a monster?"

She thrust another at him. "What about her?"

Another. "And her? Was she human?"

The impressions floated around him, but he didn't say a word, a portrait of sophistication and poise.

Sera stormed to his desk. Hot tears in her eyes, she cleared the surface in one swipe and slammed the case file down before him. "You will look at me!" Flames flared with a roar and engulfed the curtains. "You owe me that much. Look me in the eyes and tell me my life means something to you. That I wasn't bait."

He gazed at the scattered impressions. Settling back, his eyes remained on the photographs before him and never lifted to hers or the flames that shaded them in amber. He rubbed at his lips, the debate to speak heavy on his brow. Ultimately, he looked to Filip's portrait behind her, then met her stare and kept silent.

A dizzying coolness rushed down her body and numbed all in its path—her mind, her heart, her lungs, her knees. The flames around them died with a hiss, leaving Barrington and Sera to ashes, smoke, and shadows.

"That's it, then," she said, though unsure whether she'd made a sound. She nodded and straightened, anger no longer an emotion. There was nothing, just scattered dreams of a referral she would never get and a family she would never find.

One moment she was before his desk, the next she stood at the center of the room as smoke filled the space between them.

Barrington rose, and where he was supposed to have told her that her life meant something, he aimed his wand at her feet.

She fell into darkness.

wishing tree

Frozen rain tapped against the window, and though wrapped in her wool blanket, Sera shivered as if standing in the midst of the icy raindrops. For days nothing had warmed her. There was no relief from the heartache and disappointment, a vicious venom that mapped her veins.

She gazed through the icy webs fracturing the surface of her window, to the line of trees shielded by a thick fog, and shook her head. She'd been afraid of the second sight for fear Noah would find her in the afterlife, to torture her in death as he'd done in life. But now he was out there, somewhere beyond the mist, a predator lying in wait.

Barrington had known, and he hadn't told her.

A broken breath left her, forming a cloud of smoke before her mouth. Surely he had his reasons for keeping it a secret, but why bother asking for her trust?

Be a little mad and trust me, Miss Dovetail.

She shut her eyes tightly to suppress the tears threatening to fall as his low voice echoed in her thoughts and stirred her soul. But she wouldn't cry for him. He didn't deserve her tears.

One tear broke through anyway and spilled onto her cheek. She sniffled and brushed it away.

"Oh, damn you, Barrington. You should have told me," she whispered, more tears falling now. "And I should have known…"

Recalling the impressions and Isobel's body, she shivered. The savageness spoke of Noah, of his little regard for human life. But she had seen him burn. How could he be living?

She rubbed cold fingers along her temples, recalling that fateful day. It had been ages since she'd allowed herself to go there, to that place in her mind, but Sera closed her eyes and remembered.

He'd taken his time with her that morning, drinking of her magic until shadowy pinwheels flashed before her eyes, a shifting constellation of black stars in the ceiling over his bed. Lounging back, he held her as he often did, curled up at his side as he trailed a finger along the drops of blood streaming from the cuts he'd inflicted on her skin. But she felt no pain here, in the hazy in-between of consciousness and darkness where her body ceased to exist.

The bedroom door had slammed open then, and someone whisked to the bedside. Sera attempted to grasp their appearance, but it smeared into the darkness fringing her vision. She was tired, so very tired.

Voices echoed then, harsh and agitated and far away. Noah shifted her aside and rushed to his feet, whirling his black cloak on in one stroke. *What's happening?* Sera mused, but the thoughts were frail, and she couldn't reach them. She closed her eyes and followed them into blackness.

Sometime later, she opened her eyes to a strange warmth churning in her belly. *Magic*, she realized. She'd almost forgotten what it felt like; for some weeks now, Noah forbade she use it. People like her couldn't use magic; it was a sin, he'd said. He warned her to tell him when she felt it brimming and sloshing within her, so that he could take it away, could help ease the burden of her evil. So that he could cleanse her. But now her magic simmered and pricked under her skin, and for the first time in weeks, she wasn't so cold anymore.

Gripping the black iron bedpost, she pressed her feet to the floor. Her legs were weak, and bones snapped and crackled, but holding onto the nightstand, she stood. Aided by the walls, she clambered to the window. With each second, magic spread within her, flickers of warmth and energy that sparked her limbs to life and flooded her mind with sensation—the grittiness of the black damask wallpaper beneath her fingertips, the cold wooden floors underfoot. The scent of brine and sulfur wafting in from outside, trailed by shrieks and vicious cries.

A fierce voice in her head—her voice, and not Noah's invading her mind—screamed for her to go. Panic burst through her; she could not stay here. There was more beyond this room and bed and Noah. Though she didn't know what, the sensation of…of…life and reason spurred her to act. There was more, and she would find it.

She stumbled to his wardrobe and pulled it open, grabbing a robe from within. She thrust it over her shoulders and paused, caught by her reflection in the wardrobe mirror. Pale and gaunt, she hobbled toward the glass. Dark circles cradled her eyes, her cheeks sunken, her lips dry, cracked, blue. Trails of dried blood blotched her skin like spilled ink. He'd done this to her, all in the name of piety. If her magic was so evil, why did he take it? Why did it make her weaker and him stronger?

A furious conviction fanned the fire within her. Whoever she was in the past, this girl staring back at her was not it. Pressure and heat gathered in her hands. She closed her fingers into tight fists, and the mirror snapped and splintered. The stress and heat in her hands eased but mounted again, aching for freedom.

She clutched her hands tighter, and something within her roared, unrestricted. Waves of heat flowed out of her. Wild winds whipped around the room—curtains billowed in the breeze and doors rattled on the hinges. This was her magic, and if she'd managed to claim this small amount, maybe she could find the missing pieces of her past and claim her life back as well.

The door crashed open. Noah rushed inside and toured his murderous stare along the windswept room. His lips curled to a snarl.

"After all I've done for you, you defile yourself by using magic?" Confident, he raised a hand to her, the wild winds blowing his brown locks over his face. "Come, and ask for forgiveness."

Sera considered his hand and the things it was capable of. Her magic pulsed, and the windows behind him exploded. Noah flinched and ducked at the shards of glass raining around them.

He growled and straightened, drawing his wand on Sera. "Come here, now!"

Every cut, tear, and scream whirled in her mind, a hurricane of pain and death. A hurricane of him.

The fibers of his wand illuminated red. "I will not tell you again."

He wouldn't. Magic roiled within her, an uncontrollable force that clawed at her bones for release. It felt endless, infinite, and she didn't see life beyond it. Still, she lifted a hand. There was no life with him, either.

Her magic swelled and rolled up her body in a searing wave. A cloud of fire exploded out from her with a monstrous roar. Gusts of fire fanned outward and blanketed every surface in flames. Vicious fatigue swooped down on her, and she collapsed, falling into darkness surrounded by fire and Noah's screams.

Sera sighed at the memory. The Aetherium officers told her he was dead, that there had been no way he'd survived the fire or the building's collapse after they'd rescued Sera. But that had been a lie, and she'd been a fool to believe it. Of course Noah survived. He was a demon, born in the fires of the Underworld. And now she was left to suffer him alone, without her dream of a referral to bolster her. No, her dream was dead.

Sera glanced at the dark woods, and thoughts of other unfulfilled desires brushed through her mind.

Perhaps we could not be so alone...together.

A plan quickly formed in her mind. Though she could not salvage what was left of her dream, she could save what was left of Mary's. She glanced at the clock. Almost midnight. If she hurried, she would make it on time.

Sera padded across the room and dressed quickly. Gathering her cloak, she snuck out of the room. With a prayer on her lips, she made it to the library undetected. She pushed open the bookcase. The night was frigid. Barren trees *clacked* under a gust that disturbed the branches and rattled the windows. A half-moon offered little light, but she didn't need to read anything tonight. Books would not solve her problem. In Mary's words, only a Delacort would do.

She blew out a frosted breath, thrust her hood over her head, and dashed inside. Ducked low, she pressed close to the nearest shelf and inched forward, hoping the patrol schedule hadn't changed. She reached the end of the row and, for the first time in days, she smiled. Timothy leaned back against a shelf, an illuminated wand held over the open book in his hand.

Finally, a stroke of luck. She peered around the shelf, then rushed past the long tables and across the library. She reached the row where Timothy was and frowned. He was gone.

She huffed a sigh. "Wonderful."

A silver hue shone behind her. "Who goes there?"

Sera lowered her hood and spun toward him.

He stiffened, and his wand dimmed, the shadows around them encroaching. "What are you doing here, Miss Dovetail? You're lucky it was me; you could have gotten caught."

"I know, but I came to see you."

He raked a hand through his mess of black curls. "I thought we had nothing to speak about. You're happy alone, and if memory serves me right, there's no hope and I should move on." He shrugged. "What's left to discuss?"

His tone was cold and unfamiliar, but she couldn't blame him. "Look, Timothy... I know you're hurt, but there is no way we could ever go to the dance together, even if I wanted to. Mary has feelings for you, and she is my friend. I couldn't do that to her."

He looked out to the library and shook his head. "A part of me wishes you had come to tell me you didn't care for my company because you didn't like me, or thought me hideous or arrogant—annoying even—yet you choose friendship over me." His icy look was replaced by a small smile, one more of pain than joy. "Your nobility makes it hurt even more."

Her heart fluttered, but remembering Barrington and all that had happened, her shoulders lowered. If she couldn't be happy, she would find happiness in the joys of another. "Then I hope you'll find some comfort in my words, as I think there's a solution that may not change much, but at least we could all find a bit of happiness, if just for one night."

His brow lowered in question.

"I said I couldn't *go* to the dance with you," she clarified. "I didn't say I couldn't *dance* with you."

Timothy blinked. Her words seemed to register slowly in his mind, and then his brows rose. "Then you'll go to the dance?"

"Yes, I will—alone. You will escort Mary. Once there, we can share one dance. Under the guise of your father being chair of the seventhborn program, you dancing with me won't be all too shocking."

"I don't care what they think."

"I do. I must. So is it a deal, you will accompany Mary in exchange for one dance?"

"Two."

She pursed her lips.

"Please. Perhaps one for my pain and another as an early Christmas gift?" He smiled, and this time the old gleam found his eyes once more, the sadness that had plagued him for weeks dispelled.

Sera sighed. "Fine. Two dances, then. But no more."

His smile widened. "Perfect. I intend to use every ounce of my charm to show you that I deserve one more."

"Then we're in agreement?"

"You have my word."

She nodded once. "And you have mine. Ask her today so she has time to write her mama, and no one is to know of our arrangement." She unsheathed her wand.

His blue eyes narrowed. "An oath? You have my word, Miss Dovetail. Trust me, I won't tell."

The word hurt like a dagger to her heart, and she winced. "I trust no one, Mr. Delacort."

"You trust Mary enough to be here, to enter into an oath with me."

Sera held out her wand. "She has proven herself a true friend and has no reason to bring me harm."

"Neither do I," he said, "and I hope that during the course of the dance I'll be able to prove that to you." He neared and touched the tip of his wand to hers.

Their oath made, Sera cleared her throat and walked away quickly, praying and wondering whether she had done the right thing. Yet she glanced back at Timothy, and a smile touched her lips. If not happy for her own situation, at least she would be for her dearest friend.

The next night, after Mary snuck in to share the good news and ramble on about gowns and hairstyles, dancing with Timothy, and finally appeasing her mama, Sera listened absently, her mind lost to thoughts of oaths made, trust broken, and promises of dancing.

Snow blanketed the grounds. The lands around the school resembled more a puffed cloud than a forest. Sera trailed a finger along the fogged glass, as though to follow the snowflakes in their journey across the estate, the same way her tears had trailed down her cheeks for the past week. Mary's dream come true was supposed to have been a balm to her own hurt, but it hadn't worked. She swallowed around the knot in her throat, her loneliness magnified.

She glanced at her clock. There was no time for tears, not that she had any left. She slid on her gloves and hefted a sigh. *Heaven help me survive this night.* Men were capable of cruel things. She would remember this, and no dance or admiration on earth would sway her.

She paced to her bed where the yellow gown Mary secured for her was spread. Sera glanced in the mirror and smoothed down the black gown she decided to wear instead, one of Mary's hand-me-downs.

Mary would be upset, surely. "Black is Death," she had said. Sera sighed. Indeed, and ever since her fight with Barrington, she felt more like it.

She'd hated him the first night, viciously so. The second night, however, once her anger had waned, she'd thought more reasonably. Not only had she not let him explain, but he was a professor, and clearly by the spells he used to defeat his own hellhound, he was powerful. If at least for the time they had worked together, she'd been safe. And if she was to be an inspector, was the job itself not the furthest thing from safe? Whatever the risk, she would do what was necessary to find her family.

Which reminded her: Barrington's reasons were the same as well. These thoughts plagued her on the third night, when she paced in aimless circles, thinking that he should have told her. His keeping it from her did not excuse him in any way…but he would go to the ends of the earth to avenge his father and brother. Would she not do the same?

The fourth night, anger found her once more. He had betrayed her trust. How could they mend things—that is, if they could ever be mended—if they didn't have trust? And if they could fix things, did he realize just how much he was asking of her? He said he would protect her, but in turn, was he not asking her to entrust him with her life? Could she give him this? Was this not the ultimate trust?

Thoughts of this haunted her the next few nights and

into the present moment where she bit her lip, still trying to make sense of things, a feat made worse since she had yet to see him. Was he remorseful? Was he ashamed? Did he simply not care?

She thought she'd gathered her answer that morning when she returned to her room after lessons to find a delivery waiting outside her door, a small box with a yellow rose within. Her heart had quickened and pulse raced, thinking it to be from Barrington. A note, however, revealed it was from Timothy requesting she wear it to the dance that night.

Sera sighed, and plucking up the rose from her dresser, she adjusted it into her hair. No, Barrington was probably angry with her for setting his home on fire and had most likely replaced her already.

The bells tolled the hour, and she shook her head. She would have time to think of it later. Powdering her nose one last time, she adjusted her gloves and made her way downstairs to the grand staircase. Mary arrived a moment later. They shared a furtive smile; they'd agreed to show up late so they would find each other at the end of the line, a mere coincidence to everyone but them.

Any doubt she may have had over her deal with Timothy vanished the moment she looked at Mary. In a powder-blue dress with an open square neckline and V-shaped bodice, large bell skirt with ruffled lace trims, she was striking.

Sera lined up behind her; only two girls remained ahead of them. "You look beautiful," she whispered. "I'm sure Timothy will think so as well."

The first girl descended, her maroon dress dragging behind her as she vanished around the bend.

Mary reached back and squeezed Sera's hands. "Thank you, dearest."

The next girl rounded the corner.

Mary stopped shy of the last turn and sucked in a deep breath, her fan rapping at her side. "I changed my mind. You go first. I've never been so nervous in my life."

"You'll be fine. Hold on to the rail, and for all that is sacred and holy, please don't fall." Sera rounded the corner into the grand stairs and wished someone would have spoken these words to her. Timothy waited beside the stairs, a white rose in his hands.

And looming over the line of waiting boys was Professor Barrington.

Dressed in black, he towered over them like a shadow. But not even the shadows could hide the look of surprise when his eyes fell upon her. She regarded him, too, and all else ceased to exist. She'd called him the devil, but she conceded she'd been wrong. Standing there, he was more of an angel, fallen and hurting and so devastatingly beautiful. Even at a distance, the comfort of his presence swayed her, made her want to hit him and shake him and hold him all at once. And, damn it all, as angry and hurt as she'd felt and as cold and wrong as he'd been, she missed their work together and conversations — his infuriating cockiness and moments of tenderness. She missed him.

Sera gripped the banister tighter at the realization, her heart losing its rhythm. Reason told her perhaps she gazed at him for longer than was proper, but his shock quickly gave way to something else, and Sera couldn't look away. Had she not seen the expression before, she never would have noticed it, but she had — the same mix of shame and sorrow as when he looked at Filip's portrait. The expression tightened her belly, but she willed her eyes away, clutched hard at the banister, and descended. She moved from the staircase and rounded the corner to the planetarium that had been transformed to a glorious vision of a snowy palace, but stopped and peeked around the bend to watch Mary descend.

In a fitting black frock coat, Timothy met her at the foot of the stairs, dark curls raked away from his face. His cravat was sky blue like Mary's dress, and equally accentuated his eyes. A swell of joy warmed Sera's heart for her friend. Timothy was immensely attractive, and Mary would relish his company the entire night.

He handed Mary the white rose and kissed her gloved hand. "Miss Tenant, I daresay I'll be the envy of every man this evening."

Mary fanned herself, a blush bright in her cheeks.

"Shall we?" Timothy asked, offering Mary his arm. He turned them away and led her down the long corridor toward the planetarium. Sera pretended to adjust her gloves as they passed her and stopped at the threshold, admiring the grand display of magic. The theme of wishes was spread around them, beautiful orbs of light floating above, dashing along the ceiling like shooting stars in the night sky. Tables outlined the room, and couples danced in the middle as if on a cloud, a cool mist swathing the floor.

"I think I hear a waltz starting," Timothy noted. "Miss Tenant, will you do me the honor?"

Mary blushed and nodded.

Sera watched them walk away. The smile on her lips quickly withered as she glanced about the room. Groups of students sat at tables, laughing and enjoying life as they should, yet she could not bring herself to walk another step into the hall. This was not her life, and turning, she walked out, opting for the shadows in the gardens.

The gardens were desolate. A light misty rain kept everyone inside, and Sera would have had it no other way. She hugged herself against the cold that nipped at her skin and walked down the cobbled path to the tunneled archways of thick vines that led toward the Wishing Tree. Small orbs of light glowed like heartbeats, as if fireflies were trapped within the vines. The night air was frigid, but she drew in a breath, needing it to freeze the strange tightness in her stomach.

If her impending dance with Timothy hadn't been enough to make this night frustratingly nerve racking, now there was Professor Barrington. If only he'd looked angry or indifferent. She could deal with those. But no, there had been more in those eyes.

She groaned. It was impossible. Witches were losing their lives, Barrington had lost his family, and she had lost what was perhaps her only chance at a referral for the assessment. She gazed up at Mary's Wishing Tree.

"I doubt even you could fix this mess," she muttered. And even if the tree could somehow mend her and Barrington's fractured relationship, she wondered whether she would want it to. Could she ever bring herself to trust him wholly with her life? He needed her, and she needed him. She tapped her chin. Perhaps she could make demands of her own—demand there be no secrets between them. Maybe then she could grant him this trust he'd asked of her.

After her outburst, it was probably too late. She had called him a monster, a liar, a Purist, and worse than Noah. What if, in her anger, she had burned down his beloved portrait? The way he'd stared at it that night, his sadness thinly veiled…

"It's rather cold to be out here without a coat."

She bristled and turned slowly to Professor Barrington standing under the last archway. He was like one with the night, just as cold and dark, mysterious and elegant. Her mouth wavered between a hello and a thin line of uncertainty.

He entered the space enclosed by waist-high hedges. Hands at his back, he stood a distance away, which she knew was for propriety's sake. "I didn't expect to see you here," he said first.

She forced her eyes back to the tree. "I had no intention of coming, but Mary was nervous, and so I conceded. I'm sure after all that's happened, I can survive the night."

Silence.

"You look lovely," he said and cleared his throat. "And the flower in your hair."

Sera touched the rose. "Oh, yes, thank you. It was a gift from Mr. Delacort," she said, regretting it instantly but unable to tame the nerves that made her ramble.

"Hmm. Mr. Delacort has an interesting choice in color. Yellow stands for hope. What has he to hope for?" He focused back on the tree. "I would imagine his father able to purchase him any whim."

"He hopes for what we all hope for. That which not even money can buy."

He arched a brow. "I never thought you a romantic."

"It's not love I speak of, but dreams." She shrugged. "We all chase after something, and it's normally that which we can't have. Mr. Delacort is no different."

He looked to her but said nothing.

The silence deepened, a deafening, glaring thing between them. Sera bit her inner lip. Was he thinking of apologizing? A cold sweat pricked at the back of her neck. If he apologized, what would she say? Goodness, what would he? Was he even going to apologize, or sever their agreement once and for all?

Finally, he cleared his throat. "Miss Dovetail, I admit I'm not the best at this sort of thing…"

"Speaking of romantics," she cut above him, "my friend Mary was in charge of making this tree. Along the trunk are quotes of love and hope, very much like my dear Mary." She walked around the large tree, hoping he didn't continue down his road of speech. Not until she knew what to say, what to do. "And we're able to write our wishes onto those leaves there, then bind them to the tree."

"Yes, I saw it earlier. But, as I was saying—"

"Very creative, don't you think?" She leaned in to the paper bark. *Damn it.* She had to decide. Should she—*could* she trust him with her life? Her lips bowed, and she shifted back, uncertain.

He sighed. "Creative, indeed," he said, seeming to accept that she would not speak of it at the moment. He held out a blank paper leaf to her. "Would you care to try?"

She met him by the table at the base of the tree, thanked him for the paper leaf, and picked up a pencil. He did the same, and they each wrote their wishes. A light breeze soughed past as if to snatch away their secret desires, and they each respectively held down their slivers of paper. She stole a glance at his leaf and noticed that he, too, wrote something that started with the letter *F.* His fingers covered the rest, though she had no doubt he wrote *Filip*.

Her heart dulled. Did he wish to have his dear brother back even if for a day? Perhaps have the chance to tell him goodbye one last time? She lowered her eyes to her own word, *Family*, and sighed. They were more alike than she cared to admit, and his pain affected her more than she wished it did.

Barrington folded his leaf in half. "There. Makes it look more like a real leaf."

She smiled. "Now we're to send them up and bind them to the branch with our magic." Sera unsheathed her wand. Barrington did the same. They tapped the edges of their wishes, and the leaves floated upward as though time were being turned back. She was glad laziness made levitation one of her most frequently used spells, and she no longer had to speak the spell, merely think it, as the silence in that moment was magical. She sealed her leaf at the base of the third branch while Barrington clasped his beside a dark acorn that was flattened on one side.

They lowered their wands and stood in silence.

"Miss Dovetail…"

"There you are!" The sound of footsteps approached from behind, and they turned to Mary walking down the path. "Oh, good evening, Professor," she said, her face still flushed from the dance.

He inclined his head. "Miss Tenant, if you will excuse me." He turned and bowed to Sera. "Thank you for explaining the purpose of the tree, Miss Dovetail. I agree. You did a marvelous job, Miss Tenant."

Mary clapped her hands, delighted. "Thank you, Professor," she said, but he had already turned and stalked down the path toward the ballroom, his black robe billowing behind him.

"So severe a man," Mary whispered. "A pity, as he really is quite handsome." She waved a hand airily. "You must come inside! Timothy and I think you should dance at least once. Though to make me smile even wider, he said he would dance with you as many times as was proper. I said twice was fine, and I would smile brighter than the sun. Any more and people might talk." She tugged at Sera's arm. "Come, before the next dance!"

She allowed Mary to pull her away, though could not help but look to the folded leaf beside the flattened acorn one last time.

Timothy waited beside their table. He rubbed his fingers at his sides, looking utterly perfect. His hair was perfect, his attire was perfect. The way he stared and smiled as though taken by the sight of her was…perfect. And yet, Sera thanked the heavens the room was dim so he could not see the way she was more ready to flee than to dance. She was doing this for Mary, but would it backfire? Would Mary see the way he looked at her, his eyes full of devotion? Would she finally realize that the mystery girl of Timothy's desire was Sera all along?

They stopped before him, and he bowed. "Miss Dovetail, may I have this dance?"

Forcing a smile, Sera curtsied and slipped her hand into his. Butterflies tangled in her stomach, though much more over never having danced in front of so many people before—not in her limited memories, anyway. The sea of dancers parted, and eyes followed as Timothy brought them to the floor. Many scoffed and moved off the dance floor, gathering in groups and whispering to one another.

A waltz ensued. As strings were plucked and the violins whined, Sera let Timothy guide her, grateful all she had to do was follow, as she no longer heard the song or the words he spoke. There were only memories of the garden, of decisions to be made—no, a decision she *had* made, to let fear no longer guide her. She would hear out Barrington and then demand an oath of complete honesty between them. She would help him with his case, he would help her find her family, and they would then go their separate ways. She would mend what had been broken. There was no other way.

As they spun, the lights became spider threads of light, and Sera scanned the fringes of the room and found Professor Barrington in the shadows. A smile touched her lips. Where else? It was where she would be, too. They made a final turn, and as the music died, she curtsied and lifted her lashes, but frowned. The shadows remained, but Barrington was gone.

"Are you all right?" Timothy asked, straightening from his bow.

"Perfect. Absolutely perfect." She rose from her curtsy and slipped her hand from his. "Thank you for the dance, Mr. Delacort. I am…I need…I…" Her words unsaid, she shifted back and squeezed through the crowd as the next dance commenced. She could wait until tomorrow to speak to Barrington, but why wait when everything could be resolved tonight?

Mary called from behind her, but other dancers whisked past between them, and she could not follow as Sera dashed out of the ballroom. She whirled in a quick circle. Where was he? He couldn't be far. He'd only just left. She surveyed the gardens and scrutinized the shadows. He wasn't there. She spun back inside and walked across the first level, through the rectory, and into the greenhouse.

Barrington was nowhere to be found.

She turned to leave and startled. "Timothy!"

"Forgive me. I saw you run away and worried I'd done something wrong."

She pressed a hand to her forehead. "No, no. I needed air, but it was too cold outside and…a headache—I have a headache, and the music was too loud so I came to look for feverfew to perhaps make a tea." She spun to the plants and tugged off two leaves from the nearest one as he eased beside her.

He reached for one of the leaves she had just plucked and chuckled. "Obviously you haven't been paying much attention in Botany, have you? This is neem, used for rashes and other skin conditions. Not for headaches very much."

Of course it was. She hefted a sigh and let the other leaf

float down before her.

"I know it's confusing," Timothy said, taking her hand in his, "and the last thing you want is to hurt Mary, but I saw you smile when we danced. And I may not be the best empath, but I can feel strong emotions, and I felt you. You were happy. I feel the same, and I don't want to fight it anymore. Especially not after tonight."

"Timothy..." she started, but he stole the word away with a kiss.

A gasp resounded with the sprinkle of glass. They shifted away from each other and saw Mary at the greenhouse door.

"I...I thought to bring you some water, in case you felt sick..." Eyes glossy with tears, she spun and ran away into the dark forest.

"Mary, wait!" Sera made to run after her, but Timothy took hold of her hand.

"I'll find her. It's dark, and you shouldn't be out there alone—"

"You've done enough." She snatched her hand away. "She's my friend, and I will find her." Running outside, Sera drew her wand and held it above her. White fire sparked at the tip, flares of magic dancing like torch flames. In the halo of its silver light, she gathered her skirts and tunneled into the forest.

18

stay with me

The night had grown colder, winter's teeth fully bared in the mid-December night. Sera scanned her surroundings. The winds wailed, and the trees shivered.

She blinked, needing clear eyes and a clear mind to find Mary, but the tears remained, multiplied. Through the cold, heat gathered in her cheeks, shame a weight heavy on her chest. She had to find her and explain. How would she explain it? There was no excuse. No way to hide it; she had seen his kiss with her own eyes. Surely she would know Timothy accompanied her to the dance only in order to be with Sera.

Sera's heart tightened. Barrington's betrayal had broken her, and now she'd inflicted that pain upon another. Mary would never bear it. She would lose her friend forever.

"Mary!" Sera shouted. How could she have single-handedly ruined all the good in her life? Her friendship with Mary, her agreement with Barrington? Her heart begged to escape, to run through the thickets, scale the gate, and flee the Academy. What was left for her here? Her chances at a referral had been destroyed along with her partnership with the only man who'd ever given her a chance to prove herself beyond a seventhborn. And now her only true friend was gone. Her breaths caught and broke in her chest. She couldn't have ruined this, too. *No, no, no.*

She pushed through the dense brush. Things couldn't end this way. She wouldn't lose Mary, not without first apologizing. She hadn't moved quickly enough to catch Barrington, but she would find Mary if it was the last thing she did.

She held out her wand, illuminating the spaces around her. "Mary!" The winds shifted and howled. Disturbed gaunt branches made shadows dance on the ground as if to scare her. But she trudged forward. Mary had come this way, and she wouldn't turn back without her.

"Mary, please," she yelled out into the darkness. "Tell me where you are so we can talk." She whirled, hoping to catch sight of the girl or the light of her wand. The Academy spires were smaller than expected; she hadn't noticed how far she'd run. Still, she ran deeper into the dark, her magic torchlight wavering. Roots tripped her. Barren branches sliced at her face and snatched at her dress as she dashed through dense thickets. She stumbled forward into a small meadow and spun wildly. "Tell me where you are! Mary!"

She expanded her light but found no trace of her friend. Only a deep, unnatural silence. Uneasiness squeezed her bones. "Mary?"

A masculine chuckle resounded from the dark between the trees. "She isn't here."

Sera tightened her grip on her wand. "Whittaker, I have no time for your nonsense."

"Whittaker? No, he isn't here, either. But we are."

A robed figure emerged from the darkness. Sera spun slowly, watching more of them appear from behind the trees, one by one, their wands illuminated red. They wore black, beaked plague masks, and in their light, she caught sight of the emblem on their robes—ravens.

No…

Fear rushed to her limbs in a dizzying manner. Was he here? She eyed each man carefully. No, Noah wouldn't ever use a mask. He was much too proud. Much too sadistic.

Instincts flared, and she aimed her wand at them. "Don't come any closer," she warned, her eyes darting at the figures as they spread about and encircled her. She would never escape. Accepting this, she held her wand steady. They wouldn't take her alive. Not without a good fight. "I won't go with you. I'll never be your puppet."

One of the robed figures stepped into the circle. "And how do you know this, witchling? Not even the Aetherium has caught on to us." He lifted his wand to her swiftly. Shackles of magic whipped around her, scalding ropes of red. She screamed, fell back onto the damp grass, and writhed against the burn that cut through the fabric of her dress and into her skin. Blood seared as it seeped from gashes, wetting her skin. Her wand tumbled away from her, but even if she held it, no magic would come. Only pain. Eyes shut tight, she thrashed, struggled to evade the ache spreading over her skin, digging its claws into her pores. It was everywhere.

He lowered his wand, and the flow of his magic stopped. "There's nothing to be scared of. The master is certain you will help us usher in a new era, and that's a great purpose. You should be honored, seventhborn." He held out a hand to her.

The master…

In spite of the pain, Sera struggled onto her elbows, to her knees, and faced the Brother. This couldn't be her end. She couldn't let Noah reach other witches, other seventhborns. She looked into his eyes. She would survive this. She had to.

Noting her defiance, he lifted his wand to her throat. The tip was filed to a point sharp enough to slice through skin. He trailed it along her neck, the spike pricking at her pulse.

"It's a shame the master asked us to collect you. With your reserves, I could get two uses out of you."

Reserves...

Sera's mind worked like mad. He knew her reserves. And Portia mentioned she had large reserves as well. How would they have known? What did she have in common with Portia where they would know? Sera gazed up, the Academy spires like shadowy swords against the night sky. Her heart twisted. Of course. Portia had applied for the seventhborn program, where their reserves had been tested and documented, just as Sera's were documented for school purposes. The Brotherhood didn't target random seventhborns. They targeted powerful ones, with vast reserves based on the applications for the seventhborn program. It had to be, and Barrington needed to know.

"I'm being kind, seventhborn. Come."

Sera set her jaw. "No—"

She arched forward with a cry as blistering pain spiked into her body. She rolled onto her stomach and attempted to push herself up. The Brother kicked her arms from under her, and she slammed onto the ground, winded.

Magic thrashed within her, a wild beast rattling the cage of her control. She hooked her fingers into the earth and called to her magic from every part of her being, funneling it until it became a solid thing in her chest, pumping with every heartbeat. Focused, she closed her eyes and felt her pain, used it as fuel to the gathering magic. Her hands trembled;

the magic she felt churning within her held the promise of oblivion once she let it go. The last time she'd felt this way, the last time she'd released this beast of magic, she'd collapsed a building around her, nearly killing Noah and herself. Now it rattled for release. Her reserves were greater now; she may not survive it this time.

It was her only choice.

"You will come, seventhborn," he said. "You wouldn't want your friend's death on your conscience, would you?"

A gust blew. Within the wind's moan and crackling of the branches, she heard it—a grunt. The circle opened, and another hooded figure entered. He held Timothy by the neck, his wand aimed at his head.

Sera winced, yanking back the leash on her magic. She couldn't unleash it here, not with the possibility of it killing Timothy as well. "It's me you want," she said quickly, holding tight to the wild magic within her. "Let him go."

"No," Timothy said. "I'm Timothy Delacort, and it's me they want."

"Don't listen to him—"

"You want to know about the Scrolls, no?" Timothy cut above her. "I can help you. Let her go and you have my word. I'll tell you anything you want to know. My father knows people who can help."

The Brother chuckled once more. "Yes, your father knows many people. He knew us very well before he abandoned us."

Sera blinked. *Timothy's father, a Brother?*

Timothy's momentary silence told her he didn't know this, either. "I don't know what your past is with him, but he'll do anything to get me back. Let her go, and I promise he'll help you."

"A liar, just like your father," the Brother said coolly.

"No one person has the Scrolls, boy. Had your father not abandoned us, he would have known that."

The Brother grabbed a fistful of Sera's hair and yanked her to her feet. "Kill him and set his body on the Aetherium stairs—"

"No!" she screamed.

Timothy grunted and snatched his arm away from his captor. The upward movement knocked off the Brother's mask. The man stumbled. In the momentary distraction, Timothy snatched his wand and aimed it at the group surrounding Sera. She yanked herself away and lunged to the ground. A trail of heat and light dashed above her and exploded, mixed with screams and the roar of fire. She looked over her shoulder. The group of Brothers was now strewn along the field, some engulfed in flames. Their fiery bodies writhed and speared magic blindly, setting fire to the field and the trees around them.

She spun back to Timothy—

"Timothy, behind you!"

The Brother punched Timothy in the jaw, sending him whirling to the ground and the wand flying from his hand. The Brother snatched up the wand and aimed it at Timothy.

This was it.

Sera released the chain from around the magic she'd siphoned, and with a guttural cry, let the energy pour out of her. Unchecked by a wand, unfocused by desperation, governed by rage. Her wild magic fed out in a continuous flame and melded with that of Timothy's magic consuming the field. The fire roared, doubled, and devoured, both men and trees burning.

Her gathered magic running out, Sera collapsed onto her knees, her reserves dangerously low. Wracking coughs scraped her insides, the smoke a thick sheet around her.

Heat closed in, preceding the angry flames.

A shadow became visible through the vapors.

"Timothy—"

Not Timothy, but the Brother.

He sliced down with his wand. An arched blow of blinding magic cut toward her. She screamed, rolled out of the way, and groaned in agony, her arm seared in the flames. His magic spurred the fire, bringing it closer.

Through the licks, she saw him searching the flames for her, his wand in hand.

She gathered more magic, though much less than before, and lifted a bloody, scorched hand to the fire.

The flames crested and sucked the man into its void. But fire knew not friend from foe and edged closer to Sera.

The Brother lunged through the smoke, a determined hate in his eyes. She'd burned but not killed him, and now he'd kill her. Breath caught, she held up a hand, calling to her magic once more, but with her reserves near depletion and her fear of the surrounding flames, of imminent death, her energy scattered, and she was unable to focus it into another blast.

He clutched her arm and dragged her close. Sera tried to kick him, but her feet tangled in her skirts and never connected with the man.

"You will burn, witchling, but not here," he seethed, haloed by fire. She craned her neck, hoped to bite his face, his arm, anything to secure her freedom. He was taller, stronger.

The Brother seized her by the neck and whipped binds around her hands and feet. She struggled, but he sent the binds deeper. Her wrists and ankles charred, her magic once again dispersed under pain.

Their small patch of land didn't burn, but the licks of

fire crowded them, sought to reach in and devour them alive. Brothers ran in the raging flames, fiery figures trying to escape a death that had already enveloped them.

Anger bloomed in her again, and unlike the fear that scattered her magic, this rage she could hold on to. She wouldn't let them leave here alive, not to torture more witches. Hands bound, she grasped the Brother's arm, dug her fingers through his fire-shredded sleeve, and held on, her legs raw as the flames bit through her dress and sank teeth into her skin. Through the ache, she focused her magic on anger and called upon it to bind them together. A band of white whipped from her hands and wound about his arm. The way they'd done to other seventhborns. And like them, he, too, would burn.

The bands of magic around him burst into flames, and the Brother screamed, his body engulfed in fire.

Tethered to him, Sera cried out at the fiery lashes of his cloak that brushed against her face. She collapsed onto her knees, her fight clipped by pain and her need for air. Still she held on to him with all she had and willed another whip of magic to bridge them together. She hadn't guaranteed Noah was dead. She would make certain this man was.

Strange pleasure prickled her insides as she watched her skin burn, the men burn, the trees burn. She could not control these fires, but at the same time she couldn't bring herself to care.

Their binds severed, and she dragged her arm away from the fire and the dead Brother. But it didn't matter. Her reserves spent, debilitating fatigue rolled over her body, and she could barely move, barely breathe. Sera rested her head on the ashy ground, welcoming the darkness that tugged her in and out of consciousness.

Shafts of frost washed through the flames. She closed

her eyes against the coolness that pricked her seared skin, a painful balm, a blistering relief. The frost climbed over the ground, devouring the lingering fire, and crept over her skin. She turned her head. Brilliant icicles glimmered in the moonlight. Dying wouldn't be so bad here, she thought, the smoke like clouds and icy grass blades like stars.

White billows curled upward from the earth where dead Brothers were strewn among scorched and splintered branches.

A figure cloaked in black rushed through the field, gazing wildly down at every burned body. He moved unnaturally fast within the smog as though born of smoke himself. Maybe it was Death, she wondered, but the forest smeared around her—brown, blue, and gray smoke—and she conceded that perhaps this stranger was a figment of her fading wits and life.

The smoke folded outward, and she saw him clearly, the image flashing through the vapors and fog. She hauled in a weak breath. "Prof…essor."

He didn't hear her and continued his survey of the bodies on the field. She would die before he reached her, before she could tell him everything. She dug her nails into the earth and dragged herself with what strength remained, needing to go just a little farther.

She managed a short distance, but charred arms crumbled beneath her, and she met darkness, her face against the now damp ground. She rolled over and whimpered, unable to move more.

Barrington spun at the sound, the smoke a halo around him. He was beside her in an instant. Horror shaded his eyes as they traveled along her frame. She could only imagine what her body looked like, scalded and bloodied.

"Reserves," she struggled to whisper. "Seventhborns…"

"Don't speak," he ordered and pressed a hand to her forehead, to her temple. "Damn it, damn it, damn it." To her chest, to her stomach. "No." Coolness waved through her with each of his touches, but it was faint. He let out a broken breath, and she knew he failed at healing her.

Professors and groundskeepers ran out onto the field, their wands drawn. More voices sounded far away. She struggled to keep her eyes open. Her lids heavy, the world around her speckled behind frosted lashes. Barrington swept her hair back, neared his face to hers. The drain of magic made his skin pale, and in the night, he was phantomlike.

"Seventhborn…program," she said again. "Brotherhood… reserves." She met his eyes with the last of her strength, hoping he somehow understood her fragmented words, hoping that other seventhborns could be saved, even if she couldn't be.

"She must be taken inside," Mrs. James shrilled, suddenly beside him. She made to reach for Sera, but Barrington swept her into his cold arms and held her close.

"I'll transfer her to the infirmary. Secure the grounds," he thundered. And as the world vanished around them and darkness swallowed them whole, the last she heard him say was *stay with me.*

19

in pain and woe

Sunlight threaded across her eyes, and Sera frowned. This couldn't be heaven. She never imagined one could have a headache in heaven like the one settled behind her eyes. There was also no way she would ever see any pearly gates, not after the man she had killed—the man she had taken pleasure in killing. For a moment, her mind swam with all the other torturous things she would have done to him, to all the Brotherhood, were she stronger. It was a mad thought, but memory of the slain girls brushed past, and her remorse lessened.

Blinking her eyes open, she lifted a hand to ward off the light. She paused. Her hands weren't burned. She eased up the sleeve of her white nightdress and turned her arm over, then inspected her other arm. Her skin was fully healed. Only faint, reedy bruises remained where the Brother had bound her, but no burns were to be found. So she wasn't in heaven, and she wasn't dead. She lowered her arm and lolled her head sideways to confirm her next deduction.

She lay in a small, scantly furnished room that was not hers. A long table was set before the window, and on it a jug of water and a cup. Beside her bed were two chairs, one with a folded wool blanket on top. A fireplace with the Academy crest above it rounded out the space. She blew out a breath. At least she was still in the Academy, but this wasn't the infirmary...

"Finally awake, I see," Mrs. Timpton, the Academy's nurse, said from the door. She was a severe-looking woman with seedy eyes and a beaked nose, accentuated by gray-streaked black hair that she always wore in a low, rigid bun. She spoke fast, and her tone was harsh, but of all the times Sera had been to the infirmary, she had never found any cruelty in the woman.

Mrs. Timpton rolled a tea trolley into the room, then set it at Sera's bedside and poured what looked like tea. "How do you feel?"

With the nurse's help, Sera rose onto her elbows and then to an upright position, and accepted the cup. She inhaled the steam and let the warm mist fog her face, then took a quick sip. The concoction was bitter, and the first gulp felt like jagged stones scraping down her throat. "A bit sore, and my head hurts, but fine otherwise."

"Good. Great, really, considering all you've been through." Mrs. Timpton neared an illuminated wand tip to Sera's eyes and nodded to herself. When Sera set down her cup, the nurse took hold of her arm and surveyed her skin, a satisfied smile at her thin lips. "Wonderful. Perfect restoration, and in a matter of weeks. Impressive."

"Weeks? How long have I been here? Where am I?"

"You're in a room just off the infirmary. The Academy thought it best not to alarm the other students with details of your...situation," she said with a knowing arch of her brow. "You've been here for two weeks. Burns such as yours take longer to heal, but my mix of comfrey and slippery elm seemed to do the trick. It's still remarkable for you to have healed so quickly. One would think faeries slipped in here and gave you some other brew. Either faeries or that friend of yours."

Sera's heart stuttered. "Mary? How is she? And Timothy?"

She waved a hand. "Miss Tenant is fine. She's been keeping you company every night since you were brought here. Mr. Delacort was also treated and released, but I heard his father took him home."

Relief swayed Sera, and she leaned back against her pillows, her pulse finding its rhythm once more.

Voices resounded from outside of the room. Mrs. Timpton rolled her eyes. "They're like hounds, I tell you. I have to tell them you're awake," she said regretfully. "I'll be glad to have them out of my hair, to be honest."

"Who?"

Mrs. Timpton lifted the blankets to Sera's chest and pulled down her sleeves. "The Aetherium. Even the chancellor has come, and as chair to the seventhborn program, Mr. Delacort."

If meeting the chancellor was nerve racking, meeting Timothy's father was far more nauseating. Mrs. Timpton walked to the door, and once Sera nodded her approval, she opened it and addressed the men in whispers.

One by one, they walked into the room. The first was a red-haired man, handsome, with an aristocratic nose and bright green eyes framed with thick red lashes. He wore the maroon robe with black trim donned by all Aetherium inspectors.

The second man was unmistakable. Mr. Delacort shared his son's same curls and features. He met Sera's gaze and smiled, a perfect smile just like Timothy's. Although covered by blankets, goose bumps sprouted along Sera's skin; his expression did nothing to warm his eyes. It was like staring into a pit of ice. Cloaked in black, he towered above the rest of the men, including the last one to enter.

Dressed in a royal blue robe, the chancellor was a feeble man, hunched over and nothing like the impressions she had seen of him in Aetherium leaflets or his portrait hanging in the Great Hall. In those, his white hair had been combed back at either side, and he always looked straight ahead, stern and serious. The man before her didn't seem like the type who could look at anything for very long. His hair—much frizzier and silver in person—stuck out at either side like extended wings, a horseshoe shape around his head. Sera's heart dimmed. The newspapers had obviously stretched the truth about his recovery.

He was being helped by a woman she knew instantly as Mrs. York. She held a vase of flowers in her other hand, an arrangement of gorgeous purple hyacinths that matched her dress. Her hard face and high chin made Sera sit a little taller. The men, too, appeared to hold their breath, averting their eyes as she passed and helped the chancellor into a chair. She then placed the vase at the window as the chancellor stared before him, lost in his own world.

"These are my favorite flowers," she said. With a finger, she parted the arrangement down the middle. "A shame, this one has yet to bloom and looks closer to death than life. I think given a second chance, it will be lovelier than the others." She nodded as if sharing a secret with the flower, then turned. "I'm Mrs. York, the chancellor's wife. He has been somewhat under the weather and asked me to accompany him. He also thought you would feel more at ease not to be surrounded by a group of men. I hope you don't mind."

"No, ma'am. Of course not. It's a pleasure to meet you," Sera said, doubting Mrs. York would've stayed behind had her husband not invited her. She didn't seem the type to care for mending his robes as much as mending political relations.

"Wonderful." She sat beside her husband, his frail body lost within his robe. "Your file says you wish to become an inspector, yes?"

Sera nodded, confused and nervous at the sight before her.

"It's a very rigorous and demanding program. It will leave no time for, well, life. Many of our top inspectors never marry or have children."

"Then it is a good thing I don't wish for marriage or children."

"Dedication, I like that."

"Mrs. York," Mr. Delacort cut in mildly, as though addressing a child, "I believe we are here to talk about recent *incidents*. Surely I can supply you with any information you need regarding one of my seventhborn program beneficiaries, including Miss Dovetail."

Mrs. York pressed her lips into a tight smile, yet the glare she cut Mr. Delacort betrayed her anger. "Ever so helpful, Mr. Delacort."

He returned her smile, just as stiff and cold, and pressed a hand over his heart. "I live to serve the Aetherium, and all I do is with its well-being in mind."

Sera eyed them both, the tension in the room now a sixth guest among them.

The chancellor reached a feeble hand over to his wife and squeezed hers. She broke from her scowl and leaned in to him, where he whispered faint words into her ear.

"My husband says he is terribly sorry to have to do this now, but it is best when the details are fresh in your mind, yes?" She motioned for the man by the door to approach. "You may begin, Inspector Lewis."

Inspector Lewis drew a notepad and pencil from his inner cloak pocket. The sight blurred behind Sera's eyes. As boorish as he could be sometimes, it would have been a comfort to have Barrington with her.

After a few basic questions ranging from her name and age to her field of study, the inspector asked, "What do you know about the men who attacked you? Mr. Timothy Delacort said they wanted you specifically. Did you know these men?"

Mr. Delacort, though staring out the window, tensed at this question.

"They were Purists—the Brotherhood, if I remember correctly. They wore plague masks, and there were ravens on their robes," she answered. "I've heard of their history and how they persecuted seventhborns. It wasn't a hard deduction that they wanted me dead."

"Did they say anything?"

She shook her head. "They said my death would usher in a new era, and it was a great purpose, then they attempted to take me. Thankfully, Timothy Delacort arrived, and we were able to fight them off."

The man tapped his chin. "Speaking of which, how exactly were you able to fight? We didn't find you in possession of a wand."

Sera dithered. Her mind worked at an answer, but there was no way around it. "They took my wand, and I...I panicked and was forced to use my magic to defend myself. Wandless."

The inspector's brows rose at this, and he glanced at Chancellor York. The chancellor, however, sat unaffected. His wife merely nodded for her to continue.

"I didn't want to, but I knew I had to survive—to at least live long enough to say who did this. You have my word, I'll never do it again." Though Sera was unsure how she'd be able to keep this promise. She hadn't the funds for a new wand…which reminded her, without a wand, she couldn't take the Aetherium entrance exam. Her heart sank, but she swallowed her pain. There were more pressing matters to think about.

Mrs. York smiled, this time a genuine expression. "Never say never, Miss Dovetail. One shouldn't ever tire of fighting for one's life. There are things many of us are not supposed to do that we do in the best interest of our community and, sadly, of ourselves. Seventhborn or not."

The chancellor touched his wife's hand again. She leaned in and said, "The chancellor believes we do as we've been doing. Instruct the staff to keep quiet, and if anyone asks, we will say a blast of lightning set fire to the forest. Upon learning there may have been students out there, some professors ran to their aid. Nothing more." She straightened. "I agree. These Purists will not get the pleasure of any publicity."

Anger twisted Sera's core. These monsters deserved the entire Aetherium searching for them, to eradicate and destroy them. She opened her mouth to voice this, but Mr. Delacort spoke first.

"Publicity is the least of our worries. While I am relieved my son and Miss Dovetail met no serious harm at the hands of those fanatics, I must remind you that the son of the last traitor to this Academy—to the Aetherium and every magician under its law—is employed by this school. Like father, like son. We may lie about what happened in the forest, but who's to say it won't happen again with Professor Barrington still walking these halls?"

Sera stiffened but forced her muscles to relax and any expression from her face. Her heart knew no such code of conduct. It beat wildly against her chest, offense for Barrington and longing to see him spurring it on.

"We've interviewed Professor Barrington repeatedly," Inspector Lewis said, "and he has an alibi. He apprehended a couple in the library when he saw the flames through the window. Your son said he managed to kill one of the men and jumped into the flames to save Miss Dovetail without a thought."

"A criminal's remorse, surely." Mr. Delacort chuckled.

"Having personally known both Professor Barrington and his father, the chancellor and I have no reason to suspect the professor. And give the man some credit. Even he would not be so foolish as to attack his place of employment," Mrs. York said. "We must accept it as a stroke of bad luck. It is no secret the Solstice Dance was on that night. They knew the faculty's attention would be elsewhere, and they took advantage."

"This is unbelievable." Mr. Delacort's cool mask dropped, his jaw taut and eyes narrowed. "We have the son of a murderer roaming these halls, and you decide to overlook it? My son was in danger, and you claim it was *bad luck*? You're blind, and if anything ever happens to my son because of your disregard, I swear on my family's wand, York—"

"Ah, ah." Mrs. York rose, graceful and calm, though the air swelled. "Consider your next words, Delacort. Perhaps threatening the chancellor's wife in the presence of an Aetherium inspector is not the wisest of choices."

Inspector Lewis drew close to Mrs. York's side, though Sera doubted she needed him to defend her. The fire in her eyes told Sera she would cut him down in one stroke.

She smiled at Mr. Delacort. "For now, Miss Dovetail

and my husband must rest. And while I don't think more of these men will return," she said to Sera, "perhaps it is best to remain close to the Academy."

Sera blinked. Did she mean not to venture into the forest or…? No, it couldn't be she knew of her adventures with Professor Barrington.

Mr. Delacort's scowl deepened, and he stomped out the door. The tension in the room instantly lightened.

"It was a pleasure meeting you, Miss Dovetail," Mrs. York said. "I hope to soon have the pleasure again. Perhaps next time, I'll be referring to you as Inspector?"

In spite of all the trouble and confusion, a real smile met Sera's lips as Mrs. York helped her husband to his feet and ushered him to the door, followed by Inspector Lewis.

"And don't forget about the little bud," she said. "Sometimes even the smallest second chances can bloom into something beautiful. Good day, Miss Dovetail."

They exited, and the door closed behind them. Sera relaxed, and then the door opened again. Mr. Delacort strode into the room, wintry eyes fixed on his gloves left on the table by the window. Seizing them, he spun on his heels and stopped.

A slow smile spread on his lips, sending a shiver down Sera's spine. "It seems I've forgotten my gloves," he said and approached the bed. "Something you must never forget is that if any harm comes to my son, I will destroy you, Miss Dovetail."

She opened her mouth to speak—

"Don't pretend I don't know of his *feelings* for you," he cut in. "But whatever proposals he's made, put them out of your mind. You will stay away from my son if you ever wish to become an inspector. Good day."

He stalked from the room and shut the door behind him.

She stared at the door, her brow knitted. She had been right; his warm smiles and concern had been nothing but an act. It seemed Mrs. York didn't like him very much, and Sera found she didn't, either.

Sera pushed aside her blankets. Her joints felt rusted, but a good stretch helped her regain some movement. She padded across the cold floor to the window where the flowers were. And beyond them, the courtyard and the Wishing Tree.

Mr. Delacort's words were disturbing, but more so was that her conversation with the Brotherhood was still unknown to Barrington. She had to get to him immediately and make good use of this second chance. She stared down at the flowers, lifted a finger to the bud that had yet to bloom, and spoke a quiet spell of life over it the way she'd learned in Botany. The stem twirled and stretched as if waking from a slumber. All the buds followed in a like dance, sprouting outward in a gorgeous vision of purple. When it fully bloomed, she saw a thin scroll was tucked within the stem.

She slipped out the paper and unwound it. Sloppy writing marked the parchment, and a wave of warmth seeped into her chest. She sat down on the nearest chair, her hands tight on Barrington's letter.

Sometimes even the smallest second chances can bloom into something beautiful.

Her pulse warred to both quicken and slow. How much did Mrs. York know? And *how* did she know? More, why did she not care about her and Barrington's relationship if she *did* know?

Perhaps it was just a coincidence, one that could be cleared up only by talking to Professor Barrington. But first, she turned her eyes to the letter.

Dear Miss Dovetail,

I hope in earnest that this letter finds you awake and healed, your fiery spirit still intact. Forgive my absence, but not only may it be deemed improper to those who do not know of our arrangement, but as I attempted to explain before, I am awful at expressing things other than anger, displeasure, or frustration.

With circumstances being what they are, my words may mean very little now, if anything at all, but please know that what I did in taking you on as my assistant was never meant to bring you harm.

My reasons for choosing you in specific lie far beyond the realms of your birth order and imminent graduation—though they were somewhat important, but not for the reasons you think. It is true, I knew Mr. Sinclair lived, but having you near me was the only way I could ensure your safety. I imagined that if you knew, you would have frightened and fled from where I could guard you. As such, I decided not to tell you, not until I could prove to you that you could trust me with your life. But I underestimated your strength and resolve, and my actions were the ones that brought about our downfall.

More than anything, I chose you because I hoped to show you that I, too, understand a blinding desire to right a wrong, to find answers that, while may not change our situations, may help us better understand them, and in turn, free us to make something of a life with what remains.

But it is too late, and I accept that some things simply cannot be, no matter how much I desire it or bind it to a wishing tree. With this truth, you are released of our agreement. Simply say "dissolved."

*My referral is yours and will be sent to the Aetherium
when the time comes. I sincerely hope that with it, you
find what you seek. And should you need for anything,
know that you can always call on me.
Sincerely yours with my utmost respect,
Professor Nikolai Barrington*

The letter crackled, and like the very first note he had
sent, it burst into a ball of white fire that didn't burn her
skin. But as the alabaster flames warmed her hands and
licked the letter away, Sera blinked back tears, every
hesitation and uncertainty untangling within her. Once
again, anger had gotten the best of her. Once again anger
had destroyed. If only she had listened, she would have
learned these things, would have realized that they didn't
just need each other but that, in essence, they were the
same: blinded by desire and burdened by hope. And, after
all was said and done, they were mirror images of each
other in pain and woe.

With cupped ashes before her, she stared down at her
hands as though the phantom of his words lived in the
smoke.

*I accept that some things simply cannot be, no matter how
much I desire it or bind it to a wishing tree.*

She gazed out the window, down to the Wishing Tree
that still stood in spite of the snow surrounding it. What on
earth did he wish for, and what did it have to do with her?

Weary and achy, she dumped the ashes in a bin, stumbled
out of the room and to the coat-tree, and slipped on
someone's cloak.

"Miss Dovetail! You haven't been released yet," Mrs.
Timpton called behind her, but Sera walked on as fast as

she could, through the empty halls, down the stairs, and to the garden doors.

Two Night Flaggers stood by the door, though the day was early.

"No one is allowed beyond the gardens," one said. "The Aetherium forbids it."

Sera nodded. "I wish only to see the tree. It's just there."

With a curt nod, one of the boys opened the door and let her through. Out in the courtyard, she lifted her hood over her head and walked the snowy path, her bare feet entombed in the thin layer of gathering snow. But regardless of the frigid cold that bit at her legs and toes, she pushed forward to the tree.

The flattened acorn was still there, and beside it, Barrington's folded leaf. Without her wand, Sera hugged herself to hide her illicit use of magic. When a cool wind brushed past, sending a flurry of snowflakes across her face, she wriggled her fingers.

Professor Barrington's leaf swung once, twice, and snapped from the tree. As it fluttered and floated down, she moved forward, her hands cupped before her. Lifting them, she caught the sliver of paper. She turned it over in her palm, and where she had thought him to write *Filip*, she read instead, *Forgiveness*.

She clutched tight at the leaf, cursing him doubly and once more. How could she not grant him a second chance after his letter, after he wished for forgiveness? *Her* forgiveness?

"Sera?" Mary's voice came from behind.

Sera spun. The sight of her friend—hair disheveled, dark circles under her bloodshot eyes—was her undoing, and the tears that threatened finally spilled. They rushed to each other, and Mary threw her arms around her.

After some minutes, she pulled away and cupped Sera's face. "Oh, I was so worried. The nurse said you ran out here and…"

Sera shook her head, pressing a hand to her friend's cheek, regardless of who saw them. "After all I did, and you worry for me still."

"Of course. I've been worried sick; these holidays have been torture. I've been sneaking away and transferring in from the house so Mother doesn't know I've come to see you. She's being fitted for new gowns now, so I have some time. Talk to me. Tell me how you are."

"How *I* am?" Sera echoed. "I am so sorry, Mary, about everything."

Rosy cheeked, Mary bit her lip and tears filled her eyes. "We mustn't speak of it now. What matters is that you're better."

"We must talk about it. You didn't deserve what we did. I should have told you about Timothy from the second he approached me, but I betrayed your trust. The last thing I ever wanted was to hurt you."

"Oh shush, you." She clasped Sera's hands in hers as her first tear fell. "He told me what he could, and knowing you, I deduced the rest. He cares for you, Sera, and yet you gave him up because you didn't want to hurt me. How could I be angry at you for that? And I'm the cause of what happened to *you*. I was foolish for running out into the forest, but I couldn't bear the heartache. When you followed, I circled back and went to my room. I should have been brave and faced you, but I wasn't, and you nearly lost your life because of it. How dare you apologize to *me*? You want to be an inspector so that you can find your family, but you're like a sister to me, and I never would've forgiven myself had anything happened to you." She sobbed. "I'm the one who's sorry. I beg for your forgiveness."

Sera hugged her friend, embracing this added second chance. "Of course I forgive you, silly girl."

The girls held each other, and Sera winced but stifled the ache in her ribs. She would hold Mary in spite of the pain, their relationship mended. She squeezed the leaf tightly in her hand, determined to mend them all.

20

quick to anger, slow to speak

The silence in the halls was heavy, many students yet to return from winter holiday. With each step along the fourth-floor corridor, Sera relished this stillness before the unknown that awaited once she rounded the corner. Professor Barrington had dissolved their agreement, and after hours of attempting to transfer to his home, she found the spell no longer worked. No doubt he had relinquished her access, believing she'd never want to see him again.

Passing closed door after closed door, she prayed he was in his office. If not, she would be left waiting until the following week, once classes resumed. Sadly, patience was most definitely not one of her virtues. And from the moment she had read his letter and his wish, it had vanished altogether.

She turned the corner, and her eyes caught on the engraved *B* at the door. Her hands rattled, doubt finding a home in her heart. What if he didn't accept her conditions and chose not to work with her again? Yes, the referral was hers, but she needed to help these girls, those already dead and those whose lives hung in the balance.

And Professor Barrington. She wouldn't accept his charity. She would work for her referral and help him avenge his family. Oath or no oath, it was not only fair. It was right.

Nodding once to herself, she forced one foot before the other and set off down the hall.

She raised a hand to knock just as she heard the thud of tumbling books followed by a slew of curses from inside. Nerves twisted at her core at the sound of the now-familiar voice.

With a sharp exhale, she rapped at the door.

"Come in," he barked from the other side, curses audible in his next murmurs. Sera pushed the door open and, entering quickly, shut it behind her. He knelt on the floor surrounded by scattered papers and books, his back toward her. "How may I help you?"

She lowered her hood and pressed trembling fingers together at her back. She had thought over every word—rehearsed what she intended to tell him until it was branded in her mind. Now, with him no longer a phantom before her, she couldn't remember a bit.

He snatched up the papers. "I said, how may I—" He rose and turned. His light eyes fixed on hers, and no more words came. It seemed he failed to breathe, as did she, the only sound the pops of the fire. The only movement the licks of the flames.

His hair was tousled this way and that with the look of one who had raked and tugged it many times. He was pale, worn, and tired, the telltale signs of many sleepless nights. He set down his papers slowly, his gaze never leaving hers. As though if he looked away for just a moment, she would disappear.

"Miss Dovetail…"

"I got your letter," she said quickly, hoping not to lose her nerve.

He lowered his head. "I see. You didn't have to come all this way. You merely needed to say the word 'dissolve,' and you were free. Forgive me if I didn't make that clear enough—"

"You did, but please, before you say or explain anything else, allow me to speak."

He nodded, and coming around the desk, he sat back on the edge, hands clasped in his lap.

"The day in your office, after I heard you speaking to Rowe, I hated you. Every reservation I had in trusting you had somehow manifested, and I couldn't believe I was standing there, with every fear come true. I wanted to hurt you, to burn everything down around you so that you would know what it felt like to lose your greatest dream. But then some days passed, and I realized, you already do."

He met her eyes at this, nodded gently, but said nothing.

"What I know of you, of your past…what you're doing for your father and brother, are the same things I would do to find my family, and as much as it hurt that you would keep the truth from me, I understand why and forgive you—but it still doesn't excuse you in any way," she said before he spoke. "When—*if* we decide to continue on with our partnership—I have a condition."

She steeled her spine and faced him squarely. "There will be no secrets between us in regards to our work. I am privy to the same information as you, regardless of whether you think it will hurt me to know it, or scare me. You said I had to be a little mad to trust you. Now I ask the same of you. Be a little mad and trust me."

He straightened and walked back around his desk,

stealing away her breath with his retreat. Sera swallowed. Was he searching for the best way to turn her down? To tell her that regardless of her conditions, their agreement could be no more?

Opening a drawer, he slid out a long box and met her by the door. "I wanted to send it with the letter, but whereas the letter would burn if anyone else found it, this wouldn't have." He opened the box, parted the silk inside, and held it out to her. "I owned it when I was about your age. I was not in the Academy at the time, but someone I treasure greatly mentored me and helped me hone my abilities. This wand was the perfect medium and my friend through it all. It will allow you a bit more freedom until you learn to control your full powers."

Breathless, she reached for the wand, a beautiful piece of tan wood threaded tightly together with lighter wood, so tight it resulted in one smooth piece. Highlights upon the wood spoke of its age.

"It's a mix of birch and oak. The birch allows your magic to conduct faster, and the oak is perfect for control and a consistent outflow of magic. They are also the best types of wood for conducting fire. I think it will suit you well."

Sera trailed her hand along it, her magic hot pinpricks sparking to life at her fingertips. She reached the casing, and her hands froze. Though the wand was old, a new silver cap rounded out the rod, upon which was the Academy crest, and below it her name engraved.

She needed the wand for the entrance exam, yet she shook her head. "I—I can't accept this. It's beautiful, but it's yours."

"It's the least I can do."

"No, you don't owe me anything. What happened was not your fault."

"Not directly," he said, sitting back onto his desk once more. "But had I told you the truth from the beginning, perhaps none of this would have happened."

"Yes, but I never gave you the chance to explain." She marched to his desk and handed the wand back to him. "I was quick to anger—"

"And I was slow to speak." He eased her hands back, warm fingertips brushing against hers. "It's yours, and you will need it. You will not be able to take the Aetherium exam without it." He straightened and walked back around his desk.

The words should have eased her, and yet she trembled. It was over. The wand was for her exam. A parting gift. She pressed it tightly in her hands and turned away so he wouldn't see her eyes water, her nose redden, or hands shake. "Yes, the exam, of course."

"And," he said behind her, "I can't exactly have a wand-less assistant, can I?"

A smile quivered on her lips, and she turned to find him at his desk, wand in hand. Mischief glimmered in his eyes and, for that moment, his sorrow vanished. He held his wand out to her and inclined his head. "Your amendment to our oath?"

She eased toward his desk and raised her new wand to his. "We will keep no secrets in regards to our work, and we have both entered into this oath willingly."

His gaze locked on hers. "Wholly."

The strands of birch in her wand lit up first, a gorgeous amber, her magic akin to blood filling its veins. The oak threads followed then, a deeper, hotter red. Coils of magic whirled from his, a slow dance of blue and white. Whereas before their oath was but a simple exchange of magic, their respective twirls of magic now twisted about each other like hundreds of small, individual oaths made in secret. Her magic then faded into his wand, while his twined around hers. It brushed past her fingers like a cool mist, then absorbed into her wand.

A heavy silence stretched between them, their wands still touching. Something about this oath was unlike their other. Personal, thrilling, and frightening all at once. He seemed to sense it, too; his stare caught on hers as he lowered his wand.

Sera swallowed, everything so terribly unfamiliar. Knowing about his life, about his past, about his reasons in choosing her was supposed to have made things easier. It was a start, and all trust needed a real foundation, however small. Yet when he looked at her, it was as if she'd fastened her corset too tight. Though the same man—flesh and blood, sad eyes and stern face—he seemed different. A sense of relief and gladness that had been absent before settled over his frame. In a way, she understood it—understood him and how good it was not to feel so alone.

He sat and, setting aside his wand, cleared his throat. "The night of the attack, you were trying to tell me something."

Sera sighed, glad to move past their uncertainty. She sat and divulged all that had happened and what the Brother had said. Barrington rubbed his lips, considering each of her words. He stood and paced behind his desk.

"So these seventhborns they use are plucked from the list of applicants for the seventhborn program. It makes sense. A great deal of power is needed to perform necromancy, and the longer a soul is dead, the more power it takes to raise it. Not to mention the longer the secret has been kept, the greater the consequence of breaking it."

"*And* they're breaking a blood oath, which is already a great feat."

Barrington hummed. "Hence the seventhborns. Not only

do you possess the second sight, yes, but you are all also born through death, which makes for a faster connection." He shook his head to himself. "Morbid and cowardly, but rather brilliant."

Sera's hand tightened around her wand. "It reeks of *him*. He thought he did me a favor in draining my magic, said he was cleansing me somehow." She scoffed, remembering the Brother's words. "*A great purpose.*"

"They will keep going until we find what they're looking for."

"Timothy mentioned the Scrolls, and the Brother said that not one person had them. Could that be what they are searching for?"

"Perhaps. It would explain raising body after body, and that's information worth torturing for. I believe the Scrolls have been split up somehow. These corpses know where the pieces are. If they have yet to find the next piece, then they must be close to it. Mr. Sinclair may be a sadistic, Purist bastard, but I don't think he would risk his men to get you unless it was extremely necessary. We need to find out what they know."

"How do you suppose we do that?" she asked. He continued to pace. Sera squeezed her eyes, nearly dizzy at following his path that now extended around the entire room.

"Timothy Delacort said he knocked off one of their masks. He was unable to see the man's face in the scuffle, and the man managed to escape. Did you see this happen? Did you see his face?"

She nodded.

"Grand. I'll need you to show me."

"And how would I do this, exactly?"

"The way you channeled the corpses' memories. I need

you to do this with your own memories. I understand if you're tired and would like to try later—"

"No, now is fine. The longer we wait, the greater the chance he'll disappear and we won't catch him."

"Very well. I don't have Rhodonite crystals on hand, but since this memory is yours, it will be easier to conjure and cast it." He strode to the windows, shut the curtains in one snap, and motioned for her to join him in the space before the window. "First thing?"

"Wand casing." Sera removed the casing and set it on his desk. She then flipped her wand around, grasping the pointed tip.

"Perfect. Now, when casting your own memories, you must pick an item to focus on, like you did with the impressions. This time, it will be me. Imagine you're telling me of the events, but instead of using words, you use magic. Guide it, form it into the images in your mind."

She blinked. "But what if I hurt you? It's a new wand and—"

"I trust you, Miss Dovetail. You will do fine." He took a step back. "And if it makes you feel any better, I'm not only smart and charming but quite strong as well. Now, focus on me," he said. "Only me."

She locked her eyes on his and nodded.

Like the previous time, her fingers burned and grew numb, her magic fighting to enter the narrow tip of the wand. It fed out much faster than before, and within seconds, thick vines of smoke whipped out from the blunt end.

"Guide your magic. Close your eyes and tell it what you see."

Sera closed her eyes. Moving quickly through the events of that night in her mind, she paused on the moment Timothy struggled with the man. "Mr. Delacort's just knocked off the man's mask… He has a very pronounced chin and brows, and a large nose. His eyes are deeply set. I think they're brown."

"Hold the image," Barrington said, his tone low so as to not disturb her concentration. "Now open your eyes."

The moment her lids parted, her breath caught. A cloud of smoke whirled before her and displayed within it was the masked Brother, the scene of Timothy knocking off his mask repeating itself over and over. She lowered her hand slowly and walked around the suspended cloud. The more she learned to control her magic, the more she loved it.

"Brilliant," Barrington said. "You may call back your magic."

In doing so, the image before her evaporated, and her wand lost its glow.

Barrington stalked to his desk, fierce and determined. "You've given me much to work with." He gathered up papers in a dash. "I must consult with a friend and will call for you upon my return."

"Is it Mrs. York?"

He stopped, but then shook his head. "Mrs. York is an old family friend, one of the few who remained after my father…after he was accused of crimes he didn't commit. She's our Aetherium source, but it's Gummy whom I seek."

"Oh." A strange nudge twisted Sera's stomach at the thought of Gummy, but she swallowed it down. Who Barrington chose for company was no concern of hers, regardless of how much the woman's presence pricked her skin.

"Is there a problem with Miss Mills?"

"Not a problem, no. I was surprised, however, that a woman of Mrs. York's standing approved of our partnership."

He grinned and slid on his overcoat. "Not everyone is who they seem, Miss Dovetail. You will see that more and more when dealing with the Aetherium. Mrs. York has always been a grand supporter of all magicians, regardless of birth order. She was the one who asked me to look after you when sightings of Mr. Sinclair surfaced. She feared he might come for you and tasked me to do all I could to keep you within the safety of the Academy—or what we imagined was safe."

Sera's brows rose. "Mrs. York asked *you* to protect *me*?"

"Indeed. For your well-being to be sure, but also for her husband's campaign. A kidnapping of a student from the Academy coupled with a series of necromantic murders would be disastrous for him and would empower those who believe he's unable to rule due to his declining health."

Sera nodded, understanding the need to keep events at the Academy quiet.

"That is why I asked you to be my assistant, ignorant to the two cases being related." He slid his wand into the metal holder. "When she learned of the first murders, she summoned me and asked me to discreetly investigate, as well as bound the investigating officers to secrecy of it."

"Smart woman. And the chancellor?"

"His prognosis is grim, which is why we must hurry. Mrs. York is a talented healer and doing her best to delay his illness, but many in the Aetherium will soon petition that he is no longer fit to rule, namely Mr. Delacort, who no doubt will campaign for the position once the chancellor is removed."

Sera remembered the events at the infirmary, and the rather odd exchange between Mrs. York and Mr. Delacort took on new meaning.

She replayed Mr. Delacort's words in her mind. *I live to serve the Aetherium, and all I do is with its well-being in mind.* She scoffed. The only well-being he had in mind was his own.

"Once he is succeeded, Mrs. York will be unable to secure us what we need for our investigations." Barrington walked around his desk. "I should go. I will not be gone for long. Will you be all right here at the Academy?"

"I'll be fine. Mary is on holiday, but she comes to visit every day."

He nodded. "Nevertheless, stay vigilant." He slid his papers into his case. "If you run into any trouble or feel endangered in any way, transfer to the house immediately. Rosie may not wear an Invocation ring, but she's one of the strongest witches I know. I'll tell her you may come unexpectedly"—he smiled—"though I'm sure she expects that by now."

Sera mirrored the gesture, her cheeks warm. "I'll wait for your call." She flipped her hood over her head and opened the door. "Good night, Professor."

He lifted his eyes from his things and nodded once. "Good night, Miss Dovetail."

She closed the door behind her, a smile still on her lips. A good night, indeed.

21

the last man

The library was empty, save for the librarian whose nose was buried in one of the romance novels she was known for hiding beneath her desk, and Mary who sat on the couch beside the window. Though Sera warned her against gossip should anyone see them together, Mary insisted that after all that had happened, she was done with hiding their friendship.

With *The Unmitigated Truths of Seventhborns* on her lap, Sera stared out to the open fields, not seeing the snows that melted and slowly gave way to patches of wet, dead grass. There were only the faces of passersby, and the haunting thoughts of the one face she had yet to see.

Two days and no word. No letter. Had she not the hyacinths in her room and the wand in her holder, she would have thought it all a dream.

"You can ask about him, you know," Mary said quietly from over her book, twirling a lock of brown hair around a finger.

Sera pressed closer to the window, her heart quick. Just

there, a man exited the teacher's hall. Tall...black hair... black cloak...confident stride...

It was only Professor McKinney, the Ethics of Magic professor. She gritted her teeth and eased from the window. "What did you say?"

"Timothy."

Sera's attention whipped back to Mary. "What about him?"

"Oh, don't play coy with me. You've been searching for him since the first day of classes. I've seen you, and it's perfectly fine." Mary set aside her notes and books and inched closer to Sera. "I won't be hurt if you ask about him. Who am I to stand in the way of true love?"

"I'm not—I don't love him." Sera shifted away and gathered her things in a rush. "Love is poison. A nasty little thing that infects and destroys and—"

"Drives you absolutely mad."

Sera rolled her eyes and stood. Mary grinned and followed her out of the library. "Fine, fine. Tell yourself you're not in love until you believe it, though I never will. I see the way your face flushes whenever you think you've seen him. There is only one thing that makes a girl react that way, and it is love."

She opened her mouth to argue but quickly shut it. Better to lie about Timothy than have her suspect anyone else. "It doesn't matter whether I love him or not. I told you what his father said. Mr. Delacort will all but kill me if I dare go near him—"

She turned and collided into a tall figure and tipped back, her books tumbling to the ground around her, along with papers that were not hers. Strong hands came about her wrists and kept her from falling to the floor.

Professor Barrington helped her straighten, then bent

and picked up the books and scattered papers. He stuffed some of the pages into her books, dumped the books into her arms, and stepped back. "Your notes are in your book. Next time, mind where you're walking."

He spun on his heels and vanished into the library.

Sera glowered. "*He* bumped into me, and *I* need to mind where I'm walking?"

Mary hummed, a small smile on her lips that spurred Sera's pulse.

"And why are you smiling? He nearly took off my head with how hard he bumped into me."

"Oh, nothing," she said, blushing.

"That is not a nothing hum or a nothing blush."

Mary turned away quickly and rushed up the stairs. "You'll think me mad if I say it."

A cold sweat sprouted along Sera's brows. There was no way Mary could suspect anything…

"Say it anyway," she pressed, trailing her up the tower stairs and into her room. "And let me be the judge."

Mary fell back on Sera's bed and let out a breath.

Sera's eyes narrowed, her fear of Mary suspecting a relationship between her and Barrington giving way to another suspicion. One that made her stomach a little sick as she hoped against it. She knew Mary's sigh—the dreamy, infatuation sigh. She'd heard it for the past year whenever Mary thought or spoke of Timothy. "Mary…"

Her friend rose onto her elbows. "I just think he would make a good candidate is all."

Sera slid off her cloak. "Who is *he*, and what is he a good candidate for?"

"Professor Barrington." Mary hid her face with her hands. "For marriage."

Sera opened her mouth and closed it, the cloak nearly

falling from her hands. She'd suspected it, but...but this was...

"Mary, no."

"What?" She sat up. "Don't look at me that way. He's very handsome, if you look past that constant scowl. And think of it. He's unattached, wealthy, and in spite of some gossip about his family some years back, he's the perfect match." She sighed and blushed again. "Did you notice his eyes when he glared at you for bumping into him?"

"He bumped into me."

"Such a lovely shade of gray," she went on. "Oh, and a voice that commands attention. You know, I'm beginning to think it rather good that things with Timothy didn't work out. I think Mother would be proud. He may not be a Delacort, but an Academy professor is nothing to scoff at."

Sera blinked. She couldn't be hearing this. "He's the last man I would consider a good match. He seems moody and reserved. You're a ray of sunshine. He's a gloomy, annoying, humid night where it won't stop raining and your hair frizzes."

"I don't think it's moodiness. He's lonely. Besides" — Mary grinned — "I don't mind the night or the rain." She giggled. "Oh, this will be fantastic! And maybe, if I can charm him before the end of the year, I can convince him to sign your referral papers. Think of it, Sera!"

She swept from the bed and rushed to the door. "I'm going to see if he's still in the library. Wish me luck!" She closed the door behind her before the last word was said.

"Good luck," Sera murmured. She would need it with a man like Barrington. "Voice that commands attention — ha! *Your notes are in your book*," she mocked him and paused. "I had no notes..."

Sera gasped and opened her books quickly to find some of Barrington's notes and, between them, a letter. She smiled.

She tore open the envelope and slipped out the cream-colored note.

8:00 Tonight.

He was waiting in his office when she arrived, her veiled hat in his hands. "Miss Dovetail, we leave right away. We've much to do tonight." He handed her the hat and gloves and strode downstairs, his speed that of a man with a fire lit beneath him.

She followed the professor to where Lucas held open the carriage door.

He tipped his hat. "Welcome back, miss."

She smiled. "Wonderful to be back." And it truly was.

Barrington held out his hand to her and helped her onto the carriage steps, when suddenly his fingers tensed upon hers. Sera turned and startled; with her standing on the stair, they were now face to face, his light gray eyes boring directly into hers. Though wearing gloves, the pressure of his hand enclosing hers flared a wave of warmth through her, a rival to the bitter cold howling around them. For a moment, he didn't speak, his silence laced by the same strangeness she had felt in his office when taking their new oath, a thin line that on one side was their partnership and the other a thrilling yet terrifying unknown.

"I should have asked this before, but are you certain you feel well enough to venture out tonight?" he said, his voice a low rumble between them. Sera wished to answer but couldn't help but wonder if Barrington realized he still held her. More, was the worry in his eyes a figment of her mind or did he truly care, staring at her as though with one word he'd sweep her back into the safety of his home?

She pushed the thoughts to the back of her mind. Surely he was just being polite and her mind misconstrued it, the thrill of being back at work and at his side again skewing her judgment. "Yes, I'm perfectly fine, Professor. I won't let the Brotherhood scare me."

A small smile touched the left side of his mouth. "Glad to hear it."

He helped her into the carriage. She sat in her usual corner, Barrington diagonal from her. Lucas closed the door and, in moments, they were on their way. Nerves rattled her insides, and Sera let out a trembling breath.

"Cold?" Barrington reached over and lifted the seat, securing her a brown blanket that she then wrapped about her shoulders.

"Thank you. A pity one cannot light a fire in a carriage. Portable heat. Can you imagine it?"

He smiled, but gazing out of his window to the gnarled trees and the darkness between them, his eyes grew distant. "Why fire?"

"Why fire for heat?"

"No, why fire for magic—your magic? Magic manifests itself as light or smoke typically, yet you always choose fire."

"I wouldn't say I choose it, rather it has chosen me." She shrugged. "I've always felt comforted by it. I dream of it sometimes—often. When I think of my life before Noah found me, all I see is a wall of flames, and I can't break through it no matter how hard I try."

Barrington reached into his inner coat pocket and retrieved his notebook and pencil. "You have been trained before, of that I'm sure. Your ease in using wandless magic is impressive, save when your emotions get the best of you.

The fact that you're able to employ many spells without speaking or writing them tells me that you're familiar with magic above that of an Academy witchling. Then there's your run-in with the Barghest, and the binding-spell chamber. They all confirm my suspicions that you were trained by a very powerful magician. That will help in finding your family. I can seek out magicians who had students go missing, those capable of building intricate binding spells, and so forth. I'll figure it all out," he said in her silence.

Sera smiled sadly. "Am I a case now, too, Professor?"

He grinned over his notebook, a slight arch of his lips and crinkles at the sides of his eyes. "My most difficult puzzle yet."

Sometime later, the city came into view, stained in ash and soot. Dwellings crowded the skyline and a bell tower rose above them all as if seeking out the fresh air above, but the dark sky was gloomy and the air thick with lingering smoke. Lucas weaved the carriage through numerous narrow, empty streets that vanished into a thick smog soon after they'd passed them. Not that Sera minded. The dwellings were squalid and dilapidated—and downright depressing. She released the curtain and settled back. An uneasy thought sprouted in her mind. She'd never considered that, perhaps, her family came from such a place.

The scent of ocean soon met her nose, and harbor bells tolled in the distance. "We're back by the pier?" she asked.

The carriage rolled to a stop, and Barrington slid on his hat. "Not the same one. Miss Mills owns various establishments." Sera stiffened, the thought of seeing Gummy again most disagreeable.

Lucas opened the door. Barrington descended the carriage first and held a hand to her.

"You wish for me to go with you?"

"For a moment, yes. There's something I need you to confirm."

She slipped her hand into his and stepped from the carriage. Barrington ushered her to the door where, like before, Gummy leaned against the frame of the establishment—Mayson's, as opposed to Rosetta's.

She gave Sera a once-over, then grinned in Barrington's direction. "Thought you'd changed your mind."

"Of course not. Please take Miss Dovetail inside. I'll be right in," he said. His eyes met Sera's, a firm look there that promised no danger would come to her. Sera nodded and accompanied Gummy inside while Barrington spoke to Lucas.

A light mist of smoke shrouded the circular parlor, scented almost too sweetly of vanilla, as though to mask another smell. A shiver rustled Sera's frame, the coldness of the space lending itself to her morbid deduction that it was Death they sought to hide. Portraits of naked women lounging on settees hung in gold frames along the maroon walls. The women strewn about the room were not much different, dressed in sheer robes with next to nothing at all underneath. Women whom, upon closer inspection, were all pale and beautiful. There was something about them she couldn't quite place. The men they enamored wore dazed, unfocused expressions, their frames gaunt and tired as though their lives had been sucked out of them.

One man by the bar sauntered over, a lazy smile on his thin lips. "What's this, Gumm-o? You didn't tell us you had a new one." He tilted his head and appraised Sera slowly. "Ain't been used too much, I see. I can help with that." He reached for Sera's arm.

She jerked it back. "Remove yourself from before us, *sir*, or I'll remove your hand from your arm. The choice is yours."

"Ah, fiery." He grinned. "I'll be sure to teach you how to talk to a man, among other things." He made to reach for her again, but Barrington appeared and clutched the man's arm.

"Is there a problem here?" His gaze was fierce under his top hat, a look Sera would never want to be on the other end of.

Gummy swayed before the man. Breasts pressed against his chest, she trailed a hand along his jaw. The other she used to pull his arm from Barrington's hold.

"Come now, Tobias," she purred, her lips brushing against his with each word. "I suggest you listen to her, or the gentleman she's with will surely remove your arm altogether. Now, why don't you go find one of my girls?" She patted his cheek like a puppy and, as such, he walked away with no further argument.

Gummy smiled over her shoulder and winked. "Nothing beats a little womanly persuasion."

"I'm sure," Sera muttered. A hand came onto her lower back. She jumped and made to turn, but Barrington kept her fixed, his hand splayed there. He nodded once, and she knew his hand at her back was a sign to all that she was, for all intents and purposes, spoken for. She followed behind Gummy, thanking the heavens for her veil that hid her fierce blush.

They went out the back door of the brothel. Just across a gated alleyway was another building, a one-story gray edifice with no windows and a burly man at the entrance. He stepped aside and inclined his head.

"Gummy, Professor, Miss."

Barrington patted the man's shoulder in passing. "Good to see you again, Brutus."

Sera nodded her hello, glad to be in Barrington's company. Brutus didn't look like a man you crossed, his frame double Barrington's size. A white sleeveless shirt revealed boulder-like muscles, an anchor tattoo on one arm, and a scantily clad woman on the other.

Once inside, they encountered another room, this one shielded by a thick velvet curtain. Through a narrow slit, Sera saw it to be more of a storage area. Long boxes and crates were stacked throughout. They didn't enter but walked beside the curtain to a flight of stairs.

"Your friend is this way." The rickety stairs squeaked under their weight as Gummy led them down and into the damp basement. There was one room in the open space, crates stacked along the walls. The door to the room was closed and another muscular man stood before it, taller than the last.

Gummy stopped short before him and turned. "Whether this is the man or not, our deal still stands, Barry."

"Barrington," he said, "and yes, it still stands. It will be ready by the end of the week."

She pursed her lips and nodded over her shoulder. The guard turned the knob and opened the door. A man sat in the middle of the dark room, gagged and bound to a chair under the halo of a single hanging lantern. He lifted his face, and a chill washed down Sera's body, comingled with a furious wave of heat.

"I take it that's one of the men from the forest," Barrington confirmed. She nodded, her hands tense. Half of her wished to reach for her wand and set him on fire, the other half warred for control, knowing this man had answers they needed.

Barrington cleared his throat and closed the door, cutting off her view of him. A different air swept over him, an eerie calmness as he put his hand on her back once more and ushered her upstairs.

"What are you doing?" she asked as Brutus opened the door and Barrington guided them out. "Aren't we going to question him?"

Without a word, he marched forward, steering them back through the brothel and outside to the carriage. Sera stopped short and snatched herself away. "We can't leave. It was him. I'm sure of it. He was there."

Barrington jerked open the carriage door, his mouth set hard and frame rigid. "We aren't leaving, Miss Dovetail. I will question him while you stay here with Lucas."

"I'm not staying behind. I have as much right to be in there as you." He spun to leave, but she gripped his arm and stayed his retreat. "You promised there would be no secrets between us, and yet you ask me to stay here? Why can't I be there when you question him?"

"You can." He turned steeled eyes down at her, a piercing vulnerability there. "But I fear you will no longer see me in the same light if you do."

She lowered her hand from his arm, all words caught in her throat. Before she could ask why, he strode inside and vanished into the smoke.

Lucas opened the carriage door, and Barrington entered. Part of Sera wished to interrogate him the moment he settled in, but violence radiated from his frame, his demeanor tense and stiff. His cloak was off-kilter, his shirt peeking out from beneath his vest, and his hair tousled and wild. A handkerchief was wrapped tightly around his hand, dots of blood staining the fabric. Sera swallowed her questions, unable to find the courage to speak them. Not to *this* Barrington. This wild and fallen man was not *her* Barrington.

He rested back against the seat slowly—too slowly— then lowered the curtain and didn't say a word. He acted as if she wasn't there. As if she didn't exist. But Sera realized, he didn't even see her. Caught in his mind, he focused straight ahead, staring at nothing at all, his fists clenched tightly on his lap and his breaths eerily measured, as though he sought to force himself back to normal. Back from the beast she knew had emerged the moment he'd left her.

A sick feeling overcame her, and she curled into herself. Whatever happened in that room was not a part of him he wished for her to see. Mindful of the changes in him, of the blood that stained his cuffs, Sera was half glad she hadn't.

Still, she slid from her seat and moved beside him. He'd been there for her when she hurt the Barghest, and now she would be here for him, too. She reached out and took hold of his hand. Barrington flinched, turning a feral gaze to Sera, and made to snatch back his hand, but she held it firm and met his look measure for measure.

After a moment, awareness washed over his stare, as if he finally realized it was she who touched him. He averted his stare but didn't fight her as she lifted one flap of the white fabric, then another. Pain twisted her heart, but she forced any reaction from her face as she beheld the cuts that split open the skin above his knuckles. He hadn't used magic to hurt the Brother, but his bare fists. Striking him over and over again.

Setting the blood-stained handkerchief aside, she slid her fingers over the wounds and closed her eyes. Having never taken her Water-level courses, all she knew of the healing art was what she'd learned from books and Mary. She never mastered healing gashes but did learn to soothe pain. Recalling these teachings, she cleared her mind of all thoughts and focused on comfort and healing. Instantly her magic took on a different feeling, a gentle warmth coursing through her veins. She guided it down to her fingers, and soon a cloud hovered over Barrington's hand, then was absorbed into his skin.

She slid her hand away. "I never learned to heal," she said softly, "but I hope it doesn't hurt you anymore."

Barrington looked at her, eyes still wild, but Sera noticed undercurrents of shame in his stare. He shook his head.

"Good." She folded the handkerchief back over his knuckles, moved across to her seat, and they spoke not a word about what happened.

22

the next man

The carriage stopped once more. Sera moved the curtains aside, confused, the ride much shorter than she'd remembered it. They weren't back at the manor but at an indistinguishable townhouse among a row of identical houses. She turned to Barrington, who had since relaxed, though he was still pale.

"What is this place?" she asked.

Lucas opened the door.

"It's where the men who hurt you were staying. The Brother we caught said they were all gone, but I suspect they fled in a hurry and may have left some evidence behind. I'll make sure all is clear and then signal for you." Barrington descended and, drawing his wand, eased the front door open and vanished inside.

Hands held tightly around the wand in her lap, Sera moved to the edge of her seat, her eyes fixed on the house through a part in the curtains. To ease her nerves, she opted to count the windows. There were four along the first floor, two whose curtains were half closed. On the second floor were three, a smaller one in the middle. Professor Barrington's figure came into view then, his light illuminating the first-floor room. He paced around the quarters and then exited. The window fell into darkness once more.

Sera blew out a breath. At any moment he would signal for her and they would investigate the scene. She bit her lip, hoping she could once again prove useful.

He appeared again, on the second floor this time, when a figure in white brushed past a first-floor window. Sera sat up, a sense of wrongness settled in her belly. She pushed the carriage door open and jumped down.

"Miss—"

"I saw someone," she whispered to Lucas, who quickly climbed down, "on the first floor, but the professor is on the second."

The gangly boy drew his wand. "Stay here and scream if you need help." He jogged toward the townhouse, then slipped in through the slit in the door. Within seconds, his outline became visible through the window as he inspected the first-floor room. It soon disappeared.

Nerves rattling at her core, Sera kept her own wand tight at her side. Professor Barrington had moved on to the room next door...and in the room next to him was a hooded figure in white. She gasped. Where was Lucas?

There was a chance Lucas knew the intruder was there, but clearly Barrington did not. Gathering her skirts, Sera ran for the house and squeezed through the partly open door. The dark foyer and first floor were in shambles, all drawers open and haphazardly emptied. Paintings were scattered about the floor, knocked from the walls whose wallpaper was also ripped. Spells were visible in the tears. Discarded trunks, books, and papers left a trail through every room she could see and up the stairs.

On tiptoes she ascended the stairs. Low muffled voices resounded from the room nearest the staircase—Barrington's and a woman's voices.

"...know more than that. Why play games when we're after the same thing?"

Sera peeked through the space in the doorway. The hooded woman stood behind Professor Barrington, her wand pressed firmly at his back. On her sleeve was the signet of a dove. Sera aimed her wand, all hairs on end. A Sister of Mercy.

"Tell me what he told—" The woman stopped, finally aware of Sera, who entered the room slowly, her wand aimed at the woman's head.

"Set down your wand, now," Sera demanded.

The woman turned her head slightly, a smirk on her thin lips. She had a willowy pale face, her whitish hair draped over slender shoulders. "I could disarm you while holding this wand at his back." Her gray eyes glinted with challenge.

Anger soured Sera's mouth, but she managed a grin. "I don't need a wand to kill you, believe me."

Their eyes locked, a battle of wills. Sera never wavered.

"Seems we've reached an impasse where you're outnumbered," Barrington said. He nodded his head to Lucas at the door that linked the rooms.

The woman sighed and let her wand tumble to the floor. Professor Barrington spun and kicked it away to Sera's feet.

"Would you like to question her here, or bring her with us?" Lucas asked, his fingers clawed into the woman's shoulders.

"My Sisters would not have sent me if they didn't think I could protect myself. I'm not here to fight," she said.

Barrington laughed humorlessly. "Is that so? And

threatening me with a wand at my back was your invitation to chat?"

She grunted as Lucas pushed her down onto a chair. A quick flick of his wand and he wound a luminous rope of magic around her wrists, waist, and ankles.

"All I want is to find out where the man who lived here has gone," she said. "I've been watching him for some time and noticed acquaintances of yours drag him away. I would very much like to speak to him."

Barrington leaned back against the windowsill. "I doubt he'll say anything more."

Sera looked to him. The same flash of anger swept over his features, but adjusting his waistcoat, he said, "However, nothing makes a preacher out of a thief like a man under the gallows."

The woman arched a brow. "Then how about we share tales? You wouldn't be here if you knew what they were after. But I know, and I will tell you in exchange for his location."

"I'm all for a trade, contingent on the value of your information of course, Miss…?"

She smiled, clearly not prepared to offer her name.

"Very well. He did mention a few things, namely that they were seeking members of your cult—"

"We are not a cult. We have existed longer than your precious Aetherium and Academies."

Barrington rubbed his chin. "What do you want with the vile creature who lived here?"

"He has information regarding something we value greatly."

"The Scrolls, I know." Barrington crossed his arms at his chest. "Seventhborns are dying, the men who lived here were responsible for their kidnappings and murders, and yet you speak to me of myths."

"Do I not sit here before you? Trust me, Professor. The Sisters of Mercy and the Brotherhood are very real. So are the Scrolls. I'm sure your father would agree."

Barrington slid a cold gaze along her face. "My father is dead. While alive, I admit he had a rather obsessive fascination with these tales—enough to have left him labeled a lunatic. Like him, *cults* such as yours have tried to find these supposed Scrolls for years and have met no success. Do you see why I have a hard time believing you?"

"Your disbelief is fear and nothing more. I think you're afraid to consider the truth for your own sake, and the sake of the memory of your brother and father—who was responsible for a great number of deaths, including those of many Sisters."

Barrington's mouth drew to a thin line.

"You speak in riddles. While the professor extends you the most patience, I myself have none," said Lucas as he tightened the binds around the woman's legs and arms. "Tell him what you know."

The woman's eyes narrowed, sending a chill down Sera's spine. There was no doubt she would kill them if given the chance. "I'll explain it all in exchange for the location of the man who lived here. Now an oath that you will give me the man's location."

Barrington mirrored her smile, a grin Sera could envision as the very devil's, just as cold and beautiful. "Don't insult me. I will not give you your wand to swear an oath. But I'm a gentleman, and you can trust my word."

She stared at Barrington, and he at her. Sera forced her hand to steady, the tension in the room heavy on her chest.

"I suppose I have no choice." The woman settled back. "There are many things that happened before our time that are not mentioned in your beloved books. Yes, when

Angus Aldrich's daughter, Freya, stole the Scrolls from her father, she ran away and never looked back. But it wasn't for the lies purported by your dear historians. She ran away because it was her father, Angus Aldrich, who wanted to use the spells in the Scrolls to obtain power over time. When she discovered what her father was doing, she locked him inside his mind with a spell, burned his research, and sought sanctuary with our order, the Sisters of Mercy. For years the Brotherhood sought her, scrying for her, but because of our wards and magic, they were unable to find her. However, Freya knew that once she died, a necromancer with enough power could summon her spirit. Once she grew old, she decided the only way to keep the spells safe was to use the Forgotten Spell."

Barrington hummed. "So once she told her secret, it would be wiped from her memory. Strong spell."

"Precisely. But since the spells in the Scrolls of the Dead were so powerful, she thought it too risky for one person to have them all. She chose seven Sisters of Mercy and appointed each a spell, thus creating the Keepers. Once they memorized their spell, they took a blood oath never to write the spell again, never to try it themselves, never to tell the spell to another until it was time for them to pass it on to the next Keeper, and never to reveal the name of the next Keeper. In passing down the spell, they died for breaking the oath. Broken oath, broken life."

Sera sucked in a gasp. Isobel had uttered those same words.

"These Sisters scattered around the world, protecting the spells with their lives. They carried on this tradition of passing down the spell, forever ensuring it was safe. Over time, the story grew to a myth, but then a Brother arose who once again sought the spells. He breathed new life into the Brotherhood movement, radicalized them with Purist ideologies, and they waged their war against us. We protected Freya's grave, but we were outnumbered against their black magic."

"Why not burn her body?" Sera ventured. She hated asking, but Barrington said they were in this together, and she had to know.

"It untethers the soul from the body and makes it easier to summon. A skilled necromancer could then trap the spirit within another body or object. With a body intact, the necromancer must use the bones to summon the spirit. It's a good way to protect someone in death," Barrington explained, his gaze trained on the Sister.

"Ah, so you're familiar with necromancy. Why am I not surprised? You are your father's son, after all."

Barrington's jaw tightened. "You were saying…"

She sighed. "Yes, yes. He siphoned magic from hundreds of seventhborns in order to summon Freya. You might know this as the beginning of the Persecutions."

Barrington scoffed. "Lovely tale, but fear of plague was the reason for the Persecutions, not necromancy or black magic."

"Or so your books tell you. Necromancy was still an underground magic during those times; no one knew the effects of it. I'm sure you've seen what happens to a witch drained of magic, the rotting skin and emaciated bodies?"

Sera shivered, remembering her own gaunt appearance at Noah's hand.

"When body after body of dead seventhborns began to appear, people grew frightened. They thought it was yet another curse placed on seventhborns and, unless they eradicated them, it would soon spread to other magicians. The Patriarch at the time called for all seventhborns to be killed, and it proved very convenient for our necromancer. He had his choice of seventhborns to syphon. Eventually he amassed enough power to summon Freya and learn what she had done."

Sera's jaw clenched, her hand tight on her wand. The longer a soul was dead, the more magic was needed to summon it. He must have used hundreds of innocent seventhborns whose only crime was their birth order.

"Thankfully Freya wasn't able to tell him the spells, as they had been forgotten when she passed the spells on to the Keepers, but they did find out who she appointed as Keepers. Since then, they have been trailing the line of Keepers, using seventhborns to raise body after body, and here we are today."

Sera's blood ran cold, and she glanced at Barrington. Though stoic, his eyes betrayed him; his faraway look told Sera he was putting together the pieces of this horrid puzzle. The murders, the Brotherhood targeting powerful seventhborns...

"How many Keepers have they found?" he asked.

"Isobel was the sixth. There is one left."

"Dear God," Sera whispered, breathless at all the pieces coming together in her head.

"Now you see why I must find this man. If they were desperate enough to infiltrate the Academy and hunt down a powerful seventhborn, then it means they know the location of the next body or are close to it." She settled back. "That's all I'll share. Now it's your turn."

Barrington straightened, a fiery determination in his stare. "A deal is a deal, Sister. The man you seek was a pile of ash the last time I saw him, ashes that have been scattered into the Lore River. Best of luck to you in finding him." He whirled, slipped on his hat, and motioned for Sera to exit.

She moved out of the room, his words ricocheting in her mind, tangled with the memory of his bloodied cuffs, of his controlled fury. She had been right; he had been wild and fallen. Death incarnate.

"You bastard," the Sister said through gritted teeth. "What of my binds?"

"You should've thought about that before you shoved your wand to my back, threatened my assistant, and insulted my father."

She grunted, struggling against the binds. "We had a deal!"

Barrington paused at the door. "We did. I said I would tell you where the body was — well, what's left of it, anyway. I never said I would release you. You said your Sisters wouldn't have sent you if you didn't know how to protect yourself. Prove them right."

The ride back to the house was quiet, the only sounds the crunch of rolling wheels and hoofbeats on the turf and the faint tinkling of harness bells. The heavy, unsettling silence surprised Sera, considering all they had learned. But however much she wished to discuss things, one look at Barrington told her it wasn't the time. He sat in the corner of the carriage, his mouth bowed to a frown, staring out the window as the city gave way to shadowy forests that then thinned to moors stretching into the darkness. The faraway look in his eyes told Sera he saw none of it. Wherever his mind carried him pulled down his brow and darkened his stare. His mood made the shadows in the carriage appear darker and the space smaller, or so thought Sera, who stifled a sigh of relief when they arrived at Barrington's home and

Lucas opened the door.

Snapping from his brooding, Barrington exited the carriage and held out a hand to her, helping her down. She walked a few steps toward the house, but noticing Barrington did not follow, she turned to find he spoke to Lucas, though she could not hear what was being said.

Sera curled into her cloak and stared out to the moorlands. The stillness was fierce, somehow heavy and crowded, alive and ominous. The snow on the ground had since frozen to a blanket of jagged and cracked crystals, stifling all heather and undergrowth. The land was feral, untouched and dangerous to those unknowing how to navigate it. Sera glanced at Barrington; the land was so much like the man who owned it.

Barrington approached her, but Lucas did not leave.

"I won't be coming in. There is something I need to do," Barrington said, his gaze fixed on the moorlands behind her.

"Shall I come tomorrow or await your call?" Sera asked. They had so much to discuss.

"Yes, wait for my note. We must find where the body is first."

"What do you intend to do?"

He sighed, a cloud of white gathering at his mouth before vanishing. "I'm not certain yet, but I must go."

To Gummy surely. A strange twinge nudged her heart, and helplessness answered back. The thought of him finding solace in that place—with that woman—bothered her in the strangest of ways. But she nodded. He was adrift and in need of an anchor. And if Gummy was his anchor, what could Sera possibly do?

"Of course. Good night, Professor." She turned away, hoping he didn't sense the vast disappointment that swelled in her chest.

Barrington took hold of her hand, his fingers tightening about hers and drawing her back.

She turned to him, her pulse quick. But he still did not look at her, rather at her hand within his.

"What I did tonight was inexcusable," he started, his voice low and weak against the soughing breeze. "I lecture you on self-control, and tonight I had none. Forgive me. If what I've done disgusts or scares you..."

He released her hand and never finished the phrase, though the words echoed loudly between them; if what he did disgusted or scared her, she was free to leave. His eyes remained downcast, shadowed by his top hat, and his frame rigid. Bracing.

A knot birthed in Sera's throat, the desire to hold him like electric currents skimming her skin. She forced her hands to remain at her sides. It wasn't her place to touch or comfort him...and yet, here he was, once again, asking for her forgiveness. Warmth spread through her, melting away her indecision. Her forgiveness meant something to him. And however little or much, she meant something to him, too. It *was* her place to comfort him, one she had somehow earned in his life, and she would not vacate it so easily again.

She reached out and touched his arm.

Barrington lifted his eyes to her, and she couldn't find another breath. Shame swelled in his stare, and so much pain.

She shook her head, barely. "He was the monster, not you."

He stared at her—truly and fully, as though he sought her soul. "Thank you."

Although the cold cut through her layers and bit into her skin, a fierce blush pricked her cheeks.

A gust wheezed past and blew a strand of her hair onto her lip. He lifted a finger to her face, stroking the tress away. His hand lingered on her cheek, and Sera's stomach knotted, his closeness and the rise and fall of his chest a reel drawing her closer. The strangeness that enveloped them in his office emerged once more, fierce and burning. He sensed it, too, his gaze taking in every inch of her face. She saw the hesitation in his stare, felt it in his touch, to not leave her. To stay and discover whatever this was warming the space between them.

One of the horses whinnied, and Barrington blinked. Seeming to remember where he was, and who they were, he lowered his hand and moved away, the moment broken.

"I must go," he said, his voice hoarse.

Sera gulped, her next breath an agonizing chore. "Of course. Good night, Professor."

She turned to leave, a sharp pain jabbing her chest. Her body screamed for her to return to him, to discover more of the intoxicating warmth that had swathed them, but she forced herself forward. It was madness. Nothing good lay that way, not for her heart or for her dreams, however much she wished to discover it.

"And Miss Dovetail…"

She stopped and faced him, and her heart throbbed. Whatever existed before was gone, leaving Barrington to his sadness once more.

"What the Sister said about my father… He was a good man." He turned his head down and nodded, a weary gesture of someone with the burdens of the world on his shoulders. "A good man."

"I know, Professor."

He climbed back into the carriage, quickly vanishing behind the shadows within. Lucas mounted and spurred the three black stallions.

"I know," Sera whispered to herself, watching his carriage leave the gates. And though he said it to her, she entered the house and wondered whether he said it to convince her or himself.

necromancy

Ten days felt like an eternity…until another note requested
her presence. Sera watched it burn in her hands, cursing
her heart that instantly forgot its function. She'd promised
herself his touch that night had meant nothing, neither had
his lingering gaze, regardless of how the feel of his fingers
lived on her skin in their days apart. Shaking it off, she
moved to the corner of her room and transferred to his home.
Matters of the heart had no place between them. She would
focus on her dream and nothing—not even a handsome
professor and his kindred sorrow—would sway her.

When Sera arrived, Barrington was not in his office,
rather Rosie who tidied up the workroom.

"He went out last night, but I never know when he's in
or out. For all I know he's holed up in that room of his." She
waved her duster airily toward the black door. "Sometimes
he'll vanish in there for days at a time."

Sera eyed the door keenly like one able to stare through
to the other side. "What's in there?"

Rosie shrugged and finished dusting the telescope by the window. "Never been in there myself, to be honest. The last I saw of the room was when he dragged in trunks and trunks of his father's work. Research probably. Just as dedicated as his father. Other than that, I haven't a clue what goes on in there."

Something illegal, I'm sure, Sera thought to say but decided against it. Whatever orders he spoke of with Rowe and Gummy were none of her business. It would remain a mystery, both the room and the man.

"Ring if you need me," Rosie said and excused herself. Moments later, the door in question groaned open, and Sera startled. Barrington exited the room, fully dressed.

He stopped short at seeing her. "Good evening, Miss Dovetail."

A reply edged on her lips, but instead of answering, Sera scrutinized his gaze, searching for signs of the man who had stood before her the other night, his stare warm and touch gentle. Her heart dimmed. Though she was happy his sorrow from that night was gone, the man from that night was gone, too. She sighed. She had been right to push the thoughts of that moment to the back of her mind, and she would think no more about it, even if a little bitterness tinged her heart.

Barrington arched a brow in her silence. "Is everything all right?"

Sera cleared her throat and steeled her spine. "Yes, yes, everything is fine, Professor. I didn't know you were there. Rosie said she didn't hear you come in."

He closed the door behind him. "I got in quite early. Needed lots of rest for what we'll be doing."

"And what will we be doing?" she asked as he set a Gladstone bag on the worktable and opened it. There were some vials within it, filled with a blood-like liquid. "What are those?"

"What we are doing, Miss Dovetail, is going to Straight-water Cemetery," he said as he walked to the bookcase. He plucked out a book and thrust it into the bag. "It's a rather long drive, but that's where our next body is. I would transfer us there, but depending on what we encounter, our reserves may be too low for us to transfer back. I will not take the risk. As for those, they're blood vials used for healing—among other things."

Sera blinked. *Blood magic?* That was just as forbidden as necromancy, but she shook her head. Little should've surprised her about Barrington anymore. "Right. And what are we to do with this body?" She froze. "Surely you don't mean for me to raise it."

"Don't be ridiculous," he called out from the pantry. He exited with a handful of candles and set them in the bag. "You will not be raising any bodies."

She hefted out a sigh. "Good—"

"I will."

"What?"

He took inventory of the bag while Sera looked to him expecting—hoping—to find jest on his face. He shut the bag and surveyed his notebook.

Sera sank onto the stool, her heart in her stomach. "You can't do this. You heard what happens. Once the spirit tells its secret, you'll burn and die." She crossed her arms, mulish. "No. That's beyond all bounds. You may be my superior but… but you're not raising that body."

He paused in his work, a smile on his lips.

"You're smiling?" she asked under a narrow gaze. "How is any of this amusing?"

"You're worried about me."

She opened her mouth and then shut it, a blush prickling her cheeks. "After all I said—that you can *die* in doing this—

all you gathered is that I'm worried about you?"

His smile widened, and her hands clenched tighter. "I'm flattered that you worry for me, Miss Dovetail, but it must be done, and I'm the only one who can do it."

"I would fear for anyone doing this, because it's mad and dangerous, and it fazes you not in the slightest."

He stuffed the notebook into his inner pocket. "We have no other choice. We need to know who the next Keeper is before the Brotherhood or the Sisters of Mercy discover it. I must raise this body, and you will keep it from killing me."

"How? I'm not trained in healing. Quite lousy at it, to be honest. You've seen my file."

"I'm not talking about healing. When I raise this body, I must create a connection by touching it. The spirit will fight me, but it's not my first summoning from the Underworld. I can handle it for a slight longer to gain its secret. The moment it breaks its oath and tells its secret, you must snatch my hand from the body. This will untether the soul from me before it has had a chance to drag me into the Underworld with it. Timing is of the essence. A few seconds is the difference between life and death." He smiled, a perfect row of white teeth. "Easy enough."

Sera's mouth gaped, a series of words garbled in her throat.

With a quick rake of his hair, he slid on his hat. "Ready?"

"No. No, I'm not *ready*. How can you be so calm? What if I can't save you?"

He grabbed the Gladstone bag. "If I had any doubt in your ability to do this or anything else I've ever asked you to do, I never would've requested you help me." He held her veiled hat out to her. "If there's anyone capable of the most dangerous tasks, it's you, Miss Dovetail, and I trust you with my life."

At any other moment, these words would have meant the world to her, yet she gazed down to the hat and wavered. She was his only protection against losing his life, and that chilled her soul. But she accepted the hat and slipped it on. He'd asked her. Not Gummy or Rowe, but her. She would pass this test and keep him safe, come the Brotherhood or the Underworld itself.

Straightwater Cemetery came into view in the distance, a seaside burial ground seemingly as abandoned as the bodies interred there. Feathery weeds trembled in the gusts that swept in over the water. The ocean roared and forewarned the imminent storm blackening the sky. Sera pulled down the brim of her hat, the hairs at the back of her neck on end. She'd been taught the importance of omens. Taught to heed them as a magician's connection with nature. While divination was her worst subject, this intuition squeezed her belly. They shouldn't be there, and every fiber within her knotted at this fact.

Barrington, however, read over his notes at ease. If the weather was an omen, it eluded him altogether. Either that, or he simply didn't care.

"How did you learn to do necromancy?" she asked, desperate to add sound to the terrible silence between them. Anything to drown out the violent crashing of waves underscored by rumbling thunder in the distance.

"When I was younger, my father tried to recruit me into his studies on the Brotherhood and Purists, but I was more interested in other…aspects of magic."

"Black magic."

He nodded. "I wanted to understand it, to see what was so evil about it. It all seemed to be a matter of self-control to me, like wandless magic. My mentor taught me in all of the branches of magic, the basics of necromancy being one of them. Alchemy, however, became my passion."

Sera meant to ask why, but the carriage stopped.

There was but a half-moon in the sky, and the night favored deeper shadows. A mist hovered around the cemetery like a spell meant to keep the souls prisoner behind the rusted bars.

Sera surveyed the sacred land where tombs looked more like sleeping monsters, the moss strangling the headstones the dried blood of their victims—those who dared trespass and disturb their rest. The stillness was tense, and she curled into her cloak.

"Why couldn't we have had the body taken elsewhere?" she muttered.

"Unlike the beasts that commit these crimes, I have respect for the dead. I'm already waking them from their slumber, but to also desecrate their place of rest?"

She rubbed her arms. "I suppose. I've never been fond of cemeteries, especially not now that I can see the dead."

Barrington grinned at her as he pushed aside the run-down wrought-iron gate. "Fear not, Miss Dovetail. If you see a soul and wish for it to leave, command it to go. As for the bodies here, they can't come back to life—save for the one we'll be raising, of course."

She rolled her eyes and, with the lantern held before her, ducked in through the small entryway he managed to create in the gate. "I'm glad you still have a sense of humor."

A path of cobblestone damaged by time and vegetation led through the maze of headstones, broken pillars, and wingless angels. Beyond the fence, jagged rocks marked the shore. In the shadows there were more stone monsters in wait, either protecting the dead from those who sought to plunder their graves or protecting the sea from spirits who wished to escape death and run into it.

"The one we seek is this way, closest to the sea I was told." He climbed down a small, crumbling hill and offered a hand to her. "Her name is Georgiana Egerton."

Sera accepted his help, but the ground beneath her gave way, and she tumbled forward. Barrington's arms came around her waist, a firm hold that kept her upright and warmed her in an instant.

"Miss Dovetail, are you all right?"

"My foot was tangled in my skirts." She broke away, thankful for the veil that hid her blush. "I'm amazed they found her so quickly."

"The Brother spoke quite a bit before his death. We had her name, and with a bit of help, some of Gummy's sources were able to track her down."

"Good thing she has a lot of friends," Sera muttered into a passing gust.

"Pardon me?"

"I said how can we be sure it's her?" she lied as he continued forward.

Barrington stopped before a crumbling, mossy tombstone, a stone dove perched atop. "The bird is a good indication."

Sera shone the lantern to the headstone. "So is the name." Georgiana Egerton was carved into the stone, as was a dove surrounded by the seven elemental signs.

Barrington knelt before his bag and took inventory, then pulled out a worn leather book. Untying the straps that kept it closed, he opened to a page somewhere in the middle and handed it to Sera.

She lifted her veil to get a better look. There was a

protection circle, but around the border was another spell. "What are these outer ciphers?"

"An unearthing spell. Fastest way to dig out the body. Once done, aim your wand and ignite the spell using the word 'exhume.'"

"Whatever happened to no magic for personal gain?"

"Would you prefer to dig her out by hand? If so, then ladies first."

Eyes narrowed, she snatched her wand from its holder. "How chivalrous of you."

Barrington gave her a side-eye glance, a grin at his lips. "I try."

Scoffing, she bent over and traced out the symbols on the ground, the protection circle always first. Any spells performed within its borders were under her domain. Once the spell was completed, Professor Barrington came alongside her.

"Very good. Now, ignite the spell."

She aimed her wand to the ground. "Exhume."

The earth above the grave began to churn and sucked under all overgrowth. Slowly, the ground parted. Dirt rolls folded over and over as though invisible hands parted the dirt to either side. Depth developed until a wood coffin was revealed in the hole.

Barrington slipped off his coat and draped it over the headstone. Black candles in hand, he sat on the edge of the grave and jumped down. Thunder rumbled in the distance—a dire warning, or so Sera imagined. But it was too late to turn back now.

The coffin snapped open with a flick of Barrington's wand. The gray, gaunt corpse lay within, insects skittering through the various facial holes. A large beetle crawled into a vacant eye socket and Sera shivered, feeling as though it scuttled along her skin.

Once the candles were arranged strategically around the corpse, Barrington knelt beside the coffin.

"Good luck, Professor," Sera called down, her voice jagged.

He met her eyes, the reflections of the candles little lights at the cores. "*Shallow men believe in luck or in circumstance,*" he quoted. "*Strong men believe in cause and effect.*"

She frowned, and he rewarded her with a smile.

With the corpse's emaciated hand in his, Barrington pressed his wand to his wrist and murmured words out of Sera's hearing. White bands of magic twisted from his skin and wound about the corpse's bony arm.

"Follow the path of light to life," he called. "Awaken, I command thee."

The winds about them died, though the storm loomed much closer than before. This new stillness pressed down harder, and the shadows around them deepened.

"Follow the path of light to life," he called again. The bands of magic tightened. "Awaken, I command thee!"

A strong blow whipped past and devoured all warmth. Sera wrapped her arms about herself. If only it could keep her thunderous pulse steady.

Barrington closed his eyes, his brows dipped in concentration. "Follow the light to life…"

A skeletal arm flicked. Then a foot.

"Awaken, I command thee!"

The corpse crackled as it turned its head, folded at the waist, and sat upright. Sera shivered, her joints tense and hand tight around her wand.

The cadaver took in a deep breath that rattled its chest bones like tapping fingers, then exhaled. The whispery breath whisked past Sera like a frigid breeze, and the temperature dropped. The hairs on the back of her neck stood on end. Though wearing a warm dress and cloak, the cold seeped beneath her clothing and bit her flesh—an unnatural physical sensation, as if spirits dug their skeletal hands into her skin, desperate to worm inside her body and possess her. She sucked in a breath and spun, aiming her wand, but found no one there.

The corpse inhaled again, and with each crackling cycle of breath, rime crept over the ground and the walls of the grave, suffocating and devouring the earth under its hellish crust. Sera shifted back, lest it crawl up her legs and into her pores, sucking the life from her limbs and magic from her soul until she, too, withered into a gray and gaunt skeleton.

Barrington winced, the back of his vest damp with sweat. "Miss Egerton, a pleasure."

The skeleton's mouth rattled, but no sound came out.

"Ah yes, you will be granted the ability to speak, but first, you're forbidden from cursing me or using any spell against me. You will answer all of my questions with only truth, after which I agree to release you to your eternal rest."

Miss Egerton nodded, jerky movements that sprouted goose bumps along Sera's arms.

"Very well. Thank you, Miss Egerton—"

"Sissssster Egerton," replied the corpse. Her voice echoed unnaturally, a ghostly whisper. Sera surveyed their surroundings, sure other spirits had materialized to repeat her words.

"Oh, of course, forgive me. A Sister of Mercy, yes?"

The skeleton's head jutted up and down. *Crack, crack. Crack, crack.*

"I've been told you were the previous Keeper of a spell that has since been passed down to a new Keeper."

Sister Egerton turned her head to Barrington, empty

sockets boring into him. "Oath of blood…not broken in death."

"I understand, but…" Barrington cut off with a hiss. A droplet of blood streamed from his nose. He whipped out a white handkerchief and dabbed at the blood. "But you need to tell me who the next Keeper is."

The corpse thrashed its head side to side, stringy black strands like a whip to the air around her. Barrington shut his eyes tightly and pulled his shoulders in, groaning through clenched teeth. A drop of blood trailed from his ear, streaming down along his jaw.

"Professor?" Sera inched into the grave.

"I'm fine, stay where you are," he told her with some difficulty, his frame heaving with each breath. "Tell me who the next Keeper is. I demand it."

Her entire body rattled this time. "Oath of blood. Oath of blood—"

A crackle resounded in the distance, followed by the familiar blast of magic crashing against magic.

"Professor!" Lucas screamed from afar. "They're here!"

Sera straightened just as a hooded figure emerged from the shadows up the path and speared a flare of magic at her. She ducked and dove back, and the orb crashed against the headstone behind her. A rain of stone exploded into the air and grave.

Sera winced; a current of pain shot down her shoulder that had collided against a neighboring stone slab. Digging her fingers into the frigid earth, she tried to crawl back toward Barrington, but another flare struck the earth before her, then picked it up like a wave. She rolled into the shadows and curled behind one of the headstones there. After a moment of hiding, she scurried behind the neighboring gravestone, hoping to get back to Barrington. Flashes of magic illuminated the ground around her with deafening cracks and explosions.

"Lucas, cover me!" she yelled and peered around the tombstone—

She screamed, another flash darting past her. It blasted against the body of a now-headless angel statue. Sera blindly aimed her wand and speared flares of magic. In the momentary diversion, she dashed behind another tombstone, then behind the mausoleum, sandwiched between the wall and the rusted gate surrounding the cemetery.

"Damn it!" she hissed. She'd been forced too far from Barrington, and he needed her! She had to sever his connection to Sister Egerton, or she could lose him forever. Magic thrashed within her, a feral heat prickling the underside of her skin. Her body trembled under its strain. She would burn them, all of them. But she had to focus to destroy these men, to save Barrington. He trusted her with his life, and she would not fail him.

"There are four now!" Lucas yelled from somewhere in the darkness.

Four. She would obliterate four.

She peeked around the corner. A Brother dashed between Lucas's flares of magic and ran toward the grave. Sera aimed her wand. The heat coiled in her belly pulsed, and a shaft of magic shot from her wand. The force of her power feeding through the new wand knocked her back against the gate. Her head collided with the iron bars, and a loud *snap* rang in her ears. Her flare of magic blasted into the Brother, picked him up, and slammed him against a tree. He crumpled lifeless to the ground, engulfed in white flames.

Groping the turf, Sera rolled out of the way as another orb of magic dashed above her. She pressed back against the mausoleum wall. There were four, but now there were three.

With her wand tight in her hands, she hauled in a breath and started around the corner.

A growl rumbled behind her and stole away the intent. She spun slowly, to a Barghest coming around the bend, tar dripping from its jaws, and its eyes full of hate.

24

the girl she once was

Lightning crackled the sky above. In the white flash of light, Sera noted scars along the beast's body. She'd recognize those marks anywhere, put there by her own hand. The Barghest froze as though cognizant of the same.

It stepped closer, and a growl reverberated deep in its chest.

"I had mercy on you," she whispered. "I let you live. I don't have to this time."

A low rumble rolled in its throat, but it didn't move. Neither did she. There was only exploding magic and the wild winds that thrashed and howled around them.

"Help me," she pleaded, "and I'll let you go."

The Barghest whined. It glanced back as though making sure no one was present, then stared at Sera, its eyes full of fear.

"Of course, they will kill you," she realized. "Then help me, and I'll find a way to free you. Please." Tears pooled in her eyes at the thought of Barrington burning to death at the hands of Sister Egerton. "I can't let him die."

The Barghest lunged.

Sera lifted a hand to attack, but the Barghest's claws clamped at her shoulder as he pushed her out of the way and dove past her. She flipped over and scurried back, but froze at the sight of the Barghest devouring a Brother who had come around the bend. The scaly beast turned red eyes to Sera, blood dripping from its sodden snout. It lowered its front paws and head.

"Thank you." She groped the wall and stood. "I need to get to the man in the grave. Protect me from the rest."

The Barghest sniffed, then whirled into a cloud of black and dashed around the corner. A roar echoed, followed by human screams. Sera peeked around the corner. The Barghest fed on another man, a feast of blood and magic. Pulse pounding in her ears, she shot blasts of magic for cover and ran for the grave.

A hooded man did the same but never made it, instantly engulfed by the Barghest's black cloud. Fueled by the man's subsequent screams, Sera lunged into the grave. Her shoulder jammed against the coffin, and she cried out, but the sound was swallowed by a cry from Barrington, who was slumped over the corpse. The binds of magic he had created were now hundreds of spider-thin wisps tying his body to the corpse. The links had cut through his vest and shirt and into his skin.

"Tell me the Keeper's name," he groaned. "I command you!"

Sera reached for his arm to break the bond—

"No! I'm close," he panted, teeth clenched against the pain. He coughed, and sprinkles of blood dribbled at his mouth. "I need this. Don't break the bond yet." He fell forward. One hand held him up, the other grasped tight about Sister Egerton. "Tell me the Keeper's name!"

The corpse writhed, its skeletal mouth clamping open and shut, open and shut. "*No, no, no, no,*" echoed its voice in the harsh wind.

Sera pressed against the dirt behind her, her wand clutched to her chest. Sister Egerton trembled, and Barrington grunted, another roar in his throat. "You will not rest...until you tell me... Who is the Keeper?"

The body averted its face, as though physically straining to keep the secret from him.

Barrington groaned, clasped the gaunt head in his hands, and forced it to look at him. "Tell me!"

The corpse fisted Barrington's shirt with its free hand and yanked him closer, whispering something Sera was unable to hear. She then brought him face-to-face with her. "*You break my oath, I break your life.*"

Sera gasped. "No!"

Their binds became fiery shackles that whipped around his body.

She screamed and reached for him, but a violent gust thrust her back against the dirt and kept her fixed, invisible fingers forcing her to watch him scream, burn, die.

"Release him!" Sera screamed, but the wind pushed into her mouth and throat and stole away her words.

A shadow swept above them. The Barghest materialized from the smoke at the foot of the grave. It whipped its tail down into the hole and around Barrington's waist. One firm yank, and it tore him from the skeleton's hold and out of the grave.

The winds died in an instant. Sera crashed to the ground, her knees weak. "Professor!" she screamed, clawing to climb out of the hole.

"Broken oath, broken life," clacked the corpse.

Anger waved through Sera's veins. She snatched her wand from the ground and pressed it against Sister Egerton's skeletal head. The body stopped trembling and turned its empty eyes up to her.

It tilted its head slowly. "The gates will soon be open. Black magic will cloak the world in blood!"

Sera thrust a blast of magic. The skeleton's head exploded into a cloud of ash. "You're released."

A face came into view above. Sera staggered back, her wand aimed.

"It's me, miss!"

"Lucas!" She stumbled over the coffin and reached up to his extended hand. He helped her scramble from the grave. A gash over his eye bled profusely, but she swept past him to Barrington's unconscious body sprawled out on the stone-riddled ground. Beside him, the Barghest ran its snakelike tongue along Barrington's burned arms.

"Leave him," she started, but Lucas took hold of her arm.

"He's devouring the magic to make him stop burning, but we need to get him back to the manor."

"Where are the vials? He said they would help heal him." She spun around, frantic, but the ground was windswept and the vials nowhere to be found.

"They're gone, Miss, but the horses are not too far—"

"The horses can't ride fast enough to save him! We need to use a transfer spell."

Lucas hesitated, shaggy hairs waving this way and that in the storm. Before he spoke, she snatched her arm from his hold and drew the transfer spell in the ground around Barrington, a bit wider to accommodate them all.

"I'll catch up," Lucas said. "I must clear the scene of the professor's things."

Sera nodded and gingerly eased the professor into her

arms. Heat radiated from his body, the smoke a humid sheet that dampened her skin. Her heart throbbed. Blood seeped from his burns and stained her hands as she held him. His weak breath touched her cheek, and she sobbed. He was alive, but would the next breath be his last?

She adjusted him to have proper use of her wand. "You stay with me," she whispered.

A low growl came from behind them. The Barghest nudged at Barrington's burned hand with a paw.

"I'll keep my promise, but I must get him to safety first," she said. "Come back with Lucas, and I'll find a way to free you."

The Barghest bowed its head and shifted back to Lucas's side.

Sera aimed her wand. "Ignite!"

The ciphers of the spell pooled over in red, a match to the intensity of her desperation. The red hue washed the world from around them, the ground from beneath them. And as they fell, she held him tightly to her chest and begged for him to stay.

Inexperienced. Inept. Invisible.

Slumped on a chair in the hall outside of Barrington's room, Sera focused on the in and out of her breath as the feelings repeated themselves in a horrible tide-like cycle.

Once they'd arrived at the manor and Rosie heard Sera's screams, she'd quickly run in. After her share of tears and gasps, she helped Sera get Barrington to his room. Instantly she began the healing spells, some of which Sera knew, others she didn't. Inexperience became a weight heavy on her chest, caused her hands to tremble and move slowly as it laced with ineptitude. She walked out of the room, wishing to be invisible, and allowed Rosie space and silence, though prepared to help where she could.

About an hour passed when the door creaked open and Rosie walked out, weary and worn. Her puffed white hair was matted under her cap, sweat a sheen on her skin. She closed the door behind her and hefted a long sigh. Sera stared at the woman in hopes to decipher something in her stance before she opened her mouth. The odds of him surviving were low, and she turned away, struggling for another breath. She would never forgive herself if anything happened to him.

"He's resting. I managed to stabilize him, but...the burns...he needs medicine I don't have. Lucas should've known this. What's taking him so long?" she asked, but Sera knew it was not a question she wanted answered.

Instead she rubbed at her bruised wrist, sore like her neck and arms and legs, and said, "Thank you. I..." Her voice broke. "I wish I could've helped more."

"Oh, my dear." Rosie gripped a wrinkled hand over Sera's shoulder. "You were a tremendous help. Forgive me if I was cross."

She shook her head. "I was in the way. Healing isn't my talent. A small cut, perhaps, but..." Emotion stole her voice away. "Will he be all right?"

Rosie's mouth flattened to a thin line, and her hand fell from Sera's shoulder. She paced past her and sat in the other chair. "We can only wait now, and pray, of course."

"Of course," Sera whispered.

The doorbell rang a high-low melody. She put her hand above Rosie's. "I'll get it."

Rosie deflated, grateful.

Gathering her hat from the table, Sera put it on, lowered the veil, and walked downstairs. The door slammed open before she reached it. Lucas burst inside with Gummy behind him, and behind them the Barghest appeared out of a black cloud.

"Where is he?" Gummy dumped her coat into Sera's arms—or chest, rather—and scanned the open space wide eyed and hair windswept.

Sera threw the coat onto the foyer table. "What are *you* doing here?"

Gummy ignored this and took the stairs two by two. "Rosie! Where is he?"

"You flesh-mongering, venomous hobby horse." Sera tore off her hat, gathered her skirts, and darted after her. "He's resting!"

"She can help him, miss. The Master would've wanted me to call her," Lucas explained from behind her.

"Rosie!" Gummy's shrills resounded from somewhere on the second floor.

Sera found the two of them on the third floor. Lucas attempted to explain what had happened while Gummy stood before Rosie, hands on her hips as she tried to get to Barrington's bedroom door. "Let me through. You know I can help. I'm probably the only one who can save him."

"She's right," Lucas rallied. "We have to give her a chance."

Gummy stared Rosie straight in the eyes. A secret conversation flashed there, to which Rosie stepped aside resignedly.

"No one's to disturb us," Gummy ordered and opened the door. Sera toured her eyes between the two women, but with a contemptuous smirk, Gummy closed the door between them.

Sera fisted her hands. "What does she think, snogging him to death will heal him?" she asked, but Rosie walked away without an answer.

Midnight found Sera sitting by the arched windows down the hall from Barrington's room. Night blanketed the moors and silenced the house. The Barghest was curled up on the floor beside her, and though its putrid scent of sulfur at first burned her nose, Sera welcomed its company. Anything to not be so alone. To not feel so guilty.

A flash of lightning shattered the sky into fragments of light and shadow. The Barghest lifted its head at the sound. The motion revealed the underfolds of its skin where something glimmered.

"What's this?" Sera eased from her window seat, knelt beside the creature, and lifted a number of its scales. Beneath the folds of skin was a collar, red rubies studded along it. Smaller ones encircled the Brotherhood emblem.

"Is this what keeps you tethered to your master? Will it free you if I remove it?"

The Barghest tilted its head to the side and revealed a buckle in confirmation. Sera unclasped the fastener and made to remove it, but the Barghest howled, its claws dragging and tearing at the carpet.

"Hold still," she started, but droplets of blood trickled from beneath the collar and stained the rug and her fingers. She cringed, noticing the spikes that pierced the Barghest's skin and held the collar fixed to its neck.

"Those bastards." She drew in a breath. "But it has to come off if I'm to keep my word. I'll count to three and pull it free at once. It will hurt, but you won't ever need to wear it again."

The animal whined, lowered its head onto her lap, and closed its red eyes.

"One…"

The Barghest bristled.

"Two—"

Sera pulled out the collar. The Barghest released a wild wail that echoed down the halls and surely through the entire house.

"There, there," she coaxed as it writhed on the floor, the carpet now in shreds. She threw the collar aside and neared the creature.

"What was that sound?" Rosie called as she hurried down the hall, vials in her hand. She stopped short at seeing the large beast. "What's wrong with it?"

"Are those for the professor?" Sera asked. "Do any of them help with pain?"

"They are, yes. I thought it was him who yelled." Wide eyes scanned the Barghest that squirmed with doglike cries. She looked to the disposed collar whose spikes still dripped blood and handed Sera a vial. "But here, pour it along the cuts. It will stop the bleeding and help with the pain."

Sera did as told and poured the elixir on the wounds. Whatever it was, smoke curled out from the cuts, and in its midst, the gashes slowly healed.

The Barghest settled.

"There," Sera whispered, stroking a patch of hair on top of its head. Within minutes, the Barghest had fallen asleep, though its body shivered with intermittent whimpers of pain. "You're free now."

Rosie picked up the collar and wound it in a rag she pulled from her apron. Blood seeped through, staining the white fabric. "Where did you find a Barghest of all things?"

"I had mercy on him some weeks before, and this time he had mercy on me and the professor. If not for him, the professor would be dead. The Barghest would have been killed by his master for saving him."

Rosie nodded at the beast. "I remember hearing stories about them as a child. Always thought they were so abused, torn from their homes to serve warlocks. A terrible existence."

The bells tolled, and Sera's heart dropped. It was only Thursday. How would she ever survive lessons? "I don't mean to impose, but I've nowhere to take him, and I need to get back to the Academy."

"I'll have Lucas take him out into the stables once he wakes up. He helped save the Master"—her nose reddened, as did her cheeks—"it's the least we can do."

Sera eased the beast's large head from her lap and rose. "Thank you for your kindness, and for before. Had it not been for you, I don't think the professor would have…" Her words faded.

"Nonsense. Lucas told me everything. You fought courageously. We're all doing our part to save him, and you've done yours. As for healing him, it's always hard to see someone you care about suffer. Sadly, I'm used to it. I have healed him more times than I'd like."

Sera nodded, unsure she could ever get used to it.

"Is he any better?" She gazed down the hall to the closed door—closed as it had been for the past two hours. "What is she doing in there?"

Rosie's shoulders lowered with a sigh. "Whatever it is, it's for the Master's best. But you should rest now, dear."

Sera reached out and clasped Rosie's hands in hers. "Rosie, please. I can't rest until I know he'll be okay."

The woman turned watery eyes down, her cheeks and

nose flushed. "He will be, once Miss Mills is done doing whatever she's doing."

"Then why are you so worried? Why were you so resigned to her helping him?"

She pressed her lips together and, releasing Sera's hands, sat at the window seat Sera previously vacated. She gazed at the blackness outside, her stare distant as though lost somewhere in the tangles of darkness on the other side of the glass. "When the Master's brother and father passed, the Master was in a bad, bad way."

Her mien dimmed, a deep brooding Sera had never expected from someone as kind as Rosie. "Somehow— maybe due to his desperation for answers or revenge over what had happened with his father and brother—Miss Mills and her blood magic found a way into his life. He began exchanging magic-laced blood in return for information... until one day, he began using it himself."

Sera slowly sat down beside Rosie, finally aware of the orders he spoke about with Rowe and Gummy. Cases of blood in exchange for extensive help in his investigations.

"Blood magic is exceedingly addictive, and the more one dabbles in it, the more humanity you lose until you become like one of those creatures in Miss Mills's establishment, exchanging favors and dignity to satisfy the blood thirst."

Sera blinked, readily remembering the strange women strewn along Mayson's smoky room, their skin pale. And not to mention the pungent stench of death that lingered there.

"It opens up a well of information and power, sure, but it's considered black magic for a reason. It darkens the soul. The toll to use it is incredibly high and a road I never want the Master to travel again." She brushed tears from her cheeks. "At times, I think he took it just to feel more powerful than his pain, so that sadness wouldn't dominate and devour him. But since he started working on this case—since he began working with *you*—he stopped using it. The withdrawals were agonizing for him, but he managed to overcome them. I was sure he was done with it once and for all, but it seems that the one thing that was close to destroying him is now the only thing that can heal him." She shook her head, defeated. "We can only hope that this time, his journey back isn't as hard."

Sera's heart stuttered, the truth of it all squeezing the air from her lungs. She remembered the day in his office, the thin sheet of sweat over his brow and the way his hands trembled as he graded his papers. His mood swings. He must have been experiencing withdrawals while they worked. And as she learned and grew in magic, he suffered in silence, willing to teach her so she could pass her assessments and protect herself against Noah.

Her soul hurt. He was getting better, moving away from blood magic. But now, because she hadn't severed the bond in time, he was tangled back in its web, fighting for his life in the arms of his addiction.

In spite of the blame that filled her, Sera set her jaw. "This time he has the both of us, and he won't fight it alone." She squeezed Rosie's hand. "I will do everything in my power to help him."

A sad smile tipped Rosie's lips, and she cupped Sera's cheek. "If you only knew how much you've helped him already."

Warmth bloomed in Sera's chest, and a twinge of pain answered back. If only she could believe Rosie's words. If only she could believe she had helped him and not brought him within a breath of death. *If only, if only, if only…*

Hurting more than she could bear, Sera moved her face away from Rosie's touch and stood. "It's probably best I get back to the Academy." Heaven knew no good came of wondering what was going on behind those doors, whether Professor Barrington was better or not, how none of this would have happened had she broken the bond sooner, regardless of what he'd asked of her.

She moved away from the Barghest so as not to waken it when she transferred back to the school. "Please keep me informed of any changes, or if you need me for anything. Anything at all."

"Of course." Rosie unsheathed her wand and aimed it at Sera's feet. "Good night, dear."

"Good night, Rosie."

The world fell black, and a moment later, Sera stumbled and gripped her bedpost for support. Right where she stood, she kicked off her boots and peeled down the stained, damp dress. Bits of mud, dirt, and rubble gathered around her. Muscles sore and aching, she would have relished her bed but she moved to her washstand instead.

Light reflected off the water in the basin. She squeezed the cloth and ran water along her arms and face, biting her teeth into her lower lip at the frigidness that magnified her pain. She rubbed harder at the cuts and bruises, washing away her blood. The Barghest's blood. Barrington's blood.

Unable to feel clean, she slipped her nightdress over raw and reddened skin and paced to the window. She paused in the middle of the room and spun around to her surroundings. After their night, the room seemed foreign, everything about the Academy unimportant. The bed, the mirror, the wardrobe, her books were things of little value, and she could not breathe being around them—around the possessions of the girl she once was.

The old Sera—*highly emotional, insubordinate, and confrontational*—would have gone against Barrington's direction and done things her way. She would have broken his bond with Sister Egerton even if he'd asked her not to. Would have told him he was an idiot for engaging in necromancy. Would have set the workroom on fire around him to keep him from going. Had it been the old her, she wouldn't have been swayed by his kindness and company, his apologies and desires—by *him*. She would be suffering his wrath, not the possibility of his death.

But it was too late. Dazed, she walked to the window and curled up on the seat. She stared into the distance as though able to see the moors there, and in the flashes of lightning, Barrington's home. When had she become *this* girl? With this thought in her mind, she stayed awake all night and raked her memories to find the girl she once was.

Come morning, the only thing she'd found was all the regret and pain in the world, and not an ounce of sleep.

25

held

Icy rains pelted the window, an angry pitter-patter and crackle that kept Sera company as she stared out at the moonless night. The door creaked open and stole her attention. Mary paced into the room.

"Again, Sera? You've barely slept a wink in a week. And I've noticed you've been rather pale and lethargic. Are you unwell?"

She blew her own misty cloud against the glass and wiped it away with a finger. "Too much to think about."

Mary followed her gaze out into the dark woods. "Are you worried about the men from the forest?" Only a select few staff members and Timothy knew about what had happened, but there was no way she could keep it from Mary, not that part at least.

She shook her head. "Not with the Aetherium guards here, no."

"Timothy, then?" She chuckled lightly. "I should've known. You have that lovesick look about you still. But he's safe. Don't worry for him, not with his father being who he is. Mr. Delacort will never let anything happen to his son. But if it'll make you feel better, I can write to him. My mother sent a scathing letter to his father after the dance, said she thought he had better manners than to lead a girl on and then break her heart. His father assured her he would speak to Timothy. It's the perfect opportunity."

Sera shrugged and leaned her head against the wall.

Mary's eyes narrowed, then widened, awareness dawning there. "But it isn't him you worry about, is it? You love someone else?"

"I don't love…" Her voice cracked. "I don't love him."

Mary leaned forward and clasped Sera's hands. "But there *is* another!"

Sera's fingers stiffened in Mary's, her heart sore at the memory of Barrington, of his scars, of his screams as Sister Egerton sought to burn him alive. Tears filled her eyes. If only she hadn't been so stupid.

She sighed, slipped her hands away, and curled her knees to her chest. "He isn't the type of man you love."

"But you care for him?"

"He's hurt in part because of me. Of course I care."

Mary's eyes dimmed. "Will you not at least tell me who he is? I'm a healer. Maybe I can help him?"

"I wish. I promise one day I'll tell you who he is, but for now I can't. Not until I discuss it with him. He's older, and his position doesn't allow for…well, me."

Mary meditated on this for a moment. "My first guess would be a professor, but we aren't ever in the company of any—not the amount needed to develop feelings such as yours. It must be someone you met recently, as I would've sensed it before."

She murmured through Sera's clues. "His position does

not allow for you and puts him in danger where he can get hurt…" Her eyes widened. "An inspector!"

Sera started to deny it but stumbled on her words. Barrington was an inspector, though a loose version of the word. And better for Mary to think it an inspector than a professor. "He is, but that's all I can say on the matter."

"Of course. It'll never leave my mouth. If anyone finds out about it, he may be taken off your case. We can't have that. But whoever he is, I'm sure he doesn't blame you for whatever it is that happened." She smoothed down her braid over her shoulder. "I do wonder what he's like. To have captured the heart of Seraphina Dovetail, he must be quite the catch."

Sera rolled her eyes. "He hasn't *captured* my heart."

"Fine, fine, but you don't need to be in love to appreciate beauty. Tell me what he looks like."

"You won't leave this alone, will you?"

Mary smiled widely. "Never. Let me live vicariously through you."

Sera rested her chin on her knees.

"Just one thing," Mary pleaded through her guilt. "Eye color, hair, height—anything!"

Sera plucked at the frilly hem of her nightdress. Maybe she could tell Mary of his hair. That was neutral enough. Or something ambiguous like his height. Yet gazing out to the cold, dark night, she said, "He has beautiful eyes. Not just the color, but everything that goes on behind them." As though conspiring against her, images of Barrington flitted through her mind. The way his anger made his eyes darker, his sadness dulled them, how his teasing grin made them glimmer just before he'd jumped down into that grave. Now they were closed, emotionless. She swallowed tightly. "That's all. He has beautiful eyes."

Mary pressed a hand against her heart. "See, this is why we're the best of friends. I've always been a fool for eyes — blue, gray, brown, green, a mix of them all! Oh, but I do love smiles, too. A nice, wicked smile."

Mary giggled, finally bringing a smile to Sera's lips — her first in days.

Sera leaned back and listened to her friend talk about all the boys whose eyes she loved, but Barrington's were the only ones Sera could think of.

Later the next evening, a letter swept under Sera's door, a familiar crest on the seal. Heart racing, she rushed to the door and snatched it open.

A doe-eyed servant girl skittered back, pale. "You're usually at supper now," she said, small hands gathered at her chest. "Please don't tell the professor. I promised I could deliver these unseen. I need this job, miss."

"I—"

"I support my family with what the professor pays me. He will recommend my sister to the headmistress and…please." The whites of her brown eyes glinted.

"You have my word; the professor will never find out. But you must tell me, is he back? Did he give this to you to deliver to me?" Her pulse quickened in wait.

The girl shook her head, and Sera deflated.

"It was his coachman, the tall, shaggy-haired boy," she said. "I've met him only on occasion before. He told me I was to deliver it to you as soon as possible."

"So then it's been you delivering all of the notes?"

She twined her fingers before her and nodded. "It was

the only way the professor knew you were alone when you received them."

Sera smiled. Of course. He couldn't have notes materializing out of thin air with the chance of Mary sitting there with her. She pressed the note to her chest. "Thank you. It was nice to meet you—and your secret is safe with me."

The girl smiled, though her eyes still pooled with worry. But with the note in her hand, Sera cared for none of it. She closed the door and tore open the paper where she stood.

Dearest Miss Dovetail,

His condition has not improved but thankfully has not worsened. He has been murmuring in his sleep, and I thought his words may be of some importance to you. Please come at your earliest convenience.

Yours sincerely,
Rosie

Barely a minute passed, and she stumbled into Barrington's study, then rushed from the room and upstairs just as Rosie closed the door behind her.

"Miss Dovetail." Relief washed over her visibly weary frame. Rogue hairs had slipped from her swept-up bun, and dark circles cradled her eyes.

"I got your letter. How is he?"

"Restless. He didn't stop talking all night, murmurs about things in his past, and things I've no idea about. I thought maybe you could make sense of some of it. I'm at a loss." She sat in the chair just outside the room. "He's settled down now, but it doesn't last for very long. I'm able to coax him when he speaks of Filip or his father, but everything else is a mystery to me. Perhaps if you know, you could talk to him and ease his mind."

"What things did he say?"

"He mentioned ravens and Keepers, and demands someone *tell him*. If he fights to get the words through, I figure it must be important."

Ravens, Keepers…tell me. "He's reliving the scene," Sera whispered.

"Reliving the what?"

"Nothing, Rosie, forgive me. Why don't you go on and rest? I'll watch over him and call if I need you for anything."

Rosie stared at the door and then back to Sera. "You have lessons in the morning, and I would hate to impose…"

Sera squeezed her hands. "You won't be able to care for him if you're exhausted. You said he's calm now, yes?"

She nodded.

"Then I will watch over him, and the next time he begins to get agitated, I promise to call for you." She released Rosie's hand, and her lips pulled to a strained smile. "Everything will be fine."

Reaching into her apron pockets, Rosie handed Sera five vials of dark red liquid. "Miss Mills said I am to give him this when he's in pain, but don't use it unless it's absolutely necessary."

She opened the door, and Sera's heart stilled. Professor Barrington lay on a large four-poster bed, a shadow of the man he once was. His head was cocked to the side, his eyes closed. A burgundy blanket was pulled up to his chest, but if his face was any indication of the state of the rest of his body… Sera let out a shaky breath.

She entered the room that was like him in every way, from the black curtains at the windows, to the dark furnishings, to the books and files scattered on any space that could support them. Just like in his study and his office, he surrounded himself with work. Work while at the Academy and work while at home, and even when with Gummy—it was work that appeared to link them together. That, she deduced, was his anchor. Moving from one case to another to another without a chance to breathe in between. Remembering his sadness when he looked at Filip's portrait, she accepted it was a good thing he worked so hard. It was a vast and deep sorrow, and if he drifted out into those waters, Sera was unsure he'd ever find his way back.

Rosie walked over to the professor and wiped a cloth across his forehead. Sera approached from the other side and pulled up a chair beside the bed. She laid a gentle hand on Rosie's and eased the cloth from her fingers with a smile. Rosie blew out a breath and, with no further argument, walked from the room.

Sera turned back to the professor, hands frozen in her lap. If being his assistant was considered improper, this would have labeled her a loose woman. She pulled the chair close to the edge of his bed and lifted the cloth to his forehead. Her seventhborn tattoo blemished her reputation more than any scandal ever could.

She brushed damp black strands from his forehead, a half smile tugging at the side of her lips. "If Mary only knew," she whispered. What Mary wouldn't give for a chance to watch over the stern professor. To nurse him back to health.

She considered him with each stroke along his pale face. He was handsome, there was no denying that. Not like Timothy, where it was in the open for everyone to see. Barrington's beauty was as sharp as his features, buried deep behind his scowl. Anyone who dared look beyond his glower would see it, but she wondered if he'd ever want it to be found. His frown and attitude said otherwise. It was as if he wore it to intentionally keep everyone away...as though he didn't deserve them, as if he felt he didn't deserve to be cared for.

"Why did you have to be so damned stubborn?" She blotted the cloth over his cheeks and under his eyes. "I should've convinced you not to raise that body."

His chest lowered with a long exhale. "Body," he murmured. "Tell me."

"What would you like me to tell you?" She set aside the cloth and eased closer. "What would you like to know, Professor?"

He turned his head away, wincing. "Tell me."

Sera blinked. If he was reliving the scene in his mind, maybe she could use the Rhodonite crystals and cast out his memories the way Mrs. Aguirre had taught them in Mysteries of the Mind.

If they are merely unconscious, you can appeal to them, as their spirits can still hear you and allow you entry into their minds...

Sera slipped off her shoes, then rushed downstairs and into the pantry. There was a chance this wouldn't work, but it was worth the risk. With the Rhodonite crystals secured, she ran back to his room and bolted the door.

"If you can hear me somewhere in there, tell me what happened. We vowed there would be no secrets between us." She scattered some Rhodonite dust on his pillow and forehead. "I call upon that oath now. I need you to remember that night. Remember all that happened, right until the very end. Can you do that for me?"

"Keeper," he whispered. "Tell me."

"Yes, tell me." Unsheathing her wand, she removed the casing and held on to the narrow end like he'd taught her. She let out a steady stream of magic. The dust at his forehead illuminated, shading his face in a pinkish hue. He inhaled deeply and dragged in the smoky currents of her magic.

He exhaled, and Sera froze. His breath was now a white cloud, and in its midst were images. Each of his breaths joined a collective of clouds gathered over his body, his memories displayed within it for her to see.

The first scene she remembered, though it was from another angle. He gazed at her where she arched a brow at him. "How chivalrous of you," she had said, to which he replied, "I try."

The image of her smile faded and gave way to the corpse refusing him.

"*No, no, no, no,*" it clattered.

Barrington began to tremble in his bed. Sera forced her wand steady, moved beside him, and knelt on the edge of the mattress. "I'm here," she whispered. "Concentrate on your memories. She can't hurt you anymore."

He turned to her, his body tense with pain. In his memories, the skeleton came closer, opened its mouth, and uttered one name.

"*Timothy Delacort.*"

Sera gasped. Her heart pounded. It couldn't be. Timothy Delacort…a Keeper?

"*Broken oath. Broken life.*"

Barrington buried his face against her waist, digging his fingers into her side. She hissed in pain but forced herself to remain still as he unleashed a muffled roar against her. "Burn," Barrington groaned, writhing beneath the now-damp sheets.

"Shh," she coaxed and dragged back her magic. "You're all right now." She brushed the Rhodonite crystals from his face and pillows, her movements stiff, as he had yet to release her. "I've sent them away."

"Sera," he whispered. His hands eased from around her,

though not enough to release her.

"I'm here." She turned slightly and settled his head on her lap as his body shivered beneath the sweat-drenched sheets. "I'm here, and you're safe," she assured him, stroking his damp hair until his breath settled into the even rhythm of sleep. She drew up the blanket he'd kicked off and covered him with the thick fabric.

Leaning back against the headboard, she held him as he held her, hoping he knew, though unconscious, that in spite of his past, of what he believed, he deserved to be cared for, too.

Morning dawned to Sera pacing madly to and fro in her room. Barrington had fallen into a deep sleep after her spell and seemed to have finally found peace in his dreams. Now it was she who murmured, haunted by his memories.

How? How could the answer have been before them this entire time? Even the Brotherhood had the person they sought under their noses — more, in their hands — and they failed to see it.

She threw her wand onto the bed. The signs had been there. He'd said they both had secrets they wished they could erase. He'd told the Brotherhood he could help them find the Scrolls in exchange for her safety —

Sera froze in place. Revealing his secret would have killed him. He would have died for her. It was no wonder his father was so worried and hadn't allowed him back to school. He must have known Timothy was a Keeper. But the Brotherhood was getting too close, and he sought to ensure Timothy's safety.

And now Professor Barrington wasn't there to help her

with any of it.

The door opened, and Mary entered the room, face still puffy from sleep. "Good morning—"

"I need your help, desperately." Sera swept to the door, kicked it closed with her foot, and dragged Mary to the bed. Unable to keep still, she paced before her. "There is something I'm about to ask of you, something important I need you to do. I can't tell you much, but I swear I wouldn't ask for your help if it weren't important."

"You're scaring me, Sera…"

"I must speak with Timothy at once. Will you still write to him for me?"

Mary blinked. "Timothy? But I thought—"

"I need to speak to him, Mary. His life could be in danger if I don't."

Her eyes widened. "Danger? What? Why? Did your inspector tell you this? Tell me what's happening. I'm scared. Are you in some sort of trouble?"

"No, I'm not, but Timothy is if I don't get to him before—"

Mary paled. "It's the men from the forest, isn't it? What do they want with him?"

Sera sat down beside her, forcing herself to remain calm. "There's something he knows. Something they want and have been searching ages for, but he will die if he tells them. That's all I can tell you. Can you do this for me?"

"Of—of course. I will write him." She swept to the writing desk, snatched up Sera's quill and paper, and began the letter. "I'll tell him that I…that I wish to speak to him about the Solstice night. I'm sure he'll take any opportunity to learn of how you've been." She spoke as she wrote. "Is there anything I should mention that will clue him in to it being you who wants to see him?"

Sera weaved hands into her hair. "Tell him to meet you

in the room where he asked you if there was hope."

Mary's hand paused mid-stroke. "But he didn't ask me if— Oh! Very clever."

"Tell him that you changed your mind and want to discuss things with him again."

Mary wrote in haste and signed her name at the end. Folding the note, she rose. "I will have this sent to him right away, marked urgent. But please, stay safe." She strode to the door, but Sera stopped her and hugged her.

"Thank you for everything, Mary. I don't know what I'd do without you."

She smiled widely, though something of sadness clouded her eyes. "What are friends for?" Mary stuffed the letter into her cloak pocket. "I will meet you in class."

Sera closed the door behind Mary and leaned against the wood. There was no way she could survive class that morning. All she had the strength to do was to pray their letter would be enough to keep Timothy safe and that, after all she had done, prayers still worked for someone like her.

Forgiveness was granted her later the next day in the form of Mary bursting through the door. She held a letter up in the air, triumphant. She met Sera halfway into the room, and they both collapsed onto the floor. Mary tore open the Delacort seal.

My beautiful Mary,

It seems you've enchanted fate, as my father was out

when the postman arrived and the letter came straight to me. I've been thinking of you, constantly. Imminent exams or thoughts of a future hold little weight next to the future I hoped to have with you, a future I still think of. A future I will not give up on. I will meet you at our place and hopefully come morning, you and I will no longer be a dream.

I leave with you my heart and love,

Timothy

"Oh, Sera." Mary pressed the note to her heart. "Are you sure not one ounce of you can love him? Not even the edge of a nail or a strand of hair? These words are a dream."

Sera frowned and snatched the letter from her hands. "Focus, Mary. This is about keeping him safe. If it breaks his heart to know I lured him in, I will take all the blame, but I'm sure he will be happy to know that in spite of my deception, I've done it with his well-being in mind." She strode to the fireplace, but Mary intercepted her and snatched back the letter.

"May I keep it? One real love letter—a true love letter."

"Mary…"

"Please, Sera. If my mother asks, I can appease her with this. Give me this, please."

Sera looked to the letter in Mary's hands and nodded. It was the least she could do—give her this one taste of true love, even if only borrowed.

26

It Was You

Midnight dawned just as the girls reached the door hidden behind the Astronomy bookcase. Even in the dark, Sera discerned Mary's wide eyes and palpable excitement. Not to mention she declared it every other step.

"This is exciting and so romantic. I hope we're not caught," Mary whispered for the umpteenth time.

"We will be if you aren't quiet," Sera murmured over her shoulder.

"Sorry. I'm nervous. My heart is beating in my throat."

Sera stopped. "Are you sure you want to do this? After we enter the library, there's no turning back. If we are caught…"

"If we're caught, I can pretend it was me who snuck out and you were trying to get me to turn back. The headmistress will be much more lenient with me than you." She nodded, determined. "You need me here."

Sera let out a breath and pressed her wand to the wall. "Very well. By the stars."

The door clicked, and the bookcase opened. Sera peeked inside, keenly focused on the long shadows cast by the threads of silver moonlight. The library was, for the time being, empty. She ushered Mary inside and through the aisles to the Ethical Magic section. She touched her wand to the books there. "Right above all else."

The bookcase creaked open. Mary took firm hold of Sera's hand and squeezed inside. Sera rushed in behind her but bumped into her best friend and ricocheted back against the now-closed bookcase.

She rubbed at where her head had collided with the wall. "Goodness, Mary, why did you stop—"

She cut off. A hooded figure stood in the alcove before them, its shadow a monster against the wall. Sera's hand flinched to her wand.

"Cool it, Dovetail." Whittaker lowered his hood. "Timothy asked me to escort you down to the tunnel."

Sera shifted before Mary. "Why should we trust you?"

He shrugged wide shoulders. "How else would I have known he plans on meeting you two here? Now can we go? I've done enough to make sure we aren't caught. I made a huge mess in the potions laboratory, the rectory, and the greenhouse. The servants were called to clean it up, so these halls will be clear for now. If you hurry, we can be in and out in no time."

Still, she lingered. Mary looked to her, awaiting their next move. "Why are you doing this?"

"I may have no allegiance to you, but Timothy's my friend." He cast a quick glance up and down the hall. "Besides, if I do this for him, I won't need to worry about the Aetherium entrance exam. He will make sure his father signs off on my entrance papers. Seems like I'll be an inspector before you, Dovetail. Who knows, maybe one day you'll be working under me."

He winked, and bile rushed into her throat. The boy was a parasite. "Let us hope not. Lead the way."

Wand at his side, he spun to the labyrinth of halls. "If anyone sees us, pretend I caught the two of you sneaking around. I'll tell them I'm taking you to the headmistress. You play along."

Sera and Mary eyed each other. Mary shrugged.

"Fine, but the moment I feel you're up to no good—"

"You'll set me on fire. Yes, I've been on the other end of that before, seventhborn."

They moved this way and that, their bodies tight against the wall and Mary's hand firm in her own. Sera remembered the path loosely and was glad to find Whittaker didn't lead them astray. Finally they approached the plain stone wall where the hall branched off into two. Timothy swept through it like the wall didn't exist. Relief flooded her. Shock followed as Timothy brushed past Whittaker and Mary and took her into his arms. Face buried in the crook of her neck, he hauled in her scent, his hold firm. Sera stiffened but forced herself to relax and hug him back.

Whittaker made a sound of disgust. "How about we move this to somewhere more private, you know, where we won't get expelled if we're caught?"

Timothy released her slightly and, inching back, ran his gaze along her face. He tangled his fingers with hers, led the group to the stone wall, and pressed his wand against it.

They swept inside, all except Whittaker. "I'll patrol the halls and keep everyone from this way. Signal when you need me."

Once safely inside, Timothy walked to the library door, but Mary didn't follow.

"I'll stay here," she said.

"No one can see through the wall," Sera said. "You don't need to guard it."

"And there is plenty of space inside," Timothy added and opened the door to prove his point.

Mary glanced inside and shrugged sheepishly. "Still, it's been weeks since the two of you last saw each other. I'll wait out here. Go, I'll be fine."

Sera noted the pain in her eyes, the desire to disappear if she could. She squeezed her hand. "We won't be long."

Timothy stepped aside and allowed Sera to enter, then closed the door behind them.

"Mr. Delacort," she started, but his head came to a rest at the back of hers, and she silenced. His hands smoothed onto her shoulders, gentle, as if he feared she would break if he held her any tighter.

"I've missed you so much." He spoke into her hair. "I thought I'd lost you the night of the dance, but when I got your letter…"

Sera spun, realizing then just how close he was, to where her nose brushed his when she gazed up at him. "We need to talk."

"In a minute," he whispered and pressed his lips against hers.

Sera gripped his lapels and pulled away gently. "Please, we haven't much time."

"What's so important that it can't wait one minute?" he said against her lips.

"I know who you are."

He smiled. "The man who loves you?"

She met his eyes. "A Keeper."

He blinked, the simple action destroying the joy that had shaded his stare. Stiff, his hands fell away from her. His throat pulsed as he gulped, all color fading from his face.

"Timothy…"

He released a shuddering breath and shifted back. Sera reached a hand for him, but he snatched his arm away and walked across the room.

"Timothy, please."

"Who are you?" He sat down before the great fireplace, hands clasped between his knees, and stared at the flames. "Did they send you? Are you here to kill me?"

Firelight made the shadows in the room dance and seemed to bring the tapestries to life. Sera crossed the room under the watchful gaze of the seven Guardians whose eyes she felt followed her as she sat at his side. "That's what I'm trying to prevent. I would never and have never meant you any harm."

He chuckled bitterly. "Funny, as it's always been you to cause me the greatest pain."

"I never meant to."

"A lot of things were never meant to happen, yet they did." He shrugged. "I was never supposed to know this damned spell, yet here we sit."

"How *did* you come about the spell? I thought it was passed down from Sister to Sister, but you're clearly not a Sister."

"When the Brother in the forest mentioned knowing my father, I wanted it to be a lie. I asked my father about it, and he confessed everything—that he was involved with the Brotherhood and he…" Timothy let out a shaky sigh and looked at Sera. "He hunted Sisters of Mercy and seventhborns alike. Until one day he was away and two Sisters found their way into my home. I was five. They told me they had a secret to tell me and that I had to guard it with my life. They said I was special, chosen." He smiled, pained. "I thought they were angels, and in my innocence, I agreed. We made an oath, my first oath. A blood oath. The Sister died instantly and was taken away by the other. I was left to tell my father that I was the next Keeper."

A myriad of curses swelled in Sera's throat. "You were just a child. Why curse you for what your father did?"

He shrugged and leaned forward, elbows to knees. "Can you blame them? For ages they've been hunted." He motioned weakly to the portrait of Professor Barrington's father and other Purists by the door. "My father and Professor Barrington's father ultimately led this bloody campaign against the Sisters, searching for these spells. Not to mention their research in the dungeons..." He fisted his hair and shook his head. "They tortured seventhborns so that they could perfect the black magic they would use to raise the Keepers."

"Dear God..."

"The Sisters did what they thought was best to stop them. Once I told my father what had happened, he cut off all ties with the Brotherhood and distanced himself—*reformed* himself, even if it was all a lie. He loved me above the Brotherhood. I was the one thing he wouldn't sacrifice.

"Professor Barrington's father refused to let him abandon their cause, so my father—now an *upstanding member* of the Aetherium and a champion of seventhborns—blamed him first and let him take the fall. No one believed Professor Barrington's father afterward."

Sera cupped her mouth. Could she believe a story told by Timothy's father? That Professor Barrington's father was truly a madman, a murderer? She shut her eyes, briefly recalling Professor Barrington's somberness as he professed his father's goodness. Pain spread in Sera's chest. If Barrington heard this tale, surely it would destroy him.

"He did it so I would be safe, but all those lives lost...

How could I ever forgive him?"

"As long as the Brotherhood and the Sisters of Mercy exist, you will never be safe. But I know someone who can help."

Pity saturated his next smile. "My father is on the Aetherium council, Sera. If I needed to be hidden, they'd be able to keep me safe."

She rose quickly. "Then you must go to him, now. Your spell is the last the Brotherhood needs, and whether it's a myth or not, they are determined to get it. In spite of everything, you have to go to your father."

He gazed up at her, defeat in his eyes. "So that I'll be forced into hiding? To never live a normal life? To never see you again, all for the sake of some ridiculous feud and secret?"

"No, not for some ridiculous feud and secret, but for *your life*. Whatever you think you feel for me is not worth that. You have to go, let them protect you."

He shook his head slowly. "You're the best thing that ever happened to me, and now you're asking me to just disappear? I can't—how can I? Since the day of your entrance exam, I haven't been able to keep you from my thoughts."

She stumbled back as if pushed. "You...you were there?" There had been a room full of robed, stern-faced, icy-eyed men in a semicircle, asking her to perform basic magic. They'd then demanded her to tell what little she knew of the life she remembered, and of her experience with Noah. They'd watched her in disgust as she detailed his cruelty, and with each word the room felt to close in around her. Her stomach had roiled, a mix of nerves and anger at being put on display like a caged animal. A pariah. Anything but human.

She spun and tugged her cloak closed as though she stood naked before him. "You should've told me you were there."

Timothy caught her gently by the shoulders. "I wasn't supposed to be. My father allowed me to watch from the upper level, to see what went into the selection process of the next seventhborn. You never once gazed up at me, but I saw you, and since that day you're all I see."

He twined his fingers in hers and drew her down next to him. "The way you go about your life, never needing anyone, carrying the weight of being a seventhborn on your shoulders. You've never once let it sway you, never once let it stop you or break you down. I thought—no, I *knew*—you would be the only one to understand what it is like to live with this burden I carry. You inspired me. I began to think that if you still dreamed above your own situation, I could, too, come what may." He brushed a thumb lightly against her jaw. "You changed my life."

She opened her mouth but no words came.

"Come with me," he said, his forehead against hers, a cool hand at her cheek. He encouraged her face upward. "You're in as much danger, and I won't forgive myself if anything happens to you. We will be safe. You saved me the day of your entrance exam. Let me save you."

She gripped his lapels, wishing she could shake him and make him understand. "Timothy, I can't. Believe me, I am safe. It's you that you should be worried about."

"I want only you."

Sera swallowed tightly. What could she possibly say to that? She had to get him out of there, and she needed to contact Barrington somehow—if he was awake. This was what they had worked for, bled for, nearly died for.

Wake up, she prayed. The memory of holding him sent

a tingle down her arms. *You needed me, and now I need you.*

"Sera?"

She shook away her prayers. Barrington would want her to focus on the case.

"Will you come with me?"

To do what was needed.

She clasped her fingers over his. "Yes."

His mouth twitched with a smile, his eyes the brightest she had ever seen them. "Yes?"

She nodded, a broken smile at her lips. She would protect him just as he'd protected her and loved her in silence all these years. Even if her heart were incapable of loving him. Even if she vanished into thin air after securing his safety. "I'll go with you, but we must leave now. I fear the Brotherhood will manage to find out your identity."

Before the last word was said, he caught her lips in a slow kiss filled with the tenderness of a person savoring and memorizing their ultimate wish. Sera stiffened yet forced herself to ease and yield. Once he was safe, she would leave, and the memory of this kiss was all she could possibly leave him with. Her heart lay elsewhere.

They broke apart, equally breathless.

"We should go," she said, standing. Hands entwined, they walked out of the library and into the hall. Mary waited, curled into herself against the wall. She gazed up, green eyes pooled with tears.

"Mary, what is it?" Sera knelt before her, but Mary swatted away her tears and smiled meekly.

"It's nothing. You mentioned you were both in danger, and I was worried." She took Sera's hands, and the two girls rose together.

"We are," Sera said, "and we have to leave. But as soon as I can, I will reach out to you, I promise. The people after us will not rest until they find us." Releasing her, Sera made for the stone wall, Timothy behind her.

"Where will you go? It will take little work for your father to find you," Mary told Timothy. "And Sera, they will find a way to blame you, you know this. Perhaps give it a few days. You will be safe in the Academy."

Timothy sighed. "Anywhere is safer than here. We will have to keep moving, but we will be okay," he said, giving Sera's hand a gentle squeeze. She forced a smile, her heart twisting within. He would never forgive her betrayal, but his safety came first.

"Then let me help. I know of a place—an old church not too far from my house. The church grounds are sacred, and the lands there are consecrated, so you can't transfer in and out, and scrying is out of the question. You will be safe there, for a time at least, until you can get your bearings and think of a plan."

Sera and Timothy looked at each other and nodded. Their plan was no better. "That sounds fantastic, Mary. Thank you."

Mary gave her a sad smile. "What are friends for?"

She twined her hand tight around Sera's as they walked through the wall. "Come, we will transfer out from here. Quickly, before someone comes."

"But they will trace our magic," Sera said.

"I'll do it," Mary offered. "It'll be weeks before they trace every illegal transfer that takes place in the school, and even when they do, it will be my magic they find, not yours. Believe me, it will work."

Timothy's brow gathered, uncertainty on his face, but Sera nodded. "Okay. We just need a few days to think of a plan, and we'll move. If the Aetherium tracks us down at the church, we will be long gone."

Mary nodded, and kneeling, she wrote out the coordinate spells. They moved into the circle together. Mary aimed her wand at the ground and whispered, "Ignite."

A moment later, the three of them landed neatly in an open field. The night was cool, but with her pulse quick as it was, Sera welcomed the whispering breeze that chilled her skin. The winds whisked over the patchwork hills and winding country roads spread out before them, bringing the scent of earth and cold to her nose. The lights of a village flickered in the distance like beacons, but Mary turned them away from this to a waist-high stone wall that snaked along the hillside.

"We can't transfer beyond this point," she said, leading them to a break in the stone. They hiked up the hilly terrain of dry grass and thick hedgerows.

Minutes later, they reached the top of a slope. The church stood abandoned on the hill, its skeletal structure breaking up the clear horizon.

"We're here," Mary said, her breath heaving from the walk.

The crumbling brick church looked wholly unstable, some of the flying buttresses cracked or missing altogether. Sections of the roof were also gone, a side of the one spire sunken in and rotted beams of wood visible through the gaping hole. Large windows flanked the arched doorway. Vines grew along the outside, suffocating the crumbling structure. But although abandoned and terribly ominous, Sera saw it for what it was: sanctuary.

Mary walked them toward the arched doorway. With a grunt, she shouldered the door open and held her wand before her, illuminating the space.

"Watch your step," she said, entering. Sera and Timothy lifted their wands the same, rods of light in the midst of an echoing darkness.

The pews were heaps of rotted wood, stacked upon one another like miniature pyres. Crumbling bricks would have allowed for light were it day, but in the darkness, they looked like eyes in the wall. Dirt stained the once-white tile that composed the nave all the way to the altar. Sera imagined a long carpet may have been there at one time, but clearly the days of the building's beauty were long gone.

Timothy held up his wand and walked toward the stone altar. "I think this will do nicely for now."

"Indeed." Sera turned to Mary. "Thank you."

Mary lifted a hand to Sera's cheek, her chin quivering. "I really wish it didn't have to be this way." A tear spilled from her eyes. "I'm really sorry, about all of this. I truly am."

Sera cradled Mary's hand. "It isn't your fault. We never would have found this place without you. You've been a ray of light for me at the Academy, and I will never forget it."

"I hope you remember me that way."

"How else would I remember you?"

Tears pooled in Mary's eyes. She opened her mouth to speak—

"Sera, Sera in a cage…"

Sera froze, stark cold shooting down her spine at the voice echoing around her. *No…*

"Sera, Sera wants to fly…"

Her hand tight on her wand, she spun, but his voice was everywhere, bouncing off the walls and refusing to escape through the gaping holes in the structure. No, it was meant to stay and taunt her.

"But her pretty wings are broken…"

One by one, the Brotherhood stepped out from shadows, their wands aimed at Sera and Timothy. Sera gazed up; they were on the second level as well.

Timothy ran to Sera, pulling her close behind him. They

aimed their wands, but she paused, as from the shadows at the altar a man robed in red stepped out and lifted his plague mask.

"Look at her fall from the sky."

Noah was everything she remembered. Beauty personified. Fear become flesh. And alive. Very much alive. Dread bloomed to a solid rock in her chest, an invisible hand clutched tight around her lungs, shackles fettering her to the ground. His hair was shorter, accentuating his strong nose, wide jaw, and full lips. And when that devastatingly cool gaze fell upon her, Sera shivered.

He closed his eyes and hauled in a breath, as though relieved to have finally found her. But she knew better than to hold some deluded hope that he'd missed her. Their last time together she'd nearly killed him, and she had no doubt that this time, he would try to kill her.

Opening his eyes, he smiled, but not at her. "I thought you'd change your mind. Your mother will be proud."

Timothy followed Noah's gaze, and his eyes widened. But there was no need for Sera to turn. The silence behind her said it all, as did the wand tip pressed firmly at her back.

She smiled bitterly. "So it was you."

"I'm so sorry, Sera," Mary said. "I had to."

27

broken oath, broken life

Mary snatched Sera's wand and Timothy's as well. She paced backward down the nave, careful steps leading her to Noah. He stood in front of the pulpit, a stand with carved black wings at either side of it, where for centuries so many before him spewed hateful lies against seventhborns. Behind him, the stained glass depicted a gate and six guardians of magic standing before it. And locked behind the gate was the seventh sister, haloed by a black flame.

Hands bound in whips of magic, Timothy and Sera were dragged down the nave. Timothy's voice echoed above the shuffle of their footsteps as he attempted to soothe Sera whenever she'd grunt or hiss with a bump or stumble. "Everything will be okay," he said, but nothing could ease the anger she wrestled to tame in her veins, the magic at her fingertips, hot and scalding, begging for uninhibited release. She glanced up to the crumbling bricks and rotting rafters. One wild blow of magic and she could bring this place down around them. But she'd been through this before;

she couldn't risk Noah escaping again.

She had to keep Timothy safe. And Mary…

She looked at her friend. Her sister. Her traitor. Was this what true friends—what sisters—did? Every laugh, every shared cry…had any of it been real?

Pain of Mary's betrayal jabbed Sera's heart. She winced, and her hold on her magic slipped; the glass windows around them exploded, a deafening shatter. Shards of multicolored glass rained around them. Timothy shoved the Brother holding him and started to reach for Sera, but the Brother yanked him back by his cloak.

"Enough!" Noah growled, his face contorted in anger. He lifted a hand. A shock of magic slammed into Sera's chest, clawing its fiery talons into her ribs and thrusting her into the air. She crashed against the squared base of a marble statue, its pointed edge digging into her back. A jolt of coldness rushed down to each limb. Tightness gripped her chest.

"Bring them to me." Noah's voice was calm, soft… soothing almost, though savageness radiated from every part of him.

Two Brothers dragged her to her feet and tugged her and Timothy toward the altar. Timothy struggled, but with the ache of Noah's blast radiating through her, Sera stumbled upon the beveled tiles and rubble, unable to fight at all.

They were brought to a stop before Noah. Kicked in the back of the knees, both she and Timothy collapsed onto the broken tile floor. Sera winced, a stone jammed into her knee. A Brother pressed his wand to her neck.

She imagined Noah would be angry, yet a smile pulled at his lips as he descended the altar stairs slowly, his red robe dragging behind him. She looked into his eyes to better gauge his mood, but found nothing. He was worse than a tempest.

Stopping before her, he lifted a hand to her face, a sick thrill of fulfilled longing burning in those brown eyes.

"I've been thinking of you," he said over Timothy's grunts and demands he stay away from her. He reached around and slipped a pin from her hair, his touch gentle as his fingers tangled in the brown strands. Sera braced; he never stayed tender for long. "I think of you all the time."

He removed the other pins and dropped them to the ground, one by one, until Sera's hair tumbled down onto her shoulders. "Every day."

He moved quickly, and there was a loud *snap*. Burn spread across Sera's cheek, and she crashed to the ground, rubble jamming into her palms on impact. She growled, her magic spiking. It gathered and rattled for her to let go, but she ground her teeth together. Not yet.

Noah knelt before her and smoothed a hand along his hair, raking it back into place. "I'm sorry, Sera. I'm sorry. I...I hate losing things. I hated losing you. I was worried sick they would tame you."

His words gave her pause. He'd been worried she'd be tamed? Of course. Barrington had told her such in so many words. With control, she was stronger. With focus, she could destroy him. With focus she *would* destroy him.

"Let her go," Timothy snarled, now held fixed by three Brothers, two at his sides and one behind him. "You have me; you have no need of her."

Noah's look changed then, the unnatural quick coming of a thunderstorm. Brown eyes turned to Timothy, his jaw tight. With hands clasped behind his back, he walked the few steps to where Timothy knelt with hands bound.

"It's a good thing telling me your secret will kill you, otherwise I'd be forced to skin you alive for coveting things that aren't yours." He turned his eyes to Sera momentarily, then focused his attention back on Timothy. "What is this spell that you keep?"

Timothy's eyes sparkled, though a sad smile touched his mouth. "Let her go, and I'll tell you anything you want."

Sera gasped, her heart pounding. "Timothy, you can't!" Her magic pulsed. A nearby statue burst, and stone shards crumbled to the ground, white dust wafting around them. Noah raised a hand. The binds on Sera's hands slithered like snakes up her arms, burning, and she screamed—the magic she gathered shattered under the pain.

"I told you before, it's me you want. Leave her out of this!" Timothy growled. "Swear a blood oath to me that you and your men will not hurt her, and the spell is yours."

"Timothy, no!" Sera struggled to funnel her magic into one current she could use against Noah, but it was spread everywhere within her, wanting to incinerate everything.

Noah drew a dagger from a scabbard at his side. "A blood oath it is. She will not be killed in exchange for your spell. But if you try anything once you get back your wand, you're dead, and I will use her to raise you. Mary?"

Mary tossed Timothy's wand at his knees. Hands still bound, Timothy picked up his wand and held it out to Noah. Noah sliced his palm and dripped blood onto the rod, then held the tip of the stained wand to Timothy's. "My life and those of my men in exchange for her life."

Sera was sure if she hadn't been on her knees, she would have fallen onto them anyway. How could someone who she'd barely spent time with care for her to this extreme, and yet the one who pledged to be a sister betray her in such a way? She turned her eyes from the oath being made to Mary, who lingered by the transept door. Her face was turned down, her wand clasped at her core. If not for the rise and fall of her chest, Sera would have thought her dead.

Noah lowered his wand. "Our oath has been made. Now for your secret."

The well of pain tore open to a hollow pit. Tears Sera wished didn't exist spilled from her eyes.

Timothy hauled in a breath and braced. "The Rites of Supremacy."

The words spoken were like a blow to the gut, and he cringed, collapsing onto his bound hands with a groan.

Sera winced but forced herself to watch him struggle to stay upright. "Timothy, please don't do it. Don't tell him."

"What are the Rites of Supremacy?" Noah gripped Timothy's hair and lifted him back onto his knees. Timothy's face was flushed, his mouth pressed into a tight line as pain mapped his veins. "What are they?"

Sera grunted and tried to force her magic into control. *Focus, focus, focus!*

Timothy took in a deep breath and met Sera's eyes again, as though to bolster himself against the imminent pain. "As there were seven guardians of magic, so you must also find seven sisters, each element represented. The blood of six must be shed and the seventh must drink this offering. Upon saying the following words, the gates will be opened, where you will find the ultimate power: power over time…" He cried out and fell forward onto his hands. Droplets of blood streamed from his nose to the floor, a crimson constellation on the dirty tile.

Bursts of power gathered in Sera's hands, but at the sight of Timothy in pain, of his imminent death as a result of his love for her, her heart stuttered, her magic scattered, and another statue exploded.

"What is this spell?" Noah asked greedily.

"Leave him alone!" Sera roared, and the window behind Noah shattered into a cloud of pulverized glass.

Noah flinched but straightened, his murderous gaze trained on Sera. He would make her pay for that, she knew this, but managing to gather a bit of power, she shot an orb of magic toward him, hoping to bind him—anything to engage him and give Timothy a reprieve.

Noah swept aside coolly, evading her attack. The binds whipped around a pillar behind him, and quickly fizzled. Noah clenched his hands then, and Sera cried out as the binds he'd whipped around her dug deeper into her skin. She toppled over, writhing in pain that spread like blood through her veins.

Timothy fell onto his hands and, shaking, drew out a linked set of ciphers to a spell with his blood. He groaned, the sob caged behind his clenched teeth. As much as he tried to stay strong, he heaved and retched clots of blood beside him.

Sera focused on her pain and thrust a wild flare up to the rafters. Planks of rotted wood crashed down around them, but it wasn't enough to bring them down. She knew she had to calm herself in order to gather her magic into stronger blows, but her soul clawed her insides. Things couldn't end this way. They couldn't.

Noah stared down at Timothy, unaffected, consumed. "Continue. What is the spell they must speak?"

Timothy struggled to remain upright but tumbled forward onto his hands. Blood streamed from his eyes, his gaze distant and unfocused. "*I bleed my sisters. I bleed this life. I…open…*"—he clutched his stomach—"*I open that… which has been closed. I end that which has…begun.*"

He collapsed onto his side, wheezing weak and shallow breaths. "My broken oath. My broken life."

Sera screamed. Flares of fire surged around them, erratic pyres materializing out of thin air. They blew in and vanished like ghosts until, spent, heartbroken, and hopeless, Sera fell forward onto her bound hands beside Timothy.

She bent forward, resting her forehead against his. "I'm so sorry, Timothy. I'm so sorry."

A broken, bloodied smile twitched at his lip. "My love," he whispered. He lifted a hand to her face, but with a blink of those clear blue eyes, his hand fell lifeless at his side.

"It is done," Noah whispered. "The Master will be pleased."

Sera sucked in a breath, but her lungs locked and refused it. She clutched her bound hands at his chest where his heart did not beat. "Timothy?" she croaked.

A blast cut through her mourning, then another, and another. Startled, Sera ducked into Timothy as magic clashed and burst around her, trailed by the Brothers' screams as Noah killed them all. Shots hurtled toward Noah haloed in white, but he brushed them away with ease, a flick of the hand, a wave of his wand. One orb ricocheted off the tip of his wand and crashed against the pillar beside Mary, who screamed and ducked, the rubble exploding outward. She held her arms over her head as the stone, dirt, and weeds rained down on her. Sera lifted her eyes as another blast of magic whisked past her and slammed into the last Brother behind her. He crumpled to the ground, a fire-rimmed hole glowing in his chest.

"Can't have them knowing the spell, now can we?" Noah muttered.

Breathless, Sera slumped back, her chest heaving. Noah remained standing through the haze of lingering smoke and magic, unaffected. To the right of them, Mary struggled to her feet, and Sera paused. An unnerving awareness spread within her, a heavy burden that made it hard to breathe.

Noah turned his wand at Mary.

Eyes wide, she shifted back against the pillar as if she could vanish into it. "I did what you asked," she cried, frantic and ungraceful. "I did what you—"

Noah speared a black orb of magic at her.

"No!" Sera raised a hand, meeting his flare with a flare of her own. A thunderous clash resounded at the collision that thrust his magic off course and into the wall.

Noah turned a venomous gaze to Sera, a look she'd been at the end of many times before. He whipped binds around her wrists, scalding ropes of black smoke cutting deep into her flesh. Though they'd spent years apart, their connection forged itself immediately, and at once she felt him everywhere, an impermeable mist crowding and filling her. The scars on her body scorched to life as though recognizing their maker. Sera clenched her teeth and stifled a roar. Her magic scattered under the intense pain that twisted her heart in her chest. The ache was alive and wormed its way behind her eyes and to the top of her skull. Her stomach twisted, and the same sick sensation lurched in her throat as he pushed closer, seeking to tap into her reserves.

Sera refused him and held the spool of her powers so tight, the underside of her skin burned from the strain.

A slow grin twisted his lips. *You still insist on fighting me? Let me in, little bird*, he spoke into their connection. *Nothing's changed; you won't win this.*

He wouldn't kill her, no. He swore a blood oath he wouldn't, but there in his eyes was a promise. He would drain her within an inch of her life.

Never again.

Unafraid, Sera released her hold on her powers. A surge of fire roared out from her belly—hot and angry, but controlled flames that forced his shackles from around her wrists and destroyed their connection. Shafts of fire whipped from her hands and pushed back Noah's magic.

Their warring magic spurred wild winds around them. Her hands trembled, her magic fanning outward as though splintered. Still, she struggled to keep her powers in check. One burst could deplete her reserves in an instant, and then she'd be at Noah's mercy. She didn't mind death, not with the agony and guilt that hollowed her soul. But not here. Not now. She had lost Timothy. Had lost Mary. She would not lose herself.

Determination, cold and cruel, roared upward in a wave of heat within her, and her magic pushed Noah's back. She looked at Mary pressed against the pillar, sobbing into her hands, and her eyes flooded with tears.

Memories of them together flashed quickly through her mind as if spurred by the savage winds that whipped around them. Unwittingly she cast them out into the smoke that haloed their opposing magic. Images of meeting Mary her very first day at the Academy played out like flashes of lightning. When Mary popped her head into the room, her smile a ray of light during a tempest of anger. Weekends spent in the tower room, laughing at the latest gossip…or Sera comforting her after another letter had come from her mother. All of it could have been real. They could have been real friends, real sisters.

And she'd betrayed it all.

Lost in these thoughts, the pressure in her core grew to a steady hum that vibrated along her skin. The white beam of her power focused from its erratic wisps into a single channel of white. Noah pulsed his magic again, but digging her heel into the ground, Sera shouldered against it. Still, he was stronger, and within seconds his magic had pushed closer.

She wouldn't be able to do this alone. Her pain was not enough to defeat his evil. But she knew of a pain that was…

Agatha Beechworth.
Briar Wakefield.
Catherine Yates.
Elsie Godwin.
Harriet Adams.
Winnie Forge.
Ophelia Crowe.

Holding fast to their names in her mind, Sera focused on their screams, their tears, their lives lost to this monster and his vicious cause. Pressure mounted in her temples as her power split, half into fighting Noah, the other into a summoning. White fog crept out from her shaft of magic, its phantom fingers webbing along the floor and up the walls, encircling her and Noah in a cool white cloud. Shadows appeared in the fog again, standing side by side. Wide eyed, Noah watched them materialize one by one. They were everywhere—girls and women, young and old, dressed in modern attire and clothes of a time long gone. Their smoky bodies turned to Sera; they each placed a hand on their hearts. A black line tattoo marked their wrists. Seventhborns.

Whispers crowded her mind, colliding against one another. Yet, here in the midst of her battle, Sera understood their plea.

Show you…

Barrington had warned her that channeling without an anchor was a risk, but Sera nodded. He'd grown to be her anchor, whether beside her or miles away.

"Yes, show me," she cried. "I want to feel it all."

Every tear. Every pain. Every unfulfilled dream. Every lost love.

Myriad hands came upon her, fingers gripping desperately at her limbs. Voices—sobs and prayers and mournful wails—flooded her thoughts and screamed in her mind as the seventhborns fed their pain into her consciousness, their tears and frustrations, their fears and their deaths.

A cry grew in Sera's throat. Raw heat flushed through her veins, and she felt as if she was dissolving in layers; first her clothes, then her skin. Blood and organs, veins and bones. Until only her soul remained. Here in this immaterial state, the channeled pain was blinding and heavy and terrible—it was theirs. Every ache borne over being a seventhborn bled into Sera, and the heat of her powers grew.

"No!" Noah screamed, clenching his teeth against Sera's fire overcoming his.

The pain of the gathered power crested, and she knew she had to release it or it would consume her.

She surrendered to magic.

Black spouts of smoke whirled around the funnel of her power, enveloping it, forcing it into a single shaft of pure black fire. Noah's eyes widened. The black flames overcame his and pushed closer to him, closer, and swallowed him whole.

Her reserves plummeted and weak, Sera's knees buckled, and she collapsed. The dead seventhborns surrounding her lowered their hands, and their voices faded from her head. One by one, they inclined their heads at her and turned, walking back into the cool fog that soon dissipated around her.

For some time, Sera and Mary coexisted in complete silence, the mournful howls of the wind the only sound. Her wand before her, Sera did not release Timothy's body, and Mary did not move from beside the pillar.

"Pick up your wand," Mary ordered, her voice deadened. She peeled away from the wall and walked across from Sera, a specter in the moonlight. "We can't stay in this church forever, and regardless of how tight you hold him, he's never coming back."

Sera glared at her from over Timothy's head pressed against her chest. "I won't waste my magic on you."

Mary's mouth trembled, her eyes filled with tears. "You must fight me. The Brotherhood will never let me live after this." She kicked Sera's wand closer, the plea clear in her eyes. "I will not kill you without a fair fight."

Sera chuckled into Timothy's hair. "A fair fight? You've found your morals, I see."

"This was not easy for me, either, Sera. But my father, he had unsurmountable debts. How else do you think he managed to go from nothing to a well-respected healer? The more magic he had, the more patients he could see. The Brotherhood, they promised him as much blood magic as he needed in exchange for his cooperation in the future. And they called on that debt. Don't you see? Refusing them would have been the same as signing my death sentence and my family's."

"You signed it the moment you betrayed us."

She wiped one of her tears roughly. "I had no choice—"

"How can I trust anything you say?"

Mary recoiled at the anger in Sera's words, more of her tears falling.

"You were my sister, the only thing that kept me sane in this godforsaken place. I would have died for you, I nearly did, and it was all for this? For these monsters?" Her words slurred through her own tears.

"You think I wanted this, Sera? All I've done was try to

protect you. I overheard my father say the Brotherhood sought powerful seventhborns and had their eye on seventhborns at the Academy. I knew I had to find a way to keep you safe without revealing my parents' association with them, so I told Susan about your scars, then used Mrs. Fairfax to help Whittaker break into the records room so he could steal your file. I thought you'd be too embarrassed and would leave the Academy. That way the Brotherhood couldn't hurt you."

Air rushed into Sera's chest, and her heart heaved. Mrs. Fairfax's tearful plea for forgiveness had been Mary all along?

"I tried, Sera. I tried to get you away before they came for you. Had I known they were in the forest that night, I never would have run out there. All I've ever wanted was to keep you safe, but then they requested my *cooperation*. If I didn't do what was asked of me, they would have killed me and my family. The way my mother begged me to save them… I had no choice. You have to believe me. I never wanted to hurt you. All I ever did was for you, Sera. I love you."

The church doors exploded open. Aetherium guards swept inside, their illuminated wands drawn and aimed at Sera and Mary as they encircled them. Three guards swept into the circle and lifted Timothy's body out of her arms, quickly carrying him to where Sera could no longer see him. Another guard dragged Sera up to her feet.

"Identify yourselves!" a guard demanded. He was dressed in a forest-green robe and, unlike the other guards, he carried no wand and wore an Invocation ring. Sera knew him to be a Lead Inspector. He looked at Mary. "Did this seventhborn harm you?"

Sera braced. No doubt Mary would play the victim and blame her for everything—for Timothy's death, for working with the Brotherhood—and with her word against a seventhborn's, everyone would believe her.

"No," Mary whispered, a tear streaming down her cheek. She thrust her wand on the ground. "I hurt her."

Folding one knee, then the other, she knelt down and held her hands in front of her, her wrists touching. "My name is Mary Tenant. It was me who pushed Mrs. Fairfax down the stairs at the Aetherium's Witchling Academy and tethered myself to her reserves. I then possessed her and instructed her to break into the Academy's records room. I lured Miss Dovetail and Mr. Delacort here under instructions from the Brotherhood…"

While Mary confessed to her crimes, commotion behind Sera drew her attention. She turned just as the officers parted and let Professor Barrington through. He rushed into the circle and stopped before her, his skin pale, his hair as disheveled and rumpled as his half tucked-in shirt and open cloak. Worry saturated his stare that he trailed along her quickly, as if wanting to make sure she was okay in one look.

He met her gaze and exhaled deeply, relief washing over his tense frame. "Sera."

The sound of her name from his lips was a whisper yet struck into her like a whirlwind.

"Nik." Hot tears pooled in her eyes, rendering him a speckled mess of light and shadow. Agony, shame, remorse, and mourning gripped her with a vengeance. Her chest locked, her lungs refused, and her knees gave out beneath her.

But she didn't fall.

Strong arms came around her and, proprieties aside, Barrington held her, a quiet wall supporting her as she seized his lapels, breathless, and twisted them the way her insides churned. Every tear and sob caged in her heart for years burst from the deepest parts of her soul. From Noah's evil to Mary's betrayal to Timothy's sacrifice. From a family she sought to the curse of being a seventhborn.

For the first time, she broke, wholly, with no desire to be strong.

For the first time, she allowed herself to be held, allowed herself to feel human.

Allowed herself to be cared for, too.

EPILOGUE

Sera stood before the worktable in Barrington's home, shafts of light flooding through the arched windows behind her. She set aside the book she had chosen to read that morning — *The Ethics of Hydromancy* — once again drawn to the letter she received a week ago, signaling her last day at the Aetherium's Witchling Academy. Though she'd committed its disappointing words to memory, she read them once more.

For your direct involvement in incidents leading to the death of Mr. Timothy Delacort, you have been removed from the Aetherium's Seventhborn Program effective immediately.

Heat gathered in her cheeks, but she rejected the coming tears and thrust the note into a brass crucible in the middle of the table. It was childish to pretend the outcome would have been otherwise. Timothy's father had told her what would happen if she didn't stay away from his son, and he'd been a man of his word.

Since her expulsion from the Academy, Barrington had welcomed her into his home. However temporary, she was grateful for his kindness.

She tapped the edge of the kettle with her wand and sparked a flame inside. Whirls of smoke and licks of fire billowed upward as red, fiery tentacles wound about the letter and consumed it.

"Trying to burn down my home again, I see."

Sera startled at the deep baritone and lifted her head to Professor Barrington leaning against the doorframe, still dressed in his professorial robes. After Mrs. York vouched for his being at the scene, no one suspected their relationship extended beyond that of a professor and a student, and his employment remained unaffected. Sera lowered her eyes to the note now wrapped in flames. If only she could say the same.

"I had no reason to keep it. Regardless of how many times I read it, the outcome won't ever change."

They stood in silence until the flames devoured the note and extinguished. Whirls of white smoke then twirled from within the crucible. Sera sighed and closed the book she had been reading.

Barrington glanced at the cover and hummed. "Hydro-mancy?"

"I was hoping to scry for Mary, but seeing as I missed all my Water-level courses, my progress was nonexistent. It's useless to worry, I know, but I keep wondering if the spell is truly safe." Reason told her it was. Mrs. York had all the bones found at the scene stored in a vault lest a necromancer decide to raise any of the Brothers and recover the spell. Barrington then assured her Noah's spirit could not be summoned. She might have doubted him, had she not come across a black magic spell on his desk used to bind spirits after death.

But Sera lowered her eyes to the Hydromancy book; that wasn't the only reason she scried for Mary. In addition to all Mary had confessed that fateful day at the church, later inquiries revealed her infatuation with Timothy had been nothing more than her parents' orders. If she married Timothy, her family would be protected by the Delacort name and his father's Aetherium status. Sadly, the Tenants had since disappeared, leaving Mary alone to pay for their sins.

Sera pressed a hand to her chest, the words of Mary's confession a ghost haunting her thoughts.

I did it all for you, Sera. I love you.

Everything Mary had done was to protect others, and ultimately, she took the fall. The least Sera could do was look after her. Even if she never fully forgave the girl, she still loved her, too.

"The spell is safe," Barrington said, tearing her from thought. He undid the tie of his professorial robes, revealing his all-black attire underneath. Since Timothy's death, the Academy was in mourning. Sera smoothed down the black gown she wore; a part of her would always be in mourning, too. "And so is Miss Tenant. Where she is, no one will find her."

"But how can we be sure? Her father worked with the Brotherhood. Maybe they've reached out to her somehow, perhaps threatened her. If they get their hands on the spell, I fear for any line of seven sisters."

She started to open the book again when Barrington's hand came above the cover, and he gently closed it.

"Miss Dovetail," he said, much softer this time. Sera's fingers tightened on the edge of the book, his voice a balm to her fear and kindling to her heart. "Mrs. York came to the Academy today."

"What did she say?" she asked quickly, lowering onto a stool. The worry that her dread had been confirmed—that Mary had indeed heard the spell and shared it—drummed her pulse in her ears.

He leaned on the edge of the table, his legs crossed at his ankles. "Mrs. York had Miss Tenant sent away. I am not sure where. Not many people know. It is for her safety as well. We recognize that, in the end, she was also a pawn. Miss Tenant swears she didn't hear anything, and after various questionings, Inspector Lewis believes she tells the truth. There is a chance she lies, but Mrs. York has assured me that where she is, there will be no one to tell."

A nudge of pain hurt Sera's heart. Mary with a smile like sunshine, kept in solitary confinement, her light withering away each day. But she wouldn't think of this. At least Mary was safe and could smile and sing and laugh and breathe in the midst of her darkness. Timothy, however…

Her heart stuttered, and she shook the thought away. Though a part of her would mourn him always, Timothy was finally at peace.

"Come, enough work for now." He straightened. "There is someone I want you to meet."

Standing, she peered down toward the courtyard. There were no horses or carriage, and she hadn't heard anyone transfer in. "I didn't know we had a visitor," she started, but Barrington was already by the door.

"He's been here for quite some time. Grab a cloak."

Sera frowned and met him at the door, taking a cloak from the hooks there. Why hadn't Rosie told her? And why did she need a cloak?

"Is it a new client?" she asked, putting on the mantle. He'd said he would wait before taking on new work, but

Sera wished he wouldn't. Anything to take her mind off recent events was a welcome distraction.

He gave her a side-eyed smile. "Patience."

Sera rolled her eyes. "You're purposely impossible sometimes, do you know that?"

His smile widened. "Just to you."

Pinpricks nipped her skin, but Sera lowered her head and smoothed a hand down her arm, picturing the scars beneath. She would have to work on her reactions to him, tame her heart that forgot its rhythm when he was around and the smile that he drew from her lips much too easily. Nothing good could come of her attachment to him. Nothing good ever did, not for her heart anyway, especially when his seemed to belong to Gummy.

He led her downstairs, and when she thought they were to enter the parlor to meet their guest, Barrington walked to the front door and opened it. Sera's brow furrowed, but she lifted her hood and walked out into the newly settled twilight.

They ventured down a dirt path leading away from the estate. The late winter night was brisk. A breeze rustled the surrounding tall grass for miles, scented with vegetation and the nearby ocean. Sera closed her eyes for a moment, not caring where he led her as the wind hushed around them, swept into her robe, and twined about her in the softest of touches.

When she opened her eyes, Barrington gazed down at her, a smile in those steel-gray eyes.

She averted her gaze. "Sorry, the breeze…"

"Don't apologize. The peace here is singular. I hope it is lasting for you, far beyond tonight."

She mirrored his smile, her heart and face warm. "For you as well."

A growl resounded in the distance. The Barghest sprinted down a hill and lunged for an orb of magic that Lucas speared at him. After tearing through rugs in both the parlor and library, Rosie had relegated him to the stables. The horses didn't seem to mind, and neither did Lucas. In the days under Lucas's care, the fur on his bear head had grown in longer, covering the puncture wounds on his neck. Black tar no longer dripped from his mouth, just a slobber Sera often heard Rosie bemoaning. But Sera didn't mind; he could do as he wanted. He'd saved her life, according to Barrington. After the professor woke up cognizant of Timothy being a Keeper, he transferred into the school but hadn't found her. When Timothy's father arrived at the Academy frantically searching for Timothy, Barrington said he'd known they were together and had the Barghest track her down.

Sera smiled and waved at the Barghest as Lucas thrust an orb of magic out into the field. The Barghest dashed over a slope and readily caught and devoured it.

She and the professor walked along the moors in silence until they reached the top of a hill that overlooked the ocean in the far distance. Yet it was what lay directly before them that gave Sera pause. A cemetery spread along the hill, marble headstones dotting the land.

A small path wound about the entire cemetery. They followed it to a stone bench by a willow tree. An idea of who it was they visited came to mind, but the possibility left Sera without air. Barrington brought them around the headstone, and her every suspicion was confirmed.

"I would like for you to meet my brother, Filip."

Sera swallowed. "Hello, Filip," she said, unsure if she'd made a sound.

Barrington knelt at the grave and brushed away drops

of rain that had fallen earlier in the evening. "Filip, this is my assistant, Miss Seraphina Dovetail."

He motioned to the stone bench by the tree. The seat was narrow, forcing him to sit just beside her. Sera welcomed this, the desire to touch his hand and ease his pain somewhat surprising and overwhelming.

"He was older by a few seconds, though it could have been a lifetime. It was like he wanted to be first at everything—not to outdo me in any way but rather to make sure it was safe for me to follow. To show me the right way to do things. He obeyed the rules and made our parents proud, set the prime example. Too bad I never followed."

His look grew distant with memory. "My father was always away on one expedition or another. When my mother passed, he came back and took up a position at the Academy. We were ten when Father began teaching us about our history. I had no interest in any of it, and it showed. Father tried to force me to like it, punished me if I didn't, so I did the logical thing. I rebelled and eventually got kicked out of the Academy."

Remembering Timothy's words, Sera nodded.

"Shortly after, I left my home and traveled, finding work where I could. It was hard for some time, but I met many sorts of people in my travels, including the man who became my mentor, Mr. Duncan York."

Sera gasped, all the pieces of the puzzle coming together. "The chancellor was your mentor?"

Barrington smiled. "He was, before he entered Aetherium politics. He taught me many things that eventually allowed me to take the Aetherium exam."

His smile withered, and his gaze lowered to his hands. "I returned home soon after to show Filip and my father everything I'd accomplished. All I found when I arrived was my father's house consumed in flames and someone running away into the darkness of the night. In the firelight, I saw a raven on the fleeing man's robe, but I never saw his face. I would have chased him, immobilized him with a spell, but Filip and my father were still inside. My emotions got the best of me, and I couldn't extinguish the flames. They felt to be coming from everywhere, no doubt spurred on by my father's experiments, spells, tonics… But I had to save them. I found Filip on the second floor and was able to drag him out, but…" His voice faded. "It was too late to save him. There was an explosion, and the house collapsed, taking away my father as well."

For long moments they sat in silence. The winds moaned around them as though echoing his laments.

"I'm sorry," Sera said, unable to find more words.

He smiled, though it never reached the sorrow in his eyes. "You've no reason to be sorry. It was the Brotherhood who did this, and it is them who will pay. Mrs. York says the more revenge I seek, the further I move from absolution, but I fear there is no penance for the things I've done, for leaving my brother alone, most of all. I should have been there. I was supposed to protect him, and I didn't."

Emotions swelled, and she touched his hand before she realized her actions. "What they did is not your fault. The Brotherhood is evil and care for no one. This is their doing, and you should not carry their blame."

He nodded, and with his eyes turned down to her hand on his, he folded her fingers into his. "Thank you."

Cognizant of her hand in his, Sera blushed and slipped it away. She tucked a strand of her hair back into place so he wouldn't see how her hands trembled. "It is I who should thank you, for the past months, for bringing me here and telling me of your life…" *For making me your anchor.*

"I should have brought you long before. I wanted to. I just…" He exhaled, and a gust of wind stole the breath away. "I want you to know why I do the things I do. And that just as I haven't given up on Filip, I will not give up on you. We will find your family, Miss Dovetail, and learn all there is to know about your past. And make no mistake, we *will* find the Brotherhood and make them pay for all they've done." He met her stare with an openness Sera hadn't ever seen before. "Most of all, I want you to know that while my company may not compare to Miss Tenant's friendship or Mr. Delacort's affections, I hope you will be happy here for however long you wish to stay."

At once, the world seemed to disappear. There were only his words, spoken at the foot of his beloved brother's grave, the person who gave his life meaning and purpose.

Sera wished to tell him that he was a good man, that Timothy's affections were entirely one sided, and that she was already happy in his home with Rosie and Lucas and the Barghest—*with him*—but she simply held his gaze and nodded, his words a fire that spread warmth in her chest, burned at her heart and the words she wanted to say.

Movement over his shoulder caught Sera's attention as Lucas entered the cemetery, a letter in his hands. A red line ran the length of the envelope.

"Pardon me, sir, miss." He held the note to Barrington. "Rosie said it's just come for you, sir, from the Aetherium, and it's marked urgent."

"It's always urgent with the Aetherium," the professor muttered. "Thank you, Lucas."

Barrington took the letter and opened it swiftly. He read it and hummed. "Interesting. Seems someone has been using a series of love spells to bewitch Aetherium employees." He lowered the note and explained, "With a love spell, a magician can enchant their victims into doing all sorts of things in the name of love, such as disclosing valuable information. Whoever our culprit is has bewitched three secretaries in the past two weeks. Mrs. York would like us to investigate."

Sera straightened, her pulse quick. "Do you think they're attempting to find the vault where Mrs. York put the bones, in order to learn the last spell?"

Barrington folded the note and stuffed it into his inner pocket. "Perhaps, but there's only one way to find out." Standing, he held his hand out to Sera, the thrill of a new case glittering in his eyes. "Shall we?"

Sera considered his hand and all the things it offered. Safety, companionship, and adventure with the possibility of blood, murder, and death, all the while investigating love.

She slid her fingers into his and stood. "We shall."

Love was bad enough on its own, but she'd gladly tackle it by his side.

Acknowledgments

Half of the time, writing is a solitary endeavor. The other half is reaching out to family and friends in a panic when you feel stuck and low and your characters aren't cooperating and you want to set the manuscript on fire. Those are the people I want to thank.

First and foremost, to God for the gift of life and words. For everything really.

Cliff, when we first met, you told me something that resonated and has been my driving force throughout the years. Thank you for saying those words and for existing and for loving me. I love you.

To my A-Team, my endless source of inspiration and motivation. You guys are the most amazing, smart, caring, funny, loving small humans that will grow into extraordinary adults, and I am so incredibly proud to be your mom. Just looking at you all and how you see the world makes me want to be a better person. I love you, more than you'll ever know.

Thank you to my family for your continuous support. It may not seem like a big deal, but all those times I didn't have to cook dinner so I could focus on writing made all the difference. I love you.

Alice!!! I seriously cannot imagine the past eight years without you. I'm so glad we get to share our milestones, writing and otherwise, with each other. I love you! PS—My inbox is empty.

To my Wattpad4 girls, you ladies are strong, beautiful, talented, hardworking women, and it is a privilege to be in a tribe with you and have our dreams come true together. I love you girls!

Karen, thank you so much for believing in me and this book. Your notes and comments have not only made this a better book but have also made me a better writer.

Last but not least, to Wattpad, from the awesome HQ staff to every reader who took the time to vote and comment, thank you for your support and for giving my writing a home.

Getting to this part in the book writing/publishing process always makes me a bit weepy because it feels like the book is finally over, but in reality, it's just the beginning. It will have new life now, given to it by everyone who reads its words. Thank you, reader, for joining me, Seraphina, and Barrington on this journey.

GRAB THE ENTANGLED TEEN RELEASES READERS ARE TALKING ABOUT!

KEEPER OF THE BEES
BY MEG KASSEL

When the cursed Dresden arrives in a Midwest town marked for death, he encounters Essie, a girl who suffers from debilitating delusions and hallucinations. But Essie doesn't see a monster when she looks at Dresden.

Risking his own life, Dresden holds back his curse and spares her. What starts out as a simple act of mercy ends up unraveling Dresden's solitary life and Essie's tormented one. Their impossible romance might even be powerful enough to unravel a centuries-old curse.

ILLUSIONS
BY MADELINE J. REYNOLDS

1898, London. Saverio, a magician's apprentice, is tasked with stealing another magician's secret behind his newest illusion. He befriends the man's apprentice, Thomas, with one goal. Get close. Learn the trick. Get out.

Then Sav discovers that Thomas performs *real* magic and is responsible for his master's "illusions." And worse, Sav has unexpectedly fallen for Thomas.

Their forbidden romance sets off a domino effect of dangerous consequences that could destroy their love—and their lives.

ZOMBIE ABBEY
BY LAUREN BARATZ-LOGSTED

Everyone in Porthampton knows his or her place. There's upstairs, downstairs, and then there are the villagers who tend the farms. But when a farmer is killed in a most unusual fashion, it becomes apparent that all three groups will have to do the unthinkable: work together, side by side, if they want to survive the menace. Even the three teenage daughters of Lord Martin Clarke must work with the handsome stable boy Will Harvey because, if they don't, their ancestral home of Porthampton Abbey just might turn into Zombie Abbey.

KISS OF THE ROYAL
BY LINDSEY DUGA

Ivy's magic is more powerful than any other Royal's, but she needs a battle partner to help her harness it. Prince Zach's unparalleled skill with a sword *should* make them an unstoppable pair—if they could agree on...well, anything.

Zach believes Ivy's magic is dangerous. Ivy believes they'll never win the war without it. Two warriors, one goal, and the fate of their world on the line. But only one of them can be right…

entangled teen

an imprint of Entangled Publishing LLC